the Padre Pirate

A JIMMY REDSTONE/ANGELLA MARTINEZ THRILLER

DAVID HARRY

UNION BEACH LP PUBLISHING

Disclaimers

EVERYTHING IN THIS BOOK, EXCEPT FOR THE ESTABLISHMENTS FREQUENTED BY JIMMY AND ANGELLA, AND EXCEPT FOR THE NON-FICTION ART LISTED AT THE END OF THE BOOK ARE FICTIONAL. THE WORDS SPOKEN BY STEVE HATHCOCK AND GRIFF MANGAN (WHO ARE REAL PEOPLE) ARE, OF COURSE, FICTIONAL.

Fictional Works of Art

THE FOLLOWING WORKS OF ART ARE FICTIONAL AND ANY RESEMBLANCE TO ANYTHING IN ACTUAL EXISTENCE IS PURELY COINCIDENCE.

Bucksbaum

Concentration Camp pictures created using blood drops.

Crown of Alexander

Crown crafted in Czarist Russia and passing through Nazi Germany before ending up in an Israeli cave.

Golden Booby

Blue Footed Booby crafted in the South Pacific and featured in the book Paragraphs (referenced at the end of this book, shown on front cover).

Kings Cup

Crafted in Iran and found in the tomb of Lord Aratta, a figure from the Jiroft culture, and featured in The Padre Poison (Shown on the front cover).

Pirate

A bronze statue with a troubled past; the piece was stolen in 2003 and has been missing ever since (Featured on the front cover)

Copyright

LIBRARY OF CONGRESS CONTROL NUMBER (LCCN) 2019907253

ISBN: 978-09963650-5-5 TRADE PAPERBACK
ISBN: 978-09963650-6-2 E-BOOK

PRINTED IN THE UNITED STATES AND PUBLISHED BY UNION BEACH, LP

South Padre Island & Port Isabel Etablishments
Frequented by
JIMMY REDSTONE AND ANGELLA MARTINEZ

* * *

Blue Marlin Supermarket
https://bluemarlin.iga.com

Island Fitness Center
http:/islandfitnesscc.com

Med Spa
https://medspaspi.com

Paragraphs on Padre
https://paragraphsbooks.mybooksandmore.com

Parrot Eyes
https:/parroteyesspi.com

Purple Piggy
https://www.facebook.com/Purplepiggytoysandgiftssouthpadreisland

Señor Donkey
http://www.senordonkey.com/menu

Sandy Feet Sandcastle Services
https://www.sandyfeetsandcastleservices.com

Ted's
https://www.facebook.com/pages/Teds-Restaurant/113302208702632

Wanna Wanna
https://www.wannawanna.com

Venus Nails and Spa
http://www.venusspaspi.com

Please stop by and tell them Jimmy and Angella sent you

Pittsburgh Establishments
Frequented by
JIMMY REDSTONE AND ANGELLA MARTINEZ

Altius
http://www.altiuspgh.com

Amels Restaurant
https://www.amelsrestaurantpgh.com

Charley Brown House (Bayernhof Museum)
https://www.bayernhofmuseum.com

Common Plea Catering
http://commonplea-catering.com

Falling Water (Somerset, PA)
https://www.fallingwater.org

Holocaust Center of Pittsburgh
https://www.hcofpgh.org

My Dogz On The Run
http://www.pghmydogzontherun

Murray Avenue Grill
https://www.murrayavenuegrill.com

Narcisi Winery
http://www.narcisiwinery.com

Panera Bread
https://www-beta.panerabread.com/en-us/home.html

Primanti Brothers
https://www.primantibros.com

Staghorn Garden Cafe
http://www.staghorngardencafe.com

The Commoner at the Hotel Monaco
https://www.monaco-pittsburgh.com/restaurants/commoner

Please stop by and tell them Jimmy and Angella sent you.

ONE

Jimmy was in the men's room when Joy Malcom bounced through the door, almost knocking Steve Hathcock off his feet, which was not a particularly easy task. Steve bowed deeply, swung his left arm across his body in an exaggerated entry motion, watched as Joy rushed toward me and then, with a nod in my direction, adjusted his ever-present wide-brimmed hat and disappeared into the morning sun that was shining brightly on *Ted's* front door.

It took me a few beats to realize the traditional male gesture of gallantry is to bring the right arm against the torso. Hathcock had used his left. I suppose he was using this deviation to throw Joy the middle finger.

"So where's your...your partner? Hiding in the bathroom I suppose." Malcom's smile usually tends to erase, or perhaps I should say, soften, her innate nastiness. Today she had no smile and the image

I received was downright threatening. That must have been what Steve had reacted to.

"Having a bad morning?" I inquired, not bothering to either stand in greeting or to offer her a seat at our table. My version of the middle finger.

Even the staff held their distance, everyone busy cleaning tables or filling coffee pots, their eyes elsewhere.

"Matter of fact," she responded, the harshness of her jawline abating, "it might actually be a great morning. Need to see Jimmy, though." She glanced toward the restrooms. "Mind if I take a load off my feet? He can't stay in there forever, I don't suppose."

The problem with her question was that her butt was firmly in the chair before the question was fully out of her mouth. In fact, on the way down she had managed to catch the eye of Karen who promptly placed an empty mug in front of her, filling it with steaming coffee. Black, as Joy liked it. I was about to ask her if she had been on the beach yet today, but her face came even further alive and now sported a wide friendly smile. My conclusion: Jimmy had emerged from the john.

"Just the man I wanted to see," Joy announced, standing, her arms spread wide to embrace Jimmy.

"What a...a surprise to see you here on such a gorgeous morning. Isn't this your beach walking time?" Jimmy said, his "oh shit" smile a tad crooked and fading fast. His version of the finger.

In fact, the reason Jimmy and I had picked this time for our weekly pecan-filled pancake fix was because Joy usually trolled the beach at this hour. Someone must have tipped her off that we were here. Her lawsuit over the loss of the *Kings Cup* was stalled, and she had been instructed to stay away from us, just as we had been lectured on more than one occasion to keep our distance from her.

Sure, it was possible for her to prove she had had possession of the *Cup* just before it had gone missing. And she might even be able to prove Jimmy was the person who tipped the Feds off as to its whereabouts. And certainly, she could easily prove the value to be well over a hundred million. But even with all that, proving who held valid title was going to be difficult, if not impossible, for her.

The *Cup* had surfaced over the years in many locations, in the possession of many different people, from monarchs, to emperors, to sheiks to drug lords. For a while it had been in the possession of a Shogun in the Japanese Kamakura period. In each case, the *Kings Cup* vanished without a trace. The true story of how it had come into Joy's possession is something that Jimmy believes will never see the light of day — at least not in a court of law. And most definitely not in the *Venus Nail and Spa* where court is held every day and opinions and theories are exchanged like commodities.

"Now don't look so put upon, Jimmy. I'm here waving the peace flag, and you're wishing I was somewhere else. This is your lucky day."

"If this is related to the lawsuit, I'm going to insist—"

"It is...and it isn't. Now, Jimmy, be a good neighbor and welcome me at your table and stop being such a puss."

Jimmy waved toward the seat Joy already occupied "I'm all ears," he said, sipping his refilled coffee, any pretext of a smile long gone. "Let's hear what you have to say."

Joy leaned over the table as she often did when getting ready to impart private information. Since there was no one within twenty feet, the gesture was solely for show—or dramatic effect. "Roberto sees the handwriting on the wall. Trump's wall to be exact. Once the pieces are in place, the drug traffic, at least the business Roberto controls, will be forced to change directions. He's trying to stay... shall we say, relevant."

Joy paused to wet her lips, and while she did so, I took the time to again review what I knew about Roberto Alterez Santiago, alias Morris Malcom, alias, who knows. The fact that Joy didn't refer to him as her husband, or as Morris, signaled something. Exactly what it told us I didn't yet know. Jimmy and I had put Santiago in jail, a Mexican jail no less, several years back when Jimmy was a Texas Ranger and I was a rookie on the police force here on South Padre Island.

I had been assigned by the Police Chief to babysit Jimmy as part of a murder investigation he had become involved in. Santiago, as it turned out, had a wife and family in Mexico and a *wife*, Joy, here in Texas. It also turned out dear old Santiago, or Alterez as he preferred being called, was a major drug lord. Putting him in jail for life hadn't slowed his operations one iota. In fact, it might actually have made him more powerful. Perhaps it's because he has nothing to lose by slitting a throat. Perhaps it's because he has a good percentage of Mexican law enforcement on his payroll. How he manages it I can only imagine, but his operation runs as smoothly as a well-oiled corporation, and there doesn't seem to be any delay in his receiving up-to-the-minute information.

"As I said," Joy continued after making certain both Jimmy and I were leaning across the table listening, "his team is geared to land movement. I mean, sure they use boats on the Gulf and on the river, but essentially the product gets to and from the boats by ground. His people move back and forth across the border unimpeded. The wall and more sophisticated surveillance at the crossings will change that."

"So," Jimmy said, "tell us something we don't know. So far, you sound like you're carrying Trump's water."

"My you're feisty today. My lawsuit's getting to you, is that it?"

"Your suit is bullshit, Joy, and you know it!"

"Jimmy," I said, trying to deescalate, "we have orders not to discuss this. Joy, no more legal talk, or I'm—"

"Okay. Okay. Here's the thing. Santiago is moving out of...well, he's changing directions."

I can't wait to hear what that gangster has in mind now.

"You mean he's going to peddle his crap in Belize, Guatemala and points south and not the U. S.?" Jimmy quipped. "Can't imagine the market down there's large enough for your husb... for Santiago."

"That's not what I mean and you know it." Joy's eyes scanned the room, and she leaned in even further before saying, "He's moving out of... out of...his current trade practices...and into," she paused for effect, "art. That's the real reason for the *King's Cup.* And why it's so important to him."

"You mean he's now an art collector?" I asked, trying to visualize how Santiago would manage an art collection from his jail cell no matter how luxurious his current digs might be. The best thing he has going for him is security. It's topnotch.

"No, not a collector. An agent. A facilitator. He has, as you well know, connections all around the world. Art has become a favorite pastime for many of his...his clients."

"I'll bet!" Jimmy chided. "Does any of that art come with a clear title?"

"Jimmy!" Joy said, looking truly upset.

"Well, does it? Listen, Joy, it's difficult imagining anyone buying a piece of art from a guy serving a life sentence in a Mexican jail."

"He's right," I agreed, struggling to keep from laughing. "I can't visualize a showing room in the prison. And what'll you do if you need recourse?"

"Look, it doesn't work that way. His clients, friends, get on line and pick out the art they want. They contact Santiago and Santiago arranges for the merchandise to be delivered to the buyer."

"This art...this merchandise...that his...his friends...find, is that art in a catalogue? Or art that's...that's been missing a while?"

"Art that's gone missing over the years," Joy answered without missing a beat. "Black market art, if you will. I understand that's big right now. Certainly you two are familiar with black market art."

Actually, our boss, Jack Silver, the founder and CEO of Great Southern Insurance, hired us away from Homeland Security in part because of rising art thefts feeding the traffic in black market antiquities. It was an added bonus that we know our way around both sides of the law, not to mention Jimmy's extensive background as a Texas Ranger investigating white-collar criminals and art thefts.

Jimmy sat back in his chair, studied Joy a long moment, then said, "There's a big difference between art that's already gone missing and art that's about to go missing because someone contacts Santiago."

"You certainly have a low opinion of my husband."

"For starters, Joy," Jimmy responded, his tone as harsh as I have ever heard it with Joy, "he's not your husband. And on the contrary, I hold Santiago in high esteem—when it comes to criminal activity."

"I'll let all that pass. Listen, you interested in what I have to say or not?" Joy checked her watch for the third time.

"You late for something?" Jimmy asked. "Don't let us keep you."

"As a matter of fact, yes. I have an appointment over at the *Med Spa* in five minutes. Scheduled for a vitamin-infused IV, if you must know."

"Hangover?" Jimmy asked. "Tell me you're not using again."

"Don't answer him," I said, "none of his business what you do with your time. Jimmy may not be interested in what you're telling us, but I am. Just be aware that anything you tell us..." I was going to say, 'can be held against you,' but instead, I said, "We're free to tell law enforcement."

"I understand where you're coming from on this, Angella, but nothing I tell you is illegal in any way." Joy dug a notecard out of her pocket and placed it face down on the table. "That card has the name of a person who Santiago is certain has the *Pirate* in his possession. Its worth..."

"You talking about THE *Pirate*, the one went missing back in...in oh three, worth between thirty and forty million?" Jimmy asked, now clearly interested.

"Old numbers, Jimmy. Try seventy-five," Joy said, settling back in her chair, content she now had Jimmy hooked. All that remained was to reel him in.

"How do you know about this *Pirate,* what ever it is?" I asked my partner, always surprised by what he knows.

"Bronze statue, as real looking as anything I've ever seen. Belonged to an oilman from East Texas. Crafted in Peru. The piece, at least judging from pictures I've seen, is magnificent. When the *Pirate* went missing the Texas Rangers were called in. I drew the short straw. Ate my lunch."

"Why the Rangers? Didn't know they investigated stolen artwork, not private artwork anyway. You never talked about it."

"Two deaths were attributed to the heist," Jimmy said, ignoring my question. "Wish I hadn't been involved. Most frustrating investigation ever. Ran me around in circles and in the end, I didn't know any more when I was taken off the case than I did when I was first assigned. Same with the next three Rangers assigned. It's now been delegated to the cold case archive."

"I take it you investigated the heist, not the deaths?"

"If you call what I did an investigation. But the homicide team had no better luck. Professional all the way. Well planned, perfectly executed."

"I suppose your not finding that *Pirate* is why you've never discussed it."

"Slipped my mind's all."

It didn't slip Jimmy's mind, but that's neither here nor there. And more important, Joy knew it hadn't slipped Jimmy's mind.

Jimmy reached for the card, but Joy's hand arrived first. "Not so fast, my friend. There's a price for dealing yourself in. Kind of pay to play, if you will."

Joy was toying with Jimmy. Never a good idea, but he sat back and waited. The hook had been deeply set.

"I give you the name, and you get me my *Kings Cup*. Simple as that."

Joy lost the *Kings Cup* in a DHS raid. She values it at over a hundred million and blames Jimmy for the loss. She filed suit against Jimmy, and the suit is now bogged down in the Cameron County Courts, primarily because Joy is having difficulty proving title. The question as to whether the one she had was the original or a fake is also on the table. The *Kings Cup* had been black market for years, and it is not an easy task to obtain appraisals on black market art.

"And how in the hell am I supposed to do that?" Jimmy demanded, his fingers clamping down on Joy's hand in preparation, it appeared, to yank the card from her. "I have no idea where it is or who has it!"

"Simple. The name on this card has it as well as the *Pirate*."

"Tell you what I'll promise," Jimmy responded, the hook doing its job. "If the person on that card has the *Kings Cup* and I track its location I'll let you know where it is."

"I need for you to deliver it to me. Or, if you wish, to one of Santiago's folks."

"Can't promise that. But I'll give you forty-eight hours before I notify the authorities. That is, assuming Great Southern has no interest in the *Cup*."

"I assure you, my friend, Great Southern has no interest in the *Kings Cup*."

"Then you have nothing to worry about. I give you the *Cup*'s location, you arrange to pick it up. Simple task for Santiago."

"Deal." Joy said, releasing her grip on the card and abruptly standing. "See you soon, I trust. My vitamins are waiting." She blew a kiss in Jimmy's direction and disappeared into the sunshine.

TWO

"So who's this Hugo character?" I asked Jimmy when Joy was out of hearing range. These were the first words spoken by either of us since Joy took her leave. "From your silence I take it you recognize the name."

My partner and lover had turned the card over, folded it, and shoved it into his pocket, all without a word. Instead of answering me, he laid money on the table, nodded in the direction of Karen the owner, walked out to his car, and waited for me to join him. He drove several blocks, parked in a small hard-packed sand lot, and walked across the wooden ramp over the dune to the western edge of the Gulf of Mexico. Taking his shoes off and wading in until the water lapped at his ankles, he turned south. Jimmy was clearly troubled and I thought it best to let it play out.

I followed behind, allowing the soft waves to gently cover, then uncover, my now bare feet. The cool sand combined with the unbroken rhythm of the water was mesmerizing. Jimmy had moved farther out, the water now soaking the bottom of his shorts. He was working through something private, some memory, some unfinished piece of business, something he was not yet ready to share.

The *Wanna Wanna*, a popular open-air beachfront bar and restaurant, famous for their fried shrimp, was not far south of where Jimmy stopped. Volleyball players shouted encouragement to each other as volley after volley hit the net. Beach chairs littered the sand filled with people getting an early start on the sun. A rogue wave caught me daydreaming and my shorts, like Jimmy's, got soaked. If I had been standing as far out as he was it would be wet T-shirt contest time. I took a few steps back toward shore.

It was at that moment that Jimmy decided to bring me into his thoughts. Typical of him, we were far enough from shore that we could not have been overheard even with the best of drones.

"What did you say?" I yelled, knowing I'd have to go out to him if I wanted to hear what he had to say. When the Gulf settled again, I ventured out as far as I dared. The water had quickly come up to mid-calf at its ebb and around my waist when the wavelets rolled in. I planted my feet, determined not to take another step forward. Jimmy, his eyes focused on some unseen object far out to sea, said, "Oscar Hugo is, or at least several years back, was, a Federal Marshal."

"You know him?" I said, raising my voice so Jimmy could hear over the rolling waves.

He turned toward me and realizing how far out he had actually wandered, took several steps back. "Never actually met. I was transitioning from the Rangers to Homeland Security when his name popped up in conjunction with something called the *Golden Booby*. I don't recall exactly the legend, but suffice it to say that anyone who came across the Bird, as it affectionately became known, was found dead. The Bird would then again disappear."

I was slowly walking backwards toward the shoreline, my eyes peeled for rogue waves. Jimmy was doing likewise. "What do you know about this Bird?" I called out to him.

"As I recall, a professor over at UTRGV, I believe it still was the University of Texas at Brownsville at that time, a guy by the name of Simpson Hugo. This guy Oscar Hugo, who by the way, changed his name from Oscar Lowell to Oscar Hugo, claiming Simpson Hugo was his grandfather, is, or was, the owner of the Bird. The professor was found dead, and the Bird again went missing. There was a cousin involved, a woman professor, I believe it was, and some think she made off with the prize. Some think they both did. No end of rumors."

"Did you work on the case when you were with the Rangers?"

"Actually, no. And truth is, I know very little. My old boss asked me—"

"Lieutenant Contentus?"

"Ya, Contentus. I'd been working on the *Pirate* a year or so before that, and he wanted me to brief him about dealers, channels, that sort of stuff. He fed me enough info about the Bird so I knew what was going on. I started poking into this guy Hugo, actually into both Hugos, grandfather and grandson. Then for some reason it was all shut down. About all I really recall was that the old man Hugo was teaching under the identity of a dead guy by the name of August Villanova. That's about the time I left the Rangers so I lost track of what happened. Needless to say, the Bird is long gone. And so is Hugo. Or so at least I thought he was."

"Let's have Jack Silver run him through his data base," I suggested, "and see where he's now."

"We'll need to touch base with Silver in any event if...if we move forward with the *Pirate*."

"You thinking of not pursuing the *Pirate*?"

"Doing anything with, or for, Santiago doesn't sit well with me. I'm thinking of letting it ride. Your thoughts?"

"I suggest we run Joy's conversation past the boss. If for no other reason than to let him know Santiago's going into art dealing. Besides, unless I miss my guess, Joy's take-away from this morning is that we're in. If we're not, we need to make it crystal clear. Don't want Silver getting any wrong ideas from the grapevine."

"Nothing's stopping you from calling," Jimmy replied, his tone implying I should have made that call long before now. I turned and high-stepped it to shore just in time to avoid being overwhelmed by the largest wave of the morning.

"I was about to call you, Angella," Jack Silver barked when he came on the line. "Received a call from Santiago. I understand Joy hired you and Jimmy to locate the *Pirate*. Piece's been gone for years."

"She didn't exactly hire us," I replied. "She asked us to locate that piece, as well as the *Kings Cup*, for her. Well, not actually for her, for Santiago." I went on to relay to Silver what Joy had told us about Santiago's new business plan. I then added, "She really didn't say much, other than—"

"Go for it! Listen, we have several pieces insured that have, well to be blunt, have disappeared. Now on the black market, I'm afraid. The *Pirate* is one of them. We paid it off back...back in oh nine. Eight million. Now worth minimum sixty-five. Nice piece of change if you find that piece. Listen, as I've told you both many times, Great Southern has paid off on many pieces, and with all this recent theft, our losses are going up fast. Got to stem the tide. You know my rules. If and when a piece is returned, I sell it at auction. Great Southern recovers its costs and then we split sixty-forty with the finder. You have carte blanche in this case. You need the company plane, you got it. Only thing I ask is keep me in the loop. And remember, there are more frauds out there than genuine pieces, so all valuations go directly through me. Without exception! Understand?"

"Understand," I dutifully said, not for the first time.

"I'll arrange for you and Jimmy to have access to the *Pirate* file as well as what we have on Oscar Hugo." Silver paused and the line sounded as if he had hung up. But then, in an almost apologetic voice, added, "Oh, and Angella, be careful. These are some really bad people. Really bad. And Santiago's promised to get even with Jimmy and you. In his world, grievance trumps business every time. And Jimmy putting him in jail is a major grievance. Bank on that."

"We'll certainly be careful," I replied, soothing the boss man's apparent guilt at sending his employees into harm's way for purely monetary gain. But there was no denying that this is what we had signed up for. And, as Jimmy had pointed out the first time we had been told about splitting the profits with finders, there wasn't an altruistic bone in Silver's body. He was protecting his interest. Otherwise, his investigators would simply sell a found object on the black market and keep *all* the money.

I repeated Silver's conversation to Jimmy, who responded, "Actually, I think you're misreading Silver. Giving him far too much credit. He's not concerned about us. Keeping bad press away from Great Southern's his main worry. That's why he wants us on the company plane. He can control the manifest, prove we were nowhere in the vicinity if there's a problem." Jimmy returned his gaze to the horizon, as if expecting something to appear out there where water and sky merge. With his eyes still focused in the distance, he added, "And make no mistake about it, when this much money is at stake, there's going to be problems. Our job is to be sure those problems belong to the other guy."

Preferring to dwell on a more positive side of our job, I said, "Give me magnitudes. Joy, I know, believes the *Kings Cup* is worth over a hundred million. Realistically?"

"Probably sixty million. Joy...Santiago, who really had possession of the *Cup*...could get fifty easily. Problem for him is title. His cartel most likely stole it from someone. It's that someone who wants it back. And we have no idea who that someone is."

I recalled the extensive database search we had made back when the *Cup* first went missing. Nothing but dead ends. The previous owner had covered his/her tracks professionally. "How do you plan on finding out who that someone is?"

"The old-fashioned way. Lots of snooping. Mixing it up with the artsy crowd, especially the high rollers."

"Any ideas of how to find them? These so-called high rollers? Can Joy be of help?"

"Possibly, but not likely. But Santiago can. If he's moving into that business, then he's been working this a while."

"This *Golden Booby* piece you talked about. The one Hugo was after. Value?"

"Contentus threw out the number hundred million. I have no idea if that's even the right ballpark."

"That seems way too high. Just saying."

"You know, Angella, I agree with you. But what I did learn is that art is valued at what people will pay for it. To some people, owning or controlling certain objects is far more valuable than owning or controlling the money that paid for it. Especially when legends are attached to the object. The Al Capone thing meets that criteria in spades."

"Capone?"

"May not be true, but one of the legends attached to the *Golden Booby* is that Al Capone was lured down here to the island because he was led to believe the Bird was here. Several of his men were shot to death in a trap. The *Booby* disappeared at that time, leaving behind death, as the legend suggests."

"What's the big smile for?"

"If you must know, I was just thinking if there happened to be a wet T-shirt contest, you'd win big time."

Looking down, I exclaimed, "How'd I get so wet? Don't just stand there grinning like a jerk, gimme your shirt!"

THREE

"**S**o where do we begin?" I asked Jimmy when I returned to the beach a half-hour later wearing dry clothes. Jimmy was still without his shirt, refusing to wear the one I brought for him, insisting he was working on his tan. As a concession, he allowed me to rub sun block into his skin. Jimmy had asked Jason the chair guy to move a couple of lounge chairs over to an area away from the sunbathers. We were both now sitting with open laptops, the private Great Southern page open on our screens.

Great Southern Insurance Company
PRIVATE AND CONFIDENTIAL

NAME: Oscar Hugo; name changed by court order 5-8-1996 from Oscar Lowell
Dob: April 25, 1973 Pittsburgh, PA, Dod: —
EDUCATION: West Virginia University, Morgantown, BS Forensic and Investigative Science, 1994; MS Antiquities, University of Pittsburgh, 1997

OCCUPATION: 1997-2013 Federal Marshal Service
FAMILY:
Grandfather: Simpson Hugo alias August
Villanova, Dob 6-3-1926, Dod 10-1-2013;
Grandmother: Katherine O'Connell Dob 9-27-
1929, Dod 7-5-1983
Father: Harold Lowell, Dob 2-27-1950, Dod 11-
9-2010 (Born Oow, adopted by Lowell family)
Mother: Lucy Stone Lowell, Dob 1-18-53, Dod?
LKR Valencia, PA
Known Relatives: Anabelle (Belle) Neuva, Dob
2-3-83, granddaughter of August Villanova
(Hugo)

"No record of this guy Hugo since 2013. So what's your plan?" I asked Jimmy.

"A federal marshal off the grid won't be easy to find. Might be out of the country, might be any place. But I ask myself, why'd he change names? And—"

"And what did he do between graduating WVU and going to Pitt? We're thinking alike, Jimmy. And why would a cousin's name appear in the GS database? Who the hell is she?"

"Kid got himself an undergraduate degree in forensics and investigations and then takes time off. When he comes back, he takes on a new name and a new direction. Antiquities. Maybe something. Maybe nothing."

I studied the screen again and found what I was looking for. "Here's a link, Jimmy. Grandfather's original family name was Hugo. For some reason the old man changed it to Villanova. Kid changed his to match his grandfather's *original* name, not the name the kid knew him as."

"Maybe he didn't know his grandfather at all. Seems young Oscar was raised, perhaps adopted, by a family named Lowell."

"That makes sense. See there, the grandfather never married this Katherine O'Connell woman. That might be when the grandfather left town, changed his name to Villanova and moved on with his life. Oscar's father seems to have been an inconvenient baby."

"Grandfather wasn't such a nice guy. And the mother put the baby up for adoption. Kid was apparently inconvenient for everyone."

"Grandfather was involved with the *Golden Booby*. Anthropologist or something over at Brownsville. University of Texas, I believe. Something...something unusual with him. I wasn't involved with the case, but I remember it being discussed. The old man died or something."

While Jimmy was talking, I did a Google search on the cousin. "She's a professor of antiquities at the National Autonomous University of Mexico. Runs in the family. Seems she's also an adjunct at Pitt."

"Any more info on the old man?" Jimmy asked, preferring me to do the keyboard work.

I fiddled a bit with Goggle and finally said, "The something funny...I think you said unusual... about Professor Villanova, could it be the fact that he never actually got a degree?"

"How's that possible?"

"Dude's an imposter. Took the name of a guy named Villanova who actually was a PhD. This Villanova guy died in a car accident. This was in a report filed about a year after the imposter died. A detective Vega from the Port Isabel Police Department was the chief investigator."

"Mind calling..." Jimmy began, but before I could look up Vega's number, he had his own phone out and had placed the call. I assumed he was calling this guy Vega himself, but with Jimmy one never really knew.

The wind blew his words away, so I didn't hear what transpired. When he finished his conversation, his mood had changed for the better. "Got lucky. Sarge over there owes me one big time. Saved his butt many years ago. Says Vega's gone from the department. They have no forwarding info on him, but he's apparently a person of interest."

"How so? Commit a crime? Falsify reports?" One of the biggest problems any police force has is with having officers, particularly detectives, document their investigations and observations properly and completely and without favor or malice.

"Tell you in a moment. Serge remembers Hugo coming in and making a big deal out of him being a Federal Marshal and demanding access to the files. They slow rolled it and ran a check, only to find Hugo was on leave. They showed him what they could, but Vega wasn't buying what Hugo was selling. At one point, Vega wanted a search warrant for Hugo's motel, but the captain said hunches weren't enough. Now for the disjointed part. Hugo came in one morning, announced he was off the *Booby* case and didn't need or want any more info on the Bird. Instead, he told them he had a lead on something he called a pirate. Vega willingly assisted Hugo in examining files and such. Serge remembers well the conversation where Vega said he was helping with the *pirate matter* because that could bring him closer to Hugo and perhaps uncover probable cause to search Hugo's premises."

"There's got to be more, Jimmy. Anything on why Vega left?"

"Not a lot. But he did say that about a week after Hugo left town Vega tendered his resignation and moved away. He had a woman friend on the island who professed to be as baffled as the police were about his sudden departure. They thought for a while he had been a victim of foul play, but from time to time someone would report a sighting."

"Get a new job?"

"Rumor is he's a private detective, but no licenses and no Internet. Serge says there's talk of him going in with Santiago, border muscle if you will. But nothing confirmed."

"You think his *pirate matter* is your *Pirate*? Something to do with Vega leaving?"

"Time frames don't seem right, but could be. Particularly if the imposter grandfather was deeper into dark art than anyone thought."

"Starting point," I ventured, "tracking down Vega?"

"That's one avenue. Another would be Hugo's mother."

"That's Pittsburgh," I volunteered. "Good time actually to go to Pittsburgh. Says here the Three Rivers Arts Festival starts this weekend. Want to go commercial or Great Southern?"

"Let's stay out of Silver's crosshairs as long as we can. Book us on Southwest to Pittsburgh. I'll take care of rooms and a car."

A moment later Jimmy, who had been busy making reservations, said, "As luck would have it, that Arts festival you're talking about is right across from the Wyndham Hotel and I managed to get us a room there."

"How'd you manage that? With all those artists and visitors in town the hotel has to be sold out."

"Know a guy."

I studied Jimmy a moment before again re-minding myself that when he didn't want me to know he was hiding something from me I wouldn't know it. Period. And this time was no exception. His ties with CIA and Mossad, the Israeli intelligence agency, run deep. Now's not the time for chasing that rabbit. "Great." I checked my watch and asked, "What time's our flight?"

"One ten. Brownsville to Houston and a quick change of planes, then on to Pittsburgh. Land just after rush hour."

"That does me out of the fried shrimp I was thinking of over at the *Wanna Wanna*. Barely time for a quick shower, pack, and off we go."

"That's a plan," Jimmy said. "But truth is, I was hoping to do laundry before we had to go."

"You telling me you have nothing to pack?"

"Not much clean."

It wasn't like Jimmy to be worrying about his wardrobe, so something was troubling him. He probably doesn't even know what it is, but he'll work it out. I spent about an hour searching the Internet for everything I could about the *Booby*, the *Cup*, and the *Pirate*. Precious little came up, but I did get a few leads on black market art. It's over a billion-dollar business, perhaps as high as five billion, with stolen antiquities leading the pack. A companion business is the creation of fake documents, including fake art, good enough to fool many experts.

Jimmy pulled his hat over his face, pretending to nap in the morning sun. That was out of character for him and had me worried. I took a minute to call Griff over at *Paragraphs on Padre*, the island's only bookstore, to see if he knew of any books about the missing *Pirate*. The friendly bookstore owner didn't immediately recall any, but while we were chatting, he remembered that the owner of *The Purple Piggy*, a local island toy store, had come by within the week and had asked the same question. Apparently, someone saw a made-in-China toy pirate and had asked if the store happened to have a pirate that stood about five feet tall. Man had said he wanted it for a prank to play on a friend who had investigated a missing bronze pirate several years back. The storeowner didn't get any names but seemed to recall that the investigator worked in Port Isabel. "Hey," Griff reminded me before he hung up, "check with Steve Hathcock. Man knows his history, and this is right down his lane."

Steve remembered the stories about the bronze pirate, but had no knowledge other than the little that had been reported. "Rubies for eyes, if I recall right," Hathcock added. "Menacing character, that pirate."

A commotion erupted not twenty feet away. It turned out to be a group of people, mostly children in the eight to twelve range, buckets in hand, parading back and forth to the water's edge. They were filling their buckets and happily dumping the water into a giant canvas caldron positioned almost directly behind me. Why I hadn't noticed them sooner I don't know.

Standing on a two-step ladder to give her leverage in mixing up a brew of sand, water and some mystery element, was the local sand artist and teacher, Sandy Feet.

Off to the side of the caldron was the beginning of what looked to be a fortress, a multi-level fortress, replete with a moat and dragons guarding the entrance. Portions of what I took to be a giant old man, perhaps the early stages of Neptune, perhaps a random sun God, stood guard behind the fortress, or castle, or whatever the structure was.

Lucinda, who teaches sandcastle building under the banner *Sandy Feet Sandcastle Services* saw me approaching and called out, "Angella! I thought that was you but wasn't certain. You're not often on the beach. Hey, I wish I had known for sure that was you, a guy was asking for Jimmy."

"Jimmy? When was that?"

"Just a few minutes ago. He couldn't have gone far. Told him he could find you at the *Riviera* if you were on the island. Said he tried there but the concierge, or somebody, said you were out."

"Get a name?"

"Vega. Juan Manuel Vega. Goes by JM."

"You know him?"

Lucinda stopped stirring, stepped down off the ladder and walked over to where I was standing. She lowered her voice. "Something going on I should know about?"

"Just curious."

She said nothing, allowing her raised eyebrows to speak for her. "He said Jimmy called over to Port Isabel asking for him."

"That Jimmy did. Just a few minutes ago. This Vega guy, just happens to be on the island? Did he say where we could reach him?"

"Didn't say. But he's staying at the Holiday Inn."

"You know that because—"

"JM's a detective, was a detective, over in Port Isabel. A while back he had a case brought him to the island. If I recall right, it was that *Golden Booby* bird case. Stayed at the *Sand Box*, undercover if you will. Friend of mine and he began seeing... you get the picture?"

"He been on the island a while?"

"Not that I know off. Visits my friend from time to time, but not for a while that I know."

"Any idea where he now works? Where I can find him?"

"Hey, for nothing going on you sure are full of questions. I gotta get back to my class."

I hadn't noticed until now, but the water hauling had stopped and several adults, and even more children, were watching us intently.

"You, Hank," Lucinda said looking in the direction of a large well-muscled boy, a kid of about twelve whose body was well on its way to maturity, "take this paddle and mix up the brew. Dig down deep, get it all. You others mound that sand and construct a ramp up the left side as we discussed."

The children filled buckets with sand and dumped them enthusiastically on the growing mound. The adults pitched in, one eye on the sand and one eye on us.

Lucinda moved a few feet away, and when I followed, she said, "Now I recall. JM was here working a murder over at the Port Isabel museum. The *Booby* went missing at that time and rumor was someone on the island was involved. You know how rumors are on a sand spit, four or five false ones for every accurate one."

I wanted to ask if she had any pictures of the *Golden Booby* but thought better of it. Our call to the PI police department may already have been one call too many. And we hadn't really started yet. No sense putting the *Golden Booby* in play. That would come soon enough, I was certain of that.

FOUR

Flights were on time. As airports go, Pittsburgh International Airport is a delight. As is Jimmy's custom, we don't talk much in public places, and as a rule we never discuss business where we can be overheard. Since we randomly selected the rental car, it was a safe place for us to talk, at least until we parked it out of our sight.

"You solve what's itching you?" I asked as we drove under the airport exit sign, the Pittsburgh arrow pointing to the right.

"You think I have an itch?"

"If you don't, you coulda fooled me. Ever since Joy told you how to locate the *Pirate* you've been... well, more withdrawn than usual."

"Correction. She told us who had it, not where it is."

"You just proved my point, Jimmy. That's a semantic difference. If you would rather not take on this assignment then —"

"It's as good as the next one. It's just that...well, here's the thing. Three times during my investigation of the *Pirate* I tracked down who had the damn thing. Each time we went in for it, the man, and in one case, woman, who we thought had it was dead, neck slit from ear to ear. Two dead in their beds and one sitting in a living room chair, CNN news headlines snaking across the screen. No apparent break-in, nothing stolen, nothing disturbed at any of the scenes." Jimmy paused, sucked in his breath, then continued. "Only time in my life I had a hard time sleeping was after the third one. That's when Contentus took me off the case."

And that's why Jimmy never mentioned the *Pirate* before this. He was pissed then and is pissed now. We all have demons. In a much earlier life, Jimmy had been an Army Ranger sniper, so death wasn't foreign to him. But this case had gotten to him. I changed the subject. "So what do you make of Vega tracking us down on the beach?"

"I'm not certain he really wanted to track us down. He didn't get that close and not make contact."

"What then?"

"Sending us...me...a message."

"What kind of message?"

"Have to assume he has—or had—access to my Texas Ranger's file. Certainly he knows about the murders. And he knows I was pulled from the case. Two and two."

More reason for us to drop the investigation. "Why do you think he didn't want to talk to us directly?"

"Didn't call. Didn't leave a note with the concierge. In fact, he left the message with Lucinda because he knew we were right there. My guess, he was watching to be sure you made contact, and probably close enough to overhear what was said between you."

"Only if he planted a device. The only people close enough to hear anything were Sandy's students. She'd have to be in on his game to not have told me and that's not her nature." I changed the subject back to Vega. "You know, it's not adding. I mean you said two plus two. But I get blank. What do you get?"

"He either knows where the *Pirate's* located or he intends to follow us to it."

"Then why show himself? Just stay in the shadows. We might not ever see him."

"Perhaps." Jimmy fell quiet again, then added, "If he's working for Santiago, that's his way of telling us to stay on a short leash. Remember, intimidation's their game. Without fear they can't control."

"Sounds like a politician, you ask me."

"No difference, as I see it."

We proceeded downtown to our hotel, checked in without incident, and went up to our room overlooking the park. A premier room. That was some friend who set this up for him.

I busied myself unpacking, and when I was finished turned to find Jimmy studying the scene from the window as if he had seen something important. I stood beside him to see what had captured his interest. There was activity in the park across from the hotel where white tents were being set up for the upcoming art festival. People were unloading vans and trucks and loading dollies with what appeared to be heavy crates. Several of the tent fronts were open, and artists were hanging pictures and arranging their wares on tables and shelves, all newly set up. The real festivities weren't scheduled to start until mid-day tomorrow, Friday. The doorman had said live music performances would begin mid-afternoon and run until after dark.

"Thoughts?" I asked.

"Just thinking about the folks who create art. Most are lucky to get a few hundred dollars for a work they slaved over for days. At the same time we're tracking art worth multi-millions, created by artists who may be no more talented than some who will be down there. It doesn't seem right, is all.

"Tell me about this *Pirate* piece," I asked, my hand on Jimmy's shoulder. "What about it makes it worth so much?"

"Not much to tell, actually. Stands a little over five feet. Made of bronze, with perfect human form, except where he's lost a hand or foot. Face is unforgettable with his one good bright red ruby eye a salient feature. 'Soul on fire,' I was told."

Jimmy studied the river off in the distance, then continued. "When it comes to value, art is strange. People spend millions of dollars, I'm convinced, just because they can. Sure, the piece they buy hits a nerve with them, but not always because of how it looks. Often it's the story that goes with it."

"Yeah, but not all art garners big bucks, Jimmy. You said so yourself. Why the *Pirate*? Seems around the time of the heist, a piece called *Walking Man I*, by an artist..."

"Giacometti. Alberto Giacometti. I recall that."

"...Giacometti, sold for over a hundred million. A six-foot bronze statue of a thin man walking, or striding, to be precise."

"If you're asking if the *Pirate* is a Giacometti I don't think so. No one has ever suggested that. But you raise an interesting question. Is the *Pirate*, the one that went missing, real or fake? Personally, from all I learned, I think it's very much the original. But in some circles the *Pirate's* believed to be fake. Officially, however, it's believed to be real. Didn't Silver pay off several millions?"

"Eight is what I recall him telling me."

"I suppose it could be an eight-million-dollar fake. Insurance is generally a guaranteed number. But I've found experts are often in disagreement. So the price keeps going up. As I said, it's become a sport. To some people, it's as easy financially and psychologically to write a check for a hundred million as it is to write it for a million. So why not?"

"Why don't you believe it's a Giacometti? You must have a reason."

"Hunch mostly. Nothing about Giacometti even suggests he did a pirate. Second, it's not to scale, human scale. The piece is tall, I grant you that, like the walking man. But, but the anatomy of the *Pirate* is perfect. The muscles, the face, every aspect is perfection. Giacometti's pieces, at least as far as I know are...are skewed."

"So who's the artist?"

"That's the big mystery. No one knows for certain. It just turned up one day."

"Just turned up? Art like that doesn't just turn up."

"This one did. Take my word for it. No provenance. No title chain, nothing. Some say Peru, but that story didn't grow legs."

"Artists, especially those as good as Giacometti, often change perspectives."

"That's what's at the center of the controversy. And that's what drives the price up. At some point, no one cares if it's genuine or fake. They just want it."

Just being with Jimmy felt good. I rested my head on his shoulder and we stood at the window several more minutes, each lost in our own thoughts. Then I said, "Want me to call and set up a time with Oscar's mother, Lucy Lowell?"

"Rather just drop in."

"Might not be home. Might have moved. Any one of a number of things."

"I say we take our chances. Surprise might be the right way to approach this, anyway."

I suppose Jimmy's reluctance to call ahead stems from his prior investigation into the *Pirate*, where every time he closed in on a target there was death waiting for him. I wanted to remind my partner the mother wasn't a target, but thought better of it.

"What about dinner?" Jimmy asked. "What're you up for?"

Before I could answer there was a loud knock on our door and an envelope appeared under the door.

"Tickets!" I exclaimed. "To a Pittsburgh Pirates, Atlanta Braves game! Wonder when?" I checked the date printed on the tickets and then said, "Game starts in forty-five minutes. It's just across the river. I'm game if you are."

"Who sent them?" Jimmy, always the skeptic, replied.

I looked inside the envelope and there was nothing.

Jimmy's phone sounded. A text message from Joy. MORRIS SAYS TO ENJOY THE GAME. Jimmy looked at me. "Appropriate, coming from Santiago. A Pirates game, no less."

"So, we going? Might miss the first inning. But

I haven't been to a Major League game since...since I don't remember when. Should be fun."

"Hot dogs for dinner, then," Jimmy replied. "That was an easy decision."

After the game, we walked across the Roberto Clemente Bridge, one of the Three Sisters bridges spanning the Allegheny River in the downtown area, the Andy Warhol and Rachel Carson bridges being the other two. The three bridges are all painted yellow, Aztec Gold according to a public service spiel displayed on the giant screen between one of the innings. The announcement also pointed out that these three bridges are the only trio of nearly identical bridges in the United States and were the first self-anchoring suspension bridges built in the country.

"Look at these locks," I said to Jimmy, calling attention to the hundreds, if not thousands, of locks fastened to the bridge structure. Most had a male and female name painted on the lock face, but on a fair number the names were of the same sex. "How about we go get a lock?"

"And do what with it?"

"You're so romantic, Jimmy. Lock it to this bridge and throw the keys in the river. We'll be linked forever."

I half expected Jimmy to say something to the effect that such an act would be a dumb thing to do to a perfectly good lock. But instead he surprised me by saying, "Hey, not a bad idea. Let's get a lock, a good big strong one, and come back here, maybe tomorrow."

I slipped my arm around his while we both studied the water below us. We then slowly continued across the bridge. Near the end, I spotted a flight of stairs leading down toward the river. Leaning over the side, I realized there was a wharf about thirty feet below us. "Come, Jimmy, let's walk along the river. If I'm not mistaken, the wharf leads down to the Point, which is not far from the hotel. We can check out the artists as we go."

And that's how we found ourselves on the Allegheny River wharf, directly across the river from Heinz Stadium, at twelve-ten AM on Friday, June 7th, as recorded in the Point State Park Official Incident Report.

FIVE

PENNSYLVANIA DEPARTMENT OF
CONSERVATION AND NATURAL RESOURCES
POINT STATE PARK DIVISION

Date of Incident: 7 June 2019
Time of Incident: 00:10
Ranger: Grandkowski, J.
Badge: 7913
Party 1: Angella Martinez CF
DOB: April 25, 1969
Party 2: Jimmy Redstone CM
DOB: February 3, 1958
Party 3: Unknown
DOB:
Party 4:
DOB:
Add sheets for additional parties
Environmental Conditions: Dark, Overcast, Dry.
Temp 65F.
Description of Events: Parties 1 and 2 were
walking south along east bank of Allegheny
River on their way from PNC Park to Wyndham.
100 yards north of the fountain, Party 1 noticed
unnatural movement off to her left in the nature

area among the trees. She pushed party 2 forward an instant before (in her words) "two shots from a handgun were fired." Both parties state they heard movement among the trees consistent with at least one party exiting the scene. Party 2 claims to have seen one male moving away from him. Both parties drew weapons, but both deny discharging their firearm. Party 1 called 9-1-1 at 00:10 and Park Ranger 7913 responded at 00:17.

No bullets or casings were located.

No clear evidence of a shooter was found. Canvas of hired security for the Three Rivers Art Festival revealed no observation of anyone leaving the river area at the time of the incident. Neither party has a Pennsylvania Firearm Permit. Both parties possess valid Texas LTCs. Reciprocity under 18 PA C.S. 6106 (b) (15) cannot be verified until Attorney General office opens at 09:00. Both parties claim their Texas LTC is valid in PA due to their former employment at DHS. Status verified at 06:20 by phone. Wolf.

Parties were detained until verified. Released from detention at 06:22.

John Grandkowski	June 7, 2019	06:50
Signed	Date	Time

"You buying what Grandkowski said about us stumbling into a drug deal?" I asked Jimmy as we made our way back to the hotel from the detention center. The sun was already up, and I was exhausted. Jimmy, God bless him, had managed to catch a few hours' sleep on the floor of the small office where we were being "detained." Grandkowski explained that he could not allow us to use a cot in a cell unless we were officially arrested. Which also meant the full routine, including finger printing, pictures, strip search, valuables check, not that either of us had anything of value on us. We both opted for the floor of the cramped office.

"A one-person drug deal gone bad? I doubt it. Someone tracked us from the hotel." Jimmy paused to stretch his back. "My days of doing this stuff are well behind me. Time to get me a cozy desk job."

"You'd die of boredom — or an infected paper cut. Keep your day job, my friend." Jimmy didn't even crack a smile. "You don't suppose whoever's following us will show up on the hotel surveillance video?"

"Tiny's checking that as we walk. But I highly doubt we'll be that lucky."

"Professional?"

"Absolutely," Jimmy confirmed. "For one thing, those two shots were fired entirely too close to each other to be anything but professional. For another, not a blade of grass was trampled, not a flower stepped on."

"The clincher for me, Jimmy, was the lack of casings, coupled with not one of those security folks seeing anything. I'd say very highly trained."

"Don't put a lot of faith in those security folks. They're mostly part-timers picking up a few bucks. Hired to keep people from stealing the generators and the food. Doubt if they'd even notice who came and went, as long as nothing they were assigned to watch was touched."

"Tell me about Tiny. Surprised he's even taking

our calls. I only caught part of your conversation with him, but it seemed he knew we were here."

"Seems to me, don't quote me on it, but I'd say if Santiago is involved so is Tiny. He didn't exactly know we were in Pittsburgh, but he did know the *Pirate* is on our plate."

"So he has a view into Santiago. Not surprised."

"Tiny won't say one word more than he absolutely needs to, but my thinking is that Santiago got wind of Hugo's name from a drug operation gone bad. He believes the *Pirate's* been found somewhere in South Texas and Santiago is in a bidding war for it."

"So why Tiny? Don't know if he's wearing his Secret Service hat, or his CIA hat or what."

"Santiago's new business arrangements seem to suggest Middle East connections. That spells terrorism. Enter Tiny, along with a boat load of other agencies, from Homeland Security to Alcohol, Tobacco, Firearms and Explosives over at Justice."

"I don't know if that's good or bad, Jimmy. Why the hell can't we ever investigate something simple? I'm thinking perhaps a Monet lifted from the local library by a grandma in a wheelchair at high noon."

"Talk about boring. For you, that would be no different than...than selling pottery for a living?"

"Right now that sounds delightful, you ask me."

"You'd have to drop a pot every hour or so to get enough adrenalin flowing for you to stay alive."

"Truth is, Jimmy, you're right. I'd miss what we do. But being shot at in the dark, you have to admit, is outside the job description. I just...well, I just want to know what we're getting into."

"I wish I could tell you, Angella. I really wish I could. But that incident in the park gave us more information than we were likely to get any other way. At least now we're warned. Stay on our toes."

Incident in the park. He's so casual about the fact that had I not seen the movement when I did, we'd both be on slabs in the morgue, our brain matter being scrubbed off the sidewalk. If Jimmy's become so callused to life, am I far behind?

FIVE

Three hours of sleep may have sufficed back when I went through Army Ranger training, but those days are long behind me. Longer back than I care to admit. But the pounding on our hotel room door could no longer be ignored. Angella lifted her head, one eye squinting as if instructing me to make the racket go away.

But the racket wasn't going away. At least not until I did something about it. The word *police* broke through, causing me to take the noise even more seriously.

"Open this door immediately! Police investigation! Open the damn door!"

"Grandkowski?" I yelled as I stepped out of bed, my bladder about to explode. "Hold on just a moment." To Angella I said, "Sorry, but you had better get up. Grandkowski's not here to invite us to brunch. Something's got his knickers twisted."

"I'm not presentable."

"Don't imagine this'll be a fashion show," I called from the bathroom. "Look, I'll hold him off as long as I can, but from the noise he's making out there time's not on your side."

Angella slipped into the bathroom while I wrapped myself in a white robe and headed to the door.

"Angella here?" Grandkowski demanded the moment the door opened. "Need you both. Now!"

"She's making herself...presentable," I answered, glancing in the direction of the now closed bathroom door. "And who's this here with you?" I asked, nodding in the direction of a tall, slender, black woman whose eyes had already taken in every detail of our room and were now focused intently on me.

"This is Trooper Hessle. Pennsylvania State Police. She's working with me on this matter."

"What matter? What's changed that's got you so...so agitated?"

"I'll wait for the both of you, say it once. Angella," Grandkowski commanded, "we're waiting."

I studied Grandkowski a few beats. "Hold your voice down. No need to wake the hotel. She'll be right out." Trying to ease the tension, I added, "There's no window in there to climb out of."

"Don't even think about making a break for it," Grandkowski replied, his hand now on his holster. "This isn't a courtesy call. You have your weapons here with you in the room?"

"They're here. We went through all that last night. You know we have valid permits. What's the problem? We haven't had much sleep, so you've sure picked a bad time to bust us over some ad-min crap."

"You got more sleep than I got, I can assure you. Angella," he called over my shoulder, "please—"

The bathroom door opened and Angella stepped out wearing the shirt I had worn yesterday hanging down to her knees. A long way from a fashion statement.

"Mind if I slip on a pair of shorts?" she asked. "Oh, and who are you?" She was looking directly at the tall trooper.

"That's Trooper Hessle," Grandkowski said. "She and I are working this together. Yes, of course, but make it quick." Grandkowski turned his head as if giving Angella privacy, even though the sleeping area was physically separate from the sitting area where we stood.

Angella was gone less than two minutes, and from all outward appearances it still appeared as if she wore nothing beneath the shirt.

"I need to inspect your weapons," Grandkowski announced as soon as Angella had taken a seat on the mock leather sofa. "Where are they?"

"Now, why couldn't you have asked that while I was in the bedroom?" Angella's face muscles were taut with barely concealed anger.

"Please," Grandkowski said, "yinz just cooperate. Make this a ton easier."

"And if we refuse?" I asked, having no intention of refusing, but trying to sort through what was going on.

"I'll instruct Trooper Hessle to arrest you both."

Now I was on full alert.

"Let me understand," I began, motioning to my partner to sit back down and wait a moment before complying with the gun request. "You barge into our hotel room, knowing we just got to sleep. You demand to see our weapons, weapons you returned to us just a few hours ago, all with full knowledge that we both have valid carry permits. If you had a warrant, you wouldn't have knocked. And then you threaten us with arrest if we don't comply. So it's not about carry permits—or lack thereof—I got that much. You know damn well we didn't shoot anybody. So what gives?"

"Guns first."

"Explanation first," I replied, holding my ground. Having been in their shoes all too often, I knew how to set the ground rules.

"Look at the two of you," Angella said as the silence entered its second minute. "Two alpha dogs urinating over each other's water. This continues and soon you'll be peeing directly on each other. Compromise. You tell us what's going on and we promise to produce our weapons."

"Provided he agrees not to confiscate them without our permission," I added, signaling my reluctant agreement to breaking the stalemate.

Trooper Hessle nodded in Grandkowski's direction. "Fair enough," Grandkowski said, rolling his eyes. "I'll hold you both to that promise." He looked from me to Angella satisfying himself we would cooperate. Obviously, being instructed in the middle of the night by the governor to release a potential prisoner still weighed heavily on him. "We need to examine your weapons because...because an hour after you were released, a body was pulled out of the Mon."

"Not to be glib about it, but that's not the first floater you've recovered. What's this one have to do with us? Or more accurately, our weapons?"

From behind me where Trooper Hessle was standing, came a voice, the first words Hessle had spoken in our presence. Her resonance was so deep, and so male sounding that I had to turn my head to be certain another person hadn't joined us in the room. "Not many of them found with a 9mm slug imbedded in their brain."

Now we were being detained on a homicide investigation. If it hadn't been serious before, it certainly was now. *Shut your stupid mouth* was all my brain could process. *Demand a lawyer*.

Angella came awake. "You gotta be kidding! Bet there are a million 9mm weapons floating around and you're rousting us?"

"When was the last time you fired a round?" Hessle asked without addressing Angella's comment.

Say nothing!

"At the range, about a week ago," Angella said.

"You, Jimmy?" Grandkowski asked.

Say nothing.

"Don't make us do this the hard way, Jimmy. You want us to get a warrant, we'll get a warrant. But if your weapon wasn't fired recently, then what the hell? We're going to obtain the information one way or another. You know that and we know that."

"For what it's worth, a week before that," I confessed, knowing he was right about the warrant. Only with a warrant they wouldn't stop with just a few questions. They'd tie us up for days, probing every aspect of our lives. Been there, done that.

"Both at the same range?" Hessle pressed.

"Angella goes weekly. I'm not as rigorous. Usually every other week."

"Where do you shoot?"

"Almost always over at Krispy...I mean Bill... Kreem's range over in Brownsville."

"So, to be absolutely clear about this, Angella you last fired your weapon about a week ago, and you, Jimmy, last discharged about a week before that. Is that accurate?"

"It is for me," I said, ignoring the now screaming voice that demanded I shut my mouth.

"For me as well," Angella said.

"Angella, when did you last clean the pistol?"

"The night after I last fired it."

"Jimmy?"

"Same night as Angella."

"Okay. Now may I examine your weapons? Let's do this one at a time. You first, Angella."

I nodded. Angella went into the bedroom and returned a moment later with her weapon. Trooper Hessle expertly tore it down, sniffed, ran her thumbnail across several surfaces, sniffed her nail and handed it back. She then pointed to me.

I followed Angella's lead and retrieved my Beretta. Hessle repeated her routine and while she did so I silently thanked Angella for restraining me from taking a shot at the shooter. I had actually managed to have him in my sights for an instant, and when I stopped to take the shot she had yelled not to. Later she reminded me we were no longer operating under the mantle of law enforcement, and we had no real reason to shoot someone who was running away from us. She, of course, was correct. Shooting a man in the back is never a good approach, whether or not you wear a law enforcement cloak.

From the lack of any comment when Hessle handed me back the Beretta, I assumed we had passed whatever test she had administered. "Okay. I think I have what I need," she announced, her voice now even deeper than before. "Sorry to have upset you."

Grandkowski held his hand up. "I realize I promised not to confiscate your weapons, but... but here's the thing. I need to sign the paperwork, and the Captain'll have my ass if I don't have the lab confirm. Here's what I'll do," he continued, all the while fishing two evidence bags out of his pocket. "I'll see to it the lab gets right on it and back to you by tomorrow."

"Back to us by end of the day today," I said, realizing I had no real leverage here.

"Done," Grandkowski said, slipping our weapons into individual bags, then carefully writing our respective names on the outside together with the date and time.

"So why us?" Angella asked the trooper. "You can't actually believe we shot some guy down by the river. Why in hell would we have done that?"

"Didn't say you did anything. Just tidying the ends."

"Time of death?" Angella asked. Frustration still showing around her eyes and lips.

"Nothing official yet. Best guestimate, between eight and ten tonight."

"We were at the Pirate game," Angella announced, giving away more than I would have. She fished the stubs from her bag and handed them to Hessle. "Here! Now leave us alone would you please."

"So you say," Hessle responded. "Ticket stubs alone prove nothing."

"That's bull crap! And you know it!"

But the door had already closed behind them.

"Never a dull moment," Angella said. "I suggest we shower and get on up to visit Hugo's mother sooner rather than later. Someone's obviously trying to throw roadblocks at us."

"Roadblock is a good word. This was planned to take us out."

Angella's lips pulled tight, signaling something I had said triggered a memory. "Jimmy," she began, her voice tentative, "now that I focus on it, the 9-1-1 operator responded to my report of the shooting by saying, 'You say you're at Point Park. Okay. A Park Ranger has been dispatched.' I interpreted that at the time to mean that she had just dispatched Grandkowski as a result of my call. But it could also be that Grandkowski had already been dispatched from an earlier 9-1-1 call."

"Check your cell. What time did you call it in?"

"Here it is. 9-1-1 call at 12:14. Didn't the incident report show 00:10?"

"That's four minutes before you called. Unless I'm mistaken, three minutes did not expire between the shots and your call."

"Minute, maybe two. For certain not four. And with smart phones times are electronically controlled. Not off by much at all."

"That call came in just before, or just after, the shooting."

"Not possible to be after. Shooter was moving too fast, or we would have seen him." Angella shook her head. "Or the shooter wasn't alone!"

"Those shots were intended to provoke us into firing our weapons. Had we done so, we'd be sitting in that jail right this very moment waiting for our arraignment on a first-degree murder charge! Dead guy in the river, a 9mm bullet in his brain, I assume the bullet will match our weapons, and our guns would have been recently fired. I've managed to obtain Grand Jury indictments on far less than that."

SIX

Jimmy was driving, and I was enjoying the lush scenery. Having spent most of my life in South Texas, where the predominant color is brown except in late summer when many of the fields are white with cotton, I was struck with how vivid the greens were. We had turned off of I-79 and were now on a winding roller coaster of a road snaking down one hill and up another. The GPS indicated we had 3.7 miles to go, and it seemed frozen at that number. Time of arrival was now nine minutes out. "So what do you suppose Lucy Lowell has to offer," I asked, "being Oscar's mother and all?"

"Adopted mother. Didn't you tell me his mother was Katherine O'Connell? Born without benefit of marriage."

"Jimmy, you skipped a generation. Not like you. Katherine is Oscar's grandmother. She had an affair with a guy named Hugo who, you will recall, changed his name from Hugo to Villanova when he assumed the false identity of the professor."

"Sorry, I was concentrating on the events of last night. So this guy Oscar Hugo who we're tracking is the son of this Lucy woman."

"Yes. Lucy Stone Lowell. Husband died a few years back. She's our best link to him at this point. Info we have puts her at seventy-three."

Jimmy, following the GPS instructions, turned into a community of windy roads and attached houses. Doubles actually; each cluster of two was nicely landscaped, each with a private garage and a separate front door. The area was sprawling with homes snaking off into the distance.

"Right turn in 150 feet," the British accented female voice instructed. "Destination is on the right." A moment later, "You have arrived. Navigation has ended."

Jimmy took the liberty of pulling into the driveway, and we sat in the car a moment to see if anyone would come out to greet us. Not only did the door not open, but I couldn't see anyone moving in any direction.

The community was much too well maintained to be a ghost town, but towns I had driven through in Texas had more people wandering about than this community did. All the homes were landscaped pretty much the same, everything generic green and low cut, with a few pink flowers peeking out here and there.

"Nobody seems to be welcoming us. Time to knock on the door," Jimmy announced. "See what Mrs. Lowell has to say for herself."

But Mrs. Lowell had nothing to say. Not because she refused, but because she didn't answer the door. After the third round of knocking, Jimmy took a step back to where I was waiting. I started to turn back toward the car and came face to face with a man. A large man, both in height and girth. His fists were tight and so was his face. "Bang on that door all day, you can. Get no answer. You have business here?"

"Who are you?" Jimmy demanded, reacting poorly to the man's in-your-face manner. "Neighbor?"

"What's that to you?" the man answered. "You the one wants something. You can state your business or git."

"Is this the Lowell home? Lucy Lowell?" I said, forcing my way between the testosterone-laden war of words.

"Who's asking?"

"My name's Angella Martinez. And this is Jimmy Redstone. We're...we work for an insurance company."

"Oh, insurance! Why didn't you say so sooner?" The big guy took a welcome step backward. "She's been waiting for you folks." His face softened a tad. "Sure has taken enough time."

"Why's that?" I asked, confused.

"Lucy fell last week. Broke her hip pretty nasty, she did. She's over in rehab. Called me just this morning. Wants me to bring her mail."

"And who are you?" I asked, as softly as I could manage.

"Bill Brant. Live over there." He pointed across and up the road to an indeterminate house. "Knew her husband before he passed. Nice folks."

"Where can we find her?"

"See'n as though yinz're from the insurance company, don't mind telling you. Not like those other...other thugs they were. Wetbacks, you ask me. Sent them packing, I did. Mrs. Lowell...Lucy... is over at the rehab center. Can't miss it. Sits atop the hill. Go out the complex, turn left, make the first right and keep going up the hill. Can't miss it up there."

"Thank you," Jimmy said. Then making it seem like an afterthought, asked, "And when where those...those other men...here?"

"Just last night. About seven-thirty or so. It was just starting to get dark. Maybe eight. Can't be sure."

"Has her son been by?"

Brant studied us for a while, a puzzled expression on his face. He started to ask a question, paused, then said, "Surprised you know Hugo, what you being insurance adjusters and all."

"Name's in the file as person to contact. Thought we'd talk to him about caring for his mother."

Brant's face softened again. "Thought you was being nebby, is all. Haven't seen the boy like forever. When he was working for the government he was here all the time. Lucy says he quit his job, and ever since he's hardly ever around. Seen him once since then. You can't count on him helping his mother, he's never around. And from things she's said, he's always in a hurry."

"In a hurry?"

"Comes to visit. Gets his mail and stuff and leaves. Fifteen minutes at most."

"What stuff?" I asked.

"You know, packages and things."

"Mail?"

"Not so much mail, but...but boxes. Friends drop stuff off. Like just last evening a woman came by looking for Lucy. Seen her before. Had a package all wrapped up. Sent her to the rehab center just like you. Here," he thrust a few letters rolled up in a People magazine in our direction, "take her mail to her, would ya? I can't make it today. Tell her I'll come over tomorrow."

Fifteen minutes later we were in the rehab facility, a converted monastery built in the early 1800s, standing outside room 203, the name "Lucy Lowell" clearly displayed on the door. A picture of a hip was pinned beside her name. Everything about this place was massive, from the width of the hallways to the height of the ceilings to the size of the windows.

A quick knock on the big heavy door, and in we went. The room itself was large enough for a suite, but it held only a single bed. In it lay a sleeping woman, her right leg in a cast supported from a tripod at the base of her bed. A vase of bright red roses sat on the windowsill, flanked by two pictures. One was a framed portrait of a man in his very early twenties, which I assumed was her son, probably taken when he graduated from college. The other was an unframed watercolor landscape of a flower garden as seen through the window of a building, a window very much smaller than the one this portrait was propped against.

Jimmy and I walked over to the window to get a better look at the picture.

"That's my son," a frail voice said from behind us. "He's the one sends me the flowers. And you two are?" Lucy Lowell appeared tiny, frail, the cast taking up more real estate than her entire body.

"Angella, and I'm Jimmy," my partner answered. "And we take it you're Lucy Lowell?"

"You from the insurance company? Bill, my neighbor, called a bit ago and told me you'd be along. About time, I'd say."

"Well," I began, "we're not exactly—"

"How did you break your hip?" Jimmy asked, overriding my hesitation. "Fall?"

"Tripped over a curb. Why do you ask? Isn't it in the report?"

"Just wanting to make good and sure they're

taking proper care of you. Never can be too careful, you know," Jimmy responded, his tone conveying concern for her well-being. "Healing okay?"

"Doctor says it'll take a good two months, maybe three, but I'll be good as new. He says I'll need rehab for a while after that. Want to be sure insurance will cover it."

"That shouldn't be a problem, as I see it." Jimmy said.

If you believe noses grow when lies are told, then Jimmy's nose just extended an inch or more.

"That's good, 'cause Doc says I'll be out dancing before I know it. Didn't dance before, not since my poor...oh, don't need to bore you with that stuff. I'm just worried I'll have no money to pay for all this fancy medical stuff."

"Just you work on getting better. Rehab is what it takes." Jimmy was firing on all fours. "You said that's your son in that picture. Taken a while ago?"

"Twenty or so years back. Just after he graduated college. He's a Mountaineer, you know. Just like my husband. Don Knotts went there, you know. Before he went down to Peru." She reached over to twist a straw in her direction.

Jimmy held the cup for her while she sipped the water.

"That my mail you got there?"

Jimmy nodded and placed the few mail pieces on a side table. He handed the magazine to her.

"Peru?" I asked, assuming she meant her son had gone to Peru and not Don Knotts.

"His grandfather, on my late husband's side, is...was...he's gone now, a research something or other down there. Into birds, I believe. Collected art, I understand. That's when my son changed his name. Don't know why he did that, always angered me. He worked for the government there for a while. Now...now I don't know where he works."

Not letting on we knew about the name change, Jimmy said, "Name change? From what to what?"

"Lowell to...to Hugo. I don't understand why, but he now goes by Hugo. I mean his last name is Hugo. He kept the name I gave him. Oscar, after my own grandfather."

"When did you last—"

Now it was my turn to override Jimmy. "Has he visited you here in the...the rehab center?"

"Just two days ago. Brought those lovely roses. I had him go over to my house and bring me that picture. I always liked that picture of him. It showed him...well before he...well, the way I like to see him. He's all I have left, you know."

"He paint the flowers?" I asked.

"Carrie Buck, a friend of his, brought that picture here just last night. She's in town for some showing or something. She said it was something her father painted years ago. It's for Oscar for when he comes back. She knows how I enjoy flowers, so she said I could look at it until then."

I couldn't help asking, "Does this Carrie often bring stuff for Oscar? I mean, presents and things?"

"What's all this got to do with my insurance?"

"Oh, just want to be sure you have everything you need. Is there anything else we can get for you?"

"My old hip back."

"Sorry about that.

"You haven't answered my question, young man. Will the insurance pay for all this or will I have—"

"I don't see why not," Jimmy said. "Anyone gives you a problem. Tell them to call Jimmy. Mind if I look at that picture?"

"Suit yourself, but would you please hold that water for me again? Those nurses are always too busy doing something else."

Jimmy held the water bottle while she drained it dry. "Want more? I can go get—"

"That'll hold me a while. Don't want to drink so much I have to...it's hard using that pan."

Jimmy went to the window and studied the portrait. Then he casually asked, "Know where this is? I mean, where this picture was painted?"

"I believe down in Peru. Carrie was Hugo's teacher."

"At West Virginia?"

"No. No. When he went to Pitt. That's where

he met Carrie. Nice lady. Always brings paintings and stuff for Oscar."

Jimmy studied the back of the picture a moment, then turned his concentration on the image itself. "Thank you," he finally said to the widow Lowell. "Is there anything further you need from us?"

"Not that I can think of. Jimmy and Angella you say? So I'll get rehab for my hip?"

"That's correct. Use our names if you need anything." Nodding in my direction, Jimmy said, "Okay, Angella, time to go. Mrs. Lowell needs to get some rest." Turning back to the old woman, Jimmy said, "Thank you, Mrs. Lowell. Appreciate your time. Be well."

"No, thank *you* young man. You set my mind at ease about the insurance. I'll remember your names, Jimmy and Angella. Bless you."

"So what did you see? " I asked my partner as we walked to the car.

Jimmy put his left finger beside his nose. Our signal not to believe his next words.

"Just a picture. I was interested in the colors, but nothing stood out. Just a quick watercolor sketch."

"So what's next?"

"Wish I knew," Jimmy answered. "Wish I knew. Let's head back downtown, sort it out then."

I checked to see if Jimmy's finger was still beside his nose. It wasn't. But his eyes were focused intently on a white car, I think a Prius, that had turned out of the parking lot shortly behind us. I started to speak, and his finger immediately went to his lips in the universal "be quiet" sign. He then turned to face me and gave an exaggerated wink. I nodded in response and when he was certain I understood we were under surveillance, he began, "Angella, that list of possible art storage places you compiled, I assume you locked it in the room safe at the Wyndham."

"I did," I dutifully replied, not yet following what he was talking about because we hadn't compiled any such list.

"Okay. When we get back be sure to cross off old lady Lowell. Mind making a quick stop at the mall to pick up more clothes? We didn't bring nearly enough with us."

"Shopping is always on my to do list. Don't have to ask twice." Now it was my turn to wink.

Jimmy accelerated the car but had to slam on the brakes a moment later and pull off the road almost to the barrier separating us from a nasty spill into a deep ravine in order to allow a fire truck and two ambulances to pass going in the opposite direction. When they were safely behind us and Jimmy was certain no more were coming, he then drove back onto the narrow winding road, and we continued in silence to the mall.

Before getting out of the car, Jimmy leaned close and whispered, "I'm thinking one or both of us are wired for sound. Buy two full sets of clothes, undies and all."

I didn't understand the undies part of it, thinking he had Victoria's Secret on his mind. But then I remembered back to the time when we had first begun working together, and some slime ball had actually glued ultra-small state-of-the-art mics into my bras. The thought that it might have happened again sent shivers down my spine.

SEVEN

"There's even an on/off switch on the little sucker," I said, throwing the bag with the bugged bra in the back seat. "I inserted a pin in that little hole as we were taught. It's off now."

"How do you know the switch works? Maybe its phony to make you believe it's off?"

"Don't do that to me, Jimmy! I'm upset enough. I thought about leaving it in the dressing room, but then whoever's monitoring would know we found them. This way I'm thinking we can feed them false info, like you did before. Turn it on and off as we want."

"Only if it works as you think."

"Now you have me spooked. Mind if I call Tiny and ask? I got a picture I can forward to him to make certain we're on the same page."

"Best not to at this point."

"You think the government's involved in this?"

"I have no doubt. Art objects are being used to finance terrorism, that much we know for certain. Joy so much as told us that's what's going on. We told Silver. Silver told his government buddies. That puts DHS in play, which in turn puts us in play. Crap flowing downhill theorem."

"So you think we're bait for their traps? I suppose that explains why Tiny sprung us from jail last night."

"But not before they planted mics on our stuff."

"It's possible those mics belong to Santiago's folks."

"Possible. But with that little shooting caper they pulled, they thought we'd be in government issued skivvies for a while, so no need to bug our civilian clothes. Besides, these babies are too sophisticated for Santiago."

Before I could respond, Jimmy's phone rang. A series of noncommittal "okays", "yeps" and "got-its", followed before Jimmy put the phone back in his pocket.

"So?"

"So, that was Hessle."

"And?"

"Thanking me for the tip on the safe. I called her as soon as I stripped in the changing room. So far, no one's showed up."

"So?"

"Nothing more."

Jimmy hadn't been this closed for several years. *He thinks the car's bugged.* "Your conversation was too long for just—"

"Fill you in later." Jimmy confirmed my suspicions about the car being bugged by placing his finger across his lips. We drove in silence until he exclaimed, "Oh, crap! Tire light just came on. Find the nearest Avis place, and let's get this puppy changed."

I didn't see a tire light and I certainly didn't feel any change in the ride. But changing cars was definitely the thing to do. "Hey, we're in luck. There's one over on Route 19, less than two miles from here. Think the tire will hold out, or should we call for help?"

"We'll the do the best we can. Call them if it goes completely flat."

I gave Jimmy the directions and settled back, knowing he wouldn't say anything until we were away from the car. He didn't disappoint. But he did surprise me when he turned the car in and refused the attendant 's offer of an upgraded substitute. Instead, he announced that we were going down the block to Hertz.

"Why Hertz, Jimmy?" I asked when we were half a block away. "You never use them."

"Did I say Hertz?" Jimmy smiled his best I-was-just-playing-to-the audience smile. "I meant Budget."

I checked my cell. "The nearest Budget is ten

miles away. There's an Enterprise four and a half miles back that way."

"Okay, Enterprise it is."

"We walking?"

"That's what they made Lyft for."

Twenty seven minutes later — six waiting for the Lyft, eight driving, thirteen signing the papers and waiting for the car to be washed — and we were back on the road, this time sporting a green SUV that looked more appropriate for a family of six than a couple of middle-aged insurance investigators — or whatever the hell we were this week.

"Where to now, Jimmy?" I asked as I pulled out of the parking lot. "How about finding us a new hotel, perhaps not exactly in downtown. I'd say the Pitt area, somewhere in Oakland. That's close enough to downtown, but off the beaten path, so to speak."

A few minutes later Jimmy had booked us into a Quality Inn on a street called the Boulevard of the Allies. "Place is above a Panera Bread. At least the room should smell good."

"We checking in now or what?"

"Thought we'd stop by the art show first. Find that Buck woman."

"Set it on the GPS. How 'bout we park across the river? I'm thinking one of the Heinz Field lots and walk across the bridge. No need to tip off the Wyndham watchers we changed rides. They'll figure it out soon enough."

"Call it a plan," Jimmy said, already working on the navigation app on his cell.

One hour and one funnel cake topped with white sugar indulgence later, we stopped in front of a tent displaying multicolored blown glass contained within various shaped metal housings. The housings alone were gorgeous, and when combined with the vivid glass, the whole was breathtaking. So were the prices. I didn't see a tag under ten thousand dollars. Out of our league, but I couldn't control my eyes as they went from one piece to another.

"Like the pieces, I see." The voice was soft, comforting even. It belonged to a trim woman in her mid-seventies, sitting on a tall stool in the back corner. The brim of a large hat flopped over her face. But even so, it was evident the sun had taken its toll on her skin, especially on her forehead and cheeks. She was either bald or her hair was in a bun under the hat.

"You Carrie?" Jimmy asked, moving inside the tent.

"That's me."

"Are you the artist?" I chimed in. "Your work is...creative. And it resonates with me."

"Thank you. That's what keeps me doing this. The metal patterns are copied from the Inca period."

"Peru?" Jimmy inquired.

"Actually, Ecuador."

"Ecuador?" I said. "I didn't know—"

"The Incas of Western Ecuador created distinctive shapes. These are copied from those shapes. Of course, I took artistic liberty, so you can't actually find any of these exact shapes in the literature."

"No matter, I love them." I glanced at Jimmy to take his temperature on the artwork. I had one of them in mind for the office area of our new penthouse condo atop the Riviera Hotel on South Padre Island. The thought crossed my mind that Silver might spring for the art. After all, it was Great Southern's office.

I turned to Jimmy, thinking I'd get his take on asking Jack, but his eyes were focused on a figure quickly moving away from where we were positioned. Not exactly running, but closer to running than brisk walking.

Using my phone, I snapped a few pictures of the retreating individual. Turning back toward Carrie Buck I held the screen in her direction. "Recognize this person?"

She glanced at the image and quickly answered with a shake of her head. I had the distinct feeling she was either lying or hiding something. I studied the screen a moment, noticed another man hanging out at a tent not far away, his eyes focused in my direction." And what about this man?" I asked Carrie, pointing to the man standing beside booth 97. I glanced over in that direction, and unfortunately he was now gone, having disappeared in less than thirty seconds.

"I don't know either of them," Buck said, turning her body away from me even though there was no other potential customer in the vicinity.

"Ever see him before?" I pressed.

"Can't say as I have. What's this about? Something wrong?"

"Nothing's wrong," Jimmy answered. "Just asking about a man who I believe is running away from your booth, and a man—"

"There are many booths along here," Carrie volunteered. "Why do you think he was running from mine?"

"—and a man that seems to have been standing across from your booth for a while now. You don't recognize either?"

"Who are you?" Carrie demanded.

"Friends of Lucy Lowell. She said to say hello."

"Oh, Lucy! You know her?" A proprietor's smile again appeared on Carrie's face.

"Visited with her earlier today. Saw the painting you gave her. Mind telling us about it?"

"How's Lucy doing?" Carrie asked. I couldn't determine if she was genuinely interested in the old lady or just plain stalling, trying to work out a plausible story about the painting.

"Hip's getting stronger," Jimmy said, his tone friendly as it often is when he's intent on obtaining information from a reluctant witness. "You paint that picture?"

"What...oh, yeah, the one I gave Lucy. It's from my father's collection."

Jimmy gave her a long look. His way of communicating that her answer made no sense. Her father had to be in his nineties. It's possible, I suppose, for him to be still working, but given her obvious lies about the men in the photo I had just showed her, I didn't fault Jimmy for being dubious.

"My father is—"

"Fancy bumping into you two," a deep voice from behind us said. The same deep voice we first heard in our hotel room early this morning. Without turning around, I knew it to be Pennsylvania State Trooper Sonja Hessle. Her right hand disappeared behind her and I half expected to see a weapon in her hand when it next came into view. But instead, she was holding her cell phone. But the screen was facing Carrie Buck, not me. "Recognize this?"

"Of course I do," Buck responded. "Picture I gave my friend. We were just discuss—"

"You paint it?"

"My father. I was just about to—"

"Is it valuable?"

"Define valuable?" Buck demanded. "What's valuable to one person is—"

"Stop toying with me!" Hessle demanded, her eyes going instantly hard—and scary. "What's your name?"

Carrie gave the big trooper her name, who then, using a softer voice, asked, "So this is your stall?

This your stuff? You make this? Blow the glass and all?"

"Yes, to all of it. And I'm not toying. What has value to one person may not have any to the next. All depends."

"Put a price on that picture. The one you gave your friend. Friend have a name?"

"Lucy. Lucy Lowell."

"How do you know Mrs. Lowell?"

"Through her son, Oscar. A student, former student actually, of mine. Now a good friend. What's all this about?"

"This Oscar have a last name?"

"Lowe...Hugo. He changed it to Hugo some years back."

"When did you first meet this Oscar Lowell... Hugo?"

"Way back. In another life it seems."

"Put a date on it."

"1977, I believe it was. Why all the—"

"So you just give Mrs. Lowell art work?"

"Broke her hip. Cheer her up. What's this about?"

"Art you left, was it for the mother or the son?"

"What's this—"

"Answer the friggin question!"

"Son."

"You haven't told me what's it worth. Depends is not acceptable."

"Let's just say over ten thousand."

"How far over?"

"A bit."

"You missing a few zeros? Let's try this again. If that piece of art was hanging over there on that board what would you be selling it for?"

"Not for sale."

"Not for sale. Yet you gave it as a gift."

"My prerogative. It's from my father's collection."

"So add on the zeros and give me a number. The number you would get if indeed you decided to sell it."

"Two hundred thousand, or thereabouts."

"How many thereabouts?"

"About twenty or so. Depends."

"There we go with *depends*. You say it's worth two hundred-twenty or so thousand, yet you gave it away? Pardon me for being skeptical."

"As I said, my prerogative. Now are you done with this...this inquisition?"

"And you just gave it away? Just like that, for no reason, you gave your friend Hugo a quarter of a million-dollar picture?"

"I broke no laws. I don't need to explain anything to you! Get out of here! Or, I'll call...Just get out!"

"Sorry this is such a problem for you," the big cop said, her eyes still red-hot. "Since you claim you broke no laws then why so agitated?"

"You have no right to question me. It's harassment!"

"Hardly harassment, Ms. Buck, but I will honor your request—for now." Trooper Hessle backed out of the tent and motioned for Jimmy and me to follow. Once out from under the tent, Hessle turned back to face the artist who had her own cell phone out. "Tip," Hessle called to Buck. "Don't forget to file your 709. IRS will thank you."

Buck's eyebrows shot up, as did mine, totally not understanding what Hessle meant by a 709.

"Gift Tax Form," Jimmy said, coming to my rescue. "Bet she wouldn't appreciate being audited."

"Caught Capone that way," Hessle reminded us. "Still a good tool."

"What the hell was that about?" Jimmy said. "You hit a nerve."

"As well I should have. I'm certain you recognize the picture. Right after you left the rehab center someone lifted that picture from her room."

"I had no idea it was worth what she—"

"If it's the master *Bucksbaum* it is. And maybe even more."

"A what?" I replied.

"A *Bucksbaum*. Otto Bucksbaum. Look it up."
And she was gone.

EIGHT

"The flowers of Otto Bucksbaum are remarkable for many reasons," I said, reading to Jimmy from an Internet blurb. We were sitting on a bench overlooking the Allegheny River, enjoying the sunshine and the light breeze coming off the river. "For starters, they were painted while he was incarcerated at Ebensee Concentration Camp in Austria from mid-1944 to May 6, 1945, when the camp was liberated. There were twenty-eight of them, one every two weeks, and they—"

"Twenty-eight. If each is really worth a quarter mill that means they're worth seven million—"

I started to respond, but waited until an attractive woman with a white cotton ball of a dog wearing a harness proclaiming his name to be Franco ambled by. Once she was out of hearing range, I continued. "Actually, Jimmy, well over a hundred, according to what I'm reading. But, let me finish."

Jimmy fell quiet and I continued reading. "Questions remain to this day as to how he produced the color, where the paper and brushes came from. Even how the paintings made their way out remains a mystery. It's impossible, or so it says here, to believe he had time to paint and still dig the tunnels like the other men in the camp." I skimmed the article, then said, "Here's another unanswered question: Where did he learn to paint? Apparently, he had no formal training, and no paintings of his are known to exist prior to Ebensee or afterward. In fact, he came from an iron ore mining community and lived high up in the Alps above an open pit mine. Speculation is that because the hills had been stripped of vegetation, he may never have even seen a flower. If he had, it would have been when he was a young boy."

"I'm certainly not an art expert, Angella," Jimmy replied, studying the picture he had taken of the painting on his cell phone, "but all I see here are dots of color for each flower. Two colors mainly, red and orange. The red seems predominant and the orange snakes around. Can't believe it takes much training to do this. Just saying."

"All I can tell you is the set of them are worth over a hundred mil."

"How old is this Otto?"

"He was last seen celebrating his ninetieth birthday. Lived in Ein Hod, an artist village near Haifa at the base of Mount Carmel."

"That mean he's deceased?"

"There does seem to be a bit of a mystery about his death. I see here a picture of a grave marker with the name Bucksbaum beneath what I believe are Hebrew letters. At the bottom are the dates 1918—2016. But this is what's confusing. There's a New York sighting of him in 2017, but the local Ein Hod authorities issued a statement saying that Bucksbaum was laid to rest in 2016 in the Beit Oren Cemetery."

"So what's his daughter doing giving away his art work?"

"Not exactly giving it away," the deep voice of Trooper Hessle boomed. She was still fifty feet away and couldn't possibly have overheard our conversation from wherever it was she had been stationed.

"You have a warrant for that surveillance microphone?" Jimmy said, jumping to his feet. "This is beyond tiresome!"

The two of them were eye to eye, making Hessle six feet or slightly taller. Her shoulders were even broader than Jimmy's, and from the easy way her arms hung at her sides the woman, perhaps as a man in an earlier life, had spent a good deal of time boxing. Perhaps she still did.

"Don't need it. You're in a public place with no expectation of privacy. Besides, it's not you two I'm interested in. Well, that is, unless I should be. You tell me."

"Won't dignify that with an answer," Jimmy said. "The mic off?"

Hessle tapped a pouch on her belt. "Now it is. But what the hell difference that makes to you I can't imagine."

"Humor us," Jimmy answered, taking a step backward.

"You got it. We're even."

"For what?"

"Leading us to the *Bucksbaum*."

"So you now have it?" I said, trying to piece together a puzzle without having all the pieces, and frankly, without having any of the corners or edges—or even colors.

"Not exactly. It was stolen from old lady Lowell ten minutes before I got there. Didn't want to tell you that earlier in Buck's tent. And, quite frankly, I hadn't run all the background on you two that I needed."

Jimmy waited for the cop to continue, but I jumped right in. "How'd the theft happen? Mrs. Lowell was right there with it. She musta seen who lifted it?"

"Nothing's ever that easy. You two should know that," Hessle said, letting us know she had indeed done her homework on our backgrounds. "Someone pulled the fire alarm box outside her door. They evacuated her first. The *Bucksbaum* was gone when Lowell got back. Nobody saw nothing."

That squared with the fire trucks that had run us off the road. "You alluded to us leading you to the painting," I pressed. "What's that about?"

"Let's walk. If my team can listen to you, so can theirs. And truth is, their side may be better funded than mine."

We walked north, the river on our left, with Hessle not saying a word until we were under the Clemente Bridge.

At first I thought we were heading up to street level, but Hessle stopped behind the step structure, and with the sound of car tires thumping across metal expansion plates over our heads making it almost impossible to hear each other, she said, "Cat's probably already out of the bag, but I'm here in Pittsburgh investigating a guy named Oscar Hugo, nee Lowell. Was a Federal Marshal until suddenly he wasn't. Left the service right after a piece of art his grandfather had, something called the *Golden Booby*, went missing. The homicide, actually maybe homicides, associated with that heist remains unsolved. A little birdie told me you two are looking for Hugo, perhaps because he may have some other art object—or objects—you're interested in."

It wasn't a question, but I nodded in agreement. Reminding myself you have to give to get. But I wasn't giving anything she didn't already know.

Hessle continued. "Based on that painted pony fiasco down in Jamaica you two worked on, you're well aware that art objects are now major currency in terrorist operations around the world. Not only are values skyrocketing, objects that have long been hidden away in ultra private collections, objects that no one outside of a few dealers and well-heeled billionaire collectors have ever heard of, are suddenly showing up."

"Like the *Bucksbaum*," Jimmy said.

"Like the *Bucksbaum*," Hessle agreed.

"A bunch of colored dots." Jimmy said. "I'm certainly not an art expert, far from it. But...but even I can tell that—"

"Here's the thing with the Bucksbaum collection. It's not any one picture. It's the collection. They were painted in a concentration camp by—"

"Ebensee Camp," I said.

"So, you've checked the Internet, Angella. Good for you. But what's not on there is that twelve of them show—"

"Internet says twenty-eight."

"Internet's been modified. Trust me on that. It says what we want it to say. Twelve of them show the path of the tunnels and where equipment is—was—located. The Nazis hid equipment in those tunnels in anticipation of Allied bombing. The paintings were Bucksbaum's contribution to the war effort. The other sixteen are...well...fake news."

"I don't follow," I said.

"The flowers are really just dots. Angella, your partner's right in that. Dots. Actually blood dots for the reds and oranges. Don't know about the other colors, probably dye from clothing, perhaps excrement. The theory is the deep reds are pure blood and show the actual path of the tunnel. The number of dots leading up from the bottom indicates how far from the camp the tunnel begins."

"How do you know the real pictures from the fake?" Jimmy asked.

"Red dots in both bottom corners," Hessle said. "Both corners means real. But, and here's the thing makes this fascinating, one of the paintings contains coded information of a different nature. I call it the *Master Bucksbaum*. That's the one's so valuable."

I had trouble digesting the fact that concentration camp pictures, possibly created by blood drops, would still be a mystery, a valuable mystery, nearly seventy-five years later. "What different nature?"

"Angella, for me, that's the key question. One theory is direction to a hidden treasure. Remember, a lot of silver and gold were removed from the prisoners and had to go somewhere. But then again, rumors of secret treasure maps abound. Bet you have more than your fair share down there on your island. My theory, and it's built on almost nothing, is the master contains names, coded names."

"Can't imagine names alone running the value up so high." I commented, trying to wrap my head around the whole concept. "How'd the paintings get out of the camp? There wasn't exactly a community post office."

"Money talks. Not unlike today. Not all Gestapo believed the party line. And it got worse as the war wound down. They were trying to save their own asses. Come, let's continue walking." Hessle remained quiet until we were positioned under the Warhol Bridge. There was far less noise there, and it was much easier to hear what the big cop was saying. "Where was I? Oh, you asked how they got out. This is pure rumor, but it's believed the camp commandant, a sadistic bastard by the name of SS Oberstrumführer Otto Riemer sold them to an Allied spy. Money was deposited in his name in Peru. Shortly after the deposit he got drunk and pictures of him killing several prisoners got out. He was demoted to the Post Office in the Gusen camp. Some say he orchastrated that to avoid being captured at Ebensee."

Jimmy pulled out his phone, studied the image of the picture he had taken for a moment before saying, "Looks like two red dots in the bottom corners."

"Indeed there are. Count the red dots starting in the center bottom and going up to the right."

Jimmy took his time, then said, "Twenty-two, if I counted right,"

"Bingo. Twenty-two miles to the northeast from the camp entrance is where the tunnel began."

"What's the significance?" I asked.

"Two things. First, it's the last of the twelve to come out from wherever they have been secreted.

This completes the set and for a collector there can be no greater thrill—and hence value."

"And second?" Jimmy asked.

"The dots depict a winding tunnel in that picture, actually a split tunnel, with one of the splits leading to an underground bunker where Hitler was rumored to stay."

Jimmy again studied the image on his screen, then said, "Can't make it out, but if that's true then even standing alone this picture is worth...a lot."

"So tell me exactly why you're on the trail of Hugo?"

Jimmy, in a rare display of candor, told Hessle about our discussion with Joy Malcom and about Santiago's interest in becoming an art dealer. He ended by emphasizing we were employed by Great Southern to track down art the company now owned by virtue of paying off claims for robberies. At the mention of our employer's name, Hessle's eyes rolled, but she said nothing.

"So you two have gone from working to protect the homeland to working to protect a major drug lord—a drug lord incarcerated for life in a Mexican prison. I'm having a hard time wrapping my brain around that."

"As I said, we represent Great Southern Insurance Company."

Jimmy was bristling and I hoped he would hold it together long enough to survive this interview without an altercation.

"Since it's impossible for your employer to have insured the *Bucksbaum*, I will accept your statement that this was a chance encounter. In that spirit, I will not expect you to be following up on that piece. By that piece I, of course, mean the *Bucksbaum*. Am I correct in that assumption?"

"You are correct," Jimmy responded, adding, "unless, of course, it turns out GS has insured that particular work of art. Then all bets are off."

"I doubt that's the case, but you will let me know if I am wrong. Is that clear?"

I nodded. Jimmy was busy observing something out on the water, real or not I couldn't determine.

"Jimmy?"

"Oh...yes. Yes, yes, of course."

"In the for-what-it's-worth category," Hessle began, her tone now conspiratorial, "when Hugo crossed over, he called in a ton of debts in the criminal world. He's well connected all across the country with federal criminals wanted for major crimes. The man's operating with as close to an army as a civilian can get. And, from what you just told me, Santiago is operating a cross-border venture, with Hugo playing some sort of role. Situation's as lethal as you can get."

"Thanks for the heads up," I said please to see law enforcement playing it straight up for a change.

"One more thing," Hessle said. "Does the name Juan Vega, mean anything to either of you? You might know him as JM."

Jimmy was far ahead of me on this. "Was a detective back when the *Golden Booby* murders went down. Left the force about that time. What's he got to—"

"Those rounds you fired at the range down in Brownsville. Guy by the name of JM collected several rounds from the range. Flashed a badge of some sort. Not positive yet, but sources claim JM's been seen in the Burgh. You two have made some nasty *friends* down there in Texas. Last night won't be the last time they come for you. You put Santiago away for life. He plans to return the favor. Trust me on that."

"That a threat?"

"That's a fact." Hessle looked from me to Jimmy and back again. "Either of you get anywhere near the *Bucksbaum* and *I'm* coming for you. Now that's a promise."

NINE

"I understand you're in Pittsburgh," came a very familiar voice when I answered my phone. Hessle hadn't been gone more than ten minutes; she had climbed the stairs to the Warhol Bridge and was out of sight before Angella and I made our way up to street level. My vision had her riding off on a broomstick, but Angella suggested she had had a car following us as we had walked along the wharf. When I inquired as to whether the car had been keeping a look out for her or an eye on us, Angella had responded, "Both, I would imagine."

I silently mouthed *Levi* to Angella, to let her know I was talking to Levi Ben-Yuval, a high-ranking officer of Mossad, the Israeli intelligence agency. He had been a decorated general in the Israel Defense Forces, and we had most recently been the beneficiary of his services in Jamaica. As we had learned, he had the ear of Prime Minister Netanyahu, which, in turn, meant he had access to our President. I said into the phone, "That we are, my friend. That we are."

"How about we get together?" Didn't much sound like a question.

"When and where are you thinking?"

"There's a restaurant in Squirrel Hill. On Murray Ave." He gave me the name, and said, "See you in forty minutes."

"So our Israeli friend's in Pittsburgh," I commented to Angella, as I repeated our brief conversation. "What should we make of that?"

"I don't suppose you think the three of us being in Pittsburgh at the same time is a coincidence." Angella replied, knowing how I felt about coincidences.

"And neither do you," I said and left it at that.

The Murray Avenue Grill was empty when we got there, and my first thought was that Levi had emptied the place. On second thought, he had just selected well. Angella had recently reminded me that restaurant back corners were reserved for spooks and folks stepping out on their partners. We weren't disappointed. Indeed, Levi Ben-Yuval had selected a table tucked in behind the soda dispensers, where even the waiter could lose track of us. He had a cell phone to his ear and a partially eaten bowl of half-sour pickles in the middle of the table. He motioned for us to join him, and when we did, he pushed the bowl in my direction. He held up his hand indicating he was about finished.

The pickles were excellent and the bowl empty when he finally put the phone down. "Nice to see you both. You're looking well. Thanks for joining me on...on such short notice. Sorry for being rude, but you'll benefit from what I just heard. But first, why am I here? Well, you may or may not yet know of an artist named Bucksbaum who—"

"We've heard of him. Concentration camp art, we understand."

"You can call it that, but it's far more. The critical piece is now believed to be in circulation after all these years. That's why I'm here in Pittsburgh. Israel desires to get its hands on that piece. But I'm ahead of myself. Sorry for that. I understand you two are here on the trail of a piece going by the name of *Pirate*. I also believe the *Kings Cup* is on your agenda as well. Mind confirming that for me?"

"Confirmed," I said. "Angella and I were asked to track it down the *Pirate* for...for a drug lord by the name of Santiago. But it turns out it's been insured by Great Southern and we're trying to locate it for our boss."

"Perhaps that's why the attack on your life, Jimmy. But I digress. Knowing your government, they won't tell you what I'm about to tell you."

"We're all ears," Angella said. "Can't wait to learn what our government doesn't deem important enough to tell us. Or maybe it's too important. State secret stuff."

"Not so much a secret, but your government believes certain art objects are about to be negotiated in a manner that will allow a significant amount of money, or shall I say barter currency, to become available to our mutual enemies. The *Pirate* is one of those pieces."

"And the others are?" I asked, now curious how deep this goes.

"You've heard of them all. In one way or another they're connected to your drug lord pal. The *Golden Booby*, the *Pirate*, and, of course, the *Kings Cup*."

"Before you went and put Santiago in prison, he had dabbled in smuggling stolen art objects in—and out—of your country. That's how he got his hands on the *Cup* in the first place. Your lawsuit defense alleges the *Cup* Joy had was a fake. Be careful with that defense, my friend. In the end you'll lose. Santiago may not have ownership papers, but trust me, the *Cup* that disappeared from Joy's condo is as genuine as you are. And yes, she's right about the street value, or at least the terrorist barter value, being well over a hundred million."

"Whether or not Jimmy has legal culpability for the disappearance of the *Cup* we need to leave to the judge and jury," Angella said, jumping to my defense. "All he did was take the photo of the *Cup* in Joyce's place that tipped off DHS. It's not Jimmy's doing the *Cup* went missing when they raided."

"Save it for the courtroom, Angella; it'll play better there." Ben-Yuval studied us both before continuing. "Let me shift the conversation. As you well know, border security under Trump has become a hot political issue. And smart people stay as far away from hot political issues as possible. Santiago, if nothing else, is smart. So he's moving away from drugs and prostitution into the world of terrorist financing. Banker to the bombers, if you like. And to do that he's teamed up with this guy Hugo. Oscar Hugo. Bells ringing now?"

"Loud bells," I replied.

"Santiago's built a network that extends around the world in all the wrong places. He himself has become a ghost. But make no mistake, that ghost has access to the world's billionaire collectors, not to mention several well-endowed museums. Criminals, the lot of them. I have reason to believe Hugo is Santiago's ambassador to the silk-stocking crowd."

"Based on?" I pressed.

"Based on the fact everywhere topline art is being sold or displayed Hugo makes an appearance. There's no doubt he's a player. Just don't know what team he plays on—and it could be more than one."

"Mind telling us how you knew we were in Pittsburgh?" Angella asked. "Jimmy's taught me not to believe in coincidences."

"Frankly, Angella, it is a bit of a coincidence, in that my government is trying to locate the

Bucksbaum, the *Master Bucksbaum,* and art world rumor puts it here in Pittsburgh. However, in full disclosure, there have been no creditable eyewitnesses to the one we're looking for. Seems you were shot at last night. Killed a few people as well from what I'm led to believe." Ben-Yuval was broadly smiling as his way of signaling he was pulling our chains. "You called Tiny to assist you and Tiny suggested you two might be of help with our art investigation."

"Shot at yes," I confirmed. "Never discharged our weapons though. Someone went to a lot of trouble to frame us."

"That's what Hessle told me. I've worked with her before. She's good. Nothing escapes that woman. If she's on your case, your days of freedom are numbered. But she's fair, does her homework."

"She a straight shooter?" Angella asked.

"You play it straight with her, she'll return the favor. Piss her off and you won't know what hit you. You can take that to the bank, my friend."

"She always assigned to Pittsburgh or—"

"Information sharing has its limits. But I can tell you this. Both of us, she and I, are in this town for one reason only. Because we're tracking Hugo. She for her reasons and me to find the *Master Bucksbaum.*"

"What's so important about those flowers? Bunch of dots, blood dots, I'm told. All the hidden equipment has long ago been uncovered. The location of Hitler's bunker's is now well-known. So?"

"That picture, what I call the *Master Bucksbaum*, has great value to my country. Not so much in dollar value, although that's high also, but buried in those blood dots, as you call them are the new names of several Einstazgruppen who are to this day hiding out around the world. Our government wants them, and, in some cases, they are being protected by...by your government."

Angella was quicker than I at working through what all this meant. "How in the world would Bucksbaum know the new names? He was a prisoner for goodness sakes."

"Good question. To remain alive the prisoners used their talents to support the guards. Create papers for them and such. In some places this was known as Canada, because those folks were kept in a better place than the others."

"You saying Bucksbaum was a forger?" Angella pressed.

"No, but he had privileges. In fact, he shared a bed with one of the forgers who made travel documents. The man was executed. He, for some reason, wasn't."

Angella's lips pressed together as she thought through what she had heard. "Okay, so why not just go for the *Bucksbaum*?" she finally asked. "What's Hugo have to do with it?"

"Our path to the *Bucksbaum* is through Hugo. If he's here, so is it. Look, we're pretty certain it's here in Pittsburgh, but we don't know where. I was personally tracking Hugo and lost him."

"Where?" I asked. "Where'd you lose him?"

"In Matamoras. He visited Santiago a few days ago, traveled to Brownsville, booked a flight to Dallas, boarded the plane, but never got off."

"He didn't jump, so where—"

"Used a double. Well-timed operation. Your government has arrested a TSA guy who looked the other way, but that doesn't help me. Reason to think Hugo flew to Houston and then on to Pittsburgh via Midway. Certainly not in his own name, but the surveillance footage shows someone his height and build. Facial hair, a bald wig, pair of oversize glasses, and he's on the loose here."

"So what do you want from us?" I asked. It was time to see where this was all going.

"The fact they shot at you tells me Santiago no longer needs you. That means Hugo's got the *Pirate* and the *Cup* under control. You want the *Pirate*, you say for Great Southern, so we're both now searching for Hugo. Time to pool our resources."

"What's in it for us?" I asked.

"Your lives, for starters."

"Other than Santiago, who should we be worried about?"

"You really need me to spell it out for you?" Ben-Yuval leaned forward, his eyes darting around the room. From the little I could see, it appeared that only one other table was occupied. His voice barely audible, he began, "Hugo is one. Your government is two. My government is three. Whoever shot at you in the park is four. And Santiago is five."

"Thought it was Santiago in the park," Angella said, "Now you got me going. You certain?"

"Nothing in this business is certain, Angella. While it yet might not be clear to you, you two and Hugo are playing for the same management. You folks are delivery and Hugo is purchasing and muscle. Both working for Santiago."

"So who shot at us if it wasn't Santiago's people?"

"The only thing I know for certain is that it wasn't my government. Tiny says it wasn't his government. Can't vouch for that, but I believe him."

"Best guess," I asked, noting the skepticism in his voice when he mentioned Tiny.

"The Pishtacos."

"Who the hell are the Pishtacos?" Angella, who I thought had tuned out, asked.

"Peruvian gang, based in Lima, well positioned there and here. Known to be after the *Pirate*—as well as other objects of high value. But the *Pirate* is highest on their shopping list. Confirmed buyer well over a hundred million."

"Hey," I said, my mind struggling with a vague memory of a DHS briefing I had suffered through several years back. "Isn't that the gang who was involved with the police, in...in something to do with mass kidnapping and murder?"

Before Ben-Yuval answered, Angella said, "Oh, that's right. Weren't they the ones who were killing their victims and selling their parts internationally?"

"Good memories, the both of you. It turned out to be a hoax perpetrated by the Lima police to cover another scandal. The hoax was limited to what the gang did, not to the fact that they're well organized. Our information is that the Pishtacos are run by the El Artista sisters. A couple of their members, guy named Matias el Bueno and one named Antonio Alverez are thought to be in the area now. Alverez is a naturalized citizen."

Judging from Ben-Yuval's body language, he wasn't prepared to go any further with the Pishtaco gang, so I asked, "How about a lead on where to find old man Bucksbaum? Let's go to the source."

"I can tell you where to find him, but won't do you much good. Guy's got a nice sunny plot in the old Ein Hod cemetery."

Jimmy studied Ben-Yuval's eyes.

I don't know what he was trying to determine, but if it was whether or not we were being lied to it was a useless exercise. Spooks wouldn't be spooks—or perhaps I should say, spooks wouldn't remain alive very long—if their lies and deceptions were transparent. Jimmy knew that better than I did.

For his part, Ben-Yuval didn't look away or even blink.

"Time's up. I won't be joining you for a meal, but if you're interested, the corned beef in this place is as good as it gets anywhere. Order it on rye, hot. Yellow mustard. You won't be disappointed."

TEN

Angella said she wasn't very hungry and settled for a bowl of chicken soup. I took Levi's advice and had the corned beef on rye. "Excellent," I told Angella, finishing my sandwich in silence, while I failed miserably at trying to organize my thoughts. "How's your soup?"

"Excellent, as well. Place's a keeper."

"Check's been taken care of," the waitress informed us when I signaled for the tab. "But you're welcome to leave a tip if you so desire."

My phone rang before I could argue about the bill. Angella laid a five on the table and we walked out while I struggled to hear my caller.

"What was that about?" Angella asked when we were out of earshot of everybody.

"Grandkowski. Weapons ready for pickup. He's texting the address. Said he'll meet us there."

"I trust we don't need lawyers."

"If we did, the black and white would be parked right here. But we'll know soon enough. Set the coordinates."

Angella focused on Waze and a moment later said, "Twelve minutes from the time the wheels are rolling. Doesn't seem to be any traffic."

Sure enough, fifteen minutes later we were in the office of the Commander of the Point State Park Division of the Pennsylvania Park Rangers. Only Grandkowski was nowhere to be seen. Instead, Hessle was sitting behind the messy desk. "Good news and bad news. Good news first. Your weapons pass the no-fire test. Better news. Coroner has ruled that the slugs were planted at the scene. Even better news, at least from your standpoint. Time of death occurred while you were at the game. So that's off our plate so far as you two are concerned."

"So whatever happened to 'ticket stubs prove nothing'?" Angella quipped, a touch of "up yours" clearly evident in her tone.

"Stick by that statement. Bottom of the third. Bell hit a foul ball, landed just to the left of you. Video shows Jimmy, big as life, a beer in one hand and a dog in the other. You, Angella, had a bowl of nachos on your lap. But for his hands being full, Jimmy would have had himself a souvenir."

"You folks have been busy," Angella responded, her face flushing. "Bad guys didn't count on a TV appearance for our alibi."

"Coroner's the one busting her butt on this. The murders are not on my plate. Now for the bad news."

"Can't wait," I said.

"As you know, the picture, the flower picture Buck gave the Lowell woman, was lifted from the rehab center. Trail's cold. No real leads."

"The *Bucksbaum*," Angella corrected the trooper. "Nothing on surveillance, I suppose?"

"Not exactly nothing, but an effective dead end."

"Can you run the tape for us?" I asked.

"Tapes are long gone. Digital now. It's in the computer. Here, knock yourself out." She turned her computer around to face us. Hessle hit several keys, a siren sounded in the background, and the screen displayed Lucy Lowell being escorted into a hallway from her room. Several other patients, two women and a man, were also being escorted off to the left. The group of them disappeared off screen, and almost immediately thereafter a man wearing brown slacks and what appeared to be a blue shirt, no tie, appeared from the right and walked briskly into the room. He had a plastic shopping bag in his left hand. The man was back in the hall in less than fifteen seconds, and the artwork we had seen beside the flowers was being stuffed into the bag as he walked. His pace was steady, perhaps a bit faster than the patients' had been, but that was understandable, as he traced the same path they had traveled. He, too, soon disappeared from view.

Hessle touched a few more keys and a new image formed, this one showing a large group of patients sitting in chairs, a few in rolling beds, all in front of the building. The blue-shirted man was-nowhere to be seen.

"Can we see a few minutes of the video just before this?" I asked.

Hessle leaned forward, tapped the back arrow key several times, and now the image showed the folks coming out of the front door and several men, dressed almost identically to the blue shirted man, unfolding and setting up chairs.

"In answer to the question you're about to ask, he broke into a locker in the basement to get the uniform. I believe his own clothes are in that Giant Eagle bag."

"Any footage of him entering the building?" Angella asked.

"Nothing more of any help. I sent this for image matching, but that can take a while. Often days, if not weeks."

"Would a possible name help?"

"Redstone, you damn well know the answer to that. Of course it would."

"Try Matias el Bueno or Antonio Alverez. I don't know what either of them looks like, but it's worth a shot."

Hessle pulled the computer back around to her side of the desk, sat, and typed in what seemed to be a short story, or at least a long letter.

Nothing for a few minutes, then, "Shit! You nailed it. Alverez! Where in the hell did you—"

"Does it really matter where? Let's just say in our tracking of stolen art his name surfaced."

Hessle fixed me with what best can be described as furious eyes. Her face was flushed and her forehead had turned scarlet. I thought her head would explode. Her jaw moved, but she said nothing.

"I'm not being cute about this," I said by way of apology, "but the source may be sensitive. I'll check, and if it's okay I'll put you in touch. Best I can do."

"For now that'll have to do, Redstone. But I'm being open with you. I want that coming back this way. You understand me?"

"I understand. Been there. Done that."

At the risk of really pissing Hessle off, I said, "That Alvarez looks like a guy who was hanging around the art show. I think in or near Carrie Buck's booth. Any chance of seeing video of the show?"

"Funny you should ask, Jimmy. We have reason to keep tabs on Buck, so yes we do have footage. Do you recall what time you were there?"

"Wait," Angella interrupted, "I took pictures of that guy running." She pulled up the picture on her phone and said, "That's him. The guy standing off to the side. Time stamp is three-twelve."

After watching a full ten minutes of people walking past Buck's booth, I came into view, passing directly under the camera, so that my face never appeared, but my butt, along with Angella's a few steps to my right, was clearly visible. "Stop!" I said as the man we now knew as Alverez came into view. I studied the paused image for a moment, then said, "That's him. Alverez. You agree?"

"I do," Hessle said a moment later. "Let's see if we have the one who ran. I think he was actually in the booth with Carrie." The video then continued, and seventy-six seconds later the image of a man appeared; he looked both ways, then ran away from the camera.

"Got him!" Hessle said, as she typed in another long dissertation. I assumed she was now putting in el Bueno's name.

"Blocked!" Hessle said, her face again turning red. "What the hell's going on?" Her fists clenched and I took a step back, fully expecting her to take a swing. Instead, she said, "Get me read in, Redstone. You hear? I know the *Pirate*'s involved in terrorism, but there's more going on than that. That much I do know. Some agency's up to something. And I want to know what it is!"

"I'll do what I can, but—"

"But nothing! You want to chase art for Great Southern or chase defense lawyers for yourselves? I'll tie your asses up in legal shit until you wish you'd never set foot in this state." As if she had read my mind, she added, "Governor got you out of that concealed permit charge Grandkowski concocted. Nobody'll spring you on murder charges, Redstone. Nobody! With that shooting of Badman Tex in cold blood, not even the President will spring you out on bail. So watch your sorry ass."

I know I have a few hot buttons. Well, maybe more than a few. But nothing as hair-trigger sensitive as the Badman Tex shooting where the ballistics didn't line up with my story. But the jury found me innocent, and that's all that really matters. Out of the corner of my eye I saw Angella prepare to move between Hessle and me, hoping to avoid getting either of us arrested.

I counted to five. Then to five again and took a step back. "Got to do better than that, Trooper," I managed. "Learned long ago not to pick a fight I couldn't win. You got the gun. You got the power."

"Hey!" Hessle exclaimed. "Just had a vision!"

I braced for what was coming. Something I said had set her off and I had no idea what it could be. Before I could say anything, Hessle was barking orders into her radio. Almost immediately, a uniformed officer appeared in the office and handed her a jump drive. Hessle slipped the device into the computer, and with a touch of a few buttons a ball game appeared on the screen.

Josh Bell was at bat. The count was 0-2. The pitcher wound up, and the ball was low and inside. But Bell swung and made contact, the ball flying off toward the first base dugout, landing in the tenth row. There I was, looked befuddled, not knowing whether to drop the beer or the hotdog—or both. "Not very flattering of me," I said. "That damn ball coulda taken my head off!"

"I'm not interested in you at this point," Hessle said. "Look directly behind you!"

"Alverez and el Bueno!" Angella exclaimed. "What the—"

"Just get me read in. And get it done fast!" Hessle said, her eyes setting even harder than before. "Now get the hell out of here! I have work to do."

ELEVEN

The building we had been in was located under the bridge structure that spans the Monongahela River just above where the Allegheny River merges with the Mon to form the Ohio River. Parking is spread along an old wharf that often floods if the high water marks on the abutment walls are to be believed. The water level was well below the edge so I assumed our car would be safe. That was good news, because we weren't heading for our car, not yet anyway. Instead, I was two steps behind Jimmy, who at first was walking off his Hessle-induced anger, but who, after ten more minutes, had turned and instead of walking back toward our car was apparently aiming for the art show area.

I ran to catch up. "The show's closed now, if that's where you're heading."

"Carrie's from out of town."

"So?"

"So that means she has to stay somewhere. Somewhere close."

"There's a lot of hotels and motels not far from here. You planning to canvas them all?"

"That art work of hers is heavy. I'm bettin' she has a van of some sort. Lot of these folks spend the summer in vans traveling from show to show. Van lot, at least one of them, is on the Mon wharf, the other side of that bridge, out of sight of the show, but close enough to move stuff back and forth to and from their booths. I noticed it in the surveillance video."

Indeed, Jimmy was right. Less than a hundred yards ahead of us there was a jumble of campers, vans, trucks, and cars, some in rows, and some at angles to each other. A few people were wheeling plastic milk crates of various colors toward the parking area. Other than those few, the area seemed abandoned. "I would have thought this would look like a game day tailgate party. It's more like a cemetery."

"I think these folks are all smiled out, if you ask me. Dealing with the public poking around your stuff all day would wear me out fast."

"Not your thing, Jimmy. Not your thing at all. You're better at—" His arm shot out and caught me just below my chin and my mouth slammed closed, jarring my teeth. *What the hell?* I looked over at him, ready to pounce before I realized he was signaling for me to stop walking and be quiet. His focus was on a woman pushing a two-wheeled dolly. While everyone else was moving between the display area and the parked vehicles, the woman Jimmy was watching was traveling from a parking area upriver toward the center of the jumble. I leaned close and whispered, "Whatever's on that dolly is heavy. Is that what caught your attention?"

"That woman's been having trouble all the way up that ramp. Almost lost it a few times. Much too heavy for her."

"Heavy loads around an art show are not so uncommon. Something else is bothering you. What—"

"She appears to be heading toward that white van. Can you make out the plate number?" Jimmy asked, knowing my vision was sharper than his.

"Think so." I replied, straining in the dim light to see all the numbers.

Jimmy punched in numbers on the keypad and almost immediately I heard ringing on the other end. Then Jimmy said into the phone, "Hessle?" Pause. "Good, glad I caught you. You still where we just saw you?" Pause. "Good. Here's a tip for you. A stolen art piece, a piece called the *Golden Booby*, is about to be delivered to a van in the art show lot. If you can get a warrant in the next few minutes or so we'll have a windfall. Angella will give you the plate number."

I did as instructed and handed the phone back to Jimmy. He said a few more words to Hessle, listened to her response, then stuffed the phone into his pocket.

"Hessle says the judge on duty tonight owes her one. A phone call should do it, but we'll have to wait for the paperwork to be delivered. Says she'll meet us over there when she gets it." He pointed to a street intersection a half block from where we now stood.

"How the hell you know the *Booby*'s under that plastic?"

"Weight and size primarily. Sucker's pure gold, and the shape under that tarp matches."

"Lots of things are heavy. Could be lead for all you know."

"Could be, but it's not. Hit a rut a few minutes ago. The tarp opened just enough to show a flash of blue. That's the *Booby*. Bet my ass on it."

"So why the warrant? It's outside. Just go over there and pull the tarp back. To coin Hessle's words, no expectation of privacy out here. At an art show, no less."

"Warrant's for the van. If we let her take it inside, then Hessle can search the van, see what else we uncover. Besides, we have the same problem out here. Identification of stolen artwork takes time. Without identification we can't hold it, and by the time a warrant is issued it'll be long gone."

"You can take the Texas Ranger out of Texas but you can't—"

"That who you're watching?" Hessle's distinctive voice said. I had been concentrating on the dolly and hadn't heard the big woman approach.

"That hand-truck over there? You positive it's that *Booby*? Piece's worth upwards of a hundred mil."

"Did your homework. As positive as can be. Got the warrant?"

"Judge denied it without comment. Seems favors aren't worth what they used to be. Not based on some guy she doesn't know concluding there's stolen art being moved around an art show and under a drop cloth to boot. She needs more than that, I'm afraid. Besides, the art you're concerned with is not in the van. Not until we have good reason to believe there's stolen property in the van will she consider it."

"Then what the hell we doing standing around?" Jimmy, ever the practical one, said. "Let's get over there and rip that cover off. At least we'll recover the *Booby*. That should put a smile on a few law enforcement faces."

We started across the street, but before reaching the other side, the van door opened and out stepped a woman. It wasn't the artist Buck, but someone else. She immediately went over to where the first woman was struggling with the dolly, said a few words, and the two of them bent over the covered object. Together they lifted it, their backs bent as they moved. I retrieved my cell phone and snapped several pictures. It was clear we couldn't cover the distance before they'd get inside. Our only hope was for them to stumble or set it down.

We quickly closed the distance, but, as anticipated, not fast enough. We were still twenty yards from the van when Buck opened the door from the inside, allowing the women to struggle up the last step, knees wobbling, arms shaking. They disappeared inside before Jimmy closed the distance. "Hey Carrie Buck," he called. "Got a minute?"

The artist looked up at the sound of her name. We were close enough to see her eyes acknowledge she had heard us and knew who we were. But instead of welcoming us she slammed the door, remaining on the inside.

Jimmy knocked. Then called her name. Then knocked twice more.

"Sorry, Jimmy," Hessle said, but that's as far as we can go. I advise you not to break in."

"Wouldn't dream of it." Sarcasm was in the air.

"You have me read in yet?"

I thought she was kidding, but her eyes were dead serious.

"Haven't had the chance. Sorry."

"How positive are you we just missed the *Booby*?"

"Positive is all I can tell you."

"Okay, Redstone. I'll get Grandkowski on it. Have him post someone here. The *Booby* won't be leaving any time soon."

"Mexican standoff," Jimmy replied. "No pun intended."

"Let's sit over there, Angella," Jimmy said after Hessle took her leave. "Keep an eye on the van until the cavalry arrives."

"You think she's taking you seriously, or just going along to see what you turn up?"

"We'll know if Grandkowski or his people show up. I'm betting this is our gig for the night." Jimmy grabbed his phone, found the name he was looking for and hit the speed dial button. "Went directly to voice mail," he said. "Levi. It's Redstone. Hessle wants to know where the names you gave us came from. She wants briefed. Any chance of getting that done? Promised I would try. Bye." He started to hang up, then added, "Oh, by the way, the *Golden Booby*, I suppose you know what that is, just showed up. Hugo might come sniffing. Call for details."

"I don't think he cares a nickel about the *Booby*," I told Jimmy. "*Bucksbaums* are his interest. I think his only interest. Why the hell would Israel care one iota about some Peruvian art piece?"

"Hugo is his lead to the *Bucksbaum*."

"No guarantee Hugo has anything to do with the *Booby*."

Ignoring what I had just said, Jimmy asked, "Suppose those two females, the ones lugging the *Booby*, are the El Artista Sisters?"

"Sofi and Chio del Rio? I suppose." I quickly texted their pictures to Ben-Yuval. I also texted the image of the man who ran away from the artist tent earlier in the day. The man whose identity was blocked from Hessle's inquiry.

Two hours into our vigil, and still no Grandkowski. It certainly was possible he was on the scene without our knowledge, but neither of us thought so. A shadow passed over our heads. A rather large shadow. Jimmy saw it at the same time as I did, his hand going for his weapon. The only problem being that we had emptied our weapons before turning them over to Grandkowski. And they were still empty.

"Not a good plan to draw on a friend," the very familiar voice of Tiny, our seven-foot former handler and current Secret Service/CIA operative. Secret Service when he's operating within the borders of the United States and CIA when he's working elsewhere. "Good thing I know they're empty, or we'd have a problem." His voice came from somewhere behind us, but by the time I twisted around far enough to see where he was, he had positioned himself behind a tree off to our left, as if the tree could hide his frame. But the truth is, Tiny moves faster and smoother than almost anyone else I had ever met, regardless of size.

Jimmy, I think, actually spotted him before I did. "If you'd have used a bit of common courtesy and texted us there wouldn't be any issue."

"What fun would that be? Now stop looking at me. That van is on camera and you're at the edge of the image. Sit for a moment then meet me over at The Commoner. It's in the Hotel Monaco, a ten-minute walk from here. Or you can drive over if you wish. See you there." And he was gone. Just like that. Houdini would have been proud of the big guy.

"So she did take you seriously after all," I said to Jimmy.

"Seems she did. Wonder if Ben-Yuval came through and read her in?"

"With flying colors, I'd say. If Levi is to be believed, and I see no reason not to, then all the teams have made their appearance. Ben-Yuval for the Israelis, Tiny for the USA, the El Artista Sisters for the artwork, Matias and Antonio, I believe, for Santiago. The only one missing is Oscar Hugo. And who the hell knows what team he's pitching for?"

"But seems with Carrie Buck we've come close."

"This isn't horseshoes, bocce, or hand-grenades. Close doesn't cut it. Isn't that what you've taught me, Jimmy?"

"I don't know much about the horseshoes and bocce, but if you ask me, close is all you need with grenades," Jimmy confided as we sauntered out of the park to meet up with our former handler, the man who claims to always have our backs — or at least he used to.

TWELVE

The *Commoner* was almost empty when we came in through the side door from the street, or more accurately, from the alleyway running beside the hotel. We had decided on driving, and when we pulled up to the hotel, the valet was more than happy to take the car from us.

"Go off duty at one," he said. "Stay as long as you wish. When I leave, I'll park it right over there. It'll be safe. Security camera's on all night."

Only one couple was in a far corner of the restaurant, and judging from the way they were all over each other, they were only minutes away from taking their activities upstairs to a room. The kitchen was open to the dining area, but the only person back there was a busboy studiously working the floor with his mop. The bar was off to the side, closer to the hotel entrance than the alley entrance, and the tender had his head down, busy washing, drying, and hanging glasses. A tired-looking waitress sat near the now-abandoned hostess desk, her shoulders slumped as she counted the night's tips. Glancing up, she casually waved for us to sit where we wanted, not breaking her concentration on the money spread before her.

The door from the hotel opened a moment later, and in came Tiny. He paused, but barely perceptively so, to check the surroundings before walking down the few steps and across the floor to our chosen table. The waitress trailed a step behind. Before he could pull a chair out, she said, "Welcome back, Mr. Smith. You want the Ginga Wheat?"

"Make that three, if you will be so kind." Tiny turned to us. "Introduced a few years back. Made by a young couple from a place not far up the road from here called Polish Hill. Hits the spot."

"Mr. Smith?" Angella said when the waitress shuffled off. "How the hell you keep it all straight?"

"What's hard about Smith? Nobody ever asks you to spell it, and no one writes it down. Easy name to remember—and easier to forget. More likely to get tripped up using a name like Wentworth or Winchester."

The beers showed up and the waitress said, "Kitchen's about to close, gentlemen—and lady. Menu's limited this time of night. Let me know what you need and I'll work it for you."

"Cobb salad'll do me." Tiny turned in our direction, and being careful not to use our names, said, "Anything?"

We both shook our heads no, but Tiny said, "Bring them each a Scotch Egg. If they don't eat them I will."

The waitress again shuffled off toward the kitchen. The bartender went back to polishing the glassware and the lovebirds had indeed taken their activities elsewhere.

"Warrant, huh? You're right that was the *Booby*. But Jimmy you jumped the gun with the warrant."

"Come again?" I replied. "If Hessle had gotten the warrant, she'd have found stolen art in that trailer, I'm certain of it."

"Had the warrant been issued, we would have had a real mess on our hands."

"You going to leave us in suspense?" Angella chimed in, trying to cut off Tiny's cat and mouse games.

"Your mission is to secure the *Pirate* for your company. I understand you're also attempting to return the *Kings Cup* to Santiago. Unfortunately for you, my mission is to prevent the *Kings Cup* from doing any more international damage." Tiny took a long swallow of his beer, then continued, "A hundred million will finance a great deal. That *Cup*'ll bringing even more right now, so we don't want it in underground circulation."

"So how's that tie to the warrant?" Angella asked, looking about as impatient as I was. "It was the *Booby* Jimmy had spotted."

"*Booby*'s not the only piece in that van. Jimmy's

right about the van being a windfall of stolen art. *Cup's* in there as well."

Tiny's salad arrived, and he paused until the waitress had returned to her station. I took the opportunity to sample the brew and found it exceptional. "Good stuff," I said, mostly to fill the void. But it actually was good.

"Agreed," Angella said, wiping foam from her lips.

"Great brewery," Tiny said. "You two need to spend more time in this city." He glanced around, then added, "I suppose you believe we should just go in there and clean them out."

"Hoping you'd give us the answer without our tugging," Angella said

"Hugo's the reason. Guy's sitting on several other pieces. Everything going south these days flows through him. *Kings Cup.* A piece recently uncovered called the *Crown of Alexander, Golden Booby,* and some pieces new to the market, such as the *Bucksbaums.* Well, actually only one *Bucksbaum.* We're using the art as bait."

"He seems to be elusive. What makes you believe he'll put in an appearance and not send a stand-in or two?"

"No guarantees in this business. But the *Bucksbaum* might just do it. Not sure he'll trust that to his Peruvian friends. Contrary to the popular belief, there's no honor among thieves. Take that to the bank, my friend."

There was a warning from Tiny to us in that statement, but I wasn't certain whether it was us working on behalf of Santiago or...or telling us to be wary of Ben-Yuval. Instead of following up on the warning, I said, "You talking about the *Bucksbaum* I took a picture of?"

Tiny took a long pull of his beer, savored it a moment, obviously deciding how much he could safely tell us. "You know, Redstone, that picture you took of the *Bucksbaum* is the first ever digital image of any of the *Bucksbaums*. At least the first one U. S. law enforcement knows about. Kudos."

"So why's that important?" Angella asked, her beer mug back on the table, her full attention focused on the big man.

"Because we now know that the one you snapped, the one stolen earlier from old lady Lowell was...was a decoy. Yes it was a *Bucksbaum*. But no, it wasn't the *Bucksbaum* Israel's so desperate to locate and...and decode. Not the uber-valuable *Master Bucksbaum* at any rate."

That was an interesting piece of information Tiny just shared with us. Made even more interesting because Ben-Yuval hadn't suggested anything about a decoy. I shared my thoughts with Tiny, who in response said, "There's a lot your buddy hasn't told you. The art I'm following is going south to fund terrorism against our homeland. The *Bucksbaum*, and possibly the *Crown of Alexander*, are going eastward, presumably to fund a round of missiles aimed at Tel Aviv."

"So your missions diverge," Angella observed. "What's that mean for us?"

"Whatever you want it to mean. Just watch yourselves. My back-watching days are...are numbered at best."

Now the warning was clear. What to do about it remained a mystery.

"What do you know about the *Pirate*?" Angella asked, allowing Tiny's comment to fall dead on the table.

"The *Pirate* is your business. Far as we know, it's not tied to foreign activity. But we picked up a buzz in the underground market. That Golden Booby Bird, or whatever its formal name is, is what got Hugo out of law enforcement and into the underbelly of the art world in the first place."

"*Golden Booby*," I corrected. "It's called the *Golden Booby*, and at one point Hugo's grandfather, Professor August Villanova, who taught over in Brownsville, had it."

Tiny started to ask a question but was interrupted when our egg dishes arrived. Without thinking, I cut into the concoction and took a bite. It went well with the beer and I must have been hungrier than I thought because it was gone all too soon. Tiny too focused on his salad and then looked over at Angella, who had drained her mug, but was just pushing the egg concoction around her plate.

"Hey, if you're not going to eat that, my friend, I'll do the honors."

Angella mumbled something about not being all that hungry and pushed her plate toward Tiny, who accepted it without a word, as if saying something would make her take the food back. Tiny stabbed the baked egg and dropped it onto his Cobb plate. He turned to me. "Mind showing me that picture you took? Better yet, text it to me."

He had obviously seen the picture I had taken, and I thought for a moment of refusing. But there was no point to it. More importantly, Tiny's polite request was, in essence, a direct command. "I copied you as well, Angella," I said, making certain the image was being spread around.

A moment later, both their phones buzzed signaling they had received the image. Tiny studied the picture. "I understand there are codes built into these paintings. Locations of tunnels and weapons, but truth is, I don't see enough color differential to see how a code could be embedded in here at all."

Angella, who had been looking at the image as well, replied, "I tend to agree. Those flowers are really just color dots, and if there's a code in there, I can't see it."

"Considering the circumstances, it would have had to be really subtle to go without detection," Tiny said. "But even so, there's not much there to work on. But remember, this is not the critical one. Maybe that one's different."

"Perhaps, but the difference would have to be subtle, if they're using this one as a decoy," Angella volunteered.

"Perhaps," Tiny agreed, not sounding convinced. "And perhaps, there's nothing there and Ben-Yuval's blowing smoke."

"He's a brother in arms, so to speak. Why throw smoke your way?" I commented.

"No law requires us to show all our cards all the time, Redstone. You know that as well as anyone."

"So exactly what cards did you come here to play?" Angella asked, leaning into Tiny more than normal for her.

"Isn't having a nice dinner with you enough?"

"Hate to break it to you, but when you're around my appetite goes in the dumpster."

"Sorry to hear that, my friend. Truly sorry. You want it straight, here it is. Head back to Texas and leave the art chasing to us."

"You got to be kidding."

"Serious as a stroke, I can assure you."

"So what've we done that—"

"For starters, you led them right to the bait. Hugo was supposed to visit his mother to pick up the *Bucksbaum*. You led that guy Alveraz to the mother. You know the rest."

Jimmy was silent several minutes before answering. "I suppose that's who planted the mics on us?"

"Check," Tiny said.

"I suppose also that's who shot at us, to get us detained, hoping we'd discharge our weapons."

"That actually worked out better for them than they planned. You were detained long enough for them to do a job on your clothes and car, but had you been detained for murder then you'd never have found the mother and they'd still be searching for the *Bucksbaum*. Even for the bad guys, luck is important."

"So how did the bad guys know we were here? We told nobody." My real question to Tiny was, had he known we were coming to Pittsburgh, and if so, had he somehow tipped off Alverez, or whoever had planted the tracking devices on us?

"Yes, I did know about you trying to locate Hugo. Silver, your boss, briefed me. I was betting you'd be successful—and we'd nab him. But I believe you're asking if I told the bad guys. Of course not. But—"

I was eager to hear the second part of his sentence. The all-important, "but".

"—but think about who hired you. Santiago. You put him in jail. He's eager to return the favor. That plant-the-slug caper took weeks, if not months, of planning. He's been waiting for the right time. Alverez, or whoever he's working with, saw the opportunity and jumped on it. Nobody ever said the bad guys are perfect. In fact, it's their imperfections that allow us to stay a step ahead. In my business the smarts are evenly distributed between the good guys and the bad. Those who tend to under-think or make mistakes, on both sides, are gone, retired, or dead—mostly dead. Great case study for Mr. Charles Darwin."

"You've told us to watch our backs every way you know how," Angella said when Tiny finished his lecture, having spoken more words in the past ten minutes than I could recall him speaking in all the time we've known him.

"And your fronts. Santiago is not your best buddy. Get out while the getting is good. I strongly suggest you both go back to that island of yours and play in the sand."

"We work for Silver, not Santiago."

"Want me to grease the skids with Silver? Get you assigned to some other venue?"

"I want you out of this. And I'm certain Angella agrees."

"Be careful what you wish for, my friend. Be careful. Maybe Silver will assign you to Pittsburgh."

"Seems Pittsburgh, at least for now, is a hub of illegal art activity," I said. "If that's so, this could be where we belong. Silver's wish is our command. Isn't that how it goes?"

"You decide what you want, and I'll see what I can do." Tiny drained his beer.

"Why's so much art, I mean stolen art, surfacing here?" I asked. "Has it always been this way?"

"Ever since Mr. Morris Dexter Stratis moved his company headquarters to Pittsburgh. Sixtieth floor, across the street in the US Steel Tower. Five years ago. Bought a ten-acre tract up in Cranberry, near where you visited Lowell. Built a house, mansion by my standards, and a standalone museum for his art collection. He's the center of fund raising for Butler County and for much of Allegheny as well. Getting on his invite list means you've arrived. Staying on it means you've donated to the right causes, and donated well."

"What does that have to do with what we're after? Stolen stuff?"

"Rumor has it he has ten thousand square feet underground, heavily guarded, containing a big chunk of the world's stolen art."

"How does one get invited to his fundraisers?" Angella inquired, obviously interested.

"Sixty-four-thousand-dollar question, Angella. Tell me when you find out."

"You'll be the first person we call," I replied.

"Sarcasm is not your long suit, kapish?

"Get you gentlemen, and lady, a last beer?" The waitress asked. "Kitchen's closed. Bar about to."

Indeed, even the lights in the kitchen were now off. The bartender, who to my knowledge had never even glanced in our direction, was sitting with his back to us counting something, either money or cash register tapes, I couldn't determine which.

"Get them each another beer," Tiny said, standing. When the waitress went off, Tiny said, "Thanks for a lovely dinner. Hate to eat and run, but you know how it is. Enjoy the beer. And stay away from the van."

And up the steps and into the dark night the big man went. I doubt if he even heard me say, "Goodnight, Mr. Smith. Great seeing you again."

THIRTEEN

We sat for another hour, nursing our beers and thinking. The kitchen remained dark, the bar tender was long gone and when the waitress departed, she had assured us it would be okay to remain. Her eyes suggested we'd be better off, however, taking a room. According to her, breakfast service was four hours away, but food was the furthest thing from my mind. I'm certain Angella felt the same way.

Whoever had hatched the plan to frame us here in Pittsburgh, the Steel City, had done a good job. Admittedly, it was crude, but in the right hands and executed just a little better, Angella and I could easily have been indicted for murder. Angella might have been given some benefit-of-the-doubt wiggle room, but with my having shot Badman Tex, arguably in cold blood, coupled with the amount of out-of-country travel I've done in the past few years, I'd be lucky if the judge would set bail.

Judging from what Tiny didn't say, I'm certain we couldn't count on much help from our former employers. I was seriously contemplating taking Tiny's advice and heading home. But in the end that would be Jack Silver's call. I looked over at Angella and found her deep in thought as well. "Penny for your thoughts."

"I suppose I could ask you the same. Gotta ante up more than a penny. I may be a cheap date, but not that cheap."

"Buy you breakfast."

"Now you're in the ball park." A half smile appeared at the corner of her lips. "I was just thinking, Tiny clearly doesn't want us around the van. Means he doesn't want us finding Hugo. Ben-Yuval doesn't want us around the Bucksbaum collection. Didn't say much about the *Cup* or any of the other pieces that seem to be in play, but I suppose same goes for those. Santiago wants us in jail—or dead. Whichever comes first. So what the devil we doing here?"

"That's where I come out, Angella. Great minds and all that. But I do take issue with a bit of what you said. Santiago wants the *Kings Cup*, that we know. So if he ordered our demise, and I'm pretty positive he did, then—"

"What makes you so positive? There're any number of possib—"

"He set us up with the ball tickets and positioned his thugs behind us. That way they could keep an eye on us and at the same time coordinate the timing for the river murder and the fake shooting at us. Rather brilliant, I might add."

"Okay, I see your point. You were saying?"

"I was saying that if he ordered our killing then he's already secured the art he wants. Joy sent us to find Hugo and now doesn't seem to care. Tells me Hugo doesn't have it—if he ever did. I don't believe Santiago knows or cares about the *Bucksbaums.* That's a Middle Eastern play." I paused to finish my drink.

"Hey, it's getting late, Jimmy. I'm for picking this up in the morning. Want to get a room here for the night or go back to our hotel up on the Boulevard?"

"Let's go to our place. Less chance of a tail that way."

"Speaking of tails," Angella said, rolling her eyes, "bet our car's bugged again."

"Tiny?"

"Or Alveraz. Or Hessle. Or Grandkowski? The list is getting longer by the hour."

"Or Hugo," I added. "How 'bout we Lyft and leave the car here?"

"Better yet. Let's get the car out of downtown and leave it somewhere up in Oakland, but away from the hotel. You drive so we know no one's following. We can Uber the last mile if you like."

"That's a plan." I was happy to know Angella still had her head in this and was not pressing overly hard to go back to Texas. One thing I'll say about my partner—and lover—is that beneath all her musings about putting this life behind us she's as much an adrenalin junkie as I am. At times I've come to realize that she may actually be mentally tougher than I—even without Ranger training.

We managed to fall into bed just short of three-thirty, my cell phone alarm set for ten. Needn't have bothered with the alarm. At eight sharp Hessle called. We had thought ahead and turned off incoming calls to our cell phones, but neither of us remembered the legacy room phone. Frankly, I didn't even realize those phones still worked.

With four and a half hours sleep, my conversation with the trooper didn't go well—if you judge by expletives. Despite my vigorous objections, we were given twenty minutes to be in the lobby. A testament to how sleep deprived I really was is the fact that it wasn't until we were in the lobby that I realized Hessle knew exactly where we were staying, despite all the bobbing and weaving we had been doing for the past day.

"Detectives detect," was Angella's response when I passed my thought along to her. "After all, Jimmy, we checked in under our own names. It's not as if we have work names to use. I suppose we could ask Tiny, or one of his pals, maybe Ben-Yuval, to fix us up with a stack of passports."

"Doubt if Tiny would, but don't rule Ben-Yuval out. That guy is pure silicon, you ask me."

"You thinking he has our backs on this?"

Angella broke into a large smile, the first in a few days. "Hey, you need to read Hebrew to use an Israeli passport? That could be a problem."

"Don't think for a moment he couldn't get us U.S. Passports if he wanted to. As I said, the guy's silicon. I've worked with folks like Ben-Yuval before. Fiercely loyal they are. But it comes with a price. Their loyalty is to their governments. In Ben-Yuval's case, to the State of Israel. He has your back as long as it lines up with the needs of his loyalty. The instant it doesn't, well...for both of our sakes, I hope we never see a time when it doesn't. It won't be pretty—or healthy for either of us."

"You really believe that?"

"Angella, trust me on this. It won't matter how much we've done for him up to that point, he won't pause for an instant. Think of him as a robot, programmed for one, and only one, loyalty. So long as the loyalties line up, he'll take a bullet for you without hesitation. Diverge from his mission at your own peril. No emotion involved. It's all preset."

"Come on you two," the deep voice of Trooper Hessle commanded, "we have an appointment to keep."

"Where we going?" Angella asked.

I shouldn't have wasted the effort asking, because cops never give you a straight answer.

Hessle surprised me by saying, "Eight forty-five

appointment at the Holocaust Center in Squirrel Hill. There's something you two need to see. That's six minutes from here. I'm driving."

And drive Hessle did. No lights or siren, but if she was under fifty any time in the ride I would be surprised. "This is the Panther Hollow Bridge," Hessle said, as we sped over a deep ravine between very steep tree-lined slopes. "That's Pitt over to the left. Cathedral of Learning."

Still in tour guide mode, Hessle waved her right arm a moment later, apparently pointing to a plateau on top of a hill off to our right. "And that up there is the Oval, sports fields and ice skating. This is Schenley Park we're driving through, donated to the city by Mary Schenley. And over there, just behind us," she continued, now holding up her left arm, "is Phipps Conservatory. Best flower displays anywhere."

The car made a sharp right turn a moment later, braking but not bothering to stop for the red light. Down a winding hill we sped, around several curves and then another sharp right turn. "This is the new Greenfield Bridge over the Parkway." Before the words were out, she braked hard, swerved around two cars, turned left and continued on the mostly empty city street, brick homes lining both sides of the wide street. The houses on the right were built into a hillside and could only be entered by walking up a full flight of concrete stairs.

My cell phone screen displayed the time as eight-forty-three.

We paused at the next red light long enough for Hessle to assure herself she could blast on through without being hit. I would have waited for a truck to pass, but Hessle accelerated fast enough so the truck missed us by several feet. Three more red lights, same program, same results. Into a parking lot next to what appeared to be a mini-strip mall, and Hessle was out of the car and walking toward a door.

Time: Eight forty-four and thirty-eight seconds.

"You're early," I called to Hessle, who was by now a good five steps ahead of me.

"We need to be in and out in less than ten minutes. Fifteen max," Hessle said, her finger poised to push the doorbell button mounted on the wall outside of the space occupied by the Holocaust Center.

"Don't bother ringing," a gravely weak-sounding voice said from a doorway off to my right. "Not moving fast these days."

I turned to see a man come out of the early morning shadows and shuffle toward us.

A custodian, by my assessment. Most likely a retired custodian.

"I won't introduce you," Hessle said to Angella and me. "Better that way."

As the old guy approached the door he reached deep within a pants pocket and produced a key. He proceeded to unlock the door, slowly pushed it open, went inside, and touched several buttons on a keypad. A moment later the lights came on. Coming back in our direction, the man said to Hessle. "You got no more'n fifteen minutes until they be cleanin'. Best if you be gone before they arrive. Alarm'll take care of itself." The old man shuffled past us and slowly made his way back along the side of the building in the direction he had come from.

"Come in," Hessle said, "Be careful where you step. According to my source, they're taking this exhibit down and the staff'll be here, as he said, in a few minutes to finish and clean up."

The area was small, what you would expect from a storefront exhibition space. Judging from the layout of the empty easels arranged in rows and the wall-mounted display areas, the center was equipped to display perhaps a hundred works. I walked over to a corner where a screen flashed on and began cycling through faces, some old and wrinkled, some young, but all with eyes that screamed for understanding.

"Come back when they're open," Hessle called from an office in the back of the building, "you can push that button over there and hear their stories. Most of those folks are gone now and this is their legacy."

I made a note to stop back and do just that, but right now I had to focus on why we were here. Except, I didn't know even that fact. All Hessle had told us was that we were here to view a *Bucksbaum*, not the one that I had taken a photo of, but one of the earlier ones, number six she had said. It had been on display as part of the exhibit that had just closed. It was my understanding someone was coming at nine-fifteen to pick it up.

I turned back to the central display area just as Hessle was positioning a picture very similar to the one we had seen in Lucy Lowell's room at the rehab center. In fact, to my eye it appeared the same. Same color flowers, reds, oranges, smudges of what appeared to be green. I couldn't tell the difference.

"I understand," I began, not knowing what else to say, "that these...these flower pictures... were done in a camp."

"Correct, "Hessle said. "that's my understanding as well. Flowers are drops of blood spread by a fingernail."

"The orange? And the different colors of red?" Angella said. "And the green?"

"Mixed in dirt and bits of food. Dye from rags they wore."

"How did you work that out?" Angella asked, pressing close to get a better look at the painting.

"No time now. Carrie Buck's coming for this picture, so let me show you something." Hessle picked up a sheet of what appeared to be translucent graph paper and carefully positioned it over the painting, taking care to line up the edges perfectly. "Hold this; don't move it."

Angella pinched the flimsy material against the picture using her thumb and forefinger while

Hessle retrieved a small flashlight from her back pocket. She turned the light on, but instead of the traditional white light, the tip glowed blue. A series of dots appeared on the paper when she held the light in close proximity to the easel. "Here's what I've been told, " Hessle said, her tone conveying skepticism. "By reading where those dots are relative to the graph, and assuming each level of the graph is, say, a kilometer, and assuming the brightness of a dot represents a different weapon, you can see that a certain weapon, say a mortar, is positioned two kilometers from the camp. Over here," she said, the blue light having moved to the left several inches, "is a stockpile of bombs almost three kilometers out."

"What about direction?" I asked, recalling my map-reading courses and not seeing anything indicating direction. "Could be anywhere on a circle."

"Here's where I'm baffled, and why I wanted you to see this for yourself. When it was explained to me, I came to understand there's no universal agreement as to the efficacy of these...dots. As is well documented, conditions near the end were chaotic, and stories abound. I'm not even certain there's universal agreement the *Bucksbaum*s are even...real. But the official version is that the dots are positioned to give direction. See that dot off to the right? It's near the fourth line. The fourth line is north. The third is east and so forth. So in this case, the direction from the center of the camp is mostly north and a little east."

Something was wrong with what we had just seen and it took me a few minutes to realize what it was. "I assume that's a UV light you're using?"

"Correct. It is."

"But blood doesn't luminesce."

"That's what I'm saying about confusion—and frankly to my mind, myth. I'm told that for this exhibit demo the effect has been recreated using DNA and other science. In the early forties this didn't exist."

"So who's pushing the...the dot theory?" I asked.

"As best as I can determine, Carrie Buck."

"To drive the value up?" I asked.

"That would be one reason, I suppose," Hessle replied, then added, "With the support of art dealers, speculators really, working the price up for their own purposes."

"So if the stories are true, how did Bucksbaum know what to do and how to do it?"

"The story is, the resistance trained folks in all kinds of secret activities to foil the Nazis. Bucksbaum was one of the many trained before he was deported to the camp. One theory has it that he is, or was, extremely color perceptive so he could shade the dots meaningfully. The pictures were *read* by someone with a like color perception after they were smuggled out. However it was done, it apparently worked. Munitions hidden in those tunnels were mostly destroyed by the advancing Allies."

While Hessle was talking, I noticed what at first appeared to be a discarded *Bucksbaum* sticking out from a trashcan. The color splashes are what caught my eye. But as I studied it further, I realized I was looking at a sign promoting the exhibition. Except the dates were wrong. According to the poster, the exhibition was scheduled for the full month of June. "The exhibition is closing early, according to that poster. You know why?"

"As I understand it, the director's been unable to verify the authenticity of the artwork—or of the code, so she's pulled the plug."

"Does that mean Bucksbaum didn't paint them?" Angella asked. "Or that the dots are unverified?"

"Bucksbaum painted them. That much was verified before he died. But it seems the dot patterns don't match where munitions were actually found. There's discussion about the dots having other meanings, but that's a discussion for another day." Hessle checked her watch. "Cleaning folks are about to arrive. Time to move out. Buck'll be here shorty after that to pick this up. I don't want her knowing we're on her case."

Angella and I followed Hessle out to the parking lot, fully expecting to come face to face with an early arriving cleaning team, or with Carrie Buck herself. I didn't appreciate why that would be a problem, but obviously it was for Hessle and her investigation, whatever it was she was investigating. If I had learned anything over the years, it was that investigations into illegal activities never followed a direct line. In fact, they never followed any line. *Organic,* one mentor had drilled into me. "They're organic, Redstone. Go with it. Follow your instincts. It's the rabbit trails, the dead ends, the wrong turns, the things that are *almost* right, the slightly off stuff, that's what defines the boundaries. Let the investigation lead you, not the other way around." Well, this investigation was certainly leading me. Where, I had no idea.

The good news, as far as Carrie Buck was concerned, was that the lot was empty.

The bad news, as far as our organic investigation was concerned, was that Levi Ben-Yuval was leaning against the wall across the street.

FOURTEEN

We thanked Hessle for the art education and informed her we'd prefer to find our own way back to Oakland. She had been in a hurry to position herself to observe Carrie Buck when the artist arrived and, we guessed, to tail her when she left the Center with the *Bucksbaum*. The big cop took several steps across the parking lot then abruptly turned back toward us. "I don't know why Ben-Yuval wanted you two briefed on the *Bucksbaums*, but you can ask him yourself. He's right over there. Tell him for me to keep his day job. He sucks at tailing people. Now get lost. I don't want Buck seeing you in the vicinity of the Center. Understood?"

"Message received," Jimmy said as he stepped off the curb heading toward Ben-Yuval. Knowing Jimmy, that was his way of taking leave of Hessle without committing to anything. Whether or not we allowed Buck to see us was our call and not the trooper's. There was no percentage in debating the point.

"You just happen to be hanging on this corner?" Jimmy said as he approached Ben-Yuval, his lips tight, no smile.

"Just out for my morning stroll. Come, follow me."

We followed him across Murray Avenue and turned to walk down the block in a direction away from the Holocaust Center. I glanced back in time to see two cars pull into the lot next to the Center. Two young men got out of one car and an older woman from the other. The cleaning crew, I guessed.

How far down Murray Avenue Ben-Yuval planned to go depended on his mission. If he planned to observe the Center then he'd stop soon. If not, who knew where he'd lead us?

"Here's a good place to stop," he said, turning into a driveway with a wall that shielded us from the sight of anyone coming or going into or out of the Center. The wall would allow us to observe their movements without being observed ourselves.

Jimmy nodded, obviously approving of this location as a good observation post, based on his many years of surveillance experience. When we were settled, Jimmy turned to Ben-Yuval. "You told us to stay away from the *Bucksbaums*. Then you directed Hessle to brief us. What gives?"

"Change of plans. A lot has happened in just a very few hours. People...people with lots of money riding on art, are gathering here in the city. Stuff's in play that hasn't been in play for years, lots of years actually."

"To what do you attribute that?" I asked.

"Angella, long ago I stopped asking why things happen. Comes with getting older, I suppose. Now I just accept that when things do happen, they present opportunities. Akin, I suppose to that old saw about horse manure in the barn. If you approach it with a victim's mentality you moan at the thought of mucking it all out. But...but if you think about it in terms of a gift, you immediately set out searching for the horse. I'm going for the horse."

"What's that got to do with the *Bucksbaums* and our little visit this morning?" I pressed.

"As you know, they shortened the exhibit. They're saying it's because it was unconfirmed. My take, the *Bucksbaum*'s value has gone up so much they're frightened of break-ins. Liability issues. I think also reporters have been sniffing around. And not in a good way. Carrie's been told to pick up the *Bucksbaum* by nine-thirty. Thought I'd drop by and observe."

"Plan to tail her?"

"Physical tailing's not my strength, Angella. I was trained in the plant-a-transmitter school of tailing. Do it all electronically. Less muss."

Except, it made no sense that Tiny, a top CIA agent, and Ben-Yuval, a Mossad agent, would each be doing basic surveillance legwork, either physical or electronic. No, they were on the ground because something big was in the wind.

And it had a lot more to do with things that went bump in the night than it had to do with passive art work that hung demurely on a wall.

Before I could think this through any further, Carrie's white van, or perhaps it's more accurate to say, a white van similar to the one we had seen in the art show parking area, pulled into the Holocaust Center's lot. The van parked in the spot Hessle had just vacated.

We had a good view through the van windshield to the front seats, and it appeared there was only one person in the van. But, of course, people could have been in the back. Problem was, even using the zoom function of my cell, I couldn't see the face of that one person. Apparently Ben-Yuval couldn't either because he asked if I knew who it was.

"El Bueno," Ben-Yuval said a moment later, when the driver climbed out of the van and began walking toward the Center, his head swiveling from side to side.

Not seeing anything of concern, the man Ben-Yuval had called el Bueno continued to the center and rang the bell; the door opened, and in he went.

While we waited, Ben-Yuval said, "Your friend Hessle is up the street a bit. If you want to track el Bueno with her, you better get your butts up to the corner, 'cause when he comes out he'll beat hell out of here.

Even had we wanted to tag along with Hessle, there wouldn't have been enough time, because el Bueno was back out through the door within fifteen seconds. His left hand was clamped around a tube about the size of the *Bucksbaum* we had seen earlier, his head again on a swivel. Satisfied, he ran to the van, in he went, and a moment later drove to the edge of the parking lot, turned right, drove to the corner, turned right again, and disappeared down a steep road in the direction of the Monongahela River.

Hessle was four cars behind the van. The way we had witnessed her driving, keeping up would be a piece of cake.

"Gotta go," Ben-Yuval called. He jogged across Murray Avenue, climbed into a car parked almost directly across from where we were positioned, and drove off.

"Didn't he just say it's all done electronically?" I asked Jimmy.

"Must have forgotten to install a bug."

"Or it was found," I added. "How about calling a Lyft and getting something to eat?"

Within three minutes a Maroon Kia rocked to a stop in front of us, a heavyset woman behind the wheel. Jimmy gave her directions and off we went; driving lessons courtesy of Hessle. Up a hill, around a bend, down a hill, up another hill, around another bend, the wheels never stopping, and hardly even slowing.

"Here we are, folks. Staghorn's the best in Greenfield. Enjoy breakfast. Here's my card, call me when you're ready to move on."

The coffee in the shop was self-serve and smelled heavenly. We both ordered bagels and cream cheese, Jimmy's with chives, mine plain. The coffee tasted even better than the aroma suggested, and I was on my second cup when the bagels arrived. "So quiet," I said to Jimmy. "You're either overly hungry or something's not playing well."

"Both actually. You asking because you're troubled as well?"

"I asked first."

"Big picture, first. Why the hell does Ben-Yuval care that we know how to decode an art piece we aren't even chasing? And why arrange it through Hessle? She works for the State of Pennsylvania, not Israel—or even the State Department."

"And the small picture?"

"Might just be me, but I got a vibe from Hessle. An uncomfortable vibe."

"I got the same feeling. That was a strained performance if ever I saw one."

"Jimmy, I put it down to what she said about folks trying to add value to art and using the Holocaust Center to do so. Keep in mind the Internet has several articles on the *Bucksbaums* and the buried code. So there's something there."

"The show was cancelled early for some reason. Angella, you have a point."

"Maybe Hessle was just...just nervous Carrie would see us there. The timing was tight, and she just wanted us out of there before Carrie arrived."

"The timing, not getting caught by Carrie, is our issue, not hers. Why the hell would she care if Carrie, or whoever she thought was coming to pick up the *Bucksbaum*, saw us there? It's a public place. We're the public. Nothing to her. Your take, Jimmy?"

"Something like that, I suppose."

My phone chimed. The words, 'Blocked Number' appeared. Against my better judgment I answered. It was Hessle wanting to know where the hell we were. When I told her, she instructed us to wait for her.

Jimmy was perturbed. "How the hell long does she expect us to wait? All day?"

"She said five minutes. Seven max. Said to order for her."

"Nice of her. Van must not have gone far if she'll be back here in five."

"Sounded pissed, I'd say." I went over to the counter and ordered the same as Jimmy had ordered for himself, only I changed the bagel from onion to plain.

I was on my way back from the counter when Hessle came through the door. All eyes turned to her for a moment, then looked away. I grabbed an empty chair and carried it over to our small table in the corner, motioning Hessle to follow. "This is a dispense-your-own place," I told her, nodding in the direction of the coffee bar. I decided to stifle my editorial comment that she looked as if she could use something much stiffer.

"Is it fair for us to assume the white van didn't go all that far from here?" Jimmy probed as soon as Hessle had returned with her coffee.

"Better yet, assume some jackass cut me off! Drove his freakin' rental right in front of me and stalled it out. By the time I got free of the idiot the van was long gone! A-hole!"

"Give him a ticket?" Jimmy calmly asked. It was all I could do to refrain from laughing.

"I'm not a beat cop, Redstone! Haven't used a ticket book in more years than I can count. I'da shot him sooner than ticket him. And you can take that to the bank! To top it off, the windows were dark, couldn't get a look at the driver." The server took that moment to slide the bagel I had ordered in front of Hessle. "What's that green crap on my cream cheese?"

"Chives," I said. "You said to order what Jimmy or I had. That's what I did. I had the plain bagel and Jimmy had the chives. Only his was on an onion bagel."

"Good lord. Glad you at least lost the onion! I'm famished." Hessle took a tentative bite, chewed, then announced, "Not half bad. Coffee's excellent, by the way." She proceeded to finish off her bagel without further comment.

Jimmy might not have been born with patience, but long years of tedious law enforcement investigations taught him how to wait out the other guy. He's as good as they come when he puts his mind to it—and when it serves his best interest. This was one of those times when he deemed it worth the wait, so he sipped his coffee and sat quietly. Hessle had come back to us on her own, so she wanted something. As driven as she was, she wasn't going to leave without it.

"What'd Ben-Yuval want?"

"Where you know him from?" Jimmy asked, employing his go-on-offense-when-defense-is-uncomfortable routine.

"Around."

"Around where?"

"Just around! Stop jacking with me! What'd he want?"

"Think he was watching for Carrie, same as you."

"Hope he had better luck. Only it wasn't Buck driving. It was that guy el Bueno. Listen, Redstone, one thing I know is that if Ben-Yuval wanted to track Carrie, he wouldn't have positioned himself in the middle of the street. Now what the hell did he want?" Hessle fixed her eyes on Jimmy and if they had been lasers his head would have exploded from the heat.

Jimmy calmly nursed his mug as if unaware of Hessle's boiling anger. Only I knew Jimmy better than that. He had positioned his feet in anticipation, and was ready to spring upward the instant the trooper made a threatening move. Fundamental rule of Darwinism: Never encourage a fight with an opponent who carries a gun. The corollary: If you're going to fight with such a person, get to that person before he/she has time to draw. That was Jimmy's plan.

My plan was in support of the corollary. I twisted in my chair while lifting my legs as high as I could so that my feet extended over the top of Hessle's feet. At Jimmy's first move I'd drop my legs, and with any luck Hessle would trip over my feet, giving Jimmy perhaps a half-second advantage. He might not need it—but then again, he might.

"Angella," Hessle finally said to me, her eyes remaining fixed on Jimmy. "You can put your feet down. You think I'm stupid enough to pick a fight when you two highly trained folks are ready for it? Not on your life. When—I suppose I should say, if—the time comes when it's necessary to mix it up it'll be on my terms, not yours."

Jimmy nodded and I relaxed my feet. One thing we now knew, Hessle was not a novice. In fact, she had been highly trained, just as we had been. That made her more than a State Trooper. How much more we had yet to determine. We also now knew she didn't have access to Ben-Yuval's plans and movements. That meant he was operating outside of our government and perhaps even outside Tiny's purview. Thinking of Tiny, he might also be off Hessle's radar screen.

"You two make a good team, I'll say that much." When neither of us spoke, Hessle continued. "Homeland Security lost big time when you left. So why are you so far from home? And don't tell me you're investigating Great Southern's claims."

"Investigating Great Southern's claims," Jimmy said. "What else would we be doing?"

"You tell me."

"Great Southern's paid claims on lots of lost and stolen art—and other items. We go where the trail takes us."

Hessle turned in my direction. "Angella, maybe you'll be more forthcoming. You two were shot at down by the river by someone who wants you out of the way. I want to know why. I also want to know who that someone is."

"Wish we knew those answers—and a lot more." I studied the woman across from me and thought about how she had handled herself and the behavioral patterns she displayed in the few times we had seen her. I then went out on a limb. "You're assigned to Pennsylvania, but unless I miss my guess, you were trained by the same folks who trained us. The FBI in Quantico. So are you state or fed?"

"For your purposes, consider me state."

That meant the big cop was FBI, perhaps on loan to a state task force, perhaps something else. "Have it your way. The shooting, actually both shootings, ours at the Point and the floater, is Pittsburgh's jurisdiction. Why's the state involved?"

"It happened in a State Park, so—"

"So then where's Grandkowski in all this?"

"He's not a detective."

"This your case?"

"Frankly, if 'this' means you two being shot at—or the floater—then no, it's not my case. If 'this' means black market art transactions where the proceeds escape taxation, then yes, it is my case." Hessle paused a moment, looked both of us in the eyes, this time with much less intensity than we had seen earlier. "I've laid out my cards. Mind doing the same?"

"We're investigating for Great Southern."

"Jimmy! You're trying my patience! Why Pittsburgh?"

If it was my call and my call alone, I'd tell Hessle everything we knew, which actually is precious little. But Jimmy plays things close. He would say Darwin. I would say stubborn. So I was surprised when Jimmy came clean. "Truth is, we got a tip, a credible tip, that the key to finding certain art was a guy named Hugo. Oscar Hugo. No known address, as you must know. Took a walk in the park, got shot at—and framed—and apparently led some art thief to a *Bucksbaum* when we tracked Hugo's mother to a rehab center. We took a picture of the *Bucksbaum*, went to find the

Buck woman at the art show. End of book report."

"You left out seeing someone deliver what you think is the *Golden Booby* to Carrie's van."

"As I said, you know all that."

"You left out the part about the van being under surveillance. That's why the search warrant was denied."

Truth or consequences time for Jimmy. I was glad it was him on the hot seat and not me. But had it been me I'd lock up about now.

Not Jimmy, though. "Didn't know about the surveillance until after," he admitted. "Little birdie told me."

"And this little birdie is?"

Without missing a beat, Jimmy replied, "Sources are sacred. Sorry."

To my surprise, Hessle sat back in her chair, her face again soft, or as soft as a hardened cop's face ever becomes. She said nothing.

It was Jimmy who added, "I'll ask the source. That do it for you? Mind telling us what your take on the *Bucksbaum* is?"

"Still in gestation. But I'm not yet buying the *follow the dots to the buried treasure* story."

"So what are you buying? Ben-Yuval's certainly interested."

"The buried munitions are in the past, the long ago past. He's looking to the present or the future."

"Thoughts?" I asked. No harm in trying.

"Picked up a whiff sometime back. Have no reason to believe it's true. But there is one *Bucksbaum* that contains names of some sort. I don't know if they are names of dead folks or...or names of some people important to Israel."

"Such as?" I followed up.

"Such as...wanted war criminals, want my speculation, for what its worth."

"If we find out," Jimmy said, "We'll brief you. We owe you one."

Hessle nodded. "In return, here's what I can do for you." She pulled out her cell phone, looked up a name, then said, "Here's the name of a man who's known to be interested in buying art work that...shall we say...falls within the Great Southern spectrum. Included in the text is the street name I've been authorized to give you. Don't check out of your current hotel, but you'll find a reservation for you downtown at the William Penn. The word on the street is that you folks, the new you, have street creds and can be trusted. You already have an on-line presence. Study it before you make contact." She reached into her pocket and pulled out two card cases. "Take these; you'll need them."

"Appreciate the lead," Jimmy said sarcastically when his phone buzzed in receipt of the name. "Need to clear this with Silver, our boss."

"Just don't give him the names you'll be working under. No need for him to know. And, for the record, whatever that means, not sure I did you two any favors. We've been setting this up for months; don't screw it up. Nobody in or near law enforcement has been able to get anywhere near this guy's *gallery*. Sure, I can walk into his office, or his home for that matter, and its all smiles and handshakes and pleasantries, but a steel trap when it comes to his *private* collections. Some say he controls well over three billion. Good luck."

The name Hessle had sent, the name of the art collector, was none other than Morris Dexter Stratis, who we now knew was the Chairman of Stratis Industries. His claim to fame was a window guide for use in any building over ten stories. The Stratis guide, or the Strat, as it was known in the industry, was invented by his father, and it had been protected by worldwide patents for seventeen years. The Internet story is that after the patent expired, several companies brought similar products to market and, as luck would have it, they all failed.

"Failed on their own," I said, "or helped along?"

"My guess, since they all failed, they were helped along. Bottom line, his cash register dings every time a window, or a replacement window, is installed in a high-rise building anywhere in the world. I see why his art collection runs in the billions."

"And Stratis Industries owns several other companies. No wonder everyone listens when he speaks."

FIFTEEN

We hadn't worked under an alias in a long time, and I have to admit I was nervous to be doing it now that we were civilians. I studied my new driver's license with the expectation of spotting obvious errors. But my picture was spot on, and I was impressed that we each had a different credit card and even medical insurance cards. This was a professional operation, ostensibly being run by the State of Pennsylvania. Jimmy concurred in my assessment that the operation bore the hand of Big Brother. "Enough so to make Tiny proud," was Jimmy's exact comment.

"What do we do with our rental car?" I asked. "Can't just leave it at that gas station in Oakland."

"I'm thinking we pick it up, turn it in and Lyft wherever we go. Less baggage that way."

"Speaking of baggage, Hessle says the cards are good for new clothes. It's not like we didn't just do this, but, hey, they want to outfit us, who are we to turn them down?"

"Whoever *they* are," Jimmy added.

"Okay, Mr. Summerland, I'm ready when you are. I suggest we begin with the wedding and engagement rings. Unfortunately, Hessle says they're only on loan. We sign for them and they need to be returned. Bummer. You plan to wear a ring?" This was a sensitive topic with me. Months ago I had thought Jimmy was ready to propose, but for some reason he hadn't. I had no reason to believe he's changed his mind, but yet nothing.

"Have to wait 'til the morning for the rings. The jeweler she told us to see is over in the Clark building, and nothing's open until tomorrow. In answer to whether I plan to wear a band or not I think for this mission I will. Add a nice touch, don't you think?"

I had no idea what to make of Jimmy's answer, so I put it out of my mind. We spent the remainder of Sunday performing a myriad of housekeeping chores; returning the car, checking into the William Penn Hotel, and, of course, shopping. At sunset, we rode the incline up to Mt. Washington and walked a few feet to Altius, a spectacular little restaurant recommended to us by the hotel bell captain. The food was excellent, as was the view of downtown Pittsburgh from high above. We could easily see down to the confluence of the Allegheny and Monongahela rivers as the waters from each slowly merged, forming the Ohio. Pittsburgh, at least viewed from the mountaintop where we were, is perhaps the prettiest city in the country, with its many bridges and tall buildings spreading out between the rivers as far as the eye could see.

One of the many topics at dinner was how we were to make contact with Morris Dexter Stratis, the billionaire art collector. We couldn't just call him up and ask to see his private collection. I pulled out one of the business cards Hessle had given us and laid it on the table. Engraved on the card was my name, a telephone number I did not recognize and in the lower right corner, the words, "Liaison for the Arts".

"What the hell does that mean?"

Jimmy studied it a moment. "My guess is as good as yours. We'll wing it."

"No more business tonight," I said, holding my wine glass high. "Let's enjoy the dinner, the wine, the city, and each other. Tomorrow's another day."

Indeed, we spent the next several days enjoying ourselves. Tuesday for lunch we followed the suggestion of the hotel concierge and walked a few blocks over to Heinz Hall, the home to the Pittsburgh Symphony Orchestra, and enjoyed a marvelous lunch in their lovely outdoor park-like setting, prepared by *Common Pleas Catering*.

Tuesday night, the Lyft driver suggested *Superior Motors*, a restaurant receiving good vibes in Braddock, a small town just up the Mon River. The restaurant is located directly across from the Edgar Thomson Works of US Steel whose Bessemer furnaces have been in continuous operation for almost a hundred and fifty years. The meal was indeed excellent. On Wednesday, we rented a car for the day and drove east an hour and a half to

Falling Water, the Frank Lloyd Wright home designed to blend into the hillside. Pennsylvania is a beautiful state, and this ride proved the point. In Texas, particularly South Texas, the land is mostly flat, and unless a stand of trees blocks your view, you can see forever. In the Allegheny Mountains, a hundred feet to a rock face is typical. But this is punctuated by sporadic openings in the undulating hills that yield stunning panoramic views of rolling meadows and plowed fields, with their endless rows of corn, soybeans, oats, and wheat. It all looks so very idyllic.

We were out of the car at a scenic view area where three states could be seen from a single vantage point. Jimmy had just taken several cell phone pictures when he turned to me. "I'm a water person. Something about seeing water, being near water; a lake, a river, the Gulf of Mexico down where we live, any body of water, to set my internal clock. I'm not sure I'm programmed to be away from water for any length of time."

"I hear you with the water, Jimmy, but I think I could grow to get the same sense of balance from hills and mountains."

"You know, Jimmy," I said on another of our drives, "it wouldn't take all that much to encourage me to move east. There is something... something calming about these hills. You know you're surrounded by millions of people, yet... there's an isolated peace when you look out at the rolling hills."

"Visualize all this covered with snow. And our car slipping and sliding around these bends."

"Killjoy. I see a cozy room with a fireplace blazing and you see...well, you see your car stuck on the side of the road, and you standing there trying to flag down a ride. That, Jimmy, is what I call mismatched expectations."

"That, Angella, is what I call reality."

Wednesday night we had another great dinner at a small place called Amels Restaurant. The fish was excellent. Then on Thursday we Lyfted out to something called the Charley Brown House. Seems this guy Brown built a home on top of a hill over-looking the Allegheny River just up the river from Pittsburgh proper, where he exhibited self-playing musical instruments for his friends. The house is now called the Bayernhof Museum and contains one of the world's largest collections of music gen-eration devices. It was a fascinating exhibit, but the truth was the visit to the Bayernhof had been set for Thursday for an important reason. That was the day Carmella Schenley Hampton was scheduled to be the docent and lead the tour groups.

Hessle had put us on to her, not because of her docent duties exactly, but because Ms. Hampton, "Carmine," as she introduced herself during the tour, was herself an heiress and into art collection. "Anything having to do with musical instruments," Hessle had informed us. "And that includes birds."

"Birds?" I had asked.

"Yes, birds, Angella. Birds. As in *Golden Booby* being a bird. She collects birds. If there is even a sniff around here of the *Golden Booby*, which you now assure me there is, Carmine would know about it."

"Does she have her collection on display?"

"More or less." Hessle then went on to explain about Charlie Brown's house and mentioned that some of her art collection was indeed on display there.

"All of it?" I had asked.

"That's the sixty-four-thousand-dollar question, Angella. Don't know."

I called Silver, and his take on Carmella "Carmine" Hampton was a bit more skeptical. He explained how she had only recently appeared on the art scene, but she had been well received. Then he uncharacteristically added, "Rumors have it she, like so many other major collectors, has a dark site—the term they prefer, by the way, is "private"—for much of her collection. You won't know it from talking with her, though. She seems open and salt of the earth, but don't get sucked in too far."

"Her name's Carmella Schenley Hampton. Any relation to the woman who donated the park to Pittsburgh?"

"Same name," Silver admitted. "But here's the thing about Carmella. Our research is conclusive, she's not in any way related to Mary Schenley.

According to what we turned up, she gave herself that name when her husband died, leaving her a trust fund of close to a billion dollars. That's billion with a B."

Something in Silver's voice, the way he prefaced everything about Hampton in terms of research, caused me concern. Knowing our boss as I do, I didn't think pressing him would be productive. Instead, I asked, "Why take Schenley's name?"

"Why do rich people do anything, Angella? Because they can. Good luck."

The Charlie Brown house was fascinating. The self-playing musical instruments were sensational, from the 1907 Hupfeld, which played a piano and three violins, to the 1920's Knabe Ampico Reproducing Player Piano, to the Welte Cottage Orchestrion, which dated back to the turn of the century. Every one of the instruments on display worked, or so Carmine gleefully assured us. As we toured the facility, we only had time to listen to a few of them perform. If any of the pictures on the walls, or the art objects sprinkled throughout the house, were Carmine's, she didn't say. And her eyes gave away nothing.

Near the end of our tour Jimmy glanced into a room that we were passing but not entering. There, on a desk in the far corner sat a golden bird. My first impression, as I'm certain was Jimmy's, was that we had located the *Golden Booby*. Despite Carmine's constant admonitions for the twelve of us in the group to remain together, Jimmy and I both veered off toward the entrance to the small room. The chance of this being the *Booby* was nil, but to ignore it would be irresponsible.

We hadn't taken but two steps when Carmine, who was suddenly spryer than anything we had seen in the past hour, was at our sides, her frozen smile still in place. "Step right along, you two. Can't be having stragglers, not in Charlie Brown's house, we can't."

"That bird over there," Jimmy told her, "reminds me of—"

"Step along now," our guide repeated, her words were delivered with increased authority.

"—a piece of art from Peru."

"That's just some...some Pacific water bird. Nothing special. Nothing special at all. Now come—"

Jimmy held his phone up about to snap a picture.

"Put that phone away!" Carmine snapped, not sounding like the doddering docent of a moment ago. "You know the rules. Pictures only where I say so."

"I'm really sorry," Jimmy said, pulling the phone down to his side. "I thought you said it was an insignificant...some Pacific bird or another. It caught my eye because it looks just like I remember a piece called the *Golden Booby* looking. But I see now this one has brown feet and it's bronze and gold."

Jimmy had her. Carmine's eyes went wide for a long instant. Long enough for her to struggle to pull herself back under control. "The *Golden Booby*, you say?" Her lips worked, yet no sound came. "Can't say as I ever heard of it."

But we knew better. And she knew we knew better.

Jimmy set the hook even deeper. "Let it go. I was mistaken."

Carmine studied my partner a moment, her lower jaw quivering, whether in anger or frustration I couldn't tell. She then reached in her pocket and pulled out a card. "Here. Take this and come to my house tonight at seven-thirty. Come hungry."

"About?" Jimmy pressed.

"About that bird over there. What else? We don't have time now. Need to get on back to the group." The smile was back, the eyes again distant, and the singsong tempo of her voice had returned.

SIXTEEN

Google Maps showed Louisa Street to be in the Oakland area, less than a block from our Boulevard hotel, the hotel registered to us in our real names, not the William Penn Hotel where we had been staying under assumed names since Sunday. From where the Lyft driver dropped us, Louisa appeared to be a one-block street going down a hill and ending in an upward sloping weed-covered hillside. A flight of stairs extending up the side of that hill suggested that Louisa did, in fact, have a second life at the top of the hill.

I stood for a moment, ostensibly taking in our surroundings. The massive UPMC Magee-Woman's Hospital was directly behind us at the beginning of the street. But, in truth, it wasn't the environment that I was taking in. It was Angella. And the wedding ring she wore. My thumb had unconsciously been rolling over my wedding band these past few days, and I was again kicking myself for not popping the question when we were back on our island in the Gulf of Mexico. I actually had in my bag the ring I had bought almost six months ago, and I had thought long and hard about using that ring for this charade. But the last thing I wanted was for Angella to associate our marriage with our work. Naive, perhaps, to think it could be any other way. But that's where I had come out. Trouble is, I've spent more hours second-guessing that decision than I have being content that I have it right.

"Jimmy," Angella softly said, "the address we're looking for is on the left over there. Better get with the program. You've been...well, distracted. Something wrong?"

"Just thinking." I looked to see where she was pointing. "Center one of the three attached brick townhomes," I said, as if I had been studying them all along. "I'm guessing they were built in the mid-twenties." They each had a small front yard and a front bricked-in porch. I estimated twelve hundred square feet spread over two floors. We had been led to believe Carmella Schenley Hampton was a wealthy woman, but this house gave no such indication. The neighborhood, while clean and neat, didn't appear to be overly affluent. If there were such a thing as a typical Middle America neighborhood, then this area would be eligible. "Show time," I said to Angella as we stepped up onto the porch.

We were halfway across the porch when the front door opened to reveal a woman a good ten to fifteen years younger than the docent we had met earlier in the day. Gone were the old woman's smock and slumped shoulders that had been on display earlier, having been replaced by a brightly colored tailored blouse and calf-length skirt. She had also traded the hair bun for a shoulder-length hairdo, and a masterful job of makeup had all but removed the wrinkles and creases that had been her prevalent feature at the Charlie Brown House.

"I just love people who are on time," she said. "Don't you?" Her vocal tone was now even and pleasant, a very welcoming expression having been substituted for the unnatural smile we had experienced at the museum. As good as I am with faces and facial movements, Carmine's would have gone unrecognized had we randomly met. *Was it makeup we were now seeing, or had it been makeup we saw earlier?*

"We try," Angella said, holding out the flowers we had picked up on the way over. "I'm Ange Summerland and this is my husband James."

"I know your names from the reservation file." She held her hands out to receive the flowers. "Come on in and I'll just go get a vase for these lovely flowers. This was so thoughtful of you two. Make yourselves comfortable. Be right back."

From the outside the house might have been middle-class, but from the inside it was decorated with what appeared to be antiques. Floor-to-ceiling solid oak bookcases lined the right wall. Two traditional leather side chairs were positioned on either side of a small table. Straight ahead of us, there was a cream-colored Queen Ann sofa flanked with what appeared to be gas sconce floor lamps. The art on the walls ran the gauntlet, all nice, but nothing I recognized. If we were looking for museum-quality art, we had come to the wrong place.

Our hostess returned with a tray of brie cut into bite-size chunks, a few stacks of what appeared to be whole-wheat crackers, and three glasses. She set the tray on the table, opened a compartment in the bookcase and produced a bottle of Merlot. "Either of you prefer white? I have a great Chardonnay cooling in the kitchen. But we're having lamb chops for dinner, and I thought this would go better."

"Merlot is fine with me," I said, and Angella nodded her agreement.

"Sit," Hampton said, pointing in the direction of the chairs. "My great-grandfather had them crafted for him. Been in the family a while."

I lowered myself gingerly into the antique chair, not knowing what to expect from the taut leather. The comfort surprised me.

Hampton sat on the edge of the sofa facing us. "Enjoy the museum, I take it? An interesting place."

"We did," Angella said. "That guy Charlie Brown, was...was—"

"A real character, wasn't he? Wish I would have been here and been invited to his parties, many of which he didn't even attend himself."

"How's that work?" I asked.

"He'd invite people and then make them fend for themselves. Food and beverages would be provided and the party would go on without him. Often, he'd cycle people through the house, serving different courses in different rooms. Sometimes he would even have the staff rearrange and redecorate a room, so that a later course would be served back in that room and the room would appear different."

"A bit eccentric, it sounds like," I volunteered.

"Interesting character no doubt."

"Texas is built on characters," I responded, "but Brown would rival any of them. You guide every day?"

"Only on Thursdays. My public service."

How guiding tours of Charlie Brown's mansion is a public service was a mystery to me, but if I rated all the mysteries in my life on a scale of one to a ten this would be a minus three. "The musical instruments are spectacular. And they all work. I hadn't realized that sound was made mechanically as far back as the turn of the last century. That revelation was astounding."

"Glad you enjoyed. You go by James or Jimmy?"

I had to think a moment. Had Angella called me Jimmy inadvertently? Something made Hampton ask.

"I prefer James or Jim. But Angie calls me Jimmy. I'm in trouble when I hear James from her."

"I'll remember that. I prefer Jim, if you don't mind. Had a friend James and he...he was a real toot."

"You said you weren't from here. Where did you grow up?"

"In Virginia, but that's a long story for another day."

"Where in Virginia?" I pressed.

"Actually, Hampton."

"As in your name?" Angella asked.

"As in my name. You both from Texas?"

Hampton was good. She had steered us away from what she didn't want to talk about to a topic she wanted to explore further. And if we wanted to get further with her, we had to go along, with the constant internal reminder we were playing a role and we had to adhere to the script. Angella took the lead and answered all Hampton's questions about where we lived, how we met, and all those other details women find so interesting.

It was a good thing Angella could carry this off so professionally because my wheels had begun to lose traction when I realized the Schenley part of her name matched Pittsburgh and the Hampton part of her name matched Virginia. Nothing impossible about that, but the coincidence was too high to ignore. All three of us were playing roles. My brain demanded more information on her background. I not only wanted to hear her story, but how she told it.

The chitchat between Hampton and Angella continued until the bottle was empty and the cheese plate mostly depleted. That's when our hostess stood and said, "Come on into the dining room and please entertain yourselves a few minutes while I finish the chops. You'll excuse me, please."

"So what's your take?" I asked Angella when Hampton disappeared. "Assumed name?"

"She's taken on an identity and I suspect she knows we have as well. Let's play this close for a while, see where it takes us."

The meal was served. The chops, the baked potato, the asparagus, and the salad were all done to perfection. The kitchen was small, as indeed the whole house was, and there wasn't another person around. How Hampton had managed to pull this all together in so little time with as little effort as she seemed to expend was another mystery probably never to be solved. It wasn't until she was clearing the table that she mentioned the Booby, seemingly in passing. And when she did, she simply asked what interest I had in it.

"Oh," I responded, "I once saw the *Golden Booby* when it was on display down in Port Isabel, Texas." I went on to explain that Port Isabel was on the mainland side of a causeway leading out to an island called South Padre Island. I stopped just short of mentioning that Angella and I lived on that Island. "And that bird sculpture we saw today reminded me of the *Booby*."

"Good eye, Jim. Because the one you saw today may have been patterned after the original *Golden Booby*. Artist did brown feet as you noted. But..." she lowered her voice, why I didn't know because there was no one else present, "...but they really are gold, etched to appear as bronze."

"Same artist?"

She winked at me. "A gentleman allows a lady to keep a secret."

"From my brief observation I'd say same artist, same bird as well."

"My, my, my. What am I to make of all this? You two bird collectors?"

"Birds...and other objects as well." I fished out my card and laid it on the table. Hampton studied it a while, then asked, "So tell me, what does "Liaison for the Arts" mean?"

"Means we broker art pieces. By prior arrangement," Angella answered, making it totally clear we work as a team. No picking us off individually.

"Surely it means more than that. I know perhaps every broker worth anything handling high-end art in this country. I prefer to call them dealers. Maybe around the world. And I don't know you two. Why would that be?"

I debated what to say. Angella filled the void before I resolved how to answer. "Look, Mrs. Hamp...Carmine....let's be frank. We both know there's art that's on display in public places, homes, galleries, museums. And there's art that spends its life seen by only a select few, or by no one at all. The *Golden Booby* has, unfortunately, spent a great deal of its existence in...in hiding as you well know. Our specialty is *hidden* art."

"Tell me, Angie, when was the last time you laid eyes on the *Booby*?"

"Saturday night," I answered, realizing Angella may not have actually seen the *Booby*.

"And where would that have been?"

"Won't divulge the exact location. But suffice it to say, downtown."

Hampton's eyes again went wide and this time stayed that way. "So you know it's in Pittsburgh. That, indeed, is impressive." The excitement in her voice was real. "Can you...broker a sale?"

"I see no reason why not. But truthfully, the price tag is a bit...shall we say...steep."

"How much do you consider steep?"

The woman's hands began to shake and she had to sit to contain herself. Her face was red and for a moment I thought she was about to pass out. *Was she acting*?

"Again I ask, how much do you consider steep?"

"Personally for me, any number over a hundred K would be steep. But the last I checked the *Golden Booby* carried a price tag of over a hundred million. Perhaps even more, depending on circumstances."

"Walking around money for some," Hampton said, gathering herself and standing. She looked me directly in the eye. "If you can broker a deal for that bird for me...well, all I can say's you'll never have to work a day in your life again."

"How do we know you can...pay the price?" Angella pressed, taking the measure of the woman. "And in what currency and at what location? That is, should we agree to broker it for you."

"Last first. Right here to this house. Currency will be US, unless you want it in some other currency, say Peruvian Nuevos Soles."

"To this house?" I replied, forcing her hand. "This house is not secured and is not properly lighted or ventilated. A piece such as that must—"

"You might know a thing or two about *hidden art* as you call it, but you certainly don't know bubkas about who you're dealing with." Carmine's hands were now rock steady as she retrieved a key from her pocket. She retrieved a large note card printed on both sides in something like eight-point type from a drawer in the sideboard. "Here, sign this the both of you. It's an agreement of your commission at ten percent. It also binds you both to silence and to not ever disclose what you are about to see. I assure you it's iron clad. You violate this agreement, I'll own everything you have or ever will have. That understood?"

I read it quickly, handed it to Angella who also read it, she taking more time than I had. When she was finished, she nodded, and we both then signed.

"Follow me," Hampton said, confiscating the card. She headed to the living room and pulled a book off a shelf from behind where Angella and I had earlier been seating. With the key in her right hand, she reached into the opening where the book had been, and, as seen in the movies, a portion of the wall holding the bookshelves slid sideways, revealing a tunnel-like opening. Hampton bent forward into the opening. She told us to follow her, issuing an admonishment to watch our heads. Indeed, just inside the opening there was a retaining bar five feet off the floor.

It was dark as I ducked under the bar and passed into the house next door. I could hear a faint chirping coming from our right and looking in that direction saw a blue light flashing in concert with the chirp. Suddenly, the pulse rate of both the chirp and the light increased from one-second intervals to a wavering constant.

I had witnessed this scenario first-hand when the blue light on a vest a terrorist was wearing went constant. Five seconds later the blast annihilated him along with four others in the vicinity. Luckily for me I was shielded by a brick wall, but my ears rang for two full days. Carmine was no longer in sight. We were fully exposed, with no structures to duck behind. A classic trap, and we had gone for the cheese.

I dropped to the floor, pulling Angella down against me, and rolled on top of her. I lay with Angella pinned beneath me, tensed against the blast I knew was coming. Angella, not yet realizing the danger, was fighting to get up. I was losing the battle.

"Get up, you two!" Hampton scolded. "I don't know what you expected, but even if I hadn't gotten to the panel in time the only thing that would have happened would have been a phone call to my security folks. They're never far away. Jim, you watch too many Bond movies, I'm afraid."

Lights were slowly coming up, and with them came the realization that we were in a room surrounded by art objects. My guess: Mostly stolen. I say this because an enormous piece hung on a sidewall, a piece so large that the ceiling of the room had been removed to accommodate it. Like all the other pieces, this one wasn't labeled. But it looked like one I recalled from old research, called *Just Judges.* A multi-part altarpiece by Jan Van Eyck stolen from the Saint Bavo Cathedral in Belgium in 1934. *What the hell was this doing here?*

Then I saw the Madonna of Bruges, Michelangelo's famous marble sculpture. *This is a fake*! But I couldn't take my eyes from it.

"I see, Jim, you admire my collection. Not bad for an old woman."

I wasn't about to touch the *old woman* part, but I couldn't resist saying, "And just what would the Church of Our Lady of Bruges have to say about this?"

"I suspect nothing."

"But—"

"I know what you're about to say. This is a fake. But don't be so quick to judge. The Madonna was the only piece of Michelangelo's work to leave Italy during his lifetime. It went to the church in Bruges, Belgium, as you know. But it was twice removed from there. Once to Paris during the French Revolution, and then wrapped in mattresses by the retreating German army and carried off to the salt mines of Altaussee."

"And recovered by the Allies Monuments Men and returned to Bruges."

"Would it shock you to learn that not all the stockpile of stolen art made its way back to the original owners?"

"Nothing shocks me. But the Monuments Men were noted for their honesty and dedication."

"They didn't transport every piece themselves, now did they? And all three of us in this room know the...the...shall I say, the weakness...of the human condition when big money is concerned. Some pieces fell off lorries, some just vanished, and some...some may very well have been duplicated."

"Are you saying this Madonna has—"

"I'm not saying anything other than there are now two Madonnas, both carved from Carrara marble, both identical. And I'm in possession of papers proving the authenticity of the one before you. So, as I say, I'm not as certain as you seem to be that the old church wants to really say anything. Sometimes silence truly *is* golden."

One myth was now clear. Hampton hadn't limited herself to only birds. Musical instruments seemed also to be high on her hit parade, as did mammals. In the Van Eyck it was horses. In the Madonna it was people, famous people. The good news from our standpoint is that I didn't see anything that Great Southern had paid a claim on.

"Now do you believe I have the resources to handle your commission on the *Booby*?"

"It certainly seems that way, I must admit. But... but you still haven't told us if you're the buyer... or the seller."

"All in due course. Need to proceed with...with caution. Wouldn't you agree?"

"Depends upon what you mean by caution," Angella answered.

"First things first. Let's see if we can introduce you to polite society."

"What's that mean?" I asked, smelling a trap about to be set.

"*Art* polite society. My friend Stratis is throwing a gala lawn party Saturday night at his home. Afterward, several of us will tour *his* collection. Puts this to shame, I hate to say. You know who I'm talking about, I'm sure."

"Morris Dexter Stratis," I replied, hoping I had guessed right. "Who else?"

"Pick me up at six on Saturday. I'll arrange it all. You two are going as my guests."

"You can do that?" Angella asked, more curiosity than question.

"I've no real choice but to try. You could never broker the *Booby*, or anything else of high value for that matter, without his stamp of approval. So, voila, either I make that happen or I need to find someone who can. I needn't remind you to be prompt and...and black tie for you, Jim, and cocktail dress for you, Angella."

"Got it," I said, none too happy about the attire.

"Oh, and Jim, rent a Bentley or some such thing. Arriving in an Uber is just not going to cut it with that crowd."

SEVENTEEN

It wasn't exactly a Bentley, but I didn't think Carmella Schenley Hampton, our new best friend, would be embarrassed arriving at the estate of Morris Dexter Stratis in a Porsche 911. Some things, such as how easy it had been for Angella and me to gain access to Hampton's private collection, troubled me. Hampton had practically dragged us next door to view her secret dark-art lair based on our agreement not to rat her out, coupled with a vague promise to help her with the *Golden Booby*. If that's all it took to find her private stash, then why hadn't law enforcement pulled the same stunt we had and gone in there and cleaned her out?

But for now, this mystery was down at my three out of ten level. Angella believed it a seven. We arrived at Louisa Street before I had a chance to explore Angella's concern in depth. My preliminary thought was that Angella didn't trust our new friend and certainly hadn't bought Hampton's story. Parking the car, I had another thought. "I've been troubled by that...well, the use of the attached house as a dark-art gallery. Seems off. I mean housing that kind of art in this kind of neighborhood."

"Of all the things wrong with Hampton and her facade, housing art in the shadow of the University of Pittsburgh, and not all that far from the Carnegie Museum, on a quiet middle-class street, is not one of them. Dark means dark. That art wasn't meant for public display, so housing it here makes sense to me. What doesn't make sense is why in the hell would she allow us, two people she doesn't really know, to even get a whiff of its presence. And on the first date no less. That's what doesn't make any sense, you ask me."

"Can't argue with you on that," I admitted, climbing out of the car to pick up our *date*. "Just remain alert."

"You clean up well, Jim. Great car. I approve." Hampton was all smiles when her front door opened. She now appeared another ten years younger in her perfectly tailored gown, professionally applied makeup and hair that was a perfect Jane Fonda imitation. I felt awkward in my newly acquired tux and stiff formal shirt. My lopsided bow tie gave me away as a novice formal partygoer.

Hampton obviously wasn't focused on my attire. "I'm not crawling in back. I do that and I won't vouch I can climb back out. I'm invoking the perquisites of old age."

"Not a problem," I answered, "Ange is already in the back seat."

"You two think of everything, now don't you? How sweet of you." She pinched my arm in a playful gesture.

Once we were moving, Hampton inquired if I knew where we were going and I told her Waze was already programmed.

"Do your homework on Moe?" she asked.

Took me a moment to realize "Moe" was Stratis.

"We've been following him for a while," came Angella's reply from the back seat. "Guy has quite an art collection. Rumor claims he has just as much hidden as he does for public consumption."

"I wouldn't have any way of knowing what he has offline," Hampton responded, giving away nothing. "I just know his public art collection is the best in private hands anywhere in the world."

"You know him a long time?" Angella asked.

"You might say so. We're both collectors. The field isn't all that large."

I didn't think it prudent to disagree with Hampton's premise about the number of art collectors.

What isn't large is the number of offline collectors where their collections go mostly unseen, except by them. And from what I've come to learn, there are pieces in the possession of certain collectors that have never even been seen by their owners. For those individuals, it's enough to exercise control over a masterpiece. Viewing it is secondary.

"Why so quiet, you two? You'd think we were on our way to a funeral. Actually, I've been to funerals with more levity."

"Truthfully, I'm not much for large socials where everyone tries to one up the next person while drinking too much. The ones I've attended are way too noisy to hear anything, anyway."

"Jim, I'm surprised to hear that from you. You two must spend most of your time with these folks if you're brokering art. And, in my experience, they love their cocktail parties."

"Of course we do, more than I care to admit," I said, backtracking and trying to work myself out of an unforced error. "And that's why I'm not looking forward to yet another. And besides—"

"What Jimmy means," Angella said, lending her hand at correcting my social faux pax, "is because we're not currently working with anyone...I mean anyone other than you...here in Pittsburgh right now, that makes tonight pure social. He would prefer other activities for his social life when he has the option."

"Oh, I see," Hampton replied, not buying anything we were saying. "I'm sorry to be dragging you two out here, but I thought it important to your business, and mine, to be included. And, of course, I'm certain you'll enjoy seeing Moe's collection."

"Most definitely, it's the collection we've come for, not the social on the lawn, I can tell you that," I said.

"Oh, trust me, my dear man, you'll enjoy the *social on the lawn,* as you put it. If nothing else, young, rich, single, well, maybe not all single, but certainly available, women will be on full display. Great place to go fishing. And for you, Ange, the same holds true. Lots of eligible men."

"We're happily married," Angella immediately shot back, a noticeable edge to her voice. "No interest in looking."

"That's what they all say, my dear. But truth is, the divorce rate makes all that a lie. Facts speak louder than platitudes. So, go enjoy yourselves. Put a little money in the bank, I always say."

"That why you're here, Carmine?" I replied, poking back at her. "Get yourself a live one?"

"Could be. Just could be. This old lady still has life in her. Gotta live while you can." Carmine was doing her best Auntie Mame imitation, and who was I to rain on her parade? The fact that she had managed to get us included in a Stratis show-and-tell increased her street creds—at least with me.

The turn onto the winding road leading up to the Stratis estate allowed the conversation to draw down naturally. Hampton had been right about the car we arrived in. While the Porsche 911 was not an embarrassment, it was not in the top echelon either.

We were welcomed warmly by a uniformed valet sporting three bars on each shoulder board. He addressed Hampton by name without reference to a cheat sheet. Impressive.

"These are my guests, Randall," Hampton answered, "Mr. and Mrs. James Summerland."

"Do I receive a ticket for my car, or what?" I asked the man named Randall, as he turned to greet the car behind us. Indeed, it was a white Bentley Continental.

"No need, we have your photo. When you come for your car, we'll have it ready."

Neat system. Using photo IDs makes it difficult for anyone to leave with a car they didn't arrive in. I turned to follow Angella and found her speaking with a young college-age man, dressed all in black, slacks, shirt, shoes, and tie. Before I caught up to her, a woman of roughly the same age tapped my right arm. "You're James Summerland, is that correct?" She was identically dressed all in black, the only flash of color being her emerald green eyes.

"I am."

"And I'm Samantha Rivers. I'm your hostess for the evening."

I took a step back. Samantha's eyes were alive with the vibrancy mostly wasted on youth. This story didn't promise to end well. And frankly, I wanted no part of a *hostess*, whatever the hell that meant. "I'm afraid you have the wrong—"

"If you're James Summerland, then I have it right. I'm assuming this must be your first Stratis party."

"It certainly is." *And definitely the last,* I wanted to add. "I thank you, but I'd prefer to be with my... my wife."

"My job as hostess is to introduce you around. I'm an intern at one of the Stratis companies. All of us in black are. I'm here tonight to make certain you enjoy yourself and I'm graded on how well I do. Tonight there are twelve of us, and I've been assigned to escort you."

"Does that mean you know everyone here? Or what? How does it all work?" I've been in many uncomfortable situations over the years, and this had all the earmarks of rising to the top of the worst list.

"Maybe not everyone," Rivers was saying, "but most. Certainly the folks who you're scheduled to meet I know. Of course, I also know the regulars. They don't have escorts."

"Makes it easier for the *regulars* to spot the neophytes, I'd say. That's a benefit—to them—and to Mr. and Mrs. Stratis."

"Only Mister tonight, I'm afraid. Mrs. Stratis doesn't usually come to these...these events. Come now, I see the mayor over there. Time to introduce you."

A moment later, handshakes having been exchanged, Sam, as I had been instructed to call her, introduced me to the mayor with a one-sentence bio lifted straight from my newly-created Internet profile. Hessle had been thorough in her preparations. Then Sam said, "The mayor's pet project, and I'm certain he has many others, is furnishing a senior's lounge in each ward of the city." With that, she took a step back, forcing me to pick up the conversation.

"Ambitious project," I said, not even knowing how many wards there were in the city. "How far along are you?"

"About half." He then launched into praise for the city and its people and how they support one another. He went on for a full two minutes about the wonderful generosity of people from all walks of life, taking care to work the slogan, Pittsburgh Strong, into his pitch, a reference to the unity of Pittsburghers after the tragic Tree of Life Synagogue murders. All the while, Sam stood silently off to the side. "See that man over there?" the mayor suddenly asked. "That's Franco Harris, one of the best there ever was. He's a big supporter of the city."

Indeed, I saw Franco. I also saw Angella's host, a tall thin guy, directing Angella in Franco's direction. A black-clad male host with a smiling woman in tow positioned himself and his charge directly between me and the mayor, prompting Samantha to step forward. "Come along, Mr. Summerland. Next you are to meet one of the artists here this evening. Jackie O'Rourke is right over there," Sam said, nodding in the direction of an attractive strawberry-blond woman talking with an elegantly dressed Indian woman of perhaps double her age. "Jackie," I was informed as we closed in on the blond, "is an artist who has painted portraits of Pittsburgh's most beautiful women. Several of the women she painted by the way, are here tonight as well. If you would like, and we have the time, I will be happy to introduce you."

"I don't see the need for that," I answered, still bristling at Hampton's suggestion that this would be a good place for me—or maybe she was directing her comments to Angella—to *put a little money in the bank.*

"Ms. O'Rourke, Ms. Kumar," Sam said, ignoring my comment, "please, I would like to introduce you both to James Summerland. James, please meet Ms. Jackie O'Rourke and Ms. Riya Kumar. James is a liaison for art; he travels the world in pursuit of works for clients." With that introduction, my hostess again stepped back.

"Oh, Mr. Summerland," the elegant Indian woman said, her voice carrying a hint of Colonial English, "I was told you would be here. My husband would enjoy meeting you."

"Nice meeting you, I'm sure," O'Rourke said, hardly taking notice of my presence before turning to greet a slender redhead in a gown that left nothing to the imagination. Judging from O'Rourke's crowding of the redhead's personal space, the thought struck me that this particular artist could be the one putting money in the bank. There was no doubt, she and I had the same taste in women.

"And your husband is?" I asked Kumar, forcing my mind away from the redhead.

"Surely you jest, Mr. Summerland. May I call you James?"

"Certainly."

"Please call me Riya. My husband, Sanjay, is,

as I'm certain you know full well, an important art collector. His collection rivals—"

"Oh, I do apologize," I said, trying to preserve my identity, "I hadn't put it together. Please pardon me."

Riya batted her eyes and twisted her head in O'Rourke's direction. "Jackie does have that effect on wom...people. Or was it the redhead?" Her fingers fluttered over my forearm ever so softly. "I fully understand." Riya's nut-brown almond eyes burned into me with an intensity I had rarely ever seen. Dark brown hair, almost to the point of black, framed her flawlessly smooth face in such a way as to capture my full attention.

I forced my mind back into gear, knowing that if Hampton were watching, she'd be witnessing coins collecting in the bank's moneybox. "Well, in my defense, our paths have never crossed. Mine, I mean, and Sanjay's."

"That is indeed too bad. We'll just have to change that, now won't we?" Another brush of my body with her fingers; this time my shoulder. And this time they lingered. "What is your specialty, James? You were introduced as a liaison."

"It varies from client to client." I had planned to leave it vague, but the almond eyes had collapsed to a slit, coaxing me to continue. "Recently, I've been working on a lost piece called the *Golden Booby*. Also, an interesting work called the *Pirate*."

The slits were wide open now. Was it the *Pirate*...

or the *Booby*...that had captured her full attention? I waited for her to reconnect with the present before adding, "I—actually my part...wife...and I—only work for one client at a time. We have found that is the best way to avoid embarrassing conflicts."

"Oh, I understand. I believe—"

Sam, my hostess, took that moment to interrupt. "Pardon us," she said smoothly, "but we have just enough time remaining to introduce James to one more guest, if we are to tour the garden art collection before dinner is served. And we wouldn't want to keep your dinner partner waiting."

"Goodbye for now, James," Riya purred. "I am certain we will be seeing each other again very soon." One more finger flutter, this time across the back of my hand, and the gorgeous Indian woman gathered her silk sari and flowed off toward a group gathered by the bar.

Sam introduced me to a tall lean woman with short hair wearing a tuxedo shaped very much like mine. Her name was Maxine Baker; her handshake was firmer than mine and her voice, when she said, "Pleased to meet you, I'm sure," rivaled Hessle's in its deepness.

"Ms. Baker," I said, "is this your first time here? I notice you have an intern assigned to you as well."

"Max. I go by Max. It very much is my first time, Mr. Summerland. Yours as well I note."

"James. I go by James," I replied as deadpan as I could force it. "I'm an art liaison. Broker, if you will."

"Just who I was looking for. I sold a business for...for let's say, a lot of money. I'm looking to invest in something important. Can you—"

"Come, Mr. Summerland," Sam called, "I'm terribly sorry to interrupt, but we just have time to tour the gardens before dinner. And Mr. Stratis is not pleased if we're late."

I turned to Max. "Sorry we don't have time to talk longer. Here, take my card, and please feel free to contact me."

"Nice to have met you. A friend of Morris is a friend of mine. I will call you in the next few days. Have a great night."

The garden *art collection* was massive and impressive, even more impressive than the Nasher Sculpture Center in Dallas. I had toured the Nasher shortly after it opened in 2003 as part of the Texas Rangers training program. I had just been assigned to a task force focused on stolen art. The program included security systems used to protect art pieces as well as an intensive course on recognizing art that had vanished from collections around the world. The *Pirate*, one of the pieces now on my radar, didn't go missing until April of 2006. I wasn't brought in until July and by then the trail was non-existent.

"What did you think of the art?" Sam asked, as we snaked our way to the middle of three big white open-sided tents, made unnecessary by the cooperating weather. According to Sam, they had been erected earlier in the week in the event of inclement conditions.

"Impressive. One of the finest in the world," I said, looking around and trying to catch a glimpse of Angella. I didn't see her anywhere, and concluded she was in one of the other tents. For that matter, I didn't locate Franco Harris, either. But I did see a man who was either Ben Roethlisberger or his look-alike, with a black-clad escort at his side.

"Well, here we are. Tent two, table nine, seat three. Your dinner partner should be along...oh, there she is."

Sam's eyes were focused on, of all people, the artist Carrie Buck. I hadn't recognized her with her hair down and whatever else women do when they're made up for polite company. Her gown was a simple wrap-around, but it did her figure justice. "Oh, hi again," I said.

"I didn't know you two knew each other," Sam confessed. "In that case, my job is easy."

"Met last week at the art show. Carrie's a gifted artist. Has a booth at the Three Rivers Art Festival. Glass sculpture."

"Well, okay, then. Enjoy your evening, Mr. Summerland. Goodnight, Ms. Buck." Sam turned and disappeared into the heavy twilight.

"So, we meet again," Carrie said when Sam had taken her leave. "Never did get your name."

Good thing for my cover. "James Summerland. My wife's Ange. She's off somewhere."

"Oh, that's the way Stratis likes to do it. Separates couples all the time. Says it makes for more interesting conversation. Works out well for us single folks. Who am I to complain? Commissioned a few pieces tonight already. And hey, the night's still young." She took my arm. "You can escort me to our table, seeing as though I'm your dinner companion."

"Be my pleasure," I said, extending my arm. "Table nine, seat three."

"Seat four for me. The food promises to be excellent. Always is. Don't suppose this will be any different."

EIGHTEEN

"So, Jimmy," I asked when dinner was over and we met outside the tents, "what did you learn from Buck? You two certainly were going at it hot and heavy."

"What makes you say we were going *hot and heavy?* You weren't even in our tent."

"Happened to walk by on my way to the ladies' room. And there you were, your chair twisted in her direction and all. I'd say that qualifies as hot and heavy."

"I was trying to get to the bottom of her father's art. How he made it—and why. Where it's located, that type of thing."

"Get anywhere?"

"Learned the basics, but she evaded everything else. Lives in Buffalo when not on the road. Travels the country, living in her van. Otto, her father, is indeed gone. Oh, and she's younger than she looks."

"You're on dangerous ground here. Maybe I should ask, how old does she look to you?"

"In her booth I would have said, mid-seventies."

"I agree, " I said. "Go on."

"Here, tonight, looked late sixties to early seventies."

"Agree with that as well. So?"

"Would you believe sixty-six?"

"And you're telling me this why?"

"Because that's the most significant fact I could wrestle out of her. Woman knows how to keep her mouth shut. I tried every trick I know to get her to talk about the *Booby*, or about stolen art in general. She wouldn't bite, but she had no problem talking about her father. She has a clear admiration for the man, that much is abundantly clear. She talked extensively about the colored dots in his paintings and what they meant. She was quick to point out that he only survived because of the embedded code. I have the distinct feeling the one she dropped off at the rehab center is indeed the one Ben-Yuval calls the *Master Bucksbaum*."

"What'd she say that makes you conclude that?"

"I straight out asked her if the one she *gifted* to Lowell was the *master*. First she tried to evade claiming there was no such thing as a master. Taking a clue from the fact Bucksbaum survived, as Carrie pointed out, because of the coding, and recalling a concentration camp horrible fact of life that very few, if any, survived without guard involvement, it follows that the old man must have been coding something the camp hierarchy wanted coded. I point that out to Carrie and she confessed that the so-called Master had just come out of hiding."

"She use the word *master*?"

"She did."

"Lends credence to Ben-Yuval's mission. Jimmy, you did okay, considering."

"Who was *your* dinner partner, if I might ask?"

There was just enough jealousy in Jimmy's voice to make me feel good. "Sanjay Kumar. Founder and CEO of a company called Sat Inquest. Among many other things, or so he says, his company is responsible for the orbits, launch dates, and trajectories of every non-military satellite launched or recovered from space. He's even been down on South Padre working with SpaceX for their upcoming launch. Says he stays at the Riviera when he's on the island. Small world."

"That's funny, when I mentioned to his wife I was from South Padre she didn't seem to know where it was."

A jealous spike hit me. "You met his wife? He pointed her out to me. Gorgeous woman. And that sari she's wearing is magnificent. I didn't know colors could be that vivid."

"Must travel without her, I assume," Jimmy said, not commenting on my *gorgeous* characterization, which led me to believe he agreed but didn't want to acknowledge he was aware.

"Oh, here comes Carmella, or rather, Carmine, I should say. Must be time for that private showing of Stratis' latest acquisitions. This, I've been told, is an invitation-only showing."

The woman who earlier in the week we had met as a docent at Charlie Brown's former house had undergone a transformation of sorts. Her face was flushed, perhaps from a bit too much alcohol, perhaps from something else. I didn't like the woman and didn't trust anything she said or did. She solidified my mistrust when she sidled up to Jimmy and wrapped her arm around his. "Come along," she cooed, "are you ready for the *pièce de résistance*? What a wonderful night this has been, with the best yet to come! They lock the doors when Moe begins, and that's just moments from now. Hurry!"

I trailed behind as Carmine, her arm firmly entwined in Jimmy's, led us along a winding path lit only by small LED lights positioned at intervals along the walkway. The night was now fully dark, with no moon and clouds covering the stars. The smell of rain permeated the air. The lights came on as we walked and went off behind us. If we hadn't been briefed by Hessle, I would have concluded the lights were motion sensitive. But they weren't. They were individually controlled by what she had characterized as a small private army.

We turned a corner, and there in front of us was the nondescript building Hessle had told us to expect. It could have housed an old car collection, a theater, or it could even have been a factory, perhaps for electronics manufacture or for sewing clothes. Hessle also had informed us of a distillery on the premises, and this could have been it except the building in front of us had no distilling chimneys, or at least none that I could discern. I sniffed the air to make certain, but only smelled ozone. The storm wasn't far away.

"Watch your step," Carmine said, the tone being the same as when she had been stewarding us through the Bayernhof Museum. "Two steps up, then turn to your left," she instructed.

We must have been the last ones to join the viewing because there was no one else on the path. There was a dim light inside the structure, just enough to prevent us from tripping. Carmine escorted Jimmy first to the left, then to the right. She stopped, checked her watch, and in a whisper said, "Got less than two minutes. Going to be tight."

Carmine pushed a door open, and we stepped into an elevator that already contained two men. The door quickly closed around us. Even though I knew what was about to happen, it still is never pleasant to be body scanned.

"Clear," the man who had run the scanner up and down Carmella's legs and torso said, loud enough to be heard by whoever was monitoring us from afar. I was next, and again he spoke the word "clear" out loud. Jimmy was next, and when the scan began the second man tensed, his arm moving toward his own back where I guessed his weapon was positioned.

"Clear," the first man pronounced. "Now, if you will, please hand me your cell phones and any cameras or other recording equipment you might have."

Carmine's cell was already out of her small clutch, and she placed it into the bag held by the first man. I did the same, slipping mine in beside Carmine's.

Hessle had briefed us on this, but Jimmy, playing his part, resisted. "Hey, enough's enough! Nobody takes my phone! That's private!"

The second man, instead of drawing his weapon, which I expected, reached instead for the elevator panel and hit the STOP button. "Not a choice you have, Mr. Summerland. You are a guest of Mr. Stratis by invitation only. There are conditions to the visit. You in or out? We can go back down. Your choice."

"Jim, for God's sake give it up," Carmine cried, panic setting in with the realization that she might miss the tour. "This is my once a year fix. I wait all year for this, and don't mess it up for me! They'll return your precious phone at the end. I promise you that. They always do!"

"How do I get it back?" Jimmy asked. The anger in his eyes even fooled me.

"Bag'll be in your car out front when you finish," the man said, his voice calm, measured. "Sign these non-disclosures, and you're good to go."

He reached into a box at his feet, extracted three clipboards, and waited for each of us to sign. When he had all three clipboards back in his possession he looked at Jimmy. "Slip your phone into the bag, Mr. Summerland, and don't waste any more time. In fifteen seconds the tour will begin without you."

Jimmy reluctantly pulled his phone out, carefully turned it off, and placed it in the outstretched bag. The elevator door opened and we stepped into a small foyer. Carmine immediately opened the only door available to us. We followed her out of the foyer and into a gallery with glass art pieces spaced along one wall. The only light in the hallway came from single spotlights focused on each piece.

I saw Sanjay standing in a small group with his wife Riya who was beside Carrie Buck. Next to Buck was a man I didn't immediately recognize. A few steps away stood two women who seemed to be together and beside them another couple.

"Patterned after the Guggenheim," Hessle had told us in our earlier briefing. "You'll wind your way down. I'd love for you to take pictures, but that won't be possible. They'll confiscate your cells. But memorize what you see. There will be a test."

"If you know there's stolen art in there why not obtain a warrant and raid the place?" Jimmy had asked.

"Tried that. We've had three warrants issued. Three raids. Three blanks. Court will not issue another warrant without firsthand testimony of a credible person who has personal knowledge that the gallery contains contraband."

"So I'll wear a wire. What's so hard?"

"First, they do a search."

"Plant it under my arm or something. I'll swallow the mic, if need be. Surely you guys know how to avoid searches with the tiny mics we now have."

"Surely we do. Problem is, that place is heavily armored. His business is electronics, and he's at least two steps ahead of us. You can't get a signal in or out they don't want. We might be able to plant the mic, but a recording device is easily detected. By the time we could recover the device from you and play it for a court it'll all be gone. I promise you, by sunup every piece of illegal artwork will be somewhere else."

"Track the vehicles that leave."

"We tried that last year. Found nothing of value. Guy's good. Really good. Another thing that makes this all even more difficult is, as you know, the art world is replete with forgeries. Fakes so good they often fool the experts. Even using UV fluorescence and detailed examination of the provenance, doubt often remains. That means even if an art expert swears to a judge on the proverbial stack of bibles that she saw a particular stolen art piece firsthand, the case will fall apart when the judge asks for assurance that the work is not a fake."

"So why exactly are we going in?"

"Just because we can't capture the stuff and arrest the guy doesn't mean we should give up tracking it. Need to know what's there. The ten folks who are taking the tour were selected for a reason. One or more of them is linked to the dark market and terrorist money laundering."

"So how did we get invited?"

"The dark Internet identifies you two as having close ties to the Mexican drug cartels. We believe Stratis has thoughts of using you to broker a major deal for him. Perhaps through Santiago to the Middle East, perhaps something entirely different. Chatter has it Iran is in the mix. One thing we do know, we're always one step behind. And that's on a good day."

Jimmy interrupted my thoughts by whispering, "I take it that's Sanjay over there with Riya. Those two women, the one on the right is Jackie O'Rourke. A local artist who painted portraits of some of Pittsburgh's beautiful women. With her is one of the women she painted."

"That man with Carrie is a local artist by the name of Oswald Lewis. Sanjay pointed him out," I whispered back. "Don't know that other couple."

Jimmy had Lewis in his focus. "Know that face from some—"

Before Jimmy could finish his comment, Carmine's finger flew to her lips.

Our host, Morris Dexter Stratis, began to speak. His voice was soft, welcoming, and very much alive. "Thank you all for joining us here this evening. I trust everything was to your liking. Even the weatherman has seen fit to cooperate. I don't believe the weather will hold much longer, though. But no worries. Your vehicles will be brought around, and there is adequate cover out front so we should all remain dry. If perchance it should be raining a bit too hard when it's time to leave, we will simply open the refreshment room downstairs and wait it out. So please don't allow any worries to spoil your enjoyment of this special tour." He studied each of his guests as if he were reading their minds. When he finished the circuit, he said, "And now I have the great pleasure to introduce each of you to the artworks I have acquired over the course of the last year. Many of these, after tonight, will reside in museums and private collections around the world. But alas, never again will they be seen in one place together as they are here tonight. I trust you will all enjoy this special experience."

Jimmy leaned close and whispered, "Isn't that sculpture the *Walking Man*? I was—"

"Yes, Mr. Summerland, indeed this is Alberto Giacometti's the *Walking Man I*. A particularly excellent representation of the exploration of the psyche and charged space occupied by a single human. Some say his work is a good metaphor for modern doubt and alienation. Our country is now very much alienated, so what could be more appropriate?" Our host paused, looked directly at Jimmy, then continued. "I appreciate your expertise Mr. Summerland, but if you don't mind I will conduct the tour and do the speaking. You have not been assigned any speaking parts." Stratis again paused, this time to allow the polite laughter to pass. "I assume that meets with your acceptance?"

I fully expected Jimmy to explode. But instead, he smiled his charming smile and said, "My sincere apology. But I can't help note that all but one of the known versions are in museums. Including, I might note, one here in Pittsburgh at the Carnegie Museum of Art."

"Obviously, Mr. Summerland, as you and our other guests can easily see, this one is not in a museum. Now, if it's not too much to ask of you, may I continue?"

"Yes, of course, by all means."

And those were the last words Jimmy spoke until we passed through the front door to wait for our car under the large canopy. Once outside, he said, "It's hard to believe, but unless I'm dreaming, we just witnessed well over a half billon dollars of art. That *Walking Man* alone went for over one hundred forty million, give or take a few million. And Picasso's *Boy With A Pipe* sold for over a hundred million!"

"Not to mention the piece I thought you were going to comment on, The *Crown of Alexander*. That's another long-lost piece with ties to Russia and Israel via Nazi Germany. How did you keep quiet on that?"

"Didn't want to be escorted out. Didn't think Stratis would tolerate another interruption. I baited him enough with the *Walking Man.* But the real show stopper was the *Bucksbaum*, the *Master Bucksbaum*, if you believe Stratis. To my eye, it's identical to the one stolen from Lowell."

"Carrie Buck said nothing either. Either she knew it would be here, or—"

"Or she knows it's phony. Or...well, there's lots of ors," Jimmy added, looking up to see where our car was.

"I watched her eyes, Jimmy. I'm convinced she knew it would be here."

"So the one she gave old lady Lowell was a decoy. I'll go with that. So I ask, was the decoy intended to fool Hugo—or people trailing Hugo? Remember what Hessle said about fakes and phonies. One or more of them could be a forgery."

"My money's on Stratis having the original—and Buck knowing it."

"Sucker bet if I ever heard one. I'm not—"

"Oh, there you are," Carmine said, rushing up to Jimmy, her face still flushed. "I've landed myself another ride home. Save you the trouble." She winked an exaggerated wink. "And with him," she nodded in the direction of the car in front, "I've got better odds for a nice night cap. See ya." She threw her arms around Jimmy's neck, stood on her toes and kissed him on the lips. "There, that oughta keep ya! Yinz have a great night." And off she trotted.

"Jimmy!" I exclaimed, not knowing what else to say. From my observation that had been more than a thank-you-for-the-ride kiss. "You have something you need to tell me?"

"I won't dignify that with an answer. Get in," he said as the valet climbed out of our car. "And what's up with the yinz?"

"Saw a T-shirt that read YINZ is a GENDER NEUTRAL PRONOUN. Pittsburghers have their own language, it seems."

A second valet held the door open for me while Jimmy walked around the back of the car mumbling to himself. On reflection, I think he had said, "Unless you landed a better offer." It wasn't Hampton I was worried about. Nor was it Carrie Buck, whom he had had dinner with. But the interaction between Jimmy and Riya Kumar I witnessed had just flashed into my mind. Exotic is the word that came to mind to describe Riya. Exotic. And if there was one thing I knew about Jimmy, it was that exotic was in his wheelhouse.

I came out of my funk just in time to see Hampton approach a Benz GT Class convertible. She was nimbly sliding into the passenger seat, showing remarkable dexterity for a woman of her age. I was hoping to catch a glimpse of the driver, but he—or perhaps she—was already behind the wheel. But every now and then you get lucky. The driver glanced up into the rearview mirror to adjust his dark grey beret. The light hit him just right, and I made out just enough of his upper face structure to pair it with an image I had recently memorized. Carmella Schenley Hampton's date was none other than the elusive Oscar Hugo, the man I had earlier been introduced to under the name of Oswald Lewis.

"That's Oscar Hugo!" I blurted to Jimmy, instantly putting aside my pique with him. Forgetting for a moment we were no longer DHS agents, I said, "Can we hold him? Any grounds?"

"That's one life back, Angella. But if you're right, we have now confirmed he's in town. Earlier you told me his name was Oswald Lewis."

"That's what I had been told. Didn't look too close, I suppose."

"Right then, or right now?"

"Oh, I'm right now. Bank on it."

"Enough for me. I'll call Hessle, let her know." Jimmy reached for his cell. "Where the hell? Must have...oh, almost forgot, they took them from us. Help me look for the bag." Jimmy opened the door to get light.

"Here they are!" I announced a few seconds later. "Right here on the floor." I opened the bag, put Jimmy's on the console between us and shoved mine into my purse. "Your new best friend Carmine forgot hers." I looked to the car in front, hoping to catch them in time, but the spot was now empty. The Benz was gone.

"Should I call Hampton? They're gone."

"Calling won't help. You have her phone."

Before I processed what Jimmy had said, I had

begun poking around, trying to find an ICE number in Carmine's phone. The call log was open,
and prominently displayed were several calls from
Oscar Hugo. In the TEXT log, Oscar Hugo's name
appeared several times. The last message read:
"I'll drive you home."

"Seems this wasn't such a last-minute plan on
their part."

NINETEEN

The forty-five-minute drive back downtown was spent with Jimmy leaving a long voicemail for Hessle, essentially debriefing the entire evening. For my part I, was working through my angst over Riya Kumar, heightened by Carmine's mostly, I hoped, playful kiss. But I knew I wasn't wrong reading Jimmy's body language when he was interacting with the gorgeous Indian woman. Her moist lips, the wide-open eyes, the deep concentration on every word he had said was still vivid in my mind and hard to suppress. Every aspect of that scene was frozen in place, even though I continued to remind myself that Jimmy had actually done nothing improper.

When Jimmy finally finished his debriefing, he turned in my direction. "You up for delivering Carmine's phone in person?"

"You mean now? As in, let's drive out to Oakland and knock on her door?"

"Know any other way?"

"The morning would work just as well, wouldn't it? I'm tired."

"It's just a few minutes further this time of night."

It had always served Jimmy well for him to follow his instincts, so from his perspective why change now? I only hoped that some soft spot for Carmine wasn't coloring his decisions. I reluctantly capitulated. "Okay with me if that's what you want."

We drove the remaining distance in silence, and with very few cars on the road we made good time. Jimmy rolled to a stop a few houses up the street from where we had picked up Carmine about seven hours earlier. So much had transpired in the interim that it seemed very much longer than it had actually been.

"There's Hugo's car," Jimmy said, pointing toward the Mercedes not so carefully parked in front of the three attached houses.

There was a light on in the window of the furthest house, the one that held the art collection. But I couldn't recall having seen any windows at all in that structure. "Jimmy, I'm thinking those windows are part of a facade. And that door goes nowhere."

"You're right. That whole wall is art without windows or doors. Elaborate set up."

"Puzzle me this. Why park the car in front of the house with no entrance?"

"The Benz *is* parked more in front of that house than the center house, isn't it? I hadn't noticed. A bit too much to drink?"

"Doubt it. Hugo's got too much to lose to get sloppy now."

"All crooks get sloppy. That's how we catch them."

"Need I remind you, Jimmy, there's no *we* in that sentence anymore?"

Ignoring me, Jimmy said, "I'm thinking there's an entrance. We just don't understand the interior. I'm not seeing lights in Carmine's house. They just came from an art exhibit; they may be rearranging a piece of art."

We sat for a few minutes and when nothing changed, Jimmy said, "Time to go get some sleep. Wait here. I'll go put the phone by the door and we'll get out of here."

Jimmy stepped up onto Carmine's porch just as he had done earlier, only this time, the instant he set foot on the porch, two men appeared seemingly from nowhere. One positioned himself just outside of the passenger door of our rental car and the other approached Jimmy from behind.

I pushed the car door open, but the man standing there slammed it closed with his knee. My options were extremely limited, especially since neither Jimmy nor I was armed. I thought of rolling down the window and taking a swing for his midsection, but abandoned that idea almost immediately. I'd end up with a fractured arm—or worse.

Judging from how abruptly Jimmy spun around, the man behind him must have said something or made a noise. But with Jimmy's sixth sense about danger, it might have just been his intuition. The element of surprise was on Jimmy's side for a brief instant, and he took full advantage of it. Bending low while turning, Jimmy came upright, driving his head into the man's chest and causing him to rock backward and slip off the step. From the high ground Jimmy thrust himself forward, pinning both of the man's arms to his sides and when they hit the ground Jimmy was on top. I knew Jimmy's knee had found its target when the assailant let out a blood-curdling scream.

So much for stealth at one-thirty in the morning.

The man standing outside my car door ran to help his partner, reaching behind him for his weapon as he went. I sprung from the car and yelled, "Jimmy, watch! Firearm coming!" My plan was to jump the second guy from behind as soon as I got close enough. Jimmy's body made for an easy target, and I hoped to close the distance fast enough before a shot could be fired.

The only thing stopping the second guy from firing was the fact that his partner was directly under my partner, and any bullet entering Jimmy's body would most likely pass right through into the guy on the bottom. Random thugs wouldn't care, but these guys weren't exactly random.

The guy on the ground managed to slide sideways far enough so that Jimmy's head was exposed with nothing under it. The second guy saw the opening at the same time I did and brought his gun up. I was still a half step away from being able to leap onto his back. Because the target was moving and the safety margin relatively small, the gunman stopped running in order to take aim.

In that instant, I leaped. But two things were not in my favor. The earlier rain had made the walkway slick, and my purchase was tenuous. The other and far more important factor was the age and condition of the man onto whose back I landed.

He was young, in his twenties, and built much stronger than I had expected. Instead of buckling forward as I had anticipated, he simply rotated his torso, allowing my momentum to carry me over his left shoulder. I landed in the wet grass, just missing the sidewalk. The barrel of the gun in his right hand continued its focus on Jimmy's head.

"What the hell's going on out here?" Carmine yelled, appearing on the porch of the gallery house, the house we had concluded had no functioning front door. "Stop this instant!"

The gun disappeared. The man under Jimmy stopped moving. I rolled over and climbed to my feet, all the while taking stock of the damage done to my first real cocktail dress. Thankfully, not more than a small smudge and a possible minor grass stain.

Jimmy likewise rose, but his tux hadn't faired so well. It now wasn't even a decent candidate for the Goodwill bin.

"James! And Angie! What the hell are you two doing here at this hour?"

Jimmy pointed to the bag holding her phone that was now lying at the base of the steps. "Your phone was left in my car. We came to deliver it."

"Oh...oh, yes. I had forgotten about Moe's little nonsense about no recordings and pictures." Carmine nodded in the direction of the thugs who shook their heads and without exchanging a word walked back toward our car, stepped off the curb, and continued to cross the street. "Sorry about that. With all the art thefts lately, and with my new pieces, everyone's a bit jumpy. Come in and let's clean you two up. Sorry about the tux; send me the bill and I'll see it's replaced. As for your lovely gown, Mrs. Summerland, I believe it will clean up nicely. Lucky for you."

Lucky for me, indeed.

"I think we've overstayed our welcome," Jimmy said. "We'll clean up at our hotel."

"No, no, no. I insist. Besides, you must come see my new acquisition."

This time she didn't kiss Jimmy, but she had him firmly by the arm. I took up my assigned position two steps back and trailed behind as Carmine led the way across the small patch of grass separating the middle house from the end one, her arm interlocked with Jimmy's as if they were the parents of the bride following their child down the aisle. *Or perhaps the bride and groom walking themselves down the aisle.*

As Jimmy often says, *nothing good ever happens at two in the morning*. Well, here was living proof.

The front door did open, but it led into a small hallway and not into a room. Directly ahead of us there was a flight of stairs going up and another flight going down. We took the upstairs flight, and at the top there were two large bedrooms and a cozy sitting room. There also was a full bathroom. No sign of Oscar Hugo, but one of the bedroom doors was closed.

I availed myself of the facilities first, and Jimmy followed. He spent more time than I had, but when he stepped out, the mud streaks were gone from his face, and other than the tears on the elbows and knees of his tux, he looked none the worse for wear.

"Oh, Jim, you clean up so well! Come on, follow me."

At least this time she walked down the steps ahead of us, allowing Jimmy to escort me. He held his arm out and I waved it off. Anger mixed with jealousy is not a good combination.

We actually continued down the second flight to the dimly lit basement. When both Jimmy and I were off the stairs, Carmine closed and locked a door behind us. "Can't take too many precautions, now can we?" She then flipped a switch, and a spot light came on, its rays illuminating a single small painting.

"A *Bucksbaum*," I said. "According to Stratis, this is the *Master Bucksbaum* to be more precise."

"I see you were paying attention earlier, my dear. That's good." She flipped another switch, and dots appeared on the surface of the painting just as we had been schooled at the Holocaust Center. "Bet you don't know what those are."

I didn't know if it was better if we knew or didn't know.

Jimmy didn't hesitate. "Those are what makes this so valuable. Code for buried weapons locations."

"My, you do know your stuff, big boy. So you're not just a pretty face. That's also very good." Carmine squeezed Jimmy's arm. "But it's not weapon's locations, my dear sir. It's, well, never mind the art lesson. This piece is worth over a hundred million. So, you can please pardon me for the security detail, now can't you?"

"I assume this is the same piece we saw earlier tonight?" I said. "If so, how—"

"Business is business, my dear. Let's just say, Moe and I, well, we have a business relationship that works for our mutual benefit. He does his thing and I, well...I do mine."

"Mind if I take a picture of such a...of such a great piece?" Jimmy asked, his cell already out of his pocket.

"Oh, heavens no! Now put that thing away this instant!" A schoolmarm disciplining a wayward child.

Jimmy reaching for his cell caused a noise in a far corner. A scraping noise followed by shuffling of feet. Someone, or a group of someones, was not far from us. *Here we go again.*

"Os, come over here and meet my guests." The man I had been introduced to as Oswald Lewis, and who we knew to be Oscar Hugo, nee Oscar Lowell, slowly made his way across the floor toward where we were gathered. "Oswald Lewis, this is Mr. James Summerland and his wife, the lovely Angie."

Hugo looked Jimmy up and down, held his hand out. "Pleased to meet you, Mr. Summerland. Looks like you're in need of a good tailor. Have just the person in mind." He then turned to face me, bowed his head slightly before extending his hand. "You are indeed lovely. Pleased to meet you as well." He started to bring my hand upward as if to kiss it, thought better of the idea and slowly lowered it.

This guy is the definition of energy. Shame he didn't continue with his gesture.

"I understand you're an art liaison," Hugo said, his eyes turning to Jimmy. "Mind telling me what pieces you've brokered—or should I say, liaisoned?"

"First off," Jimmy began, "Angie and I work as a team. And...and second, well, second, we make it an ironclad rule to never ever discuss what we're working on, what we have worked on, or the names of any of our clients. I'm sure you appreciate what I'm saying."

"So then, tell me clearly, very clearly, just how you get customers, if you won't discuss what you've brokered."

Jimmy took a step forward as if he were about to land a punch. I sucked in my breath. Hugo, the former Federal Marshal, held his ground, neither taking the bait nor being intimidated.

"You know, Mr. ah, Lewis," Jimmy said when his intimidation tactic failed, "we've found word of mouth works just fine. And just for the record, we don't have customers. We serve clients. We obtain for them what they want."

"And what is it they want?"

"Whatever it is, we find it, negotiate a fair price, and deliver it to the desired location, no questions asked. Simple business model."

"Your fee for all of this? Expenses?"

"Sometimes a percentage. Sometimes fixed."

"That's your fee. What about expenses? I mean your expenses, not expenses of delivery."

"Is this an interview? Or we just among friends?"

"Let's just say a little of each."

"Handled by agreement," I chimed in, signaling I was a player along with Jimmy. "We're not opposed to spending our own money investigating, but only for items over ten mil. Under that we usually don't handle unless all expenses are paid up front."

Hugo turned to face me. "Boundaries?"

"Worldwide, excluding war zones and terrorist hotspots."

"I can see why the limitation, Angie. I understand that very well."

"And how does one get in touch with you should one have a...have a burning need to acquire a particular work of art?"

Jimmy reached for his cards but came up empty. "Your friend Carmine here knows how to reach us. And how do we find you, Mr. Lewis?"

"I find you, James. I find you. Not the other way around. I assure you."

TWENTY

The church bells were announcing noon on the dot. The rain had finally stopped when Angella and I made our way downstairs to have brunch at Panera Bread. Staying at the Quality Inn in Oakland under our real names, as opposed to going back downtown to the William Penn in the middle of the night disheveled as we were, seemed at the time the better of two bad options. At least in this hotel we had guessed right about being able to navigate all the way to our room without being observed. At the William Penn, several employees would have seen us, with no chance of their forgetting the man with the ripped tux and the woman with the filthy cocktail dress. And that's not even taking into account the security tapes.

A moment after we were seated, Hessle walked through the door and headed directly for our table. This wasn't a coincidence. I couldn't begin to speculate on how the hell she knew where to find us.

"You don't seem happy for my company," she said, winking in my direction. "Heard you had a bit of a skirmish down the street. Nothing serious, I see. At least not to your bodies."

"Suppose you heard about the wrecked tux and—"

"Serves you right for prowling around in the middle of the night. You gotta learn to tuck yourselves in before the witching hour."

Angella's eyes set hard and her shoulders went back in a gesture I'd never seen before. "You're joking, and Jimmy was all but shot in the head! I'd characterize that as more than a *skirmish*."

"It may not have looked it to you, but neither of you were in any real danger. Those two wear white hats."

"From where I sat," Angella said, anger still hanging over her, "those hats were anything but white. Ruined a perfectly good cocktail dress in the process."

"I've seen the footage. Good moves, you two. I'd have expected nothing less from each of you. But, the fact is, we're all on the same team."

"You care to explain?" Angella demanded. "The man had his weapon pointed directly at Jimmy's head!"

"Happen to notice if the safety was on or off?"

"With the SIG Sauer, I think that was the P227 if I'm recalling right, the release is hidden by his hand. But truth is, there wasn't enough light."

Hessle was toying with us. I recall reading a blurb a few years back that the Pennsylvania State Police had begun a switch over to the P227s. I entered the fray. "Enough with the games. If those two belong to you, please explain why I was jumped."

"For the record, you jumped him, Jimmy. Not the other way around. As you might expect, I can't get into all of it. And I certainly can't divulge operational details. But take my word, you were never in physical danger—well, not until you initiated contact, anyway. Hey, just to show we play fair here in the Keystone State, send me the tab for a new tux and I'll see what I can do. We paid for it in the first place, but you didn't exactly use the entire allowance. No promises, but I'll try."

"Least you can do," I said.

"Knock it off already. You're not the victim here. Guy didn't even have his weapon drawn. Nice take down, I have to say that much for you. You learned your trade well, my friend. Maybe too well."

Hessle was a master at deescalating situations, judging from what I had just been party to. "Next thing you know that tape'll go viral on YouTube—or the police equivalent of YouTube."

"No comment." Hessle said, straining her eyes to read the menu board. "I'm in the mood for their Napa almond chicken salad sandwich. Think I'll do half and add in the tomato soup. Your lucky day. I'm buying."

I think it was her intention, but Hessle had just confirmed that we had stumbled into the middle of a government-backed operation. What I couldn't determine, was it state or federal? "How about I'm famished. I'm in for the whole Italian with everything on it." I glanced at my partner who was now sitting calmly to the side sipping coffee. "What's your pleasure Angella?"

Without looking up she answered, "Fuji apple salad with chicken."

Hessle stood. "Be back in a moment." In fact, it took her three minutes and ten seconds, but who's keeping track? She placed a plastic tent bearing the number 16 in the center of our table. "Coffees for all, I assume. Refill for you Angella?"

"Thanks, yes," Angella said, her mind elsewhere.

When the tall trooper returned, Angella was waiting. "So what *can* you tell us," she began, "about the operation? I assume your being here now isn't a random encounter."

"Came to debrief you both on last night, in case you didn't already know that. Be good, and I'll tell you what I can."

"Doesn't seem like an even deal," I said, "but it's never even is it?"

"Covert operations are never even. You two know that better than most."

I liked Hessle. She was tough, direct, and from all that we'd seen, fair minded. In chronological order, I told her who I had been introduced to, who said what, and who I had observed. I then started to discuss the walkway leading to the display studio when she interrupted me, saying, "Hold it a moment, Jimmy, let's first hear from Angella about her conversations and observations. We'll do the art show in a moment. You already gave me much of that last night anyway."

Angella then traced her evening, including saying hello to three former Steelers whose names I didn't recognize. No mention of Franco Harris, but lots of discussion about her dinner partner, Sanjay Kumar.

"I was hoping Stratis would pair one of you with one of the Kumars. They're major players. Sanjay has deep connections in India, but also all over the Far East. Quite frankly, he's a major target of ours."

The image of Riya Kumar instantly came front and center. "Both of them?" I asked, unwilling to question the naivety Riya projected.

"Yes, most certainly. When it comes to art, both of them. In fact, Riya may take the lead in art procurement. What you might not have known is that in the art world those two, I mean Sanjay and Stratis, are rivals. Big time rivals. Classic case of whose is bigger than whose. We're working on the premise that'll work to our advantage."

"In this context," Angella chimed in, "I'm assuming you mean art collection and not—"

"Of course, art collections. The other may have been their cup of tea in an earlier life, but now it's who owns the biggest and best. Translation: Most expensive. Because of the tremendous run-up of prices on the dark side, most of their art is never displayed or even acknowledged. That way they avoid tax problems and, frankly, money laundering problems as well."

"So how do they keep score?" I asked. "It's not like they can call in Price Waterhouse and have an official signed, sealed, and delivered audit. Apparently, you folks monitor the dark web, so they can't post their holdings on there either. So how do they advertise?"

"Glad you asked, Jimmy. That's exactly why you were there last night. You witnessed one of Stratis' scoring methods. Word of mouth. Trouble is, that's only the tip of the iceberg. What he has secreted away makes what you saw last night pale in comparison. But we take what we can get and work from there. The man has the power to manipulate art prices around the world. Collectors—and galleries—live in fear of him and what he might say or do." Hessle pulled out two note pads. "Now for that pop exam I promised. Both of you write down exactly what you saw during your stroll down the ramp. Take your time, and visualize each piece and sketch it as best you can. Note the colors and anything else of any importance. If you even think you know the name of the piece then add that as well." She stopped speaking when the server approached. When the man moved on, she continued. "You can think about it while you eat, or sketch as you go. Take your time; this is critical."

This wasn't the way I had planned to spend my day, but we were here to locate stolen art, and by all accounts, last night we had borne witness to more than our fair share, both at the Stratis showing and on Louisa Street in the false home of docent Carmella Schenley Hampton.

I couldn't see what Angella was drawing, but her head was down and her pencil was busy. For my part, my Italian sandwich required both hands to contain the ingredients and even with that I was losing the battle. Between sandwich halves I wrote down as best I could the pieces, starting from Giacometti's *Walking Man* at the top of the ramp to the *Portrait of Adele Bloch-Bauer* at the bottom. That last one I knew because of the ruckus made by the one guest, an older man with a full head of curly silver-grey hair and wearing wire-rim glasses, the one man I hadn't known. He had shouted, "That's a forgery! The real one's safely in the control of my client!"

Stratis had simply responded, "Many people have claimed forgery of many pieces, but I assure you this one has been authenticated by experts. Provenance is rock solid. And, I might add, both the UV florescence and infrared reflectography have come back positive."

"I'm not accepting that as a fact, Mr. Stratis! You certainly will be hearing from...from my client."

The outburst over the *Bloch-Bauer* had focused on a painting of a woman with rich black hair elegantly coifed atop her head and wearing a massive golden gown interlaced with small black and silver panels. Then I recalled there had been a movie made about this particular painting, called, if my memory was correct, *The Woman in Gold*.

But it wasn't the *Bloch-Bauer* that had me agitated. And it wasn't the first item we had seen, nor was it the last one. It was the object next to last. To my utter astonishment, it had been the *Pirate*, and it had been all I could do to remain calm when the light had come on over that piece and the red ruby of the left eye had seemed to focus directly on me. At one point in my years of tracking the *Pirate* as a Texas Ranger, I had almost convinced myself the *Pirate* was a hoax. Very few people had actually seen the piece in person, and fewer still had actually touched it. The owner, however, had signed an affidavit stating that he had held it personally. I had my suspicions about the validity of that affidavit, but suspicions are not evidence. Great Southern Insurance Company, which had the Pirate insured, had paid the claim after two years of investigation.

I finished writing and studied my notes while I consumed the remainder of my lunch. Finally satisfied, I pushed the pad across the table to Hessle. She had been sitting quietly, her salad long gone along with several cups of coffee. Her eyes were alive in an otherwise noncommittal face.

"Need sketches," she said, "if you don't mind."

"Stick figures at best," I replied, not happy at the prospect of my chicken scratches being ripped apart and laughed at by a fleet of lawyers.

"How about just giving me the ones vivid in your memory?"

"Fair enough," I said. "How about the *Pirate*, the *Walking Man*, and the Adele whatever."

"*Bloch-Bauer*. The Gustav Klimt work. How about sketching the *Booby* as well?"

I nodded.

"Go for it."

When I was finished, Hessle studied my drawings and compared what I had drawn to Angella's renderings. "Both of you. Keep your day jobs, at least with respect to the sketches. But as to identifying the art itself, fifteen out of twenty-two is not bad Angella. Jimmy, you got thirteen. Angella got *The Painter on His Way to Work* and *Portrait of an Old Man*. Neither of you recognized *The Pigeon with Green Peas* by Picasso; *Portrait of A Young Man*, by Raphael; and *En Canot* by Jean Metzinger. The others are unimportant for now."

"I hadn't known we were being graded," I said in defense of myself. "If so, I would've—"

"Stop complaining. Okay, here's what I can tell you." Hessle waited a moment for Angella to look up from her note pad. "Let's begin with the last first. The Klimt. First, you may know there were two *Adele Bloch-Bauers* painted by Klimt. The one you saw is called *One* and the other, of course, is *Two*. Well, as it turns out Oprah owned Two and sold it a few years ago, reportedly for a hundred fifty million."

"What makes them so...so valuable?" Angella inquired, a puzzled look on her face.

"Art's an interesting commodity. No real intrinsic value, but heritage, who painted it, where it's been, who's owned it. All that and a lot more. Sometimes it's as simple as *you have it, I want it*. In the case of the Klimts, Bloch-Bauer was his patron and he painted her at least twice. Those two, along with several others he painted for her, were owned by her at her untimely death in 1925. She willed them to her husband with instructions to donate them to the Austrian Museum. Along came the war and the Nazis confiscated the paintings before the husband had made out his will. After the war, the paintings ended up in the Austrian Museum. Bloch-Bauer's heirs sued the museum claiming they had no title to the paintings. The heirs eventually won. Go watch the movie *The Woman in Gold* if you want more details. Oprah bought Two from Christie's in a bidding war in 2006 for around eighty-eight million."

My curiosity now piqued, I asked, "And One is owned by?"

"One was bought the same year by Ronald Lauder, son of the Estee Lauder founders, for the Neue Galerie, which he founded. *The Woman in Gold* is, or was, I'm not exactly certain of the timing, the center piece of a Klimt exhibition."

Recalling the commotion over the painting, I said, "So the silver-haired guy who made all that fuss, was?"

"Rudolph Gussman. One of the Neue Galerie's art advisors."

"If Gussman is right, and I assume he must be, the *Woman in Gold* is still in the gallery. How can she also be—"

"Nobody ever said this was going to be easy. Yes, the Neue Galerie is in New York. Fifth Ave and Eighty-Seventh to be exact. And yes, at least as far as I know, the *Woman* remains safely in their custody."

Angella became suddenly alert. "Run that by me again. You say the painting is in New York and it's also here? I'm with Jimmy, confused to say the least."

"Let's sort the facts as we know them, shall we? There is *a Woman* in New York. There is also *a Woman* in the Stratis gallery. From what we know, and not just from you two, but from others as well, they're identical. Your conclusion?"

"One of them's a fake," Angella answered right on cue.

"Buy that lady a free lunch!" Hessle winked, her face softening even more than it had earlier.

"Why would Stratis deal in fakes?" Angella asked. "He has one of the world's largest collections."

"You are assuming the real *Woman* is in New York. A leap of faith on your part."

"But—"

"Hold for a moment. Let's assume your assumption is correct. Then Stratis bought, or commissioned, a reproduction. Let's also assume, if you will, that the fake is so good that it can fool even the best forensic examination. Then what?"

"Then we have a mess," I said. "A real mess. And the mess extends to insurance coverage as well as everything else."

"Wait a minute, Jimmy," Angella said, holding her hand up in a stop motion. "Insurance companies, Great Southern for example, don't insure the value. If you buy a fake and pay a million, then when you sell it and it's only worth a buck ninety-eight, you're stuck, not the insurance company."

"As Jimmy said, it's a mess, Angella. In your example, assume the art piece was, in fact, genuine when you bought it. You have papers to prove it. You paid a million for it. Now you try to sell it, and the buyer's appraiser calls it a fake. You call your insurance company and say what? The only thing you can say is that the original was stolen and a fake substituted in its place. You know how hard that would be to prove?"

"Almost impossible," Angella replied, "because if there had been any evidence of tampering with the original I would have reported it immediately."

"As I said, a mess." I looked to Hessle. "What do we know about Stratis?"

"Every year he holds this gala lawn party and every year he invites certain people to remain after dinner and tour his gallery. This is the definition of a one-night stand."

"So why—"

"I'm getting there, Angella. He puts on display the new items he's obtained. Sanjay was there because he and Sanjay are locked, as I said, in this mine-is-bigger-than-yours contest over their respective art collections. So now Stratis owns bragging rights to all the new stuff he added. This must be driving Kumar crazy. But the truth is, that's actually only one of many of Kumar's worries. He's got *beaucoup* tax issues piled on top." Hessle leaned closer, as if to impart a major secret. "But for us the more interesting situation is this. A year ago we stumbled to the fact that Stratis displays fakes at his exhibitions, although the fakes are replicas of art he intends to obtain in the next year. Whether by buying, stealing, conning, or outright fraud."

"So you're saying the *Woman in Gold* is on his... his shall we say...acquisition list?"

"That's exactly what I'm saying, Jimmy. Exactly what I'm saying."

"But that doesn't solve the question as to which *Woman* is the fake, the one he has or the one in New York."

"Bingo, Redstone. Bingo! Poor Gussman's been burning up the airwaves. That will force the Galerie to remove their *Woman* from display so they can retest and recertify."

Angella's eyes went wide. "And when that happens, the painting becomes vulnerable!" she exclaimed. "Brilliant!"

Up to this moment, I had thought we were having a nice, intellectually stimulating conversation and nothing more. I finally got around to asking myself the question as to why a Pennsylvania State Trooper was buying Angella and me lunch on a Sunday afternoon. "I suppose you're about to tell us Great Southern is the insurer of the *Woman in Gold*. Please tell me I'm wrong."

"I refer you to Jack Silver for that answer. But our records do have your company listed as one of the major insurers. Welcome to the party."

TWENTY-ONE

Hessle glanced at her watch. "It's been delightful, but time's getting away from me, I'm afraid. Just so you know, on the lists you made, the real ones are: *Portrait of A Young Man; En Canot; The Pigeon with Green Peas; The Painter on His Way to Work; The Golden Booby; and Pirate. Walking Man* is a fake, as is *The Old Man with a Beard* and the *Bucksbaum*. Schools out on the *Woman in Gold*. My thought, it's a fake, but who am I?" She stood, leaned down toward us and added, "Note that all the paintings have one thing in common. They were all stolen by Nazis and are considered *lost*. That could explain your pal Ben-Yuval poking around. Israel might be using the *Bucksbaum* as a cover for something else they're interested in. The only thing I know for certain about that crowd is that I *don't know* what the hell they're up to." Hassle let that thought settle before adding, "A couple of folks are available to brief you further. Give me about five minutes, then walk across that little park over there and then down the Boulevard toward Bates. They'll find you."

"You really want us to do this?" Angella commented. "After last night?"

"Let's let bygones be bygones. This is a new day." She winked, then said, "As you cross that little park take a look at the white square building directly in front of you. That's the Isaly's Pittsburgh headquarters. In its time it was the premier dairy store, home of the Klondike and chipped chopped ham."

"Chipped chopped ham?'

"Thin-sliced. Hey, you want to check it out, go get lunch over at the *My Dogz On The Run* vendor at the corner of Stanwix and Liberty about a block from the Wyndham Hotel. Now get going."

In exactly five minutes, Angella and I were walking across the Quality Inn parking lot, headed for the small park located between Zulema Street and the Boulevard of the Allies. We passed through the parklet and started down the Boulevard toward Bates Street, the iconic white Isaly's building directly across the street to our right. It was now being used by UPMC for OBGYN. Location makes sense, being catty-corner to Magee-Womans Hospital.

Pittsburgh is a city built on hills and it is unusual for a street to run flat for any length of time. The Boulevard is no exception. It runs downhill to Bates where a traffic light slows traffic for a moment before the roadway heads back up a hill continuing its journey through Oakland and, as we found out when Hessle drove us to the Holocaust Center, into Schenley Park and onward to Squirrel Hill.

I studied the terrain around us for signs of our rendezvous partners, but my view was mostly blocked by a set of row houses that had seen better days. The area behind the houses to our left was covered in dense foliage, making for any number of excellent hiding places. Five steps from the corner, Angella's elbow tapped my side. I didn't have to look at her to know she was signaling danger, but danger from where I didn't know. I stopped walking and tried to discern movement in the brush. Nothing.

"Eleven o'clock," she whispered. "Two men. One of them's the guy I jumped last night."

"The other?"

"Never got a good look at him, but from the build I'd say the guy you took down."

"Hessle set us up? Sunday, high noon? You still see them?"

"Gone now. Can't see for the trees and bushes."

The Army Ranger in me said hold your ground and fight to the finish. The common sense in me said get the hell outta here. And do it now!

Angella didn't have to deal with such conflicts. She had already taken a step backward and was halfway turned around when a voice from the bottom of the hill said, "Hey, we come in peace. But please keep your hands where we can see them."

They had materialized seemingly out of no-where. Cops to the core. Been around these types for most of my adult life. Even though we held the high ground, their stance was textbook perfect as was the voice. Their eyes were focused where they should have been and their hands and arms were positioned properly for any maneuver we could manage. It may not have looked like it to a bystander, but these two had us out-positioned without ever moving more than a few muscles, with which they were both well endowed.

"We're unarmed," I said. "You'll get no problem from us." Then I added, "Unless, of course, you start something." Macho dies hard.

"I'll let that slide." The man doing the talking was the one Angella had jumped last night. The other eyed me as though he had a score to settle. "We're just going to step back over here, you two continue down, cross Bates and continue up toward the park. We'll fall in behind you. Just don't make any sudden stops, and everything will go nicely. Fill you in as we go. Fair enough?"

"Fair enough," Angella answered.

I said nothing.

"Okay. One other condition. This conversation never happened. Agreed?"

"I agree," Angella said.

"Agreed," I reluctantly added, my fingers se-cretly crossed.

A moment later traffic screamed along beside us, no one paying any attention to four people out for a Sunday stroll. Just as the brass had drawn it up. We walked in silence a full block, crossed a street and continued on up the hill. In the second block the man who had been silent said, "If this was up to me, Redstone, I'd just as soon kick your butt as talk to you. Yinz had no call to jump us as you did. But, hey, I'm nothing more than hired help, so here goes. The *Bucksbaum* you saw over on Louisa last night is the real deal. Some call it the Master. For the record, it's not the same one that you saw at the rehab center. That one's a decoy, but the twerp who stole it doesn't yet know that. Imagine the blow back when he, or his boss, sells it for big bucks and it can't be decoded. Almost all of the other art, save for a few pieces, are fakes. Carmine has made deep inroads into the art community, and they come in to see her collection. We monitor their comments and observe which pieces they're interested in. The brass can determine based on what transpires in there what pieces will be sold, bartered, stolen. They've already rolled up over two hundred fifty million and counting. As you know, art is fundamental in many terrorist operations and a medium for moving money around the world. Money laundering for the upper crust. Our operation is making a big dent in art trafficking."

"How about a list of people visiting the house?"

"Negative."

"You guy's working for DHS?"

"No need to know."

"State or Fed?"

"Sorry, operational details. Can't do."

"Why tell us anything?"

"Orders.

"Let's talk about the real art work we saw," Angella said, chiming in, sensing correctly I was getting antsy. "Is the Madonna real?"

"Nobody really knows for certain. But truth is, in the art world often the fake is just as valuable as the real deal. It's the ideas, the procedures, the created image that's important. And a good fake has all the right elements. If an expert eye can't tell the difference, then I don't suppose it really matters?"

I compared what I had just heard to what I recall from my training. It all made sense. We walked in silence while I worked through what we had seen and learned in the past few days. The only real pattern that emerged, and it wasn't much of a pattern, and certainly wasn't true across the board, but a common thread, was the Nazi plundered art. That's what Hessle directed our attention to as well. I thought about that a moment, and the number six hundred thousand popped to mind. As I recall, that was the number of pieces that were stolen and all but a hundred thousand had been recovered. Talk about dark art. This was like a glacier. There was more dark than meets the eye.

We were now in the middle of a bridge over a deep ravine, tree-covered hills on either side. I could hear the rumble of a train moving far below us. From the length and direction of the train moving left to right, it was easy to deduce it was a freight outbound from downtown. Not for the first time in my life I harbored the thought of climbing aboard and going wherever the manifest took me, free of obligations, responsibilities, and most of all, time pressures to complete a job.

"What's your take on fakes," I asked over my shoulder. "Big value or not?" I wasn't thinking of fraudulent values where the buyer, thinking the fake was the real deal, paid premium dollars for the piece. Rather I was curious if Carmine had been correct, that a fake had a big value as a fake.

Several steps passed and I heard no answer. Turning to make certain they could hear me over the train noise I realized that Angella and I were alone on the bridge. The two *thugs* were nowhere in sight.

TWENTY-TWO

We continued into the park and found a comfortable and secluded spot where we sat and discussed what we had seen, heard and experienced. On the positive ledger was the fact we had located the *Pirate*, the *Booby*, something called a *Master Bucksbaum*, which hadn't been on our agenda, and a piece called the *Crown of Alexander*. We had also seen several definite fakes and one possible fake, *The Woman In Gold.* The *Kings Cup* was still among the missing, but if locating lost art was our mission, we had been wildly successful. We debated what to do with the information we had, and other than briefing Jack Silver, we had no other plans.

I have to reluctantly acknowledge I had enjoyed driving with Jimmy in the Porsche, leading me to suggest we go back to the hotel, pick up the car and tour the city for the time remaining before the car was due back to the rental agency. I even toyed with the idea of extending the lease a few more days. The Pittsburgh area was proving to be fun.

Jimmy resonated enthusiastically to my idea and within thirty minutes we were in the Porsch heading north.

Not far into the first hour of our *tour,* my phone rang. It was Silver, making an unusual Sunday call. But with Jack, we were learning, nothing was unusual.

"Jimmy there with you?" he asked when I answered the call. "You outside or something?"

"We're out driving."

"Call me back when I can hear you! And make it soon!"

I repeated to Jimmy what the boss had said. Jimmy responded by saying, "Can't help it if we're several hours from anywhere we can talk. He'll just have to cool his jets."

Patience was one attribute Silver was notoriously deficient in. I checked my watch and mentally noted ten minutes. We had no more than ten minutes to call Silver back. I told that to Jimmy and he said, "Hope we can find a parking spot in ten minutes."

But he really wasn't even trying.

"Check the Internet, see if there's any mention of the Klimt going missing," Jimmy instructed me.

"Nothing posted yet. You have five minutes."

"Not gone missing? No rumors of substitutions? Nothing?"

"I told you, nothing"

"So all's well."

"Not with Silver waiting for a call-back. And not if Stratis has a genuine fake, whatever that is. Three minutes."

"At best, Great Southern only has a piece of the Neue Galerie art collection. They're in a consortium."

"Yes, but...but Jimmy, with values what they are, this is bound to cost the boss man a small fortune. He'll be all over us. One minute. Better pull over."

"You heard what Carmine said about the Madonna. Even the duplicate has high value, and museums have no real interest in exposing the fact that their piece may be a copy."

Jimmy's instinct still works as well as it ever has. The car was now stopped, nose to the curb, wedged between two other cars whose occupants were enjoying the day somewhere other than in their car. My cell went off. Silver was as predictable as a man could be.

"I thought you were to call back! You where we can talk?"

"We are. Just found a spot. Jimmy's on as well."

"I can hear you better now, so listen up. That Klimt you saw out at Stratis' last night gives me heartburn. Big time heartburn. I need to know two things, and I need to know them sooner rather than later. First, is it the original or a knock-off? In either case it's mandatory we know if it ever was in the Neue's possession. My sources say no. The electronic log of the *Woman* from the instant it arrived at the Neue shows it to have remained in place. It's even been cleaned and worked on without moving it more than a few inches. So I'm pretty certain what they originally received is what they still have. But...but in these matters, electronics have been known to...to malfunction. And never in the insurance company's favor. Get my drift?"

"We most certainly do, sir. Angella and I have been discussing next steps. We're on our way back out to the Stratis estate, see what we can see. Keep our ears to the ground."

"Listen Redstone, you also Angella, we got a lot of money tied up in that *Woman.* You hear me? Protect it at all costs!"

Jimmy's "Aye, aye, sir," was lost to the dial tone.

We had been standing on the grass a few feet from the car when the line went dead. Jimmy rolled his eyes, opened the passenger car door for me, bowing in exaggeration as he did so. He then ran around the back, jumped in, and off we sped.

"You have somewhere specific in mind?" I asked.

"As I told the boss, taking a spin out by the Stratis property, see what we can see. If we have time, we can explore this North Park area further. Looks to me like a great place to have a picnic lunch."

"We're long past lunch."

"Picky, picky. Dinner then. Pick up some steaks and stuff, have us a real old-fashioned picnic."

"Need a grill. Charcoal, plates, that sort of thing."

"Details. Details. We can pick up what we need. There's always someone grilling in the park. Use their grill when they're done. Isn't that what neighbors do?"

"What about the car. It's due back in—"

"I thought Silver just loosened our expense allowance. He's on the hook for perhaps a hundred or so million. An extra day or two for the fancy wheels is, what did Carmine call it, chump change."

I didn't know what to make of the new Jimmy. He scared and excited me at the same time.

The road leading up to the Stratis property was even twistier in the daylight than it had seemed last night. Perhaps because Jimmy was driving faster, perhaps simply because of anticipation of what was waiting for us around the next corner. I recalled our recent drive up into the Jamaican hills to visit the mountaintop spread of an ultra-wealthy rancher with deep ties to the drug and terrorism trade. Armed guards in Jeeps had positioned themselves in front and back of us as we wound our way through the thick overhang not knowing what to expect next.

Here we didn't have an armed guard, fore or aft, and I didn't know if that was good or bad. But then again, this was Pennsylvania and not Jamaica, and I took it on faith that the difference mattered. We approached the road where we had turned off last night and noted that the police car that had been positioned there was now gone. Jimmy slowed almost to a stop trying to make certain he didn't miss the now empty road leading off to a destination we could not see.

Jimmy found what he was searching for, braking almost to a stop before turning onto the access road. He proceeded slowly so we could get a good look from a distance at the property where we both agreed the Stratis mansion was located. The problem was we couldn't see beyond a far-off strand of trees, which could have been a full forest for all the visibility they offered us.

"I think there's a truck parked down that road," I reported to Jimmy as we moved slightly past the tree line. "A van, actually."

"Well, that's in keeping with what Hessle had said about them moving the artwork out. But if that's so, then they don't seem to be in any real hurry."

I nodded. "Could have taken the hot pieces early. These could be the fakes."

Jimmy found a wide place in the road and pulled over onto the flattened grass. From where we were stopped, we could watch the van being loaded. It appeared only two men were working, and neither showed any inclination of moving quickly. "At that rate they'll be there 'til morning," Jimmy commented as the minutes dragged by.

But actually he was wrong. Ten minutes after we stopped, the slow-moving man closed and locked the van's back door. A few moments later, the van was making its way up the winding tree-lined road where we were positioned. Jimmy threw a salute to the driver as the truck rattled past us.

"Okay," Jimmy said when the van was no longer visible, "time to go pick us up picnic fixings and head over to find that park. We're off duty the rest of the day. You good with that, Angella?"

"I'm good with anything. You do the cooking. I like the off-duty part."

TWENTY-THREE

The Porsche was safely in the parking garage, or wherever the hotel parking attendant had stashed it for the night. I had to admit, Jimmy's idea for a picnic had worked out well, especially after our quick unplanned tour of the *Narcisi Winery*. Jimmy was exploring the winding roads, "off in yonder mountains", as he had begun to call the hills around Pittsburgh when he spied a sign for the winery. Off he went in search of the "perfect bottle". The vineyard is enchanting and the Noiret 2016 more than lived up to my expectations. It's a wonder we found our way back to North Park after that delightful interlude, but we did, settling for a table off by itself, but not so far from other groups that when it came time to cook our steaks Jimmy had no problem finding a hot grill. The steaks were grilled to perfection.

"And what would you have done if there were no grills about?" I had playfully asked him.

"Teach you to eat raw meat."

My nose must have curled because he added, "It's an acquired taste. You acquire it after days of eating nothing but the bugs you catch. Now say thanks for the little things in life and enjoy your dinner."

I opened the door to our room at the William Penn and walked in with Jimmy trailing a few feet behind. He pulled the door closed just as I sensed, rather than saw, a presence in the large sitting room. I stopped dead still and Jimmy, not yet aware of a problem, bumped into me.

"What..." he began, and said nothing further. I felt his body tense and knew this most likely wouldn't end well, even though we both recognized our intruder.

"Sorry to have invaded your space," the voice began as the man sitting in the far corner chair rose, "but this meeting must occur without anyone knowing. I trust I'll have your cooperation in that, Mr. Redstone, Ms. Martinez."

"How did you get in?" I asked, realizing how foolish a question it was even while I was still asking it. "A phone call would have—"

"All in good order, Ms. Martinez. May I call you Angella?"

"Call me what you want," I snapped. "I'm not happy you're here uninvited. You wouldn't be happy if you found us in your living room uninvited."

"I can assure you if you were found in my living room without invitation you would not be breathing."

"Her point exactly!" Jimmy said, years of training slowly moving his feet into attack position.

There were no bodyguards present, so I saw no reason to become physical.

"Just hear me out," our visitor said. "You are in no danger unless...unless you start with me. My folks in the next room will be more than happy to intervene should the occasion warrant."

"Mr. Stratis, that won't be necessary," I replied, sending Jimmy the message to back off. We were most likely outnumbered, but even if we weren't, Stratis wasn't here to harm us. Had he been, a weapon would have already been involved.

"Angella, please call me Dex. I'm here as a client. Jimmy, please relax and take a seat. I think you'll both be interested in what I have to offer."

Jimmy walked over to the sofa and sat. I lowered myself into the chair opposite Dex, our new best friend. The second new best friend in a week. At least we were now close enough to become physical with Stratis should the situation warrant.

"Do I have your word what we talk about here is confidential?"

"As long as it's legal," Jimmy said.

"You're not a cop any longer, Redstone. What the hell do you care if I talk legal or not legal?

All you should care about is what you and your partner do or don't do. That agreed?"

"Fine, go ahead," Jimmy conceded.

Stratis reached into his pocket and pulled out his cell, tapped a few buttons and then put the phone away. "Turned it off. That way the folks next door can't hear what we're saying. Can't be too cautious these days."

When he was satisfied all was in order he leaned toward us, his eyes intent, his demeanor demanding our full attention. This was a man who knew what he wanted and telling him no was not acceptable. "I don't know, nor do I care, who put you two up to this Summerland charade, or whatever you and your cop friends prefer to think of it as. Feds, local, state, maybe even Interpol, for all I know. They all have open files on me. But the truth is, I didn't get where I am today by being sloppy. My money's made legitimately. Government couldn't land a bomb on its own foot without my technology. And they know it. They're after me for taxes, money laundering, and can you believe it, illegal trafficking, whatever the hell that is. I've been collecting art before most of them were born and I'm not about to stop now. That show last night, that was just me having fun. Half of what you saw are fakes. Good fakes, but fakes just the same. I do, however, have my eye on the original of one or two of those fakes. Before you say anything, I of course know who you work for and...and I...know Silver has a large stake in coverage of the *Adele*."

"So what do you want from us?" Jimmy asked. "You know where our allegiance lies. You here to pony up that *Adele*?"

"Interesting choice of word, Jimmy. Interesting. Allegiances have funny ways of changing—or at least bending."

"If you believe for even a moment—"

"Please don't presume to anticipate what I want from you two. In your world you follow clues, dots if you will, until they're all connected. In your experience if you can connect the dots correctly you locate the hapless felon—or in your new life you locate a missing art piece. But the truth is, and as you well know, that only occurs if you've been blessed with a large helping of good old-fashioned luck."

Jimmy held his ground. "Luck is overrated, in my experience."

"Perhaps. But I can tell you this, nothing in life is a straight line, and the dots get corrupted along the way. So please hear me out."

"Continue," Jimmy said, "My ears are wide open."

"There is a piece of art that almost no one has ever heard of. It's called the *Crown of Alexander* and it was crafted in Russia, spent time hidden in a German salt mine, and was recently discovered in a cave in Israel. Much akin to Raiders of the Lost Ark. Actually, this is personal to me. I have reason to believe it was owned by my great-grandfather.

Unfortunately, he picked the wrong side when he went off to fight against Alexander II becoming Tsar. A classic case of to the victors go the spoils. I also have good reason to believe that lying thief Kumar has the *Crown*."

"I thought I saw it last night in your possession," I said. "Am I wrong?"

"Fake. That's my way of signaling Kumar that unless he plays ball I'll destroy the market value and he'll be driven into bankruptcy—or worse."

"Bankruptcy? Over one piece?" This sounded extreme, particularly coming from a businessman such as Stratis.

"Kumar's in way over his head. He, and that lovely wife of his, have...have overextended themselves financially. And, perhaps even more critical for them, the IRS is hot on their trail. My sources inform me they owe in excess of fifty million and counting. It's only a matter of time until...until the government rolls them both up."

I had trouble visualizing Riya in prison, but that wasn't the topic of conversation. "And you're here exactly why?"

"I thought that would be obvious to you both. I'm hiring you to broker the *Crown* back to its rightful owner."

"I take it that's you."

"Indirectly."

"What's that mean?" I asked. "Indirectly?"

"First things first, Angella. You accept?"

"Suppose we don't?" Jimmy jumped in. I couldn't determine if he was toying or serious.

"Not an option, I assure you, Redstone."

"And just why—"

"Simple. You actually said it before. I will deliver the *Adele* to you. I suppose you already know that painting you saw last night has captured your employer's heart—or at least his purse. One slip of the tongue and he'll be out more money than he can afford to lose."

"So it wasn't by accident that that guy, what was his name, Gussman? That Gussman was invited to the exhibition last night," I said, finally putting two and two together. "You staged that... that little outburst."

"Nobody is ever invited by accident, my dear. And the outburst wasn't staged. Let's just say the fireworks were expected. Did your boss at least wait until morning to call you?"

"He did," I said. "You certainly have his attention." Jimmy 's frown indicated he wasn't happy with me for imparting information, but I thought it best to show Stratis we played straight up.

"That's actually good. So here's the plan— should you choose to accept it."

"Mission Impossible," Jimmy said. "Made good TV. Refusing to accept is not particularly an option, according to you."

"You two will take immediate charge of the *Adele*. The one you saw last night. That will go well with Silver, I suspect. Keep the piece under your control until title to the *Crown* passes. At that point, the *Adele* is yours, or if you wish, Great Southern's. Keep it. Destroy it. Sell it. Display it, whatever. Keep in mind the clock is ticking. As I'm sure Silver made clear, the folks in New York have already contacted the insurance carriers who are at this very moment arranging for all manner of tests to determine—or redetermine—authenticity of the work in their possession. News of this activity will leak, and the avalanche will begin. As they say, you can't repair Humpty Dumpty."

"And what makes you believe Kumar is willing to sell the *Crown*? And if so, in any time frame that helps Great Southern?" Jimmy asked, not trying to hide his skepticism.

"Why else would he pay ninety-two million for a piece with a street value of at most fifteen? And that's on a good day. He knows its heritage and he knows I'll come for it. I set that in motion last night with the fake I put on display."

Jimmy took in that bit of information before responding. "I take it you're upping the ante significantly."

"Classic blank check, my friend. Well, not entirely blank." Stratis reached inside his jacket, produced an envelope and handed it to Jimmy.

Jimmy opened it and indeed produced a signed blank check.

"The limit in that account is one-hundred-eighty million. I expect the account to remain funded after you write in the amount."

While Jimmy was taking that all in, I asked, "Any thoughts as to where we should store the *Adele* while we are...negotiating?"

"How about right here in your hotel room? This shouldn't take but a day or so. Just don't leave the room until it does. Use room service. You have a gun. Be prepared to use it. I have confidence the *Adele* will be safe in your hands."

"What about a guard service as back up? With something this valuable you never—"

"Won't need it. My folks are across the hall. *Adele* isn't going anywhere until I say so. Oh, and just in case the thought crosses your mind to wound her in some way, I suggest you resist the temptation. Sensors will dispatch the artillery. It won't be pretty."

Threats never play well with Jimmy. I put my hand on his arm to slow his response. When he spoke it was with measured cadence. And it was to ask a question. "And our compensation is?"

"Funny you should ask that. Aren't you protecting your company's asset? I thought it wasn't ethical to dip into two pots at the same time. But the good news is that from the instant you agree, all expenses shift to me. And there are no limits—and no expense reports. Just give me the total. Nod and the *Adele* will be in your possession within minutes. Video showing her being removed from the gallery and recording every movement from then until now will come with her. All signed sealed and delivered. Keep in mind in the art world my main currency is honesty. If I say it is so, then it is so. No questions asked."

Must be nice to have such power — and confidence.

Jimmy nodded and our guest stood, shook his hand, then took mine, squeezed it and said, "I trust this is the beginning of a fruitful partnership."

This guy loves his movies.

I wasn't finished negotiating. I looked him directly in the eyes. "Partnerships go two ways. We'll do our best to negotiate for the *Crown*, but if we fail, the *Adele* still belongs to Great Southern."

"Here's a piece of advice. Don't fail."

"Easy to say. If inking a deal with Kumar is as simple as you want us to believe, you'd do it yourself and wouldn't be hiring us as intermediaries. Just call him and get it done. Or use any art dealer in the world."

"Good observation, Angella. Not so simple. He'd never sell to me. My collection drives his motivation. You're new to the game, and he has no reason to suspect you work for me. You actually will be representing not me but a successful businesswoman who lives in Canada and who just sold a business. The *Crown* will be her first major art purchase." Stratis turned to face Jimmy. "You met her last night. Name's Maxine Baker."

Jimmy closed his eyes a moment. "Tall, slender woman. Wearing a tux, if I recall."

"That's her. Don't judge her by her outfit. Max is an eclectic dresser. Tux one night, stunning gown the next. I happened to invest in her last venture, and she hit it out of the park."

Jimmy retrieved the envelope from the side table, again slipped out the check and studied it for a moment. "The Baker Foundation. Calgary, Alberta," he read. "That yours or hers?"

"Not important. You two in or out?"

"Thought we had time to decide."

"On second thought, time is not wise in this case. Kumar's still in town. At the Monaco, less than a block from here. Room ten twelve. My little fake *Crown* last night set the wheels in motion. He's already made a few calls and is desperate to sell. I've alerted the brokers and they're low balling him. If he can't get his price, he's ruined. IRS has given him until Tuesday to settle. So go get it for me. Easiest job you may ever have. And while you're at it, see what else he's willing to part with. I'm told he knows where the *Kings Cup* is stashed. That could serve your interest as well."

Now he had my full attention, and Jimmy's as well. Finding the *Kings Cup* would go a long way to extracting Jimmy from that stupid litigation with Joy Malcom. "Again, tell me, why us?" I was buying time to think, let things settle. To say I was overwhelmed is an understatement.

"As I said, Kumar's smart enough and been around the art world long enough to know who you are. Actually, more accurately, he knows who you *are not*. You're not an art dealer because he, like I, knows everyone in the world who deals in ten million dollar and up pieces. But I gave you street creds by inviting you last night. Now you're a player. He'll be curious to know just what role you do play. And, as I say, he's in too much financial trouble to scratch too deeply."

"He'll figure out who we are just as you did," I said. "Internet's got everything on everybody."

"All the better. It's a big leap from being an insurance company investigator to representing me. Look, he saw the *Adele* and he knows Great Southern has a vested interest. At best he'll think you're investigating me. You get the price up over a hundred million and with the IRS breathing down his back and with the implied threat of that fake going on the market, he'll suspend his doubts." Stratis looked from Jimmy to me and back to Jimmy, his eyes softening only a fraction, if at all. "After all, Jimmy, in the end, other than money, what else really counts? So, what'll it be?"

"We're in," I said, knowing we had to protect Great Southern at all costs and not immediately seeing another way to accomplish that.

All eyes turned to my partner.

His face remained passive for several beats. Then the beginnings of a smile appeared on his lips.

"As I believe you implied a moment ago, I think this is the beginning of a beautiful friendship."

TWENTY-FOUR

Angella remained with the *Adele* as I walked the half-block to the Hotel Monaco and rode the elevator up to the tenth floor. This was the same hotel where we had had our late dinner with Tiny a week or so ago. I paused outside the Kumars' room, debating as to whether or not this could wait until morning. But every hour that was lost could be the hour that cost Great Southern mega dollars. I reminded myself, not for the first time, I was doing this for Silver, not for Stratis.

The hallway was quiet, making it seem as if it were the middle of the night, yet my watch read eight fifty-seven. Not too late to visit, I convinced myself, as I knocked on the door. The sound reverberated through the quiet hallway causing me to rethink my decision. I took a step back in preparation of retreating toward the elevator.

The inside security chain almost immediately being slipped out of its latch was an indication it wasn't too late. And even if it had been, it was now too late to do anything about it. I paused as the door slowly pulled inward. There stood a towel-wrapped Riya Kumar, wet hair hanging down her mostly bare back, water puddling beneath her bare feet.

"What took you so...Oh! My! What are *you*...I mean I was expecting San. Why are *you* here...at this hour?"

"I am so sorry to have...disturbed you. I'm here...to see your husband."

"I thought you were San. This is not a good time." The door closed.

Had I been investigating her I would have moved my foot into the doorway. But this was a social call and I had already made enough of a mess of it. I turned to leave.

Riya, her voice back to its sexy softness, said through the door, "Give me just a moment and you can come in."

"I'm sorry, but—"

The door again opened. Riya was now mostly hidden behind the door with only her face and wet hair visible. "It's okay for you to come in. You just caught me by surprise. San is in the lobby. Went down for...for something to eat. You are most welcome to come in."

Her eyes held me captive. It took much too long before I responded, "No thanks. I'll go down and catch him downstairs."

"I know he wants to discuss a business deal with you. If you miss him just come back up here. I'll be...decent in twenty minutes."

The door swung toward its closed position, but I didn't hear it snap fully locked. Nor did I hear the safety latch reengage. Invitations come in all forms, and this certainly is one of them, for what I could only use my imagination.

But I hadn't come to engage Riya, it was Sanjay whom I had business with. I walked to the elevator, rode down to the lobby, and walked across to the stairwell leading down to the Commoner. There were people sitting at several tables eating meals; a group of men sat at the bar, all with drinks in their hands. One guy was in the midst of a story, and either it was a great one because they were all intently focused on him—or he was the boss.

I located Kumar in the far back corner and started walking toward him. Halfway across the room I realized there was another person, a man, sitting across the small table from him, his back to the room. I turned and retreated to a table where with any luck I could monitor Kumar without being noticed. I seated myself and within a minute the same waitress who had served us last week come over.

"Oh, hello. Welcome back, Mr...Mr...hey, give me a moment it'll come to me. Mr...oh, yea, Mr. Redstone. You closed the place down. You and that lovely woman. She's a keeper, she is. You were with that nice Mr. Smith. Sat right over there. Glad you came back. Want the Ginga Wheat? Oh," she exclaimed looking at the wedding ring now on my finger, "I didn't see anything. My lips are sealed."

Before I could explain, she shuffled off. Not that I could have explained it even if I had tried. In her case, working in a downtown hotel bar, explanations would be pretty much useless anyway. I was just one more untrustworthy male.

In the old days, or as they say, back in the day, I would have required a newspaper to mask my observation of Kumar and his guest. But in the modern era a cell phone is all that's required. So out the phone came and I focused my attention on the screen.

The waitress set the beer on the table and hurried away before I looked up, not even bothering to take a food order. Her version of ostracism.

At the fifteen-minute mark a fast-walking Oscar Hugo came straight for my table. I kept my eyes focused on the cell phone and slumped back into the booth a bit further. My sense was he hadn't seen me, but I wasn't certain either way. He moved directly past me, took the steps two at a time and disappeared through the door.

I looked to where Sanjay Kumar sat, and he also was on the move, although he wasn't moving nearly as fast as Hugo, because he was carrying two martini glasses. Up the steps he went, but instead of turning toward the outside of the hotel as Hugo had done, he turned left toward the elevators.

I debated joining him but thought it best if he and his wife had a moment together before I barged in. She could brief him on my earlier appearance.

Ten minutes passed before I knocked softly on Kumar's door. Sanjay opened it almost immediately but seemed surprised to see me. Over his shoulder Riya was shaking her head sideways signaling for me not to say anything about my earlier appearance.

Perhaps she was embarrassed that I had caught her wrapped only in a towel, a rather small towel at that. It could be she knew her husband would become angry knowing a man observed his wife in that state of undress and would be compelled to take action. I had learned long ago that marital relationships were private matters, and anyone who presumed to know their inner workings was bound to be in error. I also learned long ago that different cultures had different customs, and what worked for one didn't always work for another.

"To what do I...we...owe the pleasure of your visit, Mr. Summerfield? That *is* your name, is it not?" The drink in his hand most certainly wasn't the first of the evening. Nor did I think it would be the last.

"Land. Summerland. I came—"

"Sorry. Summerland then. Land, field, close enough. American names are confusing."

"I came to talk about an art object I've been commissioned to secure for a client. If this is not a good time I could come back. Say in the morning."

"This is most definitely not a good time and we'll be leaving early tomorrow, so I doubt if we'll be able to—"

"Business comes first, my dear," Riya said, her voice soft, almost a whisper. "Isn't that your rule? Business first."

Sanjay turned from the door and without a word walked back into the suite. I followed him in, pulling the door closed behind me. We were in a well-appointed sitting room, or foyer, with a white leather sofa and two comfortable-looking side chairs surrounding a metallic and glass coffee table. This was an upscale living room with a seventy-inch flat panel TV mounted on a wall opposite the sofa.

"If you are hungry, Mr. Summerland," Riya said, her voice now even more seductive than it had been at the party, "Sanjay can call room service for anything you might wish to drink. A snack maybe?"

"No, thank you. This should only require a few minutes."

Sanjay sat heavily into a chair and motioned his wife into the other chair, leaving me to either remain standing or sit on the sofa. He took a long drink from his glass. It was mostly empty when he set it on the table. Riya had hardly sipped hers. "Okay, Mr. Summerfi...Summerland...what is it that's so important you choose to disturb us on a Sunday night?"

I decided to get right to it. The man was agitated

and high, or close to it, never a good combination. "I represent an art collector who is in the market to purchase the *Crown of Alexander*. It is my understanding you own such a piece."

"Stratis owns the *Crown*. You saw that for yourself yesterday!"

"I have it on good authority his is a fake. You own the original."

"And how would you know that?" He demanded, his face darkening.

"In my business, sources are sacred. You must appreciate that. The less people know, the less they can spread rumors."

"I'm not prepared to discuss this now."

It was clear to me that Stratis was right. Sanjay was desperate to sell the *Crown*. The fact he didn't immediately deny owning it was all I needed. "You haven't denied you own the *Crown,* so unless you say otherwise, I will proceed under the assumption you own it."

Sanjay reached for his drink and drained the last of it, but said nothing.

"It is my understanding you paid ninety-two million dollars for the *Crown*. I am authorized to offer you a profit of ten million."

Silence.

The axiom is: He who speaks next loses. Axioms always have corollaries. And in this situation, the corollary for me was: I've hooked him. I've thrown a low ball. Now for a fastball right down the middle.

I pulled the blank check out, laid it on the table where Sanjay could easily read it. I took my time reaching for the pen I had brought along for the occasion. "This is the only check I have, so let's not mess this up. I plan to write one hundred—"

"Who the hell is your client?" Sanjay demanded.

"Normally I'd not divulge this, but in this case I have her permission. A woman, you probably don't know her, a woman by the name of Maxine Baker. She founded a company—"

Sanjay sat upright in his chair. His eyes cleared. "Know her! Up in Canada. Calgary. Calculator for use in GPS route selection for driving apps. Theory being the directions themselves can cause traffic jams if enough people are told to follow the same route. Brilliant algorithm. Met the woman last night. Lovely conversation. You were about to suggest a number. Go ahead."

"I am about to write down the number one hundred forty-five million. Once I do I can't change it and I have no more checks." I leaned forward, pen in hand.

"Stop! That's not enough."

"So, what number is?"

"What's your limit?"

"It's certainly not unlimited, if that's what you're asking."

"Two hundred fifty million."

We were now playing the game; warm, warmer, less warm, cold, warm, hot! "Cold."

"What's that mean?"

Perhaps they didn't play hot/cold in India, or wherever Sanjay was raised. "Way over."

"Two hundred?"

"Still cold. Hint. One hundred fifty is warm." I leaned forward again and this time I made it all the way to writing out one hundred when Sanjay called out, "Make that sixty. One hundred sixty."

From behind me Riya said, "Add five. One hundred sixty-five million and the *Crown* belongs to your client."

I turned to face her, to be certain I had heard her correctly. "Her dark eyes were alive was excitement. The vision of the money? The alcohol? Something entirely different? My job was to obtain the *Crown* for Stratis. Wrong. Actually my job, my only job, was to eliminate the possibility of an insurance claim against Great Southern for theft of the original *Adele Bloch-Bauer*. And that I was about to accomplish. As a further bonus, I was bringing it in fifteen million under my authority level. Never mind that Riya just added five million to the price, perhaps to be used by her as walking around money.

I waited for Sanjay to up the price further, but he held silent. While I held my pen paused over the check I realized how easy it is to spend someone else's money. No wonder governments squander funds as they do. "Deal," I pronounced when the silence had gone on long enough. I bent forward with my pen and neither Sanjay nor Riya stopped me when I wrote sixty-five million after the one hundred I had already written.

I handed the check to Sanjay who shook his head. "Not to me. Riya handles the art foundation. Give the money to her."

I did as I was told. Riya glanced at the check and then folded it and slipped it into a small tote bag that was on the floor beside her chair. "Pleasure doing business with you, "she purred. "A real pleasure. I look forward to many more...negotiations. I hope you do as well."

The intensity in her eyes was captivating. It took a moment before I asked, "What do you see as the next steps in transferring title?" It wasn't clear to me as to whom I should address the question so I focused my eyes between them.

Sanjay answered. "It is a simple matter of my lawyer drawing up a title transfer document in the morning. That will take no time at all. I am certain you'll demand proof of authenticity, which we will update tomorrow. Can't imagine it taking more than a day, Tuesday noon at the latest.'

"I trust you will not deposit the check until title is transferred."

"Of course not, Mr. Summerland," Riya said. "This isn't my first transaction."

I stood. "I should be going. My client is waiting to hear the good news."

"Look forward to seeing you again very soon," Mr. Summerland," Riya said, disappearing into the bedroom and closing the door behind her.

I started for the door. Halfway across the room Sanjay called, "Not so fast. We're not exactly finished. Please come back over here where we can hear each other easier."

I turned to face Sanjay, expecting him to be slumped in his chair as he had been for the past fifteen minutes or so. But he wasn't slumped. In fact, he was now standing, a smile forming on his face. The smile of a man who had just escaped disaster. "Indeed we have business to discuss. Business just between you and me."

"And just what would this business entail?" I asked, taking a tentative step toward him. I was thinking Riya had indeed told him about my earlier appearance, and he had to now uphold his honor.

"Sit with me a moment longer," he said, resuming his position in the chair. "I'm certain your... your significant-other can manage a few moments longer without you so that you and I can discuss the real business of the day. Don't you think that's true, Mr. Jimmy Redstone?"

TWENTY-FIVE

"The pretense is over, Mr. Redstone, and it's now time to get down to business. We have agreed on the price for the *Crown*, but we must work out a few...let us say...housekeeping opportunities."

"We have a deal, Mr. Kumar! If I'm mistaken, hand me back that check and I'll leave."

"Don't jump the gun. As I said, we'll authenticate the *Crown* and get the paperwork ready. But...but, and here's the full deal. I couldn't say this in front of Riya, but I'm in more tax trouble than even she knows. I'll cut to the chase. It is simply mandatory I obtain the *King's Cup*. And since you also have a...shall we say...an interest in that particular artistic piece, our interests align."

I jumped to my feet. Kumar had made it known he knew who I was. Now he was telling me I knew where the *Kings Cup* was. I didn't care to hear what else he was about to unload. "Hand me that check!" I demanded. "I'm leaving with or without it! You'll be embarrassed if you deposit it!"

"You of all people, Mr. Redstone, know full well that one can't just show up in a bank and deposit a hundred some million dollar check. There's more paperwork to fill out than buying a hotel. Sit back down and listen. You've nothing to lose and from the way I see it, everything to gain by hearing me out."

My hand was on the door when he said, "Your friend Joy Malcom asked you to keep a lookout for the *Cup*. And I take it you have every reason to keep your eyes open."

I didn't take my hand off the doorknob, but neither did I twist the latch.

"I see I have your attention. You're being sued for over a hundred million for something you claim you never did. But anyone who puts that much faith in a jury getting it right is...well there's no other way to say it...a fool. And you, Mr. Redstone, are a lot of things, but one thing you're not is a fool. So come back over here, sit down and let's go through this step by step. As I said, you have nothing to lose and everything to gain."

If this had solely been my own set of circumstances, or even had it been limited to obtaining the *Crown* for Stratis, I would have walked out without question. But I was being paid by Great Southern to protect them, and that objective was paramount, no matter how uncomfortable it became for me.

The law enforcement ethic was far too ingrained to consider anything other than blind loyalty.

Sitting once more, I said, "Okay, lay it out! All of it."

"To be perfectly frank with you, Redstone, as I said, I'm in a spot of trouble. On two fronts, no less. With the deal I just struck for the *Crown* I can buy my way out of IRS difficulty. Those vultures want your first-born and I'll now have the cash to settle."

"So that should be it then. Add strings to the deal and you won't ever get the IRS off your case. It'll all go south on you."

"Well, here's the thing. Dead is dead."

"Come again."

"You know the story about doing a deal with the devil. I did worse. Believe me when I tell you I did worse. I sold the *Kings Cup* to Santiago a few years back. Problem was, title was forged. Now he's in a lawsuit with you and he demands I produce good title, so he can win your case. I can't produce. Clock is ticking. You know what happens when you cross a guy like that?"

I knew all too well. "No, tell me."

"You come to a sticky end." He ran a finger across his neck. "Not just mine, but..." Kumar lowered his voice, "but hers as well. They'll kill her first, but not before they rape and torture her. I can't allow that to happen. Would you?"

In that instant I visualized Angella and not Riya. I shook my head to indicate no I wouldn't allow anything to happen to Angella if I could help it. "The *Kings Cup* is gone. I don't have it and I don't know where the hell it is." And that was the truth.

"Knowing where to locate it is not my problem. Paying for it is."

"You just had a big payday. Use—"

"That money's going to the IRS. You can help me on this and...and, I promise you, at the end you'll be sitting pretty the rest of your life."

Or dead. A sticky end as Kumar had put it. "So lay it out." I owed it to myself to listen to his proposition.

"Let's begin with that lawsuit Malcom...actually Santiago...has against you. They have two hurdles, one easy, one tenuous. The first is proving ownership. I told you I screwed that up, but in time I'll get that fixed. Your lawyer believes they won't ever prove ownership but trust me, it's only a matter of time." He let that settle before continuing. "The only real trouble they have is proving who stole the *Cup*. Proving you saw it in Joy's condo is easy enough. Joy has you on video. You called it in to Homeland Security. That's documented. The contents of the condo were bagged and sealed and everything delivered to DHS where it was all dutifully logged in. It seems the sealed bag containing the *Cup* was signed out to...want to guess?"

"I'm not in the mood for guessing games. Get on with it."

"What? No sense of fun, Mr. Redstone? My, my. Okay, have it your way. Your name is in the logbook. The *Kings Cup* was last documented to be in the possession of one Jimmy Redstone, authentic signature and all."

I told myself he was lying about the logbook. My lawyer had not told me this bit of bad news I assume because it didn't yet exist. But, knowing the folks working the issue, if it didn't exist as of now, it would very soon. A major operation had been going on in Mexico, a hundred fifty or so million had been involved. A fake *Cup* had been constructed, so there were moving parts going in many directions. Angella had traveled to Western Mexico and taken a train ride high up into the Sierra Mountains to track the *Cup* as it was being authenticated. She had witnessed the transfer, but then had been drugged and thrown off the train. She had fallen victim to our late nemesis, the expert disguise artist Floratine Maldos. Known in the trade as Shadowy Sal.

That was all in the past. But like everything to do with Homeland Security, or the CIA for that matter, nothing was ever lost to the past. It was all in a storage bin — or digital storage as the case may be. Documents which don't exist today will be *discovered* tomorrow. Piece of cake for this crowd.

I studied Kumar a long moment. Indeed he was central casting's ideal desperate man. "You have video of everything else," I said, "show me video of my signing out the *Cup*."

"That's the one weak point I must admit, Mr. Redstone. If that video surfaces you're nailed. How long do you think it will be before one surfaces?"

Actually, I'm surprised it already hasn't turned up. Not that I was ever close to the *Cup*, but with digital splicing today, anyone can be shown doing anything. If I required bunny ears, bunny ears I would have. I could only hope the prove-it-false crowd could keep up with the fabricate-it-to-order crowd. From what I had observed working for DHS, I doubted they could.

I started to rise again.

"Might as well stay for the final curtain," Kumar said. "The bad stuff's behind you." When I reluctantly settled back, he said, "Don't let your hair-trigger get the most of you, Mr. Redstone. You play your hand well and...well...you'll end up with twenty or so million in the bank. Oh, I don't mean under a rock or down a hole, but in a real bank, paying real taxes and spending it by writing a check instead of sneaking out at night with a shovel."

Now I was on my feet and halfway to the door. I turned to pronounce an epithet on him and his family, unusual for me, but in this situation highly justified in my mind.

Kumar didn't say anything. But he was holding a blown-up picture of the portion of the island where rumor had it I had buried the forty million dollars I supposedly had recovered from a bank robbery gone bad. Joy Malcom, for one, believed I had the money — or that I knew where it was — which is the reason for the lawsuit in the first place.

The difference between the picture Kumar was holding and other similar pictures is that this one had a large red X dangerously close to where my money would have been hidden had I hidden money anyplace. "What the hell you think you got there?" I bluffed.

"The Singer treasure? That's exactly where your island historian Hathcock believes the Singer treasure's located. You have a vested interest up there. Everyone knows that."

When I didn't respond, he said, "Let me just say this, Mr. Redstone. If you have money buried up there, it won't remain buried for long. With modern electronics, they'll sniff it out sure as we're sitting here. That is, assuming they haven't done so already. Shame to throw forty million away when I'm making it so easy for you to do good for a lot of people, including yourself."

"Don't know what...Who the hell you calling?"

"Friend of yours. I'm Face Timing her."

The phone buzzed twice and none other than Joy Malcom's face popped up. "Hi, Big Guy," she said without hesitation, "trust you're making progress on the *Cup*. Getting worried about you."

"Truth is, Joy, progress is slow. Haven't run into it yet. When I do you'll be the first to know."

"Morris is getting...well, shall I say a bit concerned."

"Truthfully, Joy, I don't—"

"Oh, Jimmy, you're always so grumpy. Relax, enjoy life. You know, get out, have fun. You never know what can happen next. Just this week a good friend just up and died. No reason. Well, maybe too much drinking, but he enjoyed his time on earth. You should enjoy your time. You never know what'll get you. That's my motto."

That was a threat if ever I had heard one. Maybe that's what the attempted murder and framing was all about? Soften me up. If it had worked, great for them; if, as it turned out, it didn't work, then onto plan B.

"Joy, let me tell you again. I didn't take your *Cup*, even assuming, which I doubt, it's even your *Cup*. And I don't have any money to give you even if you did win the lawsuit."

"Oh, Jimmy, now just you stop poor-boying yourself you hear me. You took the *Cup* alright, and you surely have the money. Now stop all that teasing and come home to mommy."

I walked away from the screen.

Kumar said into the phone, "Joy, please tell Santiago all is well on the art front. Talk soon." He hung up.

"So you and Santiago are best buds." That explains seeing Oscar Hugo downstairs with Kumar. The common element being the art world.

"I get around. Santiago wants to be a player. I plan to assist him."

"From a Mexican prison, no less! You'd better be careful, or you'll enjoy the cell across from his."

Ignoring my remark, Kumar went on. "He's got the biggest network of anyone. Guy stretches from East to West. He's moving out of drugs — might take a while, but he's hedging his bets. Every year, he moves about three billion in merchandise worldwide. Wal-Mart barely does five. But I digress. Here's the deal. You can't lose. I arrange for you to buy the *Kings Cup*. The authentic *Kings Cup*. Round numbers, you pay me thirty million. I then arrange for you to sell the *Cup*, all with Santiago's permission, for seventy-five, possibly eighty. Of that, you keep eight million after taxes. All legitimate. No more sneaking around. Share the eight with Angella or keep it for yourself. Not my concern."

"So why me? Just buy it yourself and do the deal. No extra middle man."

"Two reasons, basically. One, we need a legitimate sale with all the trappings of provenance and examination and authentication. Real, nothing phony about it."

"And second?"

"Second, until my tax liens are lifted, I can't be the actual buyer or seller. Need to have a new face, someone not being...whose finances are not so much in a tangle as mine are. You're clean. This will work. IRS isn't watching your every move."

"Count me out," I said. "Not my cup of tea."

"Look, don't be a fool. You've worked your entire life in dangerous situations. What'd you get for all that? A pat on the back and kicked out the door when they were through with you. You managed to get your hands on some money, but even then you can't enjoy it. The government's playing you for a fool and you're...well, sorry to say, you're going right along with them. You won't have much more than your social security when you're too old to work, and you'll be lucky to have that. This one transaction and your life begins over. Go where you want, do what you want, have fun."

I've heard that speech over and over all my life. Sometimes I told it to myself, more often a partner contemplating some nefarious action would deliver it. Never before had it resonated even faintly.

"Mr. Redstone, your action, or shall I say your inaction, is putting the precious *Adele* in jeopardy, not to mention your own stash. Tell you what, just go down to the Island while I work the details of the transaction. If I can negotiate for a clean title to the *Kings Cup* and the *Pirate* I'll contact you and give you the exact amounts for the buy and sell. If you agree, we have a deal."

"And if I'm not interested?"

"After you learn the details and all the road blocks have been removed, if you still can't see your way clear to go forward then I'll release the *Adele* and the *Crown* and everyone but me wins. What can possibly be fairer than that?"

TWENTY-SIX

It was slightly after ten-thirty when Jimmy got back. A lot had happened in the short time he was gone. Beside the fact that I was tired and already felt like a prisoner, the phone hadn't stopped ringing, or so it seemed. One look at Jimmy and I knew something was troubling him—big time. I popped a beer and set it on the table. "While you're winding down," I began, wanting to get all the have-to news out of the way quickly, "Silver called. Three times, actually. Thinking of blocking his number, if he calls again."

"Not surprised. There are days I think he has us wired. And there are other days I know he does. What the hell burr does he have under his saddle now?"

"He's a nervous Nellie over the *Adele*. One minute he's convinced the one here under the bed is the phony. And the next minute, well, the next minute he's convinced the real one's been stolen and replaced and the authentic one is here with us. Then a few minutes later he believes the real one never was the real one. Guy's going to have a nervous breakdown—or a heart attack—or both, if that's possible."

"He say how a painting with so much security around it winds up replaced by a fake?"

"Says it's gotta be an inside job. Guy doesn't trust anyone. He'd put a security camera on his own mother if she had a piece of his insured art. Better call him and tell him it's all taken care of?"

"Mostly."

"Mostly is not an answer, Jimmy. What the hell happened?"

"Long story. Short version. I wrote the check for one hundred sixty five."

"Left fifteen on the table. Nice going."

"Think Stratis was impressed?"

"My take of him, sorry to say, is he gets what he wants when he wants it. Who he hurts in the process is collateral damage—or worse—and he doesn't give it a thought."

"You're right. Called him on my way back over here, thinking I'd least get an attaboy. Was I ever wrong! 'You went way too high!' he scolded. 'Need to sharpen up next time.' That's when I hung up. The deal comes with a catch I haven't yet told him about. Kumar needs me to go down to SPI and negotiate a complicated transaction for, of all things, the *Kings Cup*."

"Didn't Stratis hint at something along those lines?"

"I don't know what the hell Stratis said or didn't say. They're all thieves, you ask me. Anyway, assuming we can get a flight, we're going down to the Island in the morning to see a man about a dog."

"Sorry, Jimmy, but I can't go. Silver was more than clear about that. Not until the *Adele* is in his possession can I leave its sight. That was his second call. Or was it his third? He left no wiggle room. Oh, and Abigail Johnson called. Wants you to call her back. Says it's important."

"Abigail—"

"Abby. You must remember her. Reporter for the Washington Post."

"Oh, that Abigail Johnson! It's been a long day. Haven't seen or talked to her in years. She still with the Post?"

"Didn't say. But I hadn't heard about her leaving. Leading expert on homeland security and terrorism. They'd never let her go, not with the number of Pulitzers to her name. One you handed her when she held up a story for you and you gave her an exclusive."

"Call her back tonight?"

"That's what she said. She's staying downtown, I think over at the Fairmont."

"Let's walk over and see her. It's only a few blocks, and fresh air'll do us both good."

"Can't leave. Remember? This gets old real fast. And truth be known, Jimmy, I'm not keen on you going down to the Island without me. I feel trapped."

"Won't go, then."

"Hey, I'm being a baby here. If it's critical to getting the *Adele* taken care of then you have to go. And go see Abby if you need the walk."

"No need. Call her, tell her I'm back. Meanwhile, I'll call the airlines, see if I can book something."

"Can we really talk in this room? They're monitoring the *Adele*. Who knows what else they'll pick up."

"Good point. How about we use that sound block device?"

"I forgot about that! Tiny didn't take it back after we finished the operation in Jamaica."

"Bet he didn't *forget*. Little gift that keeps on giving."

"Fifteen minutes, at max," I called to Jimmy after hanging up with the reporter. "This must be important. She's in a real hurry."

Jimmy came back from the bedroom, frowning. "You've had more luck than I. No flights available until late tomorrow afternoon. Won't get me to the Island until after midnight. I sent Kumar a text telling him Tuesday morning on the island at the earliest."

"I'm sorry it's not working out, Jimmy. What's your alternative?"

"Right now, nothing. Private jet comes to mind. But that will require Silver's approval. Work on that in the morning.

Twelve minutes after I hung up with Abby, the knock on our door came. Abby was ageless—and tireless as well. It was nearly eleven at night, and she appeared as if she had just awakened. I knew her age to be between sixty and seventy, closer to seventy, but she was moving more like fifty.

"Jimmy Redstone! Angella Martinez!" Abby exclaimed. Then noticing the wedding ring, she added, "Oh, you two are married! How nice. I hadn't heard!"

"The ring is for an operation we're running," I said, my face growing hot. I pulled the ring off. "For all the good it's doing."

"No. No, leave it on," Jimmy instructed. "We may not be fooling all the players all the time, but we might just be fooling some of them some of the time."

I expected a big smile on Jimmy's face as he mangled the words Abraham Lincoln was reputed to have said. But instead he was dead serious. "What's gotten into you? I mean with that fooling some of the people junk. You're starting to sound like Stratis."

"Never know when the ruse'll work to our benefit. As long as we're in this hotel we're married." Jimmy hugged Abby and when he released her, asked, "What's so important it couldn't wait until—"

"I'm on deadline. I was just about to release a story when Angella called. Piece is ready to go, actually been complete for several days. Working on confirmation's all."

"Thought confirmations were a thing of the past," Jimmy said, only half teasing. "You still with the Post?"

"Parted ways last year, I did. The web's the thing these days. Got a gig called Abby's World. Million clicks worldwide. You believe that? It's the go-to site for news on terrorism and, with my sister-in-law's help, we throw in military operations to boot."

"That McNaughton you talking about? Retired General Lucinda McNaughton, if my memory holds?"

"That's her. Husband had to hang it up, a bit of dementia. But Cindy's still...still as feisty as ever."

"So if you're doing your own blog, why bother with all the checks and double checks? Just go with it like they all do now."

"Jimmy, this isn't the time or the place for that discussion. But yes, I'm old school. Confirmations are key for me. That's why my blog gets all the clicks. Trust is the key. Reputation's critical."

"So, you're still working homeland security. Angella and I are out. Moved on."

"Scuttlebutt has it you've moved over to be with old Jack Silver at Great Southern Insurance. DHS's loss is Jack's gain. Heard you pulled off a nice piece of work down in Jamaica by interrupting the money operations of a terrorist operation. Congratulations to the both of you. Neither Cindy nor I saw the repercussions of that one coming."

There was more to the story then even she knew. I was thinking of ways to divert Abby's attention if that subject was broached. One sniff and Abby'd be off and running and there'd be no hauling her back into the barn.

"Heard also, Jimmy, you got thrown from a horse. You okay? What's that about?"

She was telling us she had an inside source, and knowing Jimmy, he had picked up on that message as well.

"Nothing major," Jimmy said, belying the fact that he had been airlifted out of Jamaica. "I'm fine. Great doctors. Great recovery."

"Great to hear that. I don't have to tell you financing terrorist operations are getting complicated, what with all the sanctions imposed and the money laundering rules in effect. Yet they still manage. Money flows easier than water, it seems. Art is bigger than it seems. And the field isn't just shady folks whispering in back alleys. Some of the most respectable people, people running major corporations, even people in government. I've been working on a piece for months now, and the more I peel back the more I find. And, frankly, the sicker I get."

Abby paused as if she expected Jimmy or me to fill in the blanks. Jimmy had trained me well. It wasn't my nature to volunteer, but in this situation I had no blanks to fill in.

"Museums are the worst offenders. Pay anything for a hot item. Donors give the money and take tax write-offs. Museums pay highly inflated prices for an item, even if it's not authentic, provided they have *colorable originality* and an assurance the real item will never surface."

"How do they even get such an assurance?" Jimmy asked. "It seems no one can say anything about art with any certainty."

"In some cases pretty easy, actually. A collector, a dark collector, who only wants an item because he wants it, and who keeps it locked away out of sight, can guarantee a museum that the fake piece the museum is purchasing will never be proven a fraud. Everyone benefits."

"Why?" I asked. "Why go to all that trouble?"

"These folks thrive on it, Angella, is all I can say." Abby checked her watch. "Listen, this is a topic I could discuss all night, but as I said, I'm on deadline. If I had more time I'd go into more detail, so let me just give you the highlights. Jimmy, that guy you put in jail, Santiago, is now dealing art. I suppose you know that. He's connected on every continent. That's what troubles me. His tentacles reach from Iran to North Korea and everything in between. There's an endless pool of bad actors about and with a middle man like Santiago brokering art in the, say, half a billion range, real money can flow across international boundaries relatively freely. I was tipped to a major two-way, actually three- or four-way, deal that's about to transpire. That's where you come in."

Abby paused to be certain we were following, then continued. "With Santiago in the middle, a first piece of art goes to, say, North Korea. A second piece goes to Iran. Nothing big about that. Total value of the art, about one hundred million. But then North Korea and Iran swap pieces and a billion dollars flows with it."

"That's preposterous!" Jimmy said. "You're telling me in individual hands the pieces are worth one amount, but when they exchange hands the value goes up ten-fold."

"That's what I'm saying. Correction, that's what I've been told. If it wasn't so unbelievable I would have already published."

"Corroboration?" Jimmy asked.

"Not exactly. But I will say this much. The source...well, the source is impeccable. Or rather, has been dead-on accurate in the past."

"So why the hesitation?" I asked.

Abby said nothing, but wrinkled her nose

"Translation."

"Smell a rat. Source is too...too eager."

"What are the pieces you've tracked down?"

"Confidential until released?"

"Of course." Both Jimmy and I said simultaneously, both of us eager to learn what she knew.

"Something called a *Bucksbaum*. And something called...oh, I see I hit a register. You know what a *Bucksbaum* is."

"You're good," Jimmy said. "Go on. I'll fill you in on what we know when you're finished."

"And a piece I know you're all too familiar with from a terrorist plot you broke up—or thought you did. The *Kings Cup*." Abby again checked her watch. "Down to seven minutes. Unless I pull it—or change it—the story will run as I now have it. Oh, and in this mix, I'm told with the Koreans, is a work of art called the *Adele Bloch-Bauer*. You might know it better as the *Woman in Gold*."

It was all I could do to refrain from looking toward the bed. "What do you say about the *Adele*... the *Golden Lady*? I mean in your article."

"Only that it's possible to see it leave New York for the Mideast. I think it's the piece being exchanged from Korea to Iran. Iran wants it because Israel is thought to be hot after it. Oh, the tangled webs we weave."

Jimmy checked his watch. "Four minutes," he announced. "Abby you sought us out. Please do as we ask. We've not steered you wrong before, and we won't begin now. Of the art pieces now on the international market, North Korea is not a destination to my knowledge. Nor is the *Ade... Woman in Gold*. I can confirm the *Bucksbaum* and the *Cup* are in play, but the countries you mentioned should be removed. Please don't yet discuss the possibility of a trade and for now don't list any art other than the *Cup* and the *Bucksbaum*. You will do irreparable damage if you do. The *Bauer* is not going anywhere."

"The swap is the key here," Abby said. "What do you know of a swap?"

"I can say this," Jimmy said, choosing his words carefully, "there *is* a deal in process involving the *Bucksbaum*, but the only country I know about is Israel. But I very much can see a museum buying a piece at an inflated price with the money going to Iran or some other terrorist operation. But that part is pure speculation on my part."

Abby looked Jimmy straight in the eyes, hoping to see God knows what. "Promise it isn't happening tonight. I mean an international art exchange."

"Certainly not to my knowledge," Jimmy replied. "If we're assuming the players in and around Pittsburgh are involved, then I have a high degree of confidence nothing's happening tonight."

"My source said the action is definitely centered around the Pittsburgh art community. Is it possible you're just not in the loop?"

"Of course that's a possibility. Not with the government any more, so no need to include me. But...but, Silver's well connected in the community and he's said nothing."

"And if I'm not mistaken, you two are his chief investigators?"

"For art we are," I said. "At least Silver has

said as much. That your understanding, Jimmy?"

"It is. But, in all honesty, Abby could be right, we're just bit players. Decoys if you will."

Abby laughed. "Knowing Silver as I do, you two wouldn't be the decoys. You're the best he's ever had. He wouldn't burn you that way. Look, do I have your promise you'll give me an exclusive when you know what's going down?"

"You do."

"What about you, Angella?"

"I'm with Jimmy on this."

"That's good enough for me." Abby flopped in a chair. With phone in hand, she said, "Siri, get me *Editor*." While she waited for the editor person to come on line, she said, "I'd love to run the double exchange story. The source is so good. But I'm not getting sniffs from anyone else. I was hoping you'd have something coming at this from a non-government perspective. But a day late is better than being wrong." Abby's hand shot up, indicating someone had come on line. She spoke into the phone. "I know it's a poor time to be cutting, Ray, but I have no choice. I need you to embargo the last three paragraphs of the double exchange story. Run the remainder as submitted, except in the third paragraph end the sentence with the word 'Cup'. Everything after the word 'Cup' is gone. You're authorized for form editing only. No substantive word changes. This is a sensitive piece. Okay?"

Abby listened to this guy Ray for a moment, then said, "I owe you one. Bye."

"Editor's not a happy camper, but hey, it goes with the job. Ray's as good as they make them. That's why I brought him over to the blog...actually it's a specialized on-line newspaper—on-line presence, I should say."

While Abby had been dictating instructions to this faceless guy, I was visualizing him siting around a smoke-filled room, a thousand coffee cups scattered about, orderlies running from desk to desk, a pressman pulling his hair out. I relayed my thoughts to Abby.

"You've seen too many old movies, Angella. Way too many old movies. With on-line presences, pressroom's gone. And deadlines are self-imposed for discipline. Ray's in his walkup, near Ninth Avenue and Twenty-eighth Street, sitting in front of his laptop, his dog at his feet and his wife off in another room—or in bed. And there's no longer a pressman. Well, there is for the few remaining newspapers, but not for on-line folks. And even the real pressmen are not necessarily in a press building. You'll find them siting at a desk staring at a computer screen. Everything today is button push—and lightning fast.

"Abby," I asked, my curiosity taking hold, "how'd you know we were in Pittsburgh? It wasn't exactly broadcast."

"Saw you at the Stratis fete. Hey, don't look so surprised. I get around."

"Homeland security journalist at an art function?"

"This security journalist has made a few friends over the years. Actually, I talked the young Post Gazette art beat writer into taking me as her guest. Didn't wrangle an invite to the private showing, but I sure captured photos of everyone who managed to go on the tour. And there you two were. That reminds me, there was a woman there, name of Carmella, Carmella Schenley Hampton. I believe you were with her."

"We were there as her guests." I said.

"What do you know about this Carmella?"

"Internet claims she descends from Mary Schenley. But we can't find anything on Hampton. Why?"

"I know her from someplace. I checked the Internet as well and found, I suppose as you did, that Mary Schenley and her husband, Captain Edward Wyndham, had seven children. Carmella isn't listed in any lineage that I could find. In fact, the only property she seems to have now, or ever had, is a row house out in Oakland."

"What's really troubling you?" Jimmy asked, his curiosity coming alive.

"Things like that, I mean her property records being a bit wompy, that sort of stuff, sets off my sensors. And, as I said, I know her from somewhere. Somewhere long ago. Another life, another time. I never forget faces, but hers...hers may have been...altered. But you know age does creep in, and maybe I'm just not remembering faces as fast as I used to back in the day. Oh, well, I'd better be leaving."

"Good night, Abby," Jimmy called from across the room. His eyes seemed to be focused on his phone. "I'll be in touch the moment I know anything."

"How about a coffee or a late breakfast in the morning? Fill me in on what you can tell me."

'Sorry, can't. Catching an early flight to the Island. Be gone a day or so."

"Working on this issue?"

"That's the intention."

"Well, okay. Good night you two. Be in touch."

"Thought you couldn't get a flight," I said to Jimmy when the door closed. "You have a reason for not meeting with her in the morning?"

"Kumar just made his plane available. I would've turned him down, but for this text from Silver."

Jimmy held up his cell so I could see. From half-way across the room the message read: RESOLVE THE ADELE. TIME OF THE ESSENCE.

TWENTY-SEVEN

I walked out of the hotel room slightly before nine-thirty, nine-twenty-eight to be exact. The garage had assured me the Porsche would be immediately brought around to the entrance. In this case, the working entrance was actually on the small street behind the hotel within sight of Hotel Monoco. I had declined Kumar's offer of a ride to the airport because I wanted to return the car with as much privacy as I could muster, given all the players floating in and around our business. Take-off time was set for eleven o'clock. Fifteen minutes to drive to the car dealer, fifteen minutes at most to have the car inspected, pay what I owe, and be on my way. Waze showed the time from the dealer to the airport to be twenty-one minutes. No problem.

Wrong.

Apparently, "Bring your car right around, Mr. Summerland," actually means, "we'll get around to it if and when nothing else gets in our way and if it happens not to be break time."

So instead of pulling up to the dealer at nine forty-five, it was closer to ten-ten. "Be right with you, sir," translates into the same message as at the hotel. Lyft driver arrived at ten-thirty. The walk-around ended at ten thirty-six. I slipped into my ride at ten forty-five.

"How long to the airport?" I inquired, as if asking would reduce the time.

"From here, about forty-five minutes. Barring traffic."

"No, not that airport," I said leaning forward when I noticed the big smile on his face. "AGC. The county field. Get me there by eleven?"

"Barring traffic."

"Do it. Pay you well. But, hey son, don't get stopped."

Off we went. Up hills, down hills, across bridges, up more hills around curves, dip down again, across another bridge, back up, hard swing to the left, then back to the right. The numbers on my watch face counted up steadily. Then at four minutes to the hour they seemed to freeze as we roller-coasted up and down and around several more hills. Given all these hills I couldn't imagine where this airport could possibly be located.

"You lost?" I called to the young driver, a chunky black guy with an upbeat personality who was seemingly out for a fun drive.

"Never happened, man" he quipped. "Got this covered."

A moment later, with a hard swing to the left, the kid announced, "Mission accomplished!" The car skidded to a stop in front of a small building, the words Allegheny County Air Terminal across the top. "This my first time up here at this here airport. Not so bad for an old place like this. You important or something?"

"Or something," I called to him. "Tip will be posted—and generous. Rate you tops."

"Appreciate it. Ratings important. You coming back? Here's my card. Text and I'll be here. Any time, day or night. I'm your driver. Got me covered?"

I glanced at the obviously homemade card and slipped it in my pocket. "Won't be for a while, Roger. But when I do you'll be my man with the car. Got you covered."

"It's eleven, you best hurry."

"Mr. Redstone?" A TSA woman called from the corner of the building the instant I stepped from the car.

I hadn't seen her standing there and that troubled me.

"I was asked to expedite you to Mr. Kumar's plane. You're the last to arrive and their flight plan calls for them to be off the ground right about now. Captain's a bear when he's late. May I see a photo ID please?"

I did as requested.

"Okay, looks good. Now walk over through

that door and you'll be scanned. I'll meet you on the other side, and then off we go."

I pulled the door open as instructed and entered a long narrow hall. Halfway down the hall a bored-looking guy sat in a chair in front of an X-ray machine staring at the ceiling.

"You know the drill," he said when I approached. "No metal in your pockets. Computers, phones in that basket. Belt and shoes okay."

He never moved from the chair and I don't believe his eyes ever left the light fixture he was studying. I added the Berretta, the magazine empty. Ammunition left with Angella. Had plenty at home.

"Take your stuff, you're done," he said when I passed through the X-ray without filing out the weapon paperwork. Turns out I could have brought the ammunition. So much for security.

"Follow me," the TSA woman said when I passed through the door at the end of the hall. She walked briskly down a corridor, oblivious to paint peeling from the masonry blocks. Then through a door out onto the tarmac where a grey Camry was parked, a pair of yellow lights flashing on its roof. She climbed in behind the wheel, and I trotted around to the passenger's side.

My head snapped back against the head stop when she accelerated. This woman was auditioning for Talladega. I suppose it was a safe area to do so, because the only aircraft I could see was a Cessna Citation standing alone near a brick retaining wall at the edge of the airport. We covered the ground quickly and my escort skidded to a stop just short of the jet's ramp. "All out. Enjoy your flight." She was halfway back to the terminal before I passed through the entrance door to the luxurious interior of Kumar's private jet.

Both Sanjay and Riya were aboard the seven-seater, as was another man in wire glasses who Sanjay simply referred to as 'My Lawyer'. I took the seat across from the lawyer and within two minutes the door had been closed and we were on the taxiway gathering speed. Without slowing, the plane made a ninety-degree turn onto the runway and within seconds it seemed we were in the air banking right. The ground fell away even quicker than usual. I guessed it was because the airfield had been built on top of a hill and the plane was at a thousand feet or more above "ground level" while still parked.

The lawyer was busy marking up documents and made it abundantly clear he had no intention of talking with the hired help. I hadn't brought a book to read, but that was just as well. I needed the time to work out the moving parts. First I concentrated on relationships. Joy came to mind at once, and of course her husband, whom she calls Morris Malcom, but who really is Alterez Santiago. I then linked Santiago with Kumar and also with Oscar Hugo. The natural tendency would be for Hugo to be focused on the *Golden Booby* because it had been in his family. And of course Joy and Santiago were laser focused on the *Kings Cup*.

Then there was the relationship between Sanjay Kumar and Morris Dexter Stratis. Two powerful and wealthy businessmen who don't seem to be at each other throats professionally, but according to Stratis, jealousy, perhaps envy, rules Kumar when art is involved.

And where does Riya Kumar fit into all this? Surely, jealousy didn't rule her relationship to Stratis.

Pishtacos, the Peruvian gang, the El Artista Sisters, Sofi and Chio del Rio, came to mind, as did those thugs Matias el Bueno and Antonio Alveras who, I believe, work for Santiago. Bit players or major characters? I couldn't sort them out in any meaningful way.

And Levi Ben-Yuval? I certainly didn't dare dismiss him as a bit player, so what the hell was he doing orchestrating our every move, or so it seemed? Couple that with Trooper Hessle and that character Carmella Hampton, who also had a relationship to Oscar Hugo. Full circle, from Santiago to Hugo to Hampton, and I was lost. I wasn't yet certain I had all the relationships, so I redirected my focus to the art.

The *Pirate* is still missing. The *Adele* is in play as is the *Buscksbaum.* Thinking of the *Buscksbaum*, what's it doing in the possession of Hampton and Hugo? And who the hell is Hampton anyhow? A gallery in a townhouse in a residential neighborhood; a gallery with no real front entrance and a secret passage to the attached home next door? A gallery that seems to be under $^{24}/_7$ police surveillance and the only piece of authentic art appears to be the coveted, at least by Israel, *Bucksbaum*. Still thinking of the *Bucksbaum*, what about the artist Carrie Buck, daughter of a Holocaust survivor who she claims drew the *Bucksbaum* while in a concentration camp?

I was going in circles with little or no progress.

"Mr. Summerland," the lawyer said, tapping me on the shoulder, and bringing me out of a sound sleep, "you're wanted up there." His index finger pointed to the seats in front of us where Sanjay and Riya were sitting.

I didn't know which one of the two wanted me, and truthfully right now I didn't particularly desire to speak with either of them. I delayed getting up long enough to cause the lawyer's finger to really toggle as though I had done something particularly nasty.

Reluctantly I stood and walked forward. The Kumar's seats were certainly more cushy than those I had been sitting in and looked as though they could easily be folded back into beds.

I stepped forward another step and turned to face my host or hostess, whichever Kumar it was who had summoned me. In that instant I had to force away the vision of Riya opening the hotel door wearing only a hotel towel, her hair dripping wet, her eyes alive.

"Oh, Mr. Summerland. Or do you prefer, Redstone? Please join me, won't you?" Sanjay said, tapping the seat beside him. "Riya's gone back to freshen up a bit. This will be an excellent time to chat."

The plush seat seemed to engulf me when I sat. I tensed my body to avoid sinking too far back.

"Tell me," Kumar began, when I turned to face him, "did your client, Miss Baker, appreciate the money you saved her?"

"Saved her?" I asked, not immediately focusing on who he was asking about. Quickly realizing I had forgotten Baker in my list of characters, I added, "Now that you ask, as a matter of fact, no. You pushed me to the limit of my authority. Nothing was left on the table, I assure you."

"Negotiations are over. Price doesn't ever go lower. You play the game like a pro, I have to say that much for you. Of course I left money on the table. There's always money left on the table. We both know that."

"What about value?"

"Come now, Mr. Summe...I suppose up here I should call you Redstone, or Jimmy if you prefer."

"Jimmy'll work."

"To my friends, I'm San. As I was saying, who the hell knows the value of any art piece? I'm worth over five billion dollars, give or take a few million on any given day. So if I want something, how much I pay for that thing doesn't affect my way of life one iota."

He left out his little problem of the IRS hounding him, but best to let that dog lie quiet. "But... but the less you pay for any one thing the more things you can buy. At least that's the way the laws of finance work in my sphere."

"Sorry, Jimmy, but at the billion-dollar level that rule goes out the window for many reasons. Truthfully, you know what I find so fascinating? I'll tell you. In the art world, the value is aspirational. No matter what I pay for an item I can sell that item for a profit. I suppose there's a limit, but I haven't found it yet."

"Conventional thought says there's a limit to all things."

"Think of it as Kumar's law. I'll call it: Billionaire's One-way Ratchet. BOR for short."

BORE would be more to the point, you ask me. That gem I retained for myself. This sure didn't sound like the same guy who last night professed he had no spare cash to buy the *Kings Cup* or to pay the IRS before they came down on his head. The same guy who convinced me to buy the *Cup* and *I'd* make money. That guy.

"Listen, I didn't invite you up here for economics class. Here's the deal. You round up thirty million in cash any way you can. We won't worry ourselves about where it comes from. You understand me? When you have the cash call this number." Kumar handed me a business card, on the back of which he had written a number. "Tell whoever answers the phone you have the cash.

You'll receive a time and place for the delivery. Arrive at that place exactly two hours *later* than the time set. Look for a blue Land Rover. A red flag hanging out of the driver's window means compromised.

"You're asking me to trust you with thirty million dollars! That's not—"

"Not exactly. In fact, it is I who will be trusting you. Before you deliver your first dollar, I'll deposit the *Pirate* and the *Kings Cup* to your condo."

"Authentication?"

"Authentication will be made available to you in a form I believe you'll find adequate. Don't deliver the cash until you're fully satisfied. When you've turned over the thirty mill, those two pieces are yours. At that time I'll give you instructions for delivering those pieces to the buyer. Paperwork will already have been signed, sealed and delivered. You provide me the account info at your bank and the purchase price will be direct deposited. The number is now even larger than I had told you so in the end you'll come out of this a very wealthy man. Pay your taxes, and all will be fine."

"And Santiago is good with this?"

"You'll have confirmation of that fact as well."

"Here's the thing bothers me," I replied. "The *Pirate* carries a street value of minimum twenty-five mill. Most likely closer now to forty."

"Try sixty."

"Okay. Sixty. And the *Cup,* anywhere from fifty

to some might say over a hundred. And both are mine for thirty. Understand my skepticism?"

"Believe me when I say I really screwed things up. I told you some of it last night. But I'm in a hole and this...this helps. That's why you did so well negotiating for the *Crown*. Look, Redstone. I'm quite certain your real client is that ass Stratis. Had to swallow my pride. That...that guy's not what he appears to be. He bills himself as Mr. Upright. Wants the world to believe he does everything by the book. His word is never to be questioned. All that's crap! Any player in the art world knows he has a dark gallery, and most of the world's *missing* artifacts pass through his hands. He has no qualms buying from Iran, North Korea, you name it. There's a major international transaction about to occur based in large measure on some of his art properties, involving Iran and North Korea if you can believe it. He funnels large amounts of money to those...those terrorists. And the art community, and worst of all, politicians, all hail him as a good guy! Witness all the big shots out on his overly manicured lawn Saturday night literally begging to be invited to his *private* showing. I apologize for the rant, but you hit a hot button."

I heard a rustle behind me and turned in time to see Riya slip into the far back seat and disappear from view.

I still wasn't buying any of this *poor me* crap from Kumar. "I ask again, why me? Thirty million. If the properties you control truly can command double that, why don't *you* make that sale, mask it behind some of your friends? Surely you're no stranger to false flag transactions."

"I could just say I have my reasons. But truth is, the sharks out there know I'm in trouble. I might get a bit more, but not all that much. They'll low-ball me. And...and...fact is, those two art properties are being bid up by some...shall we say...not-so-nice players. I'm being watched too closely by the powers that be. Nobody in their right mind would get involved in a North Korea-Iran transaction with someone like myself who finds himself in the crosshairs of the American government. The embargo on these types of deals spooks them as it is. Adding me to the mix makes it far too toxic."

"There's always Santiago. What the hell does he care about crosshairs and toxic? For him, the more the better."

"There for a while I thought Santiago would be the intermediary, and he yet might be. But... and here's where you come in. And why you can make a killing. You're known for being a straight arrow—a trusted partner, if you will. I can divert attention to Santiago, and meanwhile we can make the purchase and move the merchandise while all eyes are on that Mexican jail. You and the art will fly under the radar."

"Santiago's in on it?"

"He's been briefed and is very much on board. This is perfect for him and his people. He gets a major cut—and, as they say, he builds his brand. It's perfect for you as well. You can declare the transaction, pay your taxes on your gains, put your *profits* into the bank, or wherever, and never have to work again a day in your life. What could be bad about that? You'd be a fool to walk away. And one thing I know about you, Redstone, you're no fool."

"But I'm an ex-lawman. Homeland Security no less. Why in the hell would they —"

"Who the hell do you think are behind these deals? If you really believe all this goes on in the ether with no help from government types, you'd better think again. Your fellow *lawmen* are not exactly all Boy Scouts. Not to mention the politicians. Get my drift?"

TWENTY-EIGHT

Jimmy was on his way to the airport, having left me behind to babysit the *Adele*. I wasn't exactly pissed, but I wasn't exactly a happy camper either. I was peeved with Jimmy, but couldn't articulate exactly why. I was angry with Silver, but even there I had a hard time coming to grips with what he had done wrong. It wasn't so much that I was confined to quarters, after all, I could catch up on my reading, household paperwork, that sort of thing, but rather the fact that I was required to remain in one place, a prison of sorts, that annoyed the hell out of me.

It didn't help when Abby called to invite me to join her for breakfast. A *get-to-know-each-other-better* brunch she had called it. The suggestion of a round or two of champagne didn't make me feel any better about begging off. In fact, her invitation made me angrier with Jimmy. Irrational, I know, but a fact I had to deal with.

Not ten minutes after hanging up with Abby, Jack Silver called to inform me he had hired a guard service to relieve me, and that as of eleven-thirty I was off duty. I no longer had full-time baby-sitting responsibilities and was free to move out of the hotel room. The only proviso being I had to work either the three-thirty to midnight or the midnight to seven shift. I selected afternoon over night.

"Abby," I said into my cell the moment after Silver rang off, "plans have changed. If that gracious offer remains open I'd very much enjoy taking you up on it. Only, can we make it, say, twelve forty-five? Have a few errands to attend to first."

She sounded pleased with the new arrangements, and when I hung up I called the front desk and requested a room change. The hotel found a room I could move into immediately, even though the check-in time was two-thirty, as the desk politely informed me. The new guard, identified only as IB, arrived ten minutes early with another man, a short, wiry, bearded guy who examined the *Adele*, first under a strange-looking microscope, then using a fancy light, then using a small chemistry set. The little man didn't appear unhappy when he left, even though he refused to confirm any results to me.

At eleven-forty five I was told all was in order and I could move out, which I promptly did. From room 518 to room 632 I went, dropped the suitcases, locked the door and took the elevator down to the ground floor. Halfway across the ornate lobby I spotted a woman who tried too hard to be casual, but, in fact, had been studying me intently. *What's this about?*

I didn't acknowledge that I had noticed her, but instead maintained a steady pace. I resolved to deal with her, if necessary, if she followed me. Her presence had been a good warning, causing me to take precautions as I made my way the several blocks across town. To the best of my knowledge I wasn't being observed, but truth is, I've been in this business long enough to know that the good ones can tail without you ever knowing. At least I tried.

Walking across town, I thought of Jimmy, now most certainly in the air on his way to Texas. Walking lowered my anger level with him. That was good. I resolved to reserve judgment on Silver for a later date. That also was good.

Thinking of the devil, the man himself called just as I entered Abby's hotel. I stepped back outside to take the call.

Silver was on a high. His forensic expert, with ninety-five percent certainty, pronounced the *Adele Bloch-Bauer* that was in our room, actually now in my former room, a forgery. "An extremely good forgery, but a forgery nonetheless," Silver told me. "If Jimmy handles his end down on SPI then we can put this episode behind us. Keep up the excellent work, you two."

Despite taking a convoluted course across town, in and out of stores, up and down elevators, back and forth across streets, I would have arrived exactly on time had Silver's call not delayed me. As it was I was only two minutes late and found Abby sitting at a back booth, her fingers racing over the keypad of her laptop. "Oh, hi, Angella, what a nice surprise you managed to work yourself free. Give me a moment to finish this sentence." Several more keystrokes and Abby flipped the computer cover closed. "This is indeed a delight. Most of my interaction has been with your...your partner. It's nice to be able to get to know you better."

"I suppose it does no harm to tell you outright, I've had almost no experience talking to reporters and now that I'm out of the government and have no prohibition, well...well to tell the truth...I'm concerned, actually intimidated is more accurate."

"Just say to me everything we discuss is off the record and it'll be off the record. Just two friends getting to know each other better is all."

"Okay. Everything we discuss *is* off the record. Does that do it?"

"It does. Let me tell you about me. As you know I worked for the Post for many years before I went out on my own. Before I left, I earned senior investigative status. That and a few dollars will get you a Starbucks Latte. But it also meant I didn't have deadlines and wasn't limited to what I reported on. Why is this important now that I'm on the Internet? In a word: sources. The key to investigative journalism is the number of sources you develop over the years. And...and of even greater importance is the quality of those sources."

"I'm curious. When you came to our room last night you knew a lot about the art world and terrorism. It's not exactly public knowledge so am I accurate in thinking that all came from sources?"

"It does. In Washington the Post is the place to develop great sources. But here's the thing most people don't know. It's a two-way street. People in government plant stories for a whole variety of purposes. To fool the public. To fool Congress. Sometimes even to fool the President. Everybody in that city has an agenda. Some agendas work well for getting government work done. Like the use of trial balloons to see if an idea will fly. Those are planted stories, and the reporter knows it. Some planted stories, however, are used to bring down an opponent. But here's the thing. In order to plant a story, a source must have a track record of giving good info over a course of time. I have such folks, a lot of such folks who use me to plant stuff. They feed me great scoops, things that would be better off not said. They do it so I'm available to them when they wish to plant something for their personal benefit. Trump is right when he calls it a swamp."

"So why do you further their goals by publishing?"

"My job is to shine light on what the government is doing to the people and on what the people are doing to the government. Bad stuff happens in the dark—from both sides. So I try to ferret out what seems wrong and publish as much as I can as honestly as I can. Close the curtain on the

Feds and they'll run right over us. Likewise with the bad folks. That's pretty much apple pie basic, I know. But it's what I believe in and what I do."

"But how? How do you know which trails to follow? From my experience working with DHS they aren't forthcoming with their own agents, so how do you ever get the straight story? I know for a fact Jimmy and I never could. They gave us just enough to do our jobs and nothing more. Sometimes what they gave us was a flat-out lie."

"That's typical siloing. They've made it an art form. I get around their deviousness by using my extensive network, perhaps one of the biggest in the business. Much of what I get, of course, comes off the record. Some call it background, some just leak it. The background, even though I can't use it directly, allows me to understand just what's going on. You'd be surprised at what I'm told *on background* and *not for publication*. Very few real secrets are ever kept in Washington. As I said, Trump's right on. The place is a cesspool."

"Classified?"

"Much of it."

"And you can publish classified data?"

"So long as I obtain it without *my* breaking the law, such as breaking into someone's home. If my source breaks the law, it's on him—or her."

"Surveillance? Electronic?"

"Yes, all of it. We're pretty good at it, actually. Gotta stay a step ahead of big brother." Abby's computer gave a soft ding. "Speaking of big brother, let's see what this is about." She studied the screen a moment, frowned, and then typed in what I took to be a response. Finishing, she turned the screen to face me.

SAY NOTHING MORE. SOURCE BEING MONITORED. CHECK LIPSTICKS.

I dug into my bag and extracted two lipstick tubes; one was mine, and one I had never seen before. Without me saying a word, Abby reached for the false tube and dropped it into her water glass. She turned the computer back around and waited a moment. Then she said, "Got the little bugger! We're good to continue."

I had a million questions. "Who was that? How did you know which lipstick was planted? How far away is the listener? Was it recording? How—"

"Slow down, Angella. One at a time! First off, I travel with a team, and it's not uncommon for someone like your friend Tiny to monitor folks who they think are leakers."

"I'm not—"

"They monitor for lots of reasons. Second, I could tell you I knew which one was the bug because it's not your color. Too pink. But I'd be lying. That lipstick bug is standard issue with...and here's the puzzling part...Treasury."

"Treasury? IRS? But why them? I've paid my taxes. Jimmy's paid his taxes."

"Treasury does a lot more than collect taxes. Used to be they handled firearms. I think they miss the good ol' days and are searching for something more than just catching tax cheats. This could be something to do with Santiago or his army. Bad stuff's going down, that much I've been told by a source who's never been wrong before. Like it or not, you and Jimmy are in the middle of something big. In fact, according to my source, this can only work if Jimmy cooperates."

"How so?"

"Don't know all the pieces. That's why I pulled the story back last night. Can't get full confirmation and...and a few things just don't yet add up right."

"Where does Jimmy come in? And...and I'm his partner, shouldn't I be included in—"

"That's just it. Your name wasn't mentioned. Just his. That's what sent my antenna up. So tell me, is everything all right between you two? Please pardon me for snooping, but that's what I do, sorry."

This went beyond mere snooping and moved right into invasion country. Abby must have read my face because she said, "One thing I know about Jimmy Redstone is that he, and I suppose you, are intensely private people. Well, as private as two people can be who work, worked, for the government. You both hold top security clearances, which means you've been investigated every which way to Wednesday by every investigative agency our government can throw at you. And then some."

"What's *and then some* mean?"

"Mossad, but I'm certain you know that based on your dealing with Levi Ben-Yuval. Recently, the Iran Intelligence Agency ran the traps on your names as well. That's when my phone first rang."

"First rang?" I asked, her tone indicating that it had rung more than just once. "It rang more than once?"

"Oh, my phone is always ringing, so to speak. Vital to an investigative reporter. The latest with your name associated is the MSS."

The letters MSS puzzled me and I said so.

"MSS. Ministry of State Security. That's North Korea's primary counterintelligence Agency and reports directly to Kim Jong-un."

"So your *finding* us in Pittsburgh, just happening to see us at the Stratis... showing...is a cover. You were tipped to something."

"Yes, that's why I'm here in Pittsburgh. It wasn't a chance meeting."

"But what I don't understand is what Jimmy has to do with North Korea. Or with Iran, for that matter."

"I certainly could be on the wrong hunt, but my sources say a major art transaction is going down involving Iran and NK. But it's not straightforward and somehow Jimmy's at ground zero. As I told you last night, there's a force multiplier somewhere."

"Force multiplier?"

"Like art transferring hands to one party for one amount and almost immediately flipping to another party for a large multiple of that number.

And Jimmy, if my source is right, is smack in the middle of it."

"You said my name didn't come up? That's odd."

"I thought it was. I had actually thought the two of you...well, you went your separate ways. Look, Angella, often I'm given only a part of a story. Sometimes that's on purpose, but truth is, often that's all my source has—something half-baked. That's why you and I are talking. And why I didn't publish all that I was told. There are pieces of the story that just aren't right."

"But why single Jimmy out?"

"That's probably a good thing—for you."

I thought about what Abby just said but couldn't get it out of my head that Jimmy would go off and run an operation without at least giving me a heads up. It just wasn't like him. *Something's wrong with Jimmy—or with our relationship.* Or...or he's being duped.

"You sound so...so put out, Angella. And if I'm any judge of people, and I pride myself on being a good judge, something's troubling you. Or let me put it another way. Something's going down you're keeping from me."

"Nothing's going on. It's just that..." *Time to shut your mouth.* "...that...well, as I said, nothing's going on."

"How long you and Jimmy been together?"

"Going on ten years," I said, hardly believing we'd been together that long.

"Goodness. I didn't realize it's been that long." Abby glanced at my ring finger, but said nothing further on that subject. I'm sure my twisting the loaner round and round hadn't gone unnoticed. "Keep in mind the info I have came from a source totally unrelated to Jimmy—and could be all wrong."

How disconnected could the source be if he—or she—knew about the art projects Jimmy and I were working on? "It's the North Korean aspect that has me going, I suppose. The thought of Jimmy getting tangled up in that mess without me, or even with me, well, I'm agitated is all."

"But here's the thing, Angella, something's troubling you. My take, it's personal. I wouldn't be worth a damn as a reporter if I didn't read that. Try my shoulder."

"Nothing to say."

"From what I've gathered, Jack Silver has set you two up in a penthouse apartment on South Padre Island. That means you're more than partners—well, more than casual work partners anyway. The reporter in me makes me ask—don't answer if you don't want to—so why haven't you two married? I mean, after working this long—and living—together you each know exactly what you have. Last night when I thought you'd been married you were quick to point out it was just pretend. Okay, I get that. But...but a look flashed across your face. What gives?"

What do I have to lose? I really need to get this off my chest and who else do I have? "Still off the record?"

"Of course. This is personal anyway, so I'd always keep it confidential. I'm not a total blabbermouth, and I'm certainly not the gossip corner."

"I know Jimmy has a ring. He's been planning on asking me to marry him for a while now. It's just that...that every time I think he's going to pop the question he pulls back. Sometimes it's me; the time's not right because we're in the wrong place, that sort of thing. But other times...like we've had many months now of just hanging around, doing small projects for Silver, traveling, relaxing, having fun. But no ring."

"Think he's having second thoughts?"

"Frankly, I don't know what's in his mind. Jimmy's...well...Jimmy keeps his own counsel pretty much."

"And if I read between the lines, that's got you... you asking yourself questions."

Be careful, Angella, this woman has warned you, she's perceptive. And an expert extracting information others don't want to impart. "He's just private, is all. But he's a good person. A truly good person."

"You think the forty or so million he brought back from Mexico...or should I say...is rumored to have brought back from Mexico—"

"Stop!" I said, pulling myself up in my seat. "That rumor's bogus! The money that came back from Mexico went directly into the bank. Only our Government was playing stupid games and refused to allow it to be deposited in its name. So the money was being held in a bank safe when the bank was robbed. What the hell did they think would happen with everyone in the Valley knowing forty million cash is in the damn vault?"

"That part I hadn't heard. Please fill me in."

"This can be on the record because there's nothing secret about it. Bank on the island was robbed. Robber stole the money as well as a piece of artwork. The *Kings Cup*."

"How the hell'd they get the money off the island? The only way off is over the causeway as I recall."

"Halfway over the bridge they unloaded the money and the art over the side of the bridge to a waiting boat, and off they went."

"So where did the rumor start about Jimmy and the money?"

"I've been wondering the same thing. Jimmy and I did eventually track down the folks behind the robbery, but the money was never recovered." I omitted the part where Jimmy deduced that the money had never left the base of the bridge, although the *Kings Cup* had. But that was just Jimmy's theory. He might be right and the money's still buried down there, or its just plain lost out at sea. What I do know is that Jimmy spent a lot of time that year out on the bay fishing—by himself.

"So it's possible he did recover it."

"You know as well as I, anything's *possible*."

"Off the record, Angella, does he have it?"

This is certainly the bear in the room. The one question I had refused to dwell on and had studiously refrained from asking Jimmy, not wishing to put him in the position of lying. I had my suspicions, but no hard evidence. Before I could craft an appropriate response, Abby's computer beeped and she again consulted the screen. When she was finished, she said, "You seem to be a popular person. My team has now confirmed there are two sets of people monitoring you. One is a Pennsylvania task force that's been working with the feds on art trafficking. That team is headed up by a State Trooper name of Hessle. Know her?"

"Off the record?"

"If you insist. You're killing me."

"She's been feeding us contacts and keeping us in the loop."

"Contacts such as?"

"Hampton, for one. That's how we got invited to the Stratis gathering."

"Others?"

"Mossad."

Abby drained her coffee cup dry before continuing. "Thing is, Mossad is far too good to be spotted unless they wanted to be. They're sending a message."

I waited for Abby to elaborate, but she fell silent. "So who're they sending a message to?" I asked, concerned that I was a pawn in a game I didn't understand. "Me? You? The Task Force?"

"Probably all of us, I'd say. And truth is, with Mossad on the scene, I can't promise our folks have all the frequencies covered, so there's no way to know if we have all the devices. I think it best for us to say nothing further. We could be compromised. Let's agree to meet again. Another time. Another place."

That sounded good to me. I nodded and stood to leave.

"Take the lipstick with you. Dry it off and throw it back in your purse. They won't know for sure if it malfunctioned or was found. Keep 'em guessing, I always say. You may want to feed them a false lead later on." With that Abby gave me a hug and whispered, "Jimmy's a keeper. Hang in there."

TWENTY-NINE

"Port Isabel, Summerland, or whatever the hell name you're using today," the lawyer said, his hand on my arm. "Time to get your butt off this plane. Car's waiting."

I must have again dozed off after my little chat with Kumar because I don't recall much after I went back to my seat. Indeed we were parked on the weed-infused tarmac of the Port Isabel Airport, long ago abandoned to all but private planes and a few Coast Guard landings. With the Homeland Security prison just down the road the airport has become much more popular as of late.

"Car's yours as long as you need it," the lawyer said, his voice giving off a warning not to abuse the privilege. "Drop it back here when you leave town. Or leave it at the hotel and we'll pick it up. Just let Kumar know where it is."

I walked down the deployed steps and found no one in the car. The keys were sitting on the dash and the engine fired right up when I turned on the ignition. When it was clear I was going to be alone, I drove out of the airport, heading toward the causeway bridge and my condo. A little detour up island to the *Blue Marlin* to stock up on beer, chips and other necessities. I added a couple steaks, some potatoes, a bag of salad, and charcoal. It had become all too easy to order room service, so my cooking skills, what little I had managed to cultivate over the years, were in remission. Grilling in the park last night triggered a desire to recapture my proficiency.

It was slightly after seven in the evening, eight in Pittsburgh, when I settled into my favorite chair and dialed Angella. She answered on the first ring, as if she had been sitting by her phone waiting for the call.

"Hi, Jimmy, how was your flight?" I couldn't quite place the edge in her voice, but one thing was clear, the spark was absent.

I told her about both Kumars being on the plane, but that neither had disembarked with me in Port Isabel, and I didn't know where they were headed. I started to explain what Kumar had said about the art properties but Angella stopped me.

"This is not the best time for discussion," she said. "Remember why we went shopping last week? The first time. Need to go again, I'm afraid."

Slow at the controls. Took me a few seconds before I realized she was telling me our communications were again being monitored. "I see a new suit in my future," I finally responded. "And perhaps a tie or two. So how was your day?" I knew Angella would only tell me what the listeners already knew.

"Silver changed things up. I've moved out of the room we were in. But I'm back there now, waiting for a meeting. Should be over around midnight. I'll call you then."

"Okay", I said. "Oh, I almost forgot. Don't forget to..." I was about to tell Angella not to forget to return her ring before she left town. But that wouldn't be a good fact to let out. Then it occurred to me I also might be wearing a mic. This was beyond old. I'd had enough. Kumar's proposition was sounding better all the time. Broker the art pieces through him. Flip them. Pay taxes on the profits and live happily ever after. "Okay, love you. Talk to you later. Call me."

"Love you. Talk later."

I dug everything out of my pockets, examined the coins, ran my fingers along the edges of the paper money, took the credit cards, driver's license, and Great Southern badge out of my wallet. Nothing jumped out at me, but that didn't mean I wasn't bugged. It just meant I hadn't found it.

I stripped, checked the linings, then jumped in the shower, the hot water feeling good on my skin. I opened the sliding door to the private balcony and took in the wonderful salt air blowing in from the Gulf. The beach was mostly deserted, with a few couples walking at water's edge. Muffled noises filtered up from the pool where perhaps a dozen people still lounged, most of them with drinks in their hands. One woman was walking laps back and forth across the shallow end.

Miracle of miracles, the propane grill fired up on the second push of the igniter. Forty-five minutes later I popped open the Merlot, filled my glass, and sat down on the outdoor patio to a steak dinner. The only thing that could make it better was Angella being here to enjoy it with me.

Two bites into the steak and the door chime sounded. I padded across the floor, sans shoes and shirt, wearing only shorts. The door chimed a second and third time in quick succession. Patience was not a virtue of my visitor.

I opened the door from our suite and passed through the reception office, pausing to flip the lights on before pulling open the door to the hall. In stepped Riya Kumar pulling behind her a dolly bearing a large crate. The instant the crate passed across the threshold she instructed me to close and lock the door.

"Thirty million sure can make one nervous," she said when the latch snapped into place, her eyes alive and focused directly on mine. "Your hair's still wet, Big Boy." She laughed, her face lighting up. "You now know how it feels to have someone barge in on you when you are...not expecting them."

"Oh, sorry for the...lack of shirt. I wasn't exp—"

"Neither was I. But listen, I don't mind you being shirtless—in fact, if I was being perfectly honest, I very much enjoy it. Where can I stow this?"

"What's in there?" I didn't offer to help her with it. "I don't think you should be here," I added, my discomfort rising.

"And just why would that be? I thought we were...business partners."

When I didn't answer, Riya added, "Art properties. The two you are purchasing. *Pirate* and *Kings Cup*. Where should I put them?"

Now I was really uncomfortable. I didn't believe stolen art pieces should be here in Great Southern's offices, and frankly, neither should Riya. "Get them out of here!" I answered. "And do it now!" I trotted off to the bedroom to track down a clean shirt, returning a few minutes later to find Riya sitting in an office chair.

Without a word, she stood and walked past me into the bedroom, leaving the crate where it was. When she didn't immediately return, I followed in her footsteps only to find her standing at the base of the bed, her head bobbing up and down in approval.

I thought better of asking her what she was approving. There was no denying that Riya was a naturally sensuous woman. And there also was no denying we were both in committed relationships. We were on a bad trajectory that held very little promise of ending well if continued. Deciding it was useless to continue insisting she remove the artwork, I relented. "I was just sitting down to a steak dinner when you...you knocked. I can put one on the grill for you if you care to join me out on the patio."

"Actually, yes, yes, that sounds wonderful. It's been so long since...well, to tell the truth, Sanjay doesn't eat meat, so it's been forever since I've indulged. But only if it's not too much trouble?"

I was hungry, and sharing mine didn't feel right, anyway. It also hadn't felt right to not offer to share dinner.

"Happen to have another. There's a potato in the pantry. You can microwave it if you wish while I put the steak on. There's salad in the fridge. Help yourself. How do you like yours cooked?"

"Hot on the outside and cool in the middle."

The grill was still hot so, we were seated in just under fifteen minutes. While we were waiting, she had leaned on the railing, her eyes focused far out to sea. At one point her jaw quivered as if she was about to say something, but no sound came. But I did get a momentary glimpse of her eyes and for that instant the sparkle had been replaced by a deep sadness which passed just as quickly as it had come.

Breaking the silence, I said, "If you look to the south toward Boca Chica Beach you'd be able to watch the SpaceX launch if there was one tonight. That's how close we are."

"That's all so exciting, Jimmy. This is such a...a nice place you have here. You are indeed a lucky man."

I was busy with the grill and didn't respond, which was just as well, because I couldn't think of anything cogent to say. I reheated my steak and plated them both. We sat and lifted our glasses.

"To a wonderful and profitable partnership," Riya toasted, touching her glass to mine, her eyes again sparkling.

I accepted her remark by nodding my head.

"This is far too large a steak for me, Jimmy. Please promise to help me finish it."

"Just eat what you want, leave the rest."

"I don't like waste."

"It won't go to waste, I promise."

"Do you always give women what they want? I think you do, don't you?"

Ignoring her comment and the sensual facial expression that went with it, I asked, "So tell me, Riya, why exactly are you here?"

"Sanjay told you the *Kings Cup* and *Pirate* would be delivered. I'm the delivery boy."

A boy she certainly wasn't. "Again, I ask—"

"Sanjay continued on to Denver for a business meeting. His exact words were, 'Deliver those art properties up to Redstone as soon as you can. And be sure they don't disappear before he delivers the cash'. So I'm just the messenger boy, delivering the artwork. I said thirty million, but truth is the items in that crate are worth over a hundred million."

"Hate to break it to you Riya, but you and I together couldn't prevent bad guys from breaking in and doing with that crate what they will."

"Sanjay cut a deal with the hotel. There are guards posted downstairs. The elevator to the penthouse can only come up with their permission."

"Helicopter can land on the roof, be in and out in a matter of minutes. With this much money at stake any manner of stuff can happen that we can't control."

Riya slowly cut her meat, and just as slowly chewed it, apparently savoring every morsel. It was a full five minutes before she lifted her head, her eyes focused directly on mine, and said, "Nice salad."

"Thank Blue Marlin," I confessed. "Came in a bag."

"I suppose if I complimented you on the steak you'd say the same."

"I would, but with a nod toward the cow."

"You're impossible, Jimmy, you know that. I'd love nothing better than to get to know you, the real you, but...but you're determined not to allow that to happen." She shook her head, her hair flowing freely about her shoulders. "Now just why would that be?"

"Not to be rude or anything, but you're here for a reason, a reason other than getting to know me. I'm waiting for the other shoe to drop."

"A gal can't have multiple reasons, is that what you're implying?"

"I'm asking every way I know how. Why are you here? You delivered the...the properties. What further reason can there be?"

Riya put down her silverware, drained her wine glass, tossed back her head again causing her hair to fan out behind her. "I told you. To get to know you. The real you. We're business partners. I like to know what makes my partners tick. What's your favorite fun thing to do? We have all night."

"What's that supposed to mean? All night?"

"I'm to remain here with the merchandise until you take title. Deliver the money, and I'm gone. Until then let's have another drink and...and get to know each other. I asked you about your favorite pastime. So what is it?"

Being left alone is what I wanted to say. It was decision time and I was still debating. Stalling, I opened another bottle, filled our glasses for the third time, and said, "Spending time with my partner. That's my favorite pastime."

"Doing what?"

"Walking. Talking." In fact, this was the precise question I had asked myself several times over the past month. Only it was phrased as, *Jimmy, what do you want to do with the rest of your life?* I'm not certain I ever actually answered the question for myself. Some questions are all too easy to duck — and this is one of them.

"Any particular subjects you enjoy talking about?"

"Never really thought about it. How about you, Riya? Tell me about yourself. What's your favorite activity?"

"Neat way to change the topic. Okay, I'll go first. My second favorite activity," she winked, "is skiing. Actually, being active, doing physical activities. Play a little tennis, hike, that sort of thing."

My cell rang. It was Angella. I checked the time and noted it was eleven-fifteen, twelve-fifteen in Pittsburgh. I reached to answer and thought better of it. I couldn't rush her off the line and I couldn't talk to her with Riya sitting there. And Riya had already told me she wasn't leaving until I paid up. I hit the *go to message icon,* the first time I had ever done that to Angella.

When the phone rang a moment later, I let it ring. I had slid into the Kumar deal little bit by little bit until I was now in deep enough that it was more painful turning back than going forward. Not a good way to make a decision, I know, but yet I had allowed myself to be carried forward. That meant using money I considered mine because I had found it, but the law most likely considered it the banks because it had been stolen from them. It would be easy enough to get a legal opinion, but some things that appear easy from the outside are not so clear-cut from within. Forty million in cash is certainly in that category, at least for me.

Riya was sitting quietly, sipping her wine, waiting for my next move. "Where do we go from here?" I began, not wanting to affirmatively commit, yet aware I was already most of the way down the proverbial slippery slope and gaining speed. "I mean, the art pieces are sitting out there in the office. How are they to be authenticated?"

"Authentication is lined up. First thing in the morning, or we can call now if you wish, you will speak with a man I know you'll trust. Jack Silver. He had both pieces examined by experts just hours ago and they put special marks on the pieces. Hold your cell up to the pieces and everything will be verified. Simple as can be."

"I assume you have no intention of leaving the pieces in my company unattended until after payment is made?"

"Those are my orders, Jimmy. I don't suppose you would counsel me to disobey Sanjay?"

"You'd have to ask him, now wouldn't you?"

"Can't until morning, Jimmy. He has...shall we say...he has his life and I...I have mine."

THIRTY

rue to Riya's word, when I woke up in the morning I had a message from Silver to text him pictures of the *merchandise*. The time stamp on his message read six forty-eight. Without disturbing Riya, I unpacked the objects, snapped a dozen or so pictures of each object and sent them on to my boss.

It took Silver exactly three minutes to guarantee me both pieces now in my possession were genuine. In a separate text, Silver congratulated Angella and me on a nice piece of work, adding, Stratis had just removed the hotel room hold on his merchandise. Sanjay was upholding his end of the bargain that all I need do was come down to the island, and whether or not I went through with the transaction, he would complete the sale of the *Crown of Alexander* to Stratis' cutout Maxine Baker. That also meant the *Portrait of Adele Bloch-Bauer*, the one in the Neue Galerie insured by Great

Southern Insurance Company, was not under a cloud. Indeed, finding that the *Woman in Gold* wasn't going to be a huge financial hit to Great Southern, coupled with a big upside with the return of the *Pirate*, Silver had every reason to fly high. For myself, I had just taken pictures of art objects having a street value of over a hundred million. Anyway I sliced it there was a minimum of seventy million profit to be made.

I was at the bottom of the slope. Time to go get the money.

Easier thought about than accomplished. I called the South Texas Historian, Steve Hathcock, and asked him to arrange for a workboat and to be prepared to take a daylong trip up island. He had several locksmith jobs, but said he could postpone all but one. Nine-thirty was the time we would depart from Parrot Eyes.

I called Angella, but my call went directly to voice mail. I left a message telling her I had two art pieces and was going out on the bay for the day. "Call you when I get back, love you."

I then called my lawyer, Merry Ayres, and caught her in her office. She agreed to spend fifteen minutes with me if I came by immediately. I called goodbye to Riya who was now in the shower and pulled the door closed behind me. When the elevator didn't come, I let myself back into the apartment to persuade my houseguest to call down and unchain me.

"Hand me my phone, will you, Big Boy," she called through the bathroom door. "I'm indisposed."

I did as she instructed and opened the door a crack, handing her the phone with my eyes averted. "There, done, dear man," she called a moment later. "I don't know what your hurry is, but go if you must. Elevator's waiting. And so am I."

And so was Merry Ayers.

I decided to continue using Kumar's loan car and pulled into the law firm office six minutes later. Ayers, always an upbeat woman, pulled me close, hugged me, then said, "Sit. You look agitated. Tell me what's on your mind."

"Couple of copyright questions. Pertaining to art. I think you told me once you took a few courses in the subject."

"I was, in an earlier life, planning to be a copyright lawyer. That is, before I moved to the island. So, yes, fire away. But I have to confess, it's easy to stump me with copyright issues. If you manage that, I can always call my friend, Linda Merritt, up there in Dallas. She's with Fulbright & Jaworski. Actually, now that's Norton, Rose, Fulbright. She's the best there is."

"I don't think that'll be necessary, but I appreciate the offer. I'm just interested in background for now. Assume a fake artist copies a real piece of art. Say the Mona Lisa. Who does the fake piece belong to?"

"That's easy. The fake artist."

"Can the fake artist sell the fake art piece?"

"Yes." Then she added, "But let's be careful here. The fake must be labeled as a fake. Or the circumstances must be such that the buyer is aware it's a fake. For example, if I sold you the Mona Lisa for a hundred dollars, you're presumed to know it was a copy—a fake. But if I was a top art collector and sold you a Rembrandt for, say, thirty million, you would have every right to believe it was the real thing. But now we're talking about fraud and breach of trust and stuff like that. So it depends on the piece and on the circumstances. But generally speaking, I read not long ago that fakes can be worth a lot of money in and of themselves. Again, provided no fraud is involved. Did I answer your question?"

"You did, as far as it goes. Now what if I buy a piece of art believing it was genuine, and then turn around and sell it, still thinking it was genuine. But it turns out to be a fake?"

"And you did everything prudent to believe it was genuine?"

"Yes."

"I would happily defend you. And I see no reason I would lose the case."

"Is it possible to lose?"

"It's *always* possible to lose a case. It does happen. Hopefully, not all that often. But it does happen."

"How?"

"Facts are elusive critters. One person's fact is another person's wish. Different juries see things in different ways. Some judges see things different from other judges. That's why lawsuits are often crapshoots. Lawyers do their best to advise clients, but...but sometimes they're wrong."

"I have to say, from a client's perspective the law is frightening. How does a person ever know what to do?"

"Great question. First of all, I tell clients to do what feels right to them. Or to say it the other way around. If it doesn't feel right, don't do it."

"Good advice. My takeaway: As long as I honestly believe a piece of art is genuine then I can sell it as being genuine and not be worried about blowback."

"That's my advice, and I'm sticking with it."

Every question I asked raised another set of questions and I started to ask another one, but my phone rang. It was Hathcock, asking where I was. I checked my watch and realized I was already fifteen minutes late. "Be right there. Sorry. Got tied up. I have to stop for a few items so give me fifteen."

I turned to Ayers. "Thanks, counselor for making the time. Be in touch soon."

Parrot Eyes launch ramp is located next to Ted's restaurant on Padre Boulevard. I had planned to park in Ted's lot, but it was overflowing. That forced me to park across the street in the lot where

Island Fitness Center is located. I thought of Teran Hughes, the proprietor, and how he had patiently worked with me ten years ago when I was recovering from a gunshot wound.

Steve was waiting when I walked down the ramp. "I'm thinking of going alone today. You okay with that?" I asked after exchanging the customary greetings.

"Sure thing, Jimmy. Kinda anticipated that. Call when you get back, and I'll come pick up the boat. It's yours 'til this time tomorrow. An eight-pack of water and a fishing pole as you requested. I even put in two extra tanks of gas over there under the hatch cover. The shovels you asked for are under the seat. Go for it."

I pulled out my money and counted out several hundred dollars.

"What's all that for?" Steve asked. "It's not near that amount, and you can pay me later."

"It's not all for the ride." I motioned him close. "Buy a prepaid phone. Call this number." I handed him a piece of paper with Abby's number on it. "Be certain you're talking to Abby. Tell her the message is from her friend on SPI. No names. Tell her everything she heard about the value multiplier is true, except substitute *Kings Cup* for the *Adele*. Same actors. Time frame within days. Tell her I've gone fishing."

"That it?"

"That's it. Oh, keep the change, but after the call drown the phone and lose the paper."

"This isn't illegal is it? You know I'm not into..."

"Nothing I'm asking you to do is illegal. But you don't want the press breathing down your throat either. Abby already has the story. This is just confirmation."

I don't know if Steve bought my explanation, but he shrugged, wished me a good day and better fishing, then headed back to his truck.

Unless I miss my guess, the skiff he "borrowed" was once, and perhaps still is, used to carry passengers back and forth from the dock to the parasailing float anchored in the middle of Laguna Madre Bay. The boat had power to spare and a relatively flat bottom. Just what the doctor ordered.

I wasted no time firing up the twin-engine outboards, throwing off the docking lines and heading into the channel leading out to Laguna Madre Bay. From past experience this would be a bit over a three-hour trek up the bay with the wind at my back. Coming home it would take a bit longer, especially so because the boat would be heavily loaded. One of the items I picked up was a burner phone for my own use in case I needed it. I left my cell in the car. Too much was at stake, and too many people knew why I was heading up the bay. No need to make it any easier on them than need be.

THIRTY-ONE

When Jimmy didn't answer his phone, I became concerned. It was after midnight, at least here in Pittsburgh, but it had been a long day, and I was sure he was tired and had fallen asleep. But it wasn't like Jimmy to not wait up, or at least wake up when his phone sounded. But there was nothing I could do about it, so I climbed into bed and passed out from exhaustion, more emotional than physical, almost as soon as my head hit the pillow.

My cell went off somewhere around six in the morning, but it may have rung for a full minute before I realized what was making all that noise. When my mind cleared enough to reach for it, I hit the answer button without focusing on the screen name. "Oh," I blurted when the caller turned out to be Abby Johnson and not my lover. "It's you. I thought it was Jimmy calling."

"Sorry to disappoint you, Angella, but I thought you'd want to hear this. I just got a tip from someone down on the border, a guy who owes me big time."

"A tip?" I repeated, not at all certain how that involved me. "And you're telling me this because?"

"Because it appears to involve your partner."

"Something involves Jimmy? Is he okay? He wasn't hurt, was he?"

"No. Nothing like that. Look, Angella, tips don't always come signed, sealed and delivered. A bit from one, a bit from another, a smidgen from a third. Enough bits and the puzzle begins to clear. Right now I'm moving around a bunch of disconnected centerpieces. What I need are some edges. Better yet, a couple of corners to anchor this thing."

"What pieces do you have?" I pressed.

"Piece one: An agent known to have transacted deals for North Korea just crossed the border at Brownsville. Piece two: That agent listed his U.S. hotel as being the Riviera. Piece three: A recently arrived Israeli just began work at a tee-shirt shop on SPI. Piece four: Iranian chatter has mentioned the *Kings Cup* several times. Piece five: The *Cup* was delivered to Jimmy. Piece six: And this is a speculation piece, Jimmy is to be the intermediary between NK and Iran."

"Pardon me, Abby, but where do I come into this picture?"

"And piece seven: Your friend Carmella Schenley Hampton, so called docent curator at

Bayernhof, is a Treasury Department Investigator, actually, Assistant Director. I knew I had seen her somewhere before, long time ago. I finally put it together. She's underground, tracking fraudulent art transactions and money laundering for the IRS."

"I'm still lost. What do you want from me?"

"For starters, are there any pieces you're holding?"

"Nothing. I haven't spoken to Jimmy since he left yesterday morning. Wait, I take that back. We spoke for a brief moment last night, but when I called him back there was no answer."

"That might actually be a piece. If he has the art then he could be tied up. Listen, this may all add up to nothing. I've followed more than one mouse down a blind hole. And often in my trade the more the cheese smells, the bigger the trap you walk into. And the cheese smell on this story is at an all time high."

"But why Jimmy? And I asked you this yesterday, why isn't my name popping up with all your sources?"

"I know you don't want to hear this, Angella, but one of the major pieces is the rumor Jimmy has some forty-mill stashed away. That kind of cash buys a lot of art. Makes him a player."

"But that's a rumor! A bad one at that!"

"The lady doth protest too much, methinks. Another piece: Kumar is under IRS pressure and about to be indicted for money laundering.

Hampton can score a major victory if she can pressure Kumar into persuading Jimmy to expose where forty million is hidden. Kumar just might be working both sides of the street."

"Assuming Jimmy's hidden the money in the first place," I shot back, trying to hold back the horrible sinking feeling that was threatening to take me down.

"It all fits nicely, particularly if the IRS, or some other branch of our government, thinks of Jimmy as a bigger fish than Kumar. If that's so, then Kumar sets the trap for Jimmy in exchange for leniency from the IRS. It's done all the time."

"This is pure...pure speculation!" Then another horrible thought stuck. "You're not going to publish that rubbish about Jimmy! Tell me you're not!"

"Right now, Jimmy having the cash is specu-lation. I don't publish speculation. But be advised I'll publish whatever I deem worthy of publishing. Friend or no friend. That is, provided I got it on the record from a reliable source. Does my reputation no good to screw the story up until I have some form of confirmation Jimmy's name stays out of the story. That's why I need a few more corner pieces, so I can see the picture clearer."

Something Abby had said was bothering me and I hadn't been able to figure out what it was. Then it came to me. "What's the Israeli in the T-shirt shop have to do with anything?"

"Mossad. Lends credence to the Iran part of this story is all."

"How do you go about getting what you need?" I was playing for time, trying to understand what Jimmy's involvement was. But what I did know is that something was wrong, really wrong.

"That I never really know. But what always works best for me is to be as close to the action as I can get. That's why I'm leaving for South Texas at noon. I booked two seats on a private charter. I assumed you'd like to join me."

"I'd love to. But..." I had the three-thirty to midnight shift babysitting the *Adele*. Then something Abby said registered. "...but maybe I can swing it. Call you back in a bit."

First I called Jimmy, and my call went directly to voice mail. Most unusual for Jimmy, who never turns his phone off. Next I called Jack Silver. If Abby had been right that Jimmy had the *Kings Cup,* then there was a good chance the dominoes had fallen all the way back to Stratis, and the *Adele* would be released.

Silver's call went directly to voicemail as well. I sent him a text as a follow up.

I showered, went down for breakfast, but found that I was too agitated to eat anything. I sat nursing a cup of coffee and winding myself into an even tighter knot.

The more I thought of the situation surrounding my partner the sicker I felt. I knew I couldn't help Jimmy if I remained here in Pittsburgh, but my years of training refused to allow me to abandon my post. Something had to give.

Fly to SPI with Abby is the first step, that much I resolved. What I would do when I was on the island I hadn't yet worked out. But not going was no longer an option. I reached in my bag for my phone to call Silver and it literally rang in my hand.

Silver's name popped up on the screen. I resolved to leave Pittsburgh regardless of his instructions. *Jimmy comes before the job* I repeated over and over.

"Hi, Angella. Glad I caught you. Things are moving fast on my end. Got good news for you. The *Adele*'s been released to us. Pick it up in your old room, wrap it in a sheet so no one can see it and take it a few blocks to the Theo Gallery. It's all arranged. Hand it only to the owner, a woman named Therocy. In private, take a picture of her holding it—of course without the cover—and send me the picture."

"After that?"

"You've earned yourself some time off. Go enjoy."

"Thank you."

"No. Thank you. You and your partner do good work. Keep it up. If this plays out as it looks as though it will, I see a large bonus in your future. Be safe."

"Hi, Abby," I said a few minutes later. "That ride to SPI still open?"

"It is. Pick you up at your hotel, William Penn Place entrance, eleven-thirty. Plane's been confirmed for twelve-thirty departure. ETA is three-forty five CDT. Glad you can make it. I've ordered a Greek Salad for my lunch. That okay for you?"

"Can't think of anything better."

It felt good to be going home to my island— and to my partner. He'd been gone a day and it seemed a lifetime.

THIRTY-TWO

On my way north, after first traversing the wind surfers, and then skirting the kite boarders, I pushed the throttle to max. After twenty minutes flat out, I slowed, moved over toward the western shore, and doubled back on my track. No one was following, but to be on the safe side, I continued back south for six minutes, then stopped the engine entirely, broke out the fishing gear, and floated.

The solidly constructed boat sat almost motionless in the gentle wind-driven water. I had little chance of catching anything, not only because it was too late in the morning, but also because I had no bait. Several fish, however, taunted me by jumping clear out of the water and doing belly flops within feet of my line. I had to remind myself that I hardly ever did better even with bait on the hook. I thought back to a mission deep in the jungle when our squad was cutoff and hadn't eaten more than bugs and vegetation for several days.

One of the guys had passed out from hunger and we were taking turns transporting him. We were still three days from any point safe enough for extraction and two more went down. We barely had strength enough to walk, let alone carry someone else. That's when the squad leader, at first light, set off a grenade in a pond. Breakfast that morning was plentiful. We all made it home safely.

Satisfied no one was following, I hauled in the line, said goodbye to the jumpers and again set course north, keeping to the western shore. I was looking for drones, but with their recent improvement I wasn't positive I could distinguish a drone from a pelican. The saving factor was that pelicans usually flew in V-formation and in this area they typically flew low over the water. Today was no exception. While I had been "fishing", two pelican flocks had passed overhead, each behaving as expected as they made their way northward. Even as ingenious as our government is, I doubted seriously if a drone could have been secreted among either flock. But I suppose the possibility existed.

My real danger, however, came not from what I saw, but from what I couldn't see; namely, a high-flying plane—or a satellite. A satellite would be unlikely, as it only passes over an area periodically and can't be made to linger. But high-flying aircraft are another thing. Except, they would have to be scheduled and coordinated, and that could only be accomplished if someone in the government knew I was coming up this way and approximately when. That was a chance I had to take.

I knew Hathcock would never tip off the feds. And I couldn't imagine any reason Sanjay or Riya Kumar would want me arrested—especially not Riya. After all, it was Kumar's financial butt I was protecting. Why kill the golden goose? I couldn't think of anyone else who would know my timing.

I considered calling Angella on the burner, but thought better of it. She couldn't help, and because she was being monitored there was a high probability the call would be traced and my location exposed.

The burner phone wasn't sophisticated enough for navigation, so I had to navigate the old-fashioned way, by following a mental map. There are no markers indicating the burial location, so in order for me to recover my stash, I must first land on the bay side of the sand spit separating Laguna Madre Bay from the Gulf of Mexico. That landing must occur at a very particular location, itself not marked in any way. I find it by starting at Port Mansfield, which is on the western side of the bay and then doing on water what I later do on land, namely following a series of compass courses. The courses are made trickier on water by the ever-changing currents and wind, all of which must be adjusted for, the goal being to put the bow of the boat on shore within a few feet of a precise location.

Wind, tide, and current are only a few of the factors that must be gauged and corrected for. The shoreline where I would ultimately land is constantly changing as the sand shifts, erodes, and fills in. There is an old beached row boat, mostly decayed, not far north of where I need to land, but I had no way of knowing if it had moved or been totally destroyed.

I again thought of Angella and again wanted to call her. But speaking to Angella was a desire, not a necessity. Right now I had to deal only with necessities. I felt horrible, having never before not taken a call from her. But the circumstances had been entirely wrong at the time. How could I have explained Riya's presence in our apartment so late in the evening? Now I had the additional problem of explaining away her presence the remainder of the night. Thinking of bad endings, I was heading for one big time.

Lost in my thoughts, I passed up a timed direction change point. I realized my error three minutes beyond where I needed to make the course correction. *Jimmy, settle yourself!* I turned the boat a hundred eighty degrees and went back southwest for three minutes adjusting slightly for what I thought the current and wind conditions were. *Not smart, Jimmy, not smart at all.*

I reminded myself that precision was necessary—more than necessary, mandatory. After precisely three minutes, I turned onto the new course, set the timer for forty-eight minutes and promised myself no more mental Angella dialog. No more "what ifs" and '"shoulda beens". This is where my Army Ranger training was designed to kick in. It's all concentration on the mission from here on out.

But it was a lost cause. My mind returned to Angella, on our future, and on where we go from here, all overlaid with the fact that Riya was waiting for my return back at the apartment.

The timer sounded, I set the new course, reset the timer for eighteen minutes, checked the tide which now seemed to be non-existent. The wind, however, was a problem. It was gusty and sporadic. The bay was empty of boats north of Mansfield. That was a good fact. The bad fact was the shallow water and twisty nature of the course I was following.

I made the last course correction, set the timer for six minutes and hoped to hell that when the alarm sounded, the bow would be approaching a sandbar that jutted out into the bay several feet, a sandbar with a long-ago broken away buoy mostly buried near its point. If not, we would be turning for home—empty.

At the two-minute mark, I slowed the engine almost to a stop, allowing the boat to settle. Even with the sun high in the sky I had no sand bar in sight.

Thirty seconds to go, and a dark cloud blotted out the sun removing any chance of reading the bottom. "Now what?" I exclaimed, pulling the throttle all the way to the stop position. The heavy boat still made its way forward while I peered ahead, seeing land but no sand bar. Suddenly, the boat shuddered and came to full stop, throwing me forward against the coaming.

I had found the sand bar, only sand had collected on its south edge, widening what had been a point into more of a blob. There was no mistaking the location, even though I saw no sign of the wayward buoy.

I jumped out, bowline in hand, and manhandled the heavy craft as far onto the sand as I could. I buried the small anchor, retrieved the shovel and hand compass, and again checked the sky for drones—or birds— and saw neither.

So far, so good.

Using the shovel, I probed the area, trying to locate the buoy. It took several minutes before the shovel hit something. More digging uncovered the top of the buoy which had been buried less than a foot below the surface.

Now that I knew where I was, I was ready to begin the land navigation portion of my trek. The location I was heading for was not entirely random. At one time, this land had belonged to John Singer, brother of the founder of the Singer Sewing Machine Company. Singer had constructed several water wells, and I had appropriated one of those wells to my own needs.

Before taking the first step, I mentally reviewed the directions, making certain I remembered them all. Satisfied, I began to the first course.

Eighty-five degrees and ten steps.

At the tenth step I paused.

Ten degrees, fifteen steps.

That maneuver looped me around the edges of a buried boulder.

North four steps.

I studied the terrain and was satisfied everything appeared right. One last look to the sky and I gave myself permission to continue.

Thirty degrees, one hundred ten steps

This last direction had to be precise, both in compass heading and step size. I counted out loud, not trusting myself to get it right otherwise.

One hundred eight. One hundred nine. One hundred ten.

Stop! I'm here!

I stuck the shovel in the ground and again searched the sky. Texas Big Sky I called it. Deep blue and all-embracing. More sky than earth, or so it seemed. I saw nothing up there of concern — actually nothing but a few wispy high-level clouds. I gave myself permission to dig.

After several shovel loads I paused, concerned the sand wasn't packed as tight as it had been in the past. My first thought, somebody was recently here. But I saw no evidence of anything being disturbed. *Could the rain have made the sand behave this way?*

I doubted it could have, but with sand one never really knows. I again studied the terrain, this time more carefully, and again saw nothing leading me to believe anyone had been digging in this spot. No footprints, no sand piles, nothing disturbed. *The only way to know for certain whether someone has invaded my stash is to dig it up and see for myself.* So continue to dig I did.

I knew from past experience I'd be digging a minimum of an hour and a half, and possibly for as long as two hours. That's a lot of sand to remove, so I carefully carried the first shovel loads far enough away from the hole so that later I wouldn't have to step over and around large mounds.

As I worked, the area around the hole slowly grew taller with sand. It wasn't that I just had to go down twelve or so feet, but in order to get that deep I had to make the hole wide enough for me to walk down into it. That also meant creating a sloped side. At one point the perimeter sand was so high it seemed I was inside a bunker, pretty much like the bunker I had to dig out in order to rescue one of our downed pilots back in my Ranger days.

My shovel finally hit a metallic sounding object. Unless I was mistaken, this would be the first of the waterproof cases. There were nineteen more down here, each with two million. My plan was to remove fifteen and save five for a rainy day. Kind of like what my parents had taught me, but not exactly the kind of savings they had in mind.

I continued shoveling sand and extracting cases, carrying them one at a time up the ramp and piling them in stacks. When I finally had three stacks of five cases each I began shoveling sand back into the massive hole. That task was easy as compared to digging it out.

The good news when I checked the cases was that all of the seals were intact. The bad news, I had to now carry the cases, one at a time, back to the boat. When I had first brought these up here I had tried using a sand dolly. That had been a miserable failure, and the dolly was buried not far from where I now stood.

One by one, I trudged through the sand from the burial site to the workboat. No need to count steps or use the compass now because the sand retained my footprints. *Reminder to self: Cover your tracks when you finish.*

Happy with the loading job, I went back to the burial site to begin flattening it out. The job didn't have to be perfect, nor did all the sand need to fit in flat. One rain and all traces of activity would be gone. The hole now looked like a freshly covered grave with a large mound of sand above ground.

Satisfied, I began walking backwards toward the boat, sweeping the ground with the shovel as I went. In some places I got down on my hands and knees and used my palm to level the sand. In a couple of days there would be no evidence that anyone had even been here, but it was those couple of days that I was concerned about.

The closer I got to the boat, the more time I spent with my knees in the sand crawling backward being careful to erase all trace of my passage.

"Get up off that sand!" an authoritative voice commanded. "U. S. Marshal Service. Don't touch that shovel! Put your hands in the air! Keep your hands in plain sight and raise them over your head! Do it now!"

"What the—"

"Jimmy Redstone, you are under arrest for Possession of Stolen Property. Are you armed?"

Thank God I wasn't. "No."

"Have anything sharp on you?"

Other than my tongue? "No."

"Slowly lower your hands behind your back. You know the drill. No quick moves."

A slip tie went around my wrists and pulled tight, much tighter than necessary. But I knew not to complain. "Now slowly turn. Slow. No sudden moves."

I turned to face a federal marshal, a guy about five-nine. He pulled out a cred pack and flashed his badge. Not much different from the one I used to carry.

Four men were arrayed behind him, each with an assault weapon positioned across his chest. Had I been foolish enough to have made a sudden move I don't think there'd be enough of my DNA left to make a proper identification.

The bay behind them was littered with white attack parachutes, also not unlike the type I had been trained to use.

THIRTY-THREE

By the time we arrived at our SPI condo I was more confused than anything. Before leaving Pittsburgh, Abby had received a terse message, traced to a burner, purporting to come from Jimmy and confirming the North Korea and Iran deals. The gone fishing part had me very much concerned, particularly because Jimmy's never shown any propensity for fishing, except when he's troubled.

Abby and I not being allowed up in the elevator to my penthouse apartment at the Riviera sent me into a frenzy of activity, mostly directed at management. When they refused to budge, I tracked down an elusive Jack Silver, the real owner of the apartment, who had the clout to force the hotel owner into action.

In all, it took forty-five minutes before the two men stepped aside and allowed Abby and me to enter the elevator. They used a bypass key to send us up to the penthouse.

Jack had explained how the guards were there to protect the *Kings Cup* and the *Pirate*. "Don't be angry with them, Angella," Silver had said. "They're there to protect your investment. Be glad they are."

What Silver hadn't explained was why when I walked into my bedroom I found Riya Kumar sound asleep in my—and Jimmy's— bed, her clothes draped across a chair and her bra drying on a towel rack in the bathroom. From the crime scene evidence it was my immediate judgment she had been here a while—a long while. Which, in turn, explained why Jimmy hadn't answered his phone at midnight. Once again my stomach knotted—only this time the knot was not showing any sign of releasing any time soon.

"I can explain everything," Riya said, blinking herself awake. "It's only that—"

"Get out of my bed! You...you slut! I don't need explanations! I need you gone!"

"What's all this?" Abby asked, walking into the bedroom after hanging up with her editor. Looking around, she said, "It appears to me you're in the wrong bedroom, Mrs. Kumar. Angella may not want explanations, but I most certainly do."

"Who are you?" Riya asked, fear playing at the corners of her eyes. "This is between Ms. Martinez and myself. A business deal. A private business deal. Nothing more, I can assure you."

"I'm Abby Johnson, a reporter. And anything you do is indeed my business."

"I have nothing to say to reporters!" Riya pulled the covers up to her chin. "And don't you dare take any pictures! I'll sue you!"

"Mrs. Kumar, please let me remind you this is not your home. You have been found occupying a bed that does not belong to you. So any talk of suits or retaliation is foolish at best. So why don't you get yourself dressed and come out to the office? Come, Angella, let's allow your...your house guest privacy. We'll get to the bottom of this...this...situation."

It was a good twenty minutes before Riya made her appearance. If we had had a back door, I would have thought she had taken off. When she finally put in an appearance her makeup was done to perfection, not that she even needed any. Jealousy cut into me like a knife. I glared at her, trying, but failing, to contain my deep anger. "So what the hell's going on?" I demanded, "And what's that crate doing in here?"

"That crate contains the *Pirate* as well as the *Kings Cup*. They've both been authenticated and I'm here to—"

My cell sounded. "Hold that thought." It was Detective Lieutenant Carrie Malone of the SPI Police Department. "Hi Lieutenant," I said, forcing my voice to sound chipper, while at the same time glaring at Riya. "Haven't spoken to you in a while. How are—"

Abby's cell rung and she stepped across the room to answer it. A moment later she went out into the hallway for privacy.

Malone interrupted me, saying, "I have news for you that you aren't going to be happy with. I'm sorry."

"Oh, my God! Has something happened to Jimmy?"

"Yes. He's been —"

"Is he injured? Where is he?"

"Slow down a moment. Jimmy's physically okay. But I'm afraid he's been arrested. He's in federal custody. Being airlifted to Brownsville as we speak."

"Airlifted? From where? What's he...what's he charged with?"

"It says here Possession of Stolen Property. Feds applied for a search warrant of your apartment and so far it's not been granted. But it's highly unusual for a federal judge not to grant a warrant when an arrest has been made. I understand a hearing's set for when he arrives at the courthouse later today."

"Search warrant?" I repeated, struggling to get my bearings and failing miserably. "What the hell they looking for?" I followed Abby out into the hall. The less Riya heard the better.

"Standard stuff," Malone responded. "Evidence connecting Jimmy, or you, to the stolen property, which I assume is money, cash, from that Island bank robbery. Anything else they might find. Most likely they're going fishing."

That term again, going fishing. "If it's standard practice then why was it denied?"

"I'm not privy to that info. Can't venture a guess. Well, yes, actually I can. Someone got to the judge. She may know more than she's letting on. But, hey, what the hell do I know?"

It finally struck me that Malone was being all too friendly. She didn't have to tell me any of this. *Time to take command of the situation.* "I take it this call is more than a courtesy call. You want something."

"Both. Actually, it's what the feds want. To keep *you* under surveillance. Not to allow you to leave the island type of thing. Can't do that. You want to go, go. But I would appreciate it if you'd consent to come by and chat."

"You serious?"

"You ever know me to joke about police work? Bring your lawyer if you wish."

She was right, I never knew Malone to joke about anything, police work or non-police work. "How about I bring my reporter friend instead?"

"Reporter? That's a new one on me. No one brings a reporter to talk with the police. Now it's my turn to ask if you're serious?"

"You ever know me to joke about my freedom?"

"You have a point there. I sent Detective Cruz to your place to give you a ride over here. He's in your lobby. I'll let him know you and—"

"Abby Johnson from the Washington Post... formerly from the Post...now on her own."

"...and Abby Johnson formerly from the Washington Post will be down in, say, ten minutes."

"We'll only need five," I said, figuring the sooner I get to police headquarters the sooner I'll learn what's going on.

"I heard your side," Abby said when I hung up. "Here's what I know. Federal sting operation being run out of Pittsburgh. Kumar, Sanjay Kumar, don't know about that one in there, is working with the IRS on this. My sources tell me Jimmy took a boat north and dug up money buried in the sand. Money's in sealed boxes and they can't open the seals without a court order. Judge is being a stickler, wants probable cause to believe that whatever's in those boxes was obtained illegally. Certainly the boxes themselves are not stolen. She's ordered Jimmy, as well as the boxes he dug up, to be brought directly to her court the moment they land in Brownsville."

"So Jimmy should go free?"

"Not so fast. The feds just need to connect the dots a bit tighter, is all. Matter of time. This all fits with Jimmy saying he was going fishing. It also fits with what I told you about Carmella Schenley Hampton being an IRS undercover agent. Woman must have had facial work for me not to recognize her. This is one serious operation. My sources say Kumar sold out to the IRS to save his skin. Set the trap and Jimmy jumped in full body."

I called Lawyer Ayers and before I could tell her more than my name, she said, "Got it covered,

Angella. On my way over there as we speak. Say nothing to anyone."

"Did Jimmy call you?"

"He's not in Brownsville yet. Someone called on his behalf."

"Who?"

"Someone with a Middle Eastern accent. Didn't leave his name."

"Tell me where to meet you. I want to be there when you get info on Jimmy."

"Afraid that's not possible."

"Why?"

"He's been arrested for serious felonies. He'll be held separate from everyone until after they book him. I won't get much, if anything. And—"

"He's my partner! I have to—"

"Listen to me Angella. It wouldn't matter if...if you two were married. They'll get all the info from him they can long before you're allowed anywhere close to him. And—"

"What?"

"I wouldn't be a bit surprised to learn that you're also a suspect."

"I did nothing!"

"Doesn't matter what you actually did. What did you know? Feds love conspiracies, in case you haven't noticed? If you even knew where that money was hidden—or even if there was hidden money—they'll drag you in."

"I need to see him!" I pleaded. "You have to make that happen."

"That simply won't be possible. Sorry, Angella. Gotta go."

"But—"

The line went dead.

THIRTY-FOUR

I've been in the Reynaldo G. Garza and Filemon B. Vela Federal Court House in Brownsville many times, always walking in and out via the pink granite front entrance steps. Sometimes wearing a tie, sometimes just a pressed shirt and sports jacket. Even when I entered through the jail-side door I did so with my hands free and often holding the arms of a person, usually male, I had arrested for criminal activity. One thing for absolutely certain, I had never ever thought I'd be walking through these doors with my own hands shackled behind me, federal marshals clasping my elbows.

Waiting just inside the doorway was the last person in the word I expected to see. "Say nothing," Merry Ayers instructed, her voice now having a no-nonsense tone to it.

"But I—"

"Nothing! And I mean nothing!" She turned to the men guiding me. "I want to speak with my client—in private."

"Good luck with that, lady. Our orders are to deliver this weasel directly to the judge. No passing go. No passing nothing—and that means lawyers."

"Are those the boxes you found?" Ayers pointed to a dolly being pushed by a third marshal a few steps behind us. "You didn't go and disturb the seals on those boxes, did you?" I had never seen Ayers this serious and certainly never heard her speak with such force. "Not so much as a peek in those boxes, is that accurate?" she demanded.

The marshals continued walking without breaking stride. No one responded to Ayer's question.

I paused to make myself available to her, but the men at my elbows didn't, causing me to stumble forward.

"Be careful, Redstone, hate to have you injured when you're so close to your new home," the marshal on my right said. He was the one who had arrested me and who was obviously the senior person in charge.

"Hope you like orange, my man," the other marshal added, " 'cause that's your new color of choice. Better hope they put you in solitary, 'cause they don't treat former lawmen all too kindly inside."

They were goading me into lashing out. I had pulled that same stunt a time or two myself and was determined not to fall for it. We passed through several doors and then took the elevator up to the third floor. I looked for Ayers but she was nowhere to be seen.

Why it had taken me this long to focus on the big picture I don't know, but I hadn't. As I was propelled through the halls of justice, I realized that because of my arrest they were within their rights to apply for, and almost certainly receive, a search warrant for my apartment. That's when the gravity of the situation hit me. Sitting in a crate in the middle of the office were the *Kings Cup* and the *Pirate*. From their perspective, both art objects were stolen. The marshal might be more on target than he knew with his orange jumpsuit quip.

My only hope would be for Jack Silver to vouch for the art not being stolen, but that would be iffy at best. Perhaps he could do so with respect to the *Pirate,* since Great Southern had insured it, and he could claim I recovered it for him. But the *Kings Cup*? It had gone missing in the same bank robbery as had the forty million in cash, and not even Silver could create a plausible reason why it would be in my condo.

And Riya? She'd be found there as well. Angella would be long gone from my life before I could possibly explain to her what had happened — and why.

I looked up in time to read the sign on the courtroom door. Hon. Sofia Hinjosa. I've appeared in her court on several occasions. A tough-mind judge who brooked no crap from anyone. Being on the border, she sees everything life has to throw at a judge. The last time I was here it was me with *my* hand clamped around the arm of a truck driver. It was me hoping the creep would run so I could put a bullet through his brain. Not a proud thought, but the truth. The slime had been driving north from the Rio Grande when he had had engine trouble. He climbed out of the cab and proceeded north on foot leaving twelve people, including four toddlers and one infant, locked in the back. I was on stake-out duty when I caught a dispatcher on a joint frequency saying someone had just called in claiming to have heard pounding from the inside of a truck. The truck was less than a quarter mile from where I was positioned. The temperature was one hundred five when I cut the lock open. No one died, but they couldn't have survived another hour, the doctors had said.

The bench was empty and so was the courtroom, except for the bailiff who was standing by the door behind the bench, and the clerk who was sitting at a small table beside the bench. The court reporter's chair was empty.

Four men and three women appeared and took seats near the back of the small, as courts go, courtroom. A moment later the door behind the bench opened and in came a heavy-set man, mid fifties, wearing a dark suit, white shirt and dark tie. I assumed he was a federal attorney. Merry Ayers followed him through the door, which closed behind them.

The door opened again and a heavy-set woman in her forties came in and made her way to the recorder's desk. She fiddled with several devices and then nodded in the direction of the Court Clerk.

I was marched forward, through the partition that separated the front of the courtroom from the spectators and pushed down into a chair behind a table positioned slightly to the left of the centerline. The man in the suit stood behind a second table set slightly to the right of the centerline. He was quickly joined by two of the three women from the back of the courtroom, each carrying a load of file folders.

Ayers joined me at the table. "We're in the courtroom now," she barked to the marshals, you can please take you hands off my client. I promise he won't be running away."

They glared at her and looked toward the bailiff, who nodded. The marshals took two steps back. It wasn't so much that they were worried about what Ayers might do. The judge was their concern, and one negative word from the bailiff and she would lay into them.

"Here's the thing, Jimmy," Ayers said, her voice barely above a whisper, "they asked for a search warrant based on your arrest. But apparently the Federal Attorney couldn't articulate exactly what they were looking for. Actually, the cartons, cases I think they're calling them, they found, the ones you dug up, are sealed. That means they have only a guess at what's in them. You were smart enough to say nothing. From what I've been able to put together those cases do not belong to the bank that was robbed. And it's not illegal to dig things up on a beach—or to bury stuff for that matter, bizarre as it may seem. So until the feds can prove they caught you in possession of stolen property...actually let me correct that...they have to show you're in possession of the fruits of a federal crime — in this case stolen cash — she won't issue a search warrant for your residence."

"How're they going to do that?"

"My question exactly. In chambers, Jack — Jack Hendrix, the Federal Attorney — claimed the bills inside those cases are marked. He also claims they can trace the marked bills directly back to the bank heist. A stretch, but certainly possible."

"But they're sealed inside — "

"They've now asked for a search warrant to open the seals to let them search the cases. It's a close call, but that search warrant I believe Hinjosa will grant. I can think of several reasons why she'll allow those containers to be opened."

"What's the basis for allowing the cases to be opened?" I didn't think I had much hope of keeping the boxes sealed, but I wanted to explore the possibilities.

"Based on your bizarre behavior. People just don't bury boxes on sand-spits miles from civilization for the fun of it. Hinjosa is a tough cookie, but in the end she usually gets it right. Just keep your mouth shut. You got something to say, say it to me — in private. You on board with that?"

"They can't prove I buried them. Only that I dug them up," I told Ayers. "Can't be a crime to dig stuff up."

"I argued that in chambers. Judge is thinking about it."

"All rise," the man standing by the back door called.

The judge, a slender woman, no more than five three, swept into the courtroom before anyone could move and instantly motioned for everyone to remain seated. "All right, what have we here?" she called before she was even seated. "Ah, yes. The matter of a search warrant for searching the premises of a Mr. Jimmy Redstone." She looked directly at me. "If I recall right, Mr. Redstone, you have appeared in this court several times, always at the left table. Do I have that correct?"

"Yes, Your Honor," I said, expecting Ayers to kick me under the table.

"One of those times was that horrendous abandoned truck. You saved several lives that day. So what happened to you...oh, well, never mind that for now."

"It wasn't just me that saved those folks, Your Honor. But thanks for remembering." Now Ayers did kick me.

"How could anyone ever forget? Unfortunately, that hasn't been the only abandoned truck in South Texas. And unfortunately, many of the others were not so lucky." Hinjosa studied me a long moment, her lips clenched as if getting ready to scold me as a teacher might do. "And now, Mr. Redstone, you are back here in cuffs. Gone off the..." She paused, opened a file folder lying on the desk in front of her. "Let's see what we have. Attorney Hendrix I believe you filed the request for the search warrant, so please tell us what you want and why. Wait. I see this is for two warrants. One for Mr. Redstone's residence and one for those cartons over there. I suppose it's logical to begin with the cartons. So let's do that one first. The floor is yours, sir."

"Thank you, Your Honor. On..." Hendrix studied his notes. "...on, or about September 15, 2015 the First View bank on South Padre Island, Texas, was robbed of forty million dollars in cash. There is evidence that one Jimmy Redstone now has that money."

Hinjosa leaned forward. "And what evidence is that, may I ask? I mean, what evidence is there that Mr. Redstone has the stolen money? Are you claiming he's the bank robber?" She consulted her notes. "I don't see that allegation in here."

Hendrix again studied the papers on his table. "No evidence of bank robbery. At least not yet there isn't. Someone unknown at this present time removed the forty million from the bank and placed it all in an armored vehicle that had earlier been hijacked. The vehicle then drove across the causeway, which as you know, is the only motor vehicular method off the island. The police blocked both ends of the causeway, effectively trapping the armored truck on the bridge portion running over Laguna Madre Bay. The thieves lowered the money over the side of the bridge and down onto a barge or a boat of some sort. The boat got away. Days later Redstone over there found the boat and/ or the money and appropriated it to his own use."

"And just how do you know that last fact?"

"Everyone in the county knows that fact."

"I dare say, I live in the county and I don't know anything of the sort. Do you have an eye witness of Redstone dredging up the money—or even dredging up the boat?"

"No, Your Honor."

"Do you have an eye witness of Redstone carrying the money off? Or perhaps carrying off cartons or boxes containing the money?"

"No, Your Honor."

"Then exactly what do you have?"

"What we have is...is..." Hendrix looked down, then said, "classified."

"Classified! How the devil can the fruits of a bank robbery be classified?"

"They are classified is all I can tell you at this time, Your Honor."

"I see containers over there. Boxes. Is the money Redstone allegedly made off with in those... those containers?"

"We have every reason to believe it is, Your Honor."

"But you're not positive?"

"That's a correct understanding. Yes."

"Mr. Redstone," the judge said, "I'm not yet prepared to order you to do so, but would you be so kind as to open those boxes for us and save us a lot of time here? If there is a misunderstanding we can clear it up fast. Please would you show us what's in there?"

Ayers was on her feet. "Your Honor, if you will. First off, the boxes are sealed. Second, there's no evidence, no evidence whatsoever, as to whom those boxes belong to. Or who put them in the sand up there on the island. I will stipulate that my client did, in fact, dig those boxes up out of that sand. So whatever—"

"Attorney Ayers, you must admit that burying what appears to be waterproof containers, *sealed* waterproof containers, far up a beach in a remote area, is...is, shall I say, suspicious behavior at best?"

"First, let me again stipulate that we are not admitting that Mr. Redstone buried those boxes. That is a fact to be proven at a later date. As I said, we will stipulate to the fact that my client dug those boxes up today. Suspicious perhaps. A bit strange, perhaps. But, but not in any manner illegal...well, not on its face illegal, in any event."

"Granted. You do have a point. Continue Attorney Hendrix. Please explain the legal basis as to why I should order those boxes unsealed."

"Redstone was seen in the vicinity of the missing money back when it had first gone missing.

The volume inside those containers matches the volume of the missing cash."

Hinjosa leaned forward. "What do you mean Redstone was seen in the vicinity of the missing money? Who saw him? Where was he? Where was the money? Why didn't whoever see him stop him from taking the money? This is a rather large set of containers, he didn't exactly grab them and run down an alley."

Hendrix looked as if he had been kicked in the gut. He leaned over to consult with the women who were with him at his table. Every time he straightened up I thought the conversation was about to end. But he leaned forward to ask another question. And another.

"Counselor," Hinjosa finally said, tired of sitting idle. "You're either prepared to answer the question or you're not. Which is it?"

"Your Honor, I misspoke. Please excuse me. It is believed the money, all forty million of it, was transferred to these containers by the folks who took it from the bank. It was—"

"What do you mean, it is believed? By whom? Based on what? Mr. Hendrix, I need for you to move this along."

One of the women handed Hendrix a slip of paper. He studied it a moment, then said, "Satellite photos show containers having this same appearance being lowered into the bay, Laguna Madre Bay, the morning of the heist. These containers were removed from the robbery getaway truck and from all accounts appear to be the same as we have here in front of us."

"Okay, we have containers in the bay. We don't know what actually is in those containers, now do we?"

Hendrix turned to face his associates who now sat with their eyes averted. "I don't believe we do, no, Your Honor. But there is no other place for the money to have been off-loaded from the getaway truck. The truck did not have the forty million dollars when it was searched. I think it's a fair inference that the containers held the stolen money. And...and we do have—"

"Go on, Attorney Hendrix. You've dug this deep, the shovel's in your hands."

"As I was saying, the containers were lowered from the location on the bridge where the stolen truck...no, I mean the truck containing the stolen money...was parked. We can also put into evidence the serial numbers of the bills that were stolen and then simply open the containers and see for ourselves what we have. After all, this is only a probable cause hearing. We know a crime has been committed and we know the evidence of that crime is the same size as we found in Mr. Redstone's sand hiding place. And his counsel has admitted that the hiding place is suspicious. Suspicions activity can give rise to probable cause."

"Your Honor," Ayers said, "I specifically did not admit that the hole in which the containers were found was dug in any manner by my client."

"Sustained. Move on, Attorney Hendrix. Frankly, you're wearing my patience thin. It's late. Well past cocktail hour, I should note. Get a move on."

"I'm prepared to call the bank Vice-President, Mr. Randolf Escowon, to testify as to the serial numbers of the stolen property."

"You're on shaky ground here, but go ahead, but make it fast."

I watched as the little man with the big curled mustache carefully made his way to the front from the very back row. My last memory of him was when he was annunciating a thousand reasons why I couldn't deposit forty million dollars that belonged to the federal government into an account owned by the feds. My memory is that by the end of the day, and the seemingly thousands of forms he had produced for me to fill out, I was ready to shoot the little twerp.

He held up his right hand and swore that the testimony he was about to give was the truth, the full truth and nothing but the truth. To prove the point, I expected him to produce a handful of government forms for the judge to sign.

"Mr. Escowon," Hendrix began, "please tell this Court what your position was on September the fifteen of 2015."

"Do you mean my title or where I was positioned in the bank?"

"Your title, sir. Your title."

The little guy stretched to his full five-foot height. "Vice President."

"Now tell the Court where you were positioned on that day?"

"You mean on the fifteenth of September?"

"Yes on the fifteenth, sir."

"Of 2015?"

Hendrix glanced at the judge expecting to be rebuked, but she held silent. "That's the date, yes."

"At my desk in the lobby where I am every day. That is, every day I am on duty. Not on weekends or my days off."

"And what out of the ordinary happened on that day, sir?"

"Do you mean before the robbery or after the robbery?"

"Did anything out of the ordinary happen before the robbery?"

"Well yes. If you call three new accounts out of the ordinary. We don't usually get that many new—"

"Mr. Escowon," Judge Hinjosa said, "We are not here today to discuss the financial health of your bank. Was there or was there not a robbery?"

"Yes. Horrible it was, too. Men with guns! And masks. Lot of noise! People down on the ground! I still have bad dreams."

"How much money was stolen from your bank

that day?" Hinjosa asked, clearly taking over for the prosecutor.

"You mean by the robbers?"

"Is there anyone else who stole money that day?" the judge asked, clearly holding back her temper.

"I've not checked the bank records, so I—"

"Mr. Escowon!" Hinjosa exclaimed, finally having lost it. "Focus on the robbery! The one with the guns and masks. How much money was taken?"

"Forty million dollars, Judge."

"Please look at those containers over there."

"The water-stained looking ones?"

"Yes, the water-stained ones. Use your best guess, would the money stolen that day, the money placed in the armored truck, fit in those containers?"

Escowon studied the containers. Fiddled with his mustache and studied the containers again. "I'm not certain. I don't think you can get forty million dollars in those containers. I was under my desk, so I didn't get a really clear look at the money on the truck, but I think there was more money than that. We don't ever have forty million dollars at the bank, so I can't be positive."

"Okay, Mr. Escowon, use your best guess. Yes or no. Will the money stolen that day from your bank fit in those containers? Remember, yes or no."

"No. But maybe yes. I can't be certain."

"Let's move on. Do you happen to have the serial numbers of the bills that were stolen from your bank that day?"

"During the robbery?"

"Of course, during the robbery."

He reached inside his coat and produced a sheet of paper. "Here, I wrote out the numbers. It's a really long list, but I have it."

"Bailiff, will you please bring that list to me." Hinjosa turned to the witness. "Mr. Escowon you are excused. Please don't leave the courtroom, we may require your services later."

"What services?"

"Testimony."

"Does that mean I can go back to my seat now?"

"That's what it means," Attorney Hendrix said out of the corner of his mouth. "By all means, go back to your seat.

THIRTY-FIVE

Abby had received a call from an informant at the Brownsville Court House telling her Jimmy was a half-hour out and suggesting that she get over there as fast as she could. The stringer sensed a big story and wanted to ride Abby's coattails.

Abby, who had cultivated a nose for breaking news, turned to me and said, "Apparently, Jimmy's been caught with his hand in the cookie jar big time. That means he went to dig up money, big money and—"

"Jimmy doesn't have—"

"Angella," Abby said, tossing her head over her shoulder in the direction of the bedroom, "one never really knows what his or her mate has or doesn't have, or for that matter, does or doesn't do. Right now I'm putting my money on Jimmy having money stashed up north as the rumors suggest. Jimmy's relayed message to me earlier this morning essentially confirmed as much. That money is key to those two art objects in that crate over there. Listen Angella, I'm sorry but I'm going with the story. Jimmy's in the middle of a North Korea/Iran deal. Come with me or stay here. Your choice, but plan to be in that courtroom when Jimmy gets there."

With Jimmy's...paramour?...mistress?...just what to call her?...in my bedroom there's nothing to stay here for. "If I stayed here there's a good chance a homicide charge'll be filed against yours truly. I'm going with."

On the way down in the elevator, I reviewed my options as to what I could and should do depending upon how insistent Detective Cruz was about my going with him to police headquarters.

I voiced my concern to Abby, who responded forecefully, "By what authority can he possibly stop you from going where you want?" she demanded to know. "Unless he arrests you, you're a free woman. Puts his hands on either of us, I'll have his butt run off the force!"

"What about the guard Kumar hired?"

"Let him try to detain us," Abby said, digging through her purse and extracting a small can of pepper spray. "Let the bugger try."

Imagine my surprise when neither the guard nor Detective Cruz was anywhere in sight, having been replaced by none other than Levi Ben-Yuval.

"Come with me, Angella," Ben-Yuval commanded, "we must talk. Time is of the essence."

I turned to Abby, who was busy putting the spray can back in her bag and not doing a particularly good job of it. "Abigail Johnson this is Levi Ben—"

"Levi and I are well known to each other, Angella. You're looking well, Levi. Life must be treating you well."

"Getting along, thanks. You won't need that spray pepper. Kumar's guy is long gone. Won't be back. At least not until his arm mends."

"We're on our way out, gotta hurry," Abby replied, barely stopping long enough to acknowledge Levi. Story's waiting." Turning to me, she demanded, "Coming or not?"

"Angella and I have business upstairs," Ben-Yuval interrupted, pushing me back into the elevator. "Catch up with you later, Abby." Levi hit the PH button before I could manage a protest. "As I said, time is of the utmost importance, as you will see."

I started to respond, and he clamped his hand over my lips as a warning to be careful what I said. If it had been anyone other than Levi, I would have decked him. But he was one of the top agents in the world—and top agents don't easily get decked, no matter how good you are, or think you are. So I just bristled and held my tongue.

As if to soften the blow, Levi said, "We'll speak inside. I believe you say it here as we do. The walls have ears."

Indeed they do. Indeed they do. We remained silent until the Great Southern door to the hallway closed behind us. Actually the manner in which Jack Silver had constructed our space works out well. The entire top floor of the hotel is leased by the insurance company. So when someone steps off the elevator on the PH floor they end up in a hallway with only one door in it. That door opens into the Great Southern office. To get to our actual private space you must first pass through the office and then through a locked door in the far corner.

Levi casually remarked, "I assume Riya remains in the apartment."

It was all I could do to keep my calm. Unclenching my teeth I responded, "She sure as hell is! And just how would you know about *that* woman?"

Ignoring my outburst, he commented, "I see the packing material, but I don't see the actual pieces. Is there any place the *Pirate* or the *Kings Cup* could be stored out here in the office? I assume your private quarters are through one of those doors?"

"Only in the office bath," I said, pulling open the door. The small bath was empty, and I said so. "The rest of the space out here contains file drawers. The storage closet's full of supplies."

"Get Kumar out here. I assume she's made herself at home in your private suite. Won't be the first time, nor the last if I know her."

Stomach knots again.

I flung the door to the bedroom open mentally loaded for bear. Before I could say anything, Riya announced, "I'm going. I'm going! Sanjay says the deal's been completed. You now own the merchandise. Give me just a moment to gather my things, and I'll be on my way."

Not before I break your neck.

The bed remained unmade, but the skimpy nightshirt she had been wearing a few minutes earlier had been replaced with proper daytime clothes. Reluctantly, I had to admit the woman was hands down gorgeous. That didn't modulate the pain I felt over Jimmy's behavior. In fact, it made it worse—if that was even possible.

In all the time Jimmy and I had been partners I don't recall an instance where I wouldn't have given my own life to protect him. And I was certain the same thing was true in reverse. But watching this...this woman...parade around our private space, the space we were so happy in, did more damage than a nine-millimeter slug. "Enough already!" I shouted. "Take what you have and get out of here!"

"Sorry you feel this way, Angella, I don't think you understand."

"I understand all I need to understand! Get out before I—"

"I'm going, but you're making a large mistake. I delivered two very valuable art pieces to you. Thirty million is a steal. You're about to flip them for a hundred or more. Seventy million in the bank and you're...you're squabbling over...over what?"

"Get out of my bedroom before you won't be going anywhere!"

"Remind me to never do business with you again," Riya said when she was safely past me into the office. "I'd say it was a pleasure, but that, my dear, would be only half the truth." She continued through the office paying no attention to Ben-Yuval, who was sitting in a swivel chair as if waiting for the person missing from the desk in front of him to return and continue an interview.

Riya went into the hallway, and I watched as she stepped into the elevator and the door slid closed behind her. I was silently hoping for a malfunction where the entire thing lost its brakes and fell to the basement.

Now that would be karma.

No such luck.

The printer sprung to life when I turned back to face Ben-Yuval. I pulled the first page out of the tray.

ABBY'S WORLD.

The art world has always had its characters. From thieves to collectors, from museums to scholars, often scratch a bit too deeply and clandestine activities float to the surface. So it is not at all surprising that we now find a convenient cross-section of camaraderie developing between the art world and international organizations that find a need to move money around the globe—often in pursuit of terrorist activities.

Enter Jimmy Redstone, a former Texas Ranger and Department of Homeland Security Agent who was arrested today for having in his possession containers said to contain forty million dollars in cash. The cash is reported to have come from a bank heist several years back that Mr. Redstone investigated. The money was never recovered and rumors have persisted that Redstone had buried the money on North Padre Island.

Two pieces of valuable art, one known as the *Kings Cup* and the other as the *Pirate*, were observed in Mr. Redstone's South Padre penthouse condominium. These two works of art have one thing in common; they both disappeared under suspicious circumstances and they both had been investigated by Mr. Jimmy Redstone without apparent success.

Speculation is that Mr. Redstone hired a boat to travel north from the city to his secret hiding place where he had buried the treasure. Unbeknownst to him, the U. S. Treasury Department was tracking Mr. Redstone with highflying aircraft of the type employed on our Southern Border to detect and interdict illegal drug traffic.

At approximately two-sixteen this afternoon Federal Marshals parachuting from a Coast Guard plane arrested Mr. Redstone just after he had dug up waterproof money cases and was in the process of loading the cases onto his boat. Presumably, the cash was to be used in exchange for the art objects already in his possession. Mr. Redstone is being arraigned in Brownville

I reached down for the next page but the machine had jammed. "I thought everything I had said was off the record," I stormed. Was there no trust remaining in anyone? "I thought we had—"

"I don't see anything in here she used from you, Angella," Ben-Yuval commented after studying the article. "This all came from personal observation and informants. But knowing her as I do I wouldn't put anything past her. She's been known to bug places. For grins, let's do a quick scan."

Ben-Yuval pulled a small canvas pouch from his jacket, slipped a cigar-sized device from it, flipped a switch, and proceeded to walk around the office.

Within two steps a little red light began to flash. Another step and a second light flashed in synchronization with the first. He reached under the sofa cushion and extracted a bottle cap sized device. He pressed the sides together and set the device down.

"It's off for now. Actually, I was hoping she would have planted that device."

"Why's that?"

"You'll see later. Need to finish the scan." Ben-Yuval then walked around the entire office, including the bathroom, closet, and drawers and found nothing more. He then went into our quarters and motioned for me to follow, his finger across his lips. The device flashed red directly under the fan, but everywhere else it remained dark. "Great," Ben-Yuval announced. "All's clear on the spy surveillance front. And good news, the *Pirate* and the *Cup* are safe and sound in your closet."

"So no bugs?"

"Not that my scanner has picked up. But take a

quick look around. See if anything is out of order. Even the best of them leave a trail."

I opened drawers, looked under the bed and dresser and was about to announce the 'all clear' when I spotted a foreign object on a shelf where Jimmy's Berretta usually resides when he's home. "What's that...thing? Over there on the shelf. I don't recognize it."

Ben-Yuval had his back to the shelf and spun around as if the object would bite him if he didn't take action. "Which object? The lock?"

"What lock? Jimmy doesn't have a lock."

"This is one really bad ass lock. Need a plasma cutter to get it off anything without a key."

"Lock?" I repeated. "Let me see it."

Ben-Yuval handed the monster lock to me and it wasn't until I saw the words, written with my red nail polish, 'Angella & Jimmy' with the word 'FOREVER' centered below, that it finally came to me. "Oh," I exclaimed, "that's Jimmy's."

Ben-Yuval smiled. "Seems he was planning a little...little surprise."

"It's not what you think!" I felt blood rushing to my face.

"What do I think?"

"Never mind. You men are all the same." I turned away and proceeded back to the office. When Ben-Yuval joined me, I asked, "What about the one in the fan? Isn't that a problem?"

"No worries. Friendly. Go take it down if you wish."

When I returned with the device, again no larger than a bottle cap, I said, "What do you mean, friendly? Just how can something that invades my privacy be friendly? You...you've lost your sense of decency, morals—assuming you ever had them in the first place."

"Don't go getting on your high—how do you say, horse?—until you've walked in my shoes young lady. Just suck it up. We have work to do. Jimmy, and I suppose that means you as well, are now in proud possession—I don't know how proud you are, but you're certainly in unmistakable possession—of two valuable art objects. I believe it will turn out that the *Pirate* belongs to Great Southern. If that proves accurate, then if Silver does what he's done in the past, he'll sell the *Pirate* for a fair price, deduct all the costs Great Southern has incurred over the years, and then he'll split the difference with you. Usually he splits fifty/fifty, but even if it's some other ratio you'll make a nice buck on the transaction."

"Need all of it for lawyers for Jimmy," I responded, still concerned for my partner, whether out of habit or because of love for him was not something I was yet ready to decide.

"Hold that thought. Now for the complicated piece of this."

"As if this all is not complicated enough."

"Maybe not so much complicated as intricate—and very dangerous."

"I can't wait," I said, more sarcasm than brains. "If you say it's dangerous you have my attention."

Ben-Yuval walked over to the sofa and activated the device, making certain I saw what he was doing. He nodded to me and began. "You, Angella and Jimmy, if we spring him in time, are flying to North Korea to—"

"I'm not going anywhere near—"

"Hear me out, Angella. Hear me out. This is vital to my country. We have one shot at this and it better be a good one. Iran has made a deal with Kim Jung-un to deliver enough enriched uranium to allow Iran to wipe out Israel once and for all. They believe they have a way to do it without forever contaminating the desert. Our scientists doubt that claim, but once they drop the bomb on us, it makes no difference to us if they're wrong about the contamination. We're gone. To them, it's a big oops. They have such little regard for life that they most likely don't care. Anyway, the uranium has been produced in NK and Supreme Leader Kim Jong-un's just waiting for the opportunity to deliver it."

"What's holding him up?" I asked, frantically trying to figure out where I come into this. I was also trying to understand if this was for real, or if Ben-Yuval was only playing to the hidden mic.

"Who the hell ever knows what Jong-un's up to? He's playing off Trump, who, by the way, knows full well what the bastard's up to. Jong-un'd launch a nuke into Hawaii, but he knows—or at least believes—Trump will annihilate his country and half of South Korea if he does so."

"I hate to ask. What's your plan?"

"Beyond a plan, I'm afraid. Somehow, and we don't know how, why, or when, Jong-un became enamored with art. The embargo prevents him from buying or selling, but, and this is quite classified, we managed to spike his interest in the *Kings Cup*. Don't ask how, just that we did. He had demanded that it be presented to him by, and get this, an American."

"Is this for his home image?" I asked, struggling to play my part.

"Exactly. But it also works well for his international image. So here's where we are. An American will deliver the *Kings Cup* to him in a state ceremony. He wanted Trump, but that was quickly off the table. He went through a list of government officials, Secretary of State, etc. All nixed. What was tossed out for his consideration is a former government official."

"You mean—"

"Jimmy was tagged."

"I didn't know our government disliked Jimmy that much!"

"I'll let that slide. But that was on the table until...until our Treasury Department got a bug up its arse to nail Jimmy. Totally unrelated, but about to screw up a major operation. Nothing any of us, Tiny included, could do to call those SOBs off. Apparently, they messed up their budget and need to bring in big stuff fast. Forty million qualifies as big stuff. They moved so fast that even the local federal attorney, guy named Hendrix, got blindsided."

"So why not just stop it?"

"Ever since they pulled that crap in Chicago, once the public latches on it just gets worse if they try to stop it. Witness this." Ben-Yuval held up Abby's World. "No privacy anymore. In fact, the Internet drives the news cycles. Life's backwards, but, hey, can't do anything about it."

"Go on. I'm sure I've not heard the plan."

"Jimmy presents the *Cup* and...here's what's bizarre, Jong-un insists that he present Jimmy with currency, they're haggling over which currency as we speak, thirty million."

"What's that about?"

"Kim Jung-un wants to show the world he can do commerce without Trump."

"They have no money!"

"Precisely. But here's the nutty thing. He buys the *Cup* for, let's assume thirty million. A day later he turns around and sells it to the Iranians for two hundred million."

That's what Abby said was going to happen. "And the Iranians will pay that much?"

"They very much will because—"

"Because the uranium comes with the cup! And the U. S. has agreed to the art transfer?" I said, suddenly understanding exactly what was going down.

"In agreement for Jong-un announcing he is dismantling his nuke sites."

"How will the uranium be transferred? Can't imagine Trump allowing that to occur."

"Inside the *Cup*," Ben-Yuval said matter-of-factly, as if this happened every day of the year. "I can't say any more about the actual transfer than that. But trust me, it will occur."

Ben-Yuval reached over and turned the listening device off. He had set Abby up to publish the story he—and possibly Tiny—wanted published all along. *What could possibly go wrong?*

THIRTY-SIX

Ben-Yuval threw the device I had taken down from the fan into his pocket along with his bug scanner. "Now for the real operation," he said with a smile.

"That wasn't real? And do I assume that the fan bug was your doing?"

"You may if you wish."

"Do I assume also that you know Riya from... from past...shall we say...operations?"

"You know I can't discuss personnel."

"I'm not going to get shit out of you, so what about the operation?"

"Assuming your friend Abby takes the bait and publishes her information about the artwork going to Korea. She's now had all the corroboration she needs. In the old days, papers were published at fixed times, so planted stories, any stories had to wait. Now the news cycle is twenty-four/seven, and with a touch of the button Abby's story will be worldwide. U. S. eyes, and all foreign eyes will be focused like lasers on Iran. That provides an opportunity for us—Israel—to kidnap some of the remaining war criminals while your government is otherwise distracted."

"What the hell does Korea, Iran—"

"Patience, patience. First, let's fetch the art that Riya brought. As I said, it's in your master closet."

Sure enough the *Kings Cup* was sitting on the floor beside the bronze *Pirate*. What I hadn't realized was that the *Pirate* stood over five feet tall and was exquisitely crafted to look very much real. The detailing of the muscles of the body, the facial scaring, and the blood red rubies in the eyes made the *Pirate* mesmerizing—and alive.

Ben-Yuval instructed, "You take the *Cup.* I have the *Pirate*. We'll put these pieces out in the office on the desk."

When that task was completed, he said, "Okay, now for the Bucksbaum."

"What are you talking about?" I replied, knowing the *Bucksbaum* was safely secured in the *gallery* on Louisa Street in Pittsburgh. Two guards positioned across the street for good measure.

"This," Ben-Yuval announced, after rifling through several desk drawers and then holding up a picture identical to the one I had last seen at Hampton's gallery in Pittsburgh. The smile broadened across his face, as he said, "This is our little snooker of the Treasury Department. Treasury, in its zeal to prosecute Jimmy, planted the *Bucksbaum* here earlier today just after Jimmy headed north to get the money."

I thought about what Levi had just said and it made no sense—and I said so.

"Leaks go two ways. They, the IRS, set up Jimmy through Kumar. But they had no real way to know that Kumar could produce either the *Pirate* or the *Cup*. There's so much smoke and mirrors and deception in the art world that they trap themselves coming and going. Witness that little stunt by Stratis to get the piece he wanted, the *Crown of Alexander*, away from Kumar. That put enough pressure on Silver to force it to happen, one way or another."

"But why Jimmy?"

"Forty million is big money. But think of it, it's a sexy story as well. Hidden treasure, sexy woman seduces tough former agent. Think about it. What more can you want?"

I *was* thinking about it and getting sicker by the minute.

"The way I see the IRS in this is they need to divert attention away from something internal. At first I thought it was budget overruns, but maybe it's more than that. Don't know. Jimmy falls into their sights. Maybe through Santiago, maybe via someone else. It's not important. What is important is that they want to focus massive attention on Jimmy. They feed Abby stories. They get Kumar, who's in tax trouble, to suck Jimmy in, set the bait as it were. I think Stratis was also in on this with his fake *Adele*. Jimmy digs the money up, they swoop in and grab him. They get a search warrant and bingo, they find the *stolen Bucksbaum*, which they planted for extra measure. Jimmy becomes the center of attention and they divert away from whatever else is going on."

"Is that what the Korea story is all about? A diversion? Or did you make it all up?"

"Made up a bit of it. But no, that story *is* making the rounds. We just lent a little shove. Could be your so-called Deep State. But whatever or whoever it is, they're good. Maybe the Russians causing mischief."

"Your plan now?"

"Treasury will come back for the *Bucksbaum*, one way or another. Either they'll come under a warrant, or they'll come without a warrant. But make no mistake, they want this piece back. The last thing in the world they want is for it to fall into our hands."

"Why is that?"

"This *Bucksbaum* contains the identities of many of the worst Nazis, the ones who committed major war crimes. Israel wants these people captured and tried. The U. S. and many other countries are blocking the capture. Israel has exhausted its ability to find out the identities these Nazis have taken. That's why the *Bucksbaum*, the *Master Bucksbaum*, has been hidden all these years. It contains, in code, those new names. Israel's been working hard to find where it was hidden. Seems your government had it all along."

"You planning on taking the *Bucksbaum* to Israel?"

"Left to my own devices, I would. But my government says no. It is not in Israel's best interest to get cross-wise with your country. My instructions are to decipher it and leave it here."

"How are you going to read it? We saw the dot patterns at the Holocaust Center in Pittsburgh. Is that what—"

"I expect the reader any minute now. Had to fly the expert in from out of the country, and even with your very porous borders there were a few... how shall I say, hitches?"

Something was wrong with this picture but I couldn't place what it was. "You have a Plan B if the reader doesn't make it?" I asked, filling the uncomfortable silence.

Ben-Yuval checked his phone before saying, "Crossed the border forty minutes ago. There's a Space-X closing down there which could have caused an issue, but I haven't heard anything negative." He now checked his watch. "Time's tight. Reader'll need a good fifteen minutes to decode the names. My courtroom sources tell me the judge will rule on the search warrant no later than six-fifteen and possibly as early as six."

"It's almost six now. I'd say it's time for Plan B."

"Under Plan B, we borrow the *Bucksbaum* for a while. But that sets off alert bells and will make your mission even more difficult."

"My mission! What mission? You gotta be—"

"No time to argue. Listen, the two folks who will be serving the warrant to search this place are currently enjoying themselves over at *Señor Donkey*. They'll stay there until the judge issues the warrant. Once that happens, it will be printed out at the police station and your friend Malone will join them. Make it all very legal when they find stolen art at your pad. If the judge declines the warrant then they'll skip the police and come for the *Bucksbaum* directly. In any event, we have them in our sight."

"At that point, I mean if there's no warrant, we just won't let them in."

"Do you think the guard stopped them when they came to plant the piece? And finding Riya hanging around keeping watch over the *Pirate* and the *Cup* didn't slow them one bit. Unless we are prepared to use lethal force, we can't stop them either. And I am not so authorized."

"How did they—"

"Drugs. Modern stuff has memory suppressant built in. A quick shot. You go out. You wake up and you remember nothing."

"So...so when I found Riya in my bed she hadn't been there all...all night?"

"My goodness no, Angella. Never. Jimmy

wouldn't have...oh, my. You two need to talk."

"You're covering for him. Spooks fraternity and all that misplaced loyalty."

"I'll show you the video if you wish. She slept on this sofa. The bedroom door was locked all night. And Jimmy was in there."

"Video evidence, we know, can be misleading."

Before Ben-Yuval could respond, I realized what was bothering me about the *Bucksbaum*. "You said Israel wants the new names of Nazi war criminals so they can be prosecuted. Do I have that right?"

"You do."

"But, and here's where I go off track, not one of them can be much under 100, and most would be over 110."

"Well done, Angella," Ben-Yuval conceded. "Let's just say the ones we are looking for are believed to have taken certain very valuable Jewish artifacts. They may be dead but the artifacts still exist. Israel wants what was stolen from those who were murdered—and from their communities."

"What kind of artifacts are you talking about?"

"I've said too much already. But I can tell you this..." Ben-Yuval's phone buzzed. He checked the screen and took a step toward the door and pulled it open.

In stepped a young woman, twenty, no older than twenty-five, skinny as a rail, perhaps weighing all of ninety pounds. She turned around to face a wheel chair. "Grandpa," she said, her voice soft and caring, "we're here. Just a little bit further and you'll see it again."

The old man was facing backwards so I couldn't see his face, but I heard what I thought was a grunt.

The young woman then proceeded to back him into the office and turn the chair around. The man in the chair was even more emaciated than his granddaughter and was covered in a blanket up to his skeletal face. His mouth was in constant movement, but no words came out. Saliva dribbled down both sides of what remained of his chin and the woman tenderly reached over him and wiped him dry.

"*Shalom Aleichem*," Ben-Yuval said to the newcomers.

"*Aleichem Shalom*," the young woman responded, an infectious smile spreading across her rugged face.

"Angella," Ben-Yuval said, "may I present Otto Bucksbaum and his granddaughter Sophia Buck."

The old man's eyes blinked several times and his head nodded.

"He says it's nice to meet you," Sophia said, extending her hand in my direction. "Grandfather's last stroke took his speech away, but he's still got it up here." She touched her head. "Isn't that right, grandpa?"

The eyes blinked again. Eyes that even with

the passage of time and the growth of cataracts were still vibrant.

Sophia said, "I understand we don't have much time."

Ben-Yuval switched to Hebrew and a torrent of words passed between him and Sophia, ending with him saying to me, "Hand Sophia a pad and a pen or pencil, then hold the end of the painting up in front of him. Otto will decipher what names he can."

While I was retrieving the pad and pen, Ben-Yuval's phone buzzed. He studied the screen then said, "Judge's beginning to render her opinion."

Once the painting was opened in front of the wheel chair, Bucksbaum's eyes went wide and Sophia had to dry them as well as his mouth. Slowly, painfully slowly, his right hand moved out from under the blanket. The skin on the back of his hand, what little remained, was translucent, exposing blue blood vessels.

He maneuvered his hand upward, finally managing to touch the painting with the tip of a finger. He then worked his finger up to his almost non-existent lips and held it there as spittle collected and dripped into his lap.

"Grandfather," Sophia said, her voice soft, concerned, "what names can you tell me?"

The old man blinked and Sophia motioned for us to bring the painting even closer to his face. He studied it a long time and I had about given up hope that he would provide any information when he extended one finger.

Sophia studied his eyes as they began to blink. At the end of each blink burst she wrote something on the pad. This continued for many minutes until he held up a second finger.

Sophia flipped a page and continued to make marks on the pad. I looked over her shoulder, but either they were random curved fragments or perhaps Hebrew. The marks did resemble in a very loose sort of way what I remember Hebrew looking like the few times I had seen it in the past. *Or had it been Arabic?*

Twenty minutes later Ben-Yuval, after examining his phone said, "Time's expired. Afraid we must end."

Otto touched his finger to his lips and again reached forward to touch the painting. When he completed his task, he nodded and turned his head.

"Grandpa's deciphered all five. He memorized parts so only he alone could get all of it. He has lived for this day and is satisfied. He's ready to go home. I am afraid now he will—"

"Let's remain positive, shall we?" Ben-Yuval said, helping to turn the old man around and usher him back out into the hall. "Thank you for bringing him all this way and have a safe trip home. *Shalom, Sophia. Shalom, Otto. Lehit-raot.* Be well, my friend. Be well." We watched as Sophia quickly wheeled her grandfather into the elevator, and the door closed behind them.

Back in the office, Ben-Yuval said, "Let's get both the *Pirate* and the *Kings Cup* out of here and out of harm's way. When the marshals return they should only remove the *Bucksbaum,* but in the art world one never can be certain. We have..." he checked his cell, "less than four minutes. My people have slowed the marshals down all they could without risking giving our operation away. We better hurry."

I took the *Kings Cup* and Ben-Yuval held open a pillow case. I slipped it inside. He wrapped the *Pirate* in a sheet and we were off. I watched the time tick off the clock as we waited for the elevator to return to the penthouse floor where we waited, fully expecting the marshals to be on it when the doors opened.

But they weren't.

On the way down something that had been troubling me surfaced. "Tell me straight Levi, our research showed old man Bucksbaum to have been buried in Ein Hod back in 2016. If that is true then who was the man up there?"

"Internet is not infallible."

"But—"

"Let's just say Israel employed a bit of neighborly deception."

"So the U. S. would release the Master. Was that the idea?"

"Took them three years to bite. But bite they did. Now the ball's in our court as the expression goes. And unless somehow this operation is leaked we'll be wrapped before they mobilize."

We were out of the elevator and across the parking lot a few steps from Ben-Yuval's car when his phone buzzed. "Their car's just turning off the main road," he announced after reading the text.

"Close call," I said to the Israeli agent. "Too close for my liking."

"An inch is as good as a mile in this business. Get used to it my friend. Get used to it."

"What's that supposed to mean? Jimmy and I are out of government service." Sarcastically, I added, "In case you haven't heard."

"You might be pressed into service in the near future. You never know."

Ben-Yuval again studied his phone, this time with a serious look on his face. "That future might be sooner than you think."

"What the hell you talking about?"

"I'll be calling in a major favor. You know those names we just received from Bucksbaum? Once we begin the operation, it won't take your government long to figure out what's going on. At that point they'll harden the targets. Of the five names Otto provided, two are confirmed deceased, two are living in the States and one in Peru."

"And you're telling me this why?" This is one of those rhetorical questions that I knew the answer to even without asking. But I had to ask anyway.

"Because at least one of those targets will prove difficult for known professionals to penetrate. And your good friends in Israel might need you to do this."

"I have no friends in Israel—other than you that is."

"All I can say, Angella, is that what you don't know can't hurt you."

That statement has never been true and wasn't true now. I knew I wouldn't get any more from a spook than what the spook was willing to give, so I just said, "I can't speak for Jimmy, but for me I'm done. Period. Done. Understand?"

"Hate to break it to you, Angella, but you owe me a big one. A real big one."

"And just what might that *big one* be? I can't imagine."

"You won't have long to wait to find out, that much I can promise."

THIRTY-SEVEN

The clock at the back of the courtroom pointed straight up and down. Even a hard-working judge like Sofia Hinjosa didn't usually work this late, unless perhaps in her office where I wouldn't see her. There were only two spectators in the courtroom, and one of them was the bank jerk Escowon. The other, a woman in her early twenties, was busy taking notes and sketching something on a pad. *Reporter?*

My question was answered a few minutes later when Abby rushed in and took a seat next to the woman.

"Tell me again, Attorney Hendrix," Hinjosa said after examining the numbers Escowon had provided and reviewing her notes, "what were the circumstances of Mr. Redstone's arrest today?"

"Agents had reason to believe the defendant would extract the cash from the sand. He was followed north from his residence by surveillance aircraft. The Coast Guard flew two planes out over the Gulf containing marshals. When pictures of the defendant revealed he had, in fact dug up containers that matched the descriptions of the ones that we saw being unloaded from the bank robbery vehicle, marshals were dispatched and the defendant arrested."

"Now, Attorney Ayers, I presume you are of the opinion that the boxes can not be searched without a warrant."

"Yes, Your Honor."

"And exactly why not?"

"No probable cause that Mr. Redstone has committed a crime. The boxes were not themselves stolen from the bank, and we don't know what is even inside those boxes."

Judge Hinjosa sat upright. "Now here's where I get stuck. We know forty million dollars went missing. We know that money does not belong to the defendant. We know the defendant dug the boxes up at a place that is not his home. Unless, of course, he lives on the beach. He doesn't live up there on the beach by any chance, does he?"

"No, Your Honor. He does not," Ayers answered, not bothering to stand.

"So that's not his home. In fact, it's not even his property, is it?"

"Not that I know of," my lawyer said, again remaining seated.

This is slipping away, fast. I knew it. Ayers knew

it. And judging from the fact that Hendrix was now sitting tall in his chair, he knew it as well. In fact, the only one in the courtroom who didn't know it was the bank dude who was fiddling with his mustache.

Judge Hinjosa's lips tightened and her eyes squinted as if trying, and failing, to remember something from her past. I couldn't begin to imagine what it was that was causing her so much concern. She remained in this pose several minutes before picking up a writing instrument, pen or pencil I wasn't in a position to determine. "Counsel, " she said, her eyes now focused on the prosecutor, "I assume you are familiar with the laws of Treasure Trove. Are you not?"

Hendrix cleared his throat several times, glanced at his young associates who both again avert their eyes, then turned to face Hinjosa. "Perhaps not as well as I should be, but I am of the opinion that Texas does not honor the Treasure Trove doctrine."

"If it did," Hinjosa responded, "you'd agree with me that the money, if indeed it is money in those containers, would belong to the Sovereign, the State of Texas, would you not?"

"If Texas honored the doctrine of Treasure Trove, yes, Your Honor, I would."

"So then one or both of you should so brief me. Here's what I recall from law school." Hinjosa was clearly having fun now, and at my expense I might add. "The rule of Treasure Trove arose when

Roman conquerors concealed coins and bullion in the ground when they were driven from the British Isles. The Romans expected to return at a later date and reclaim their buried treasures. Treasure Trove laws were set up to allow the English King to keep any treasure it found. My recollection is that the law was changed to allow the finder to own what he/she found."

"My recollection, "Hendrix added, glancing at a note one of the clerks placed in front of him, "is that Texas does not follow the Treasure Trove doctrine, but instead, any found *treasure* would belong to the land owner, not to the finder."

"Care to give us your recollection, Attorney Ayers?"

"I'll pass on the speculation, Your Honor. But I would add that an important factor in who owns found property is whether the property is deemed lost or simply misplaced."

"Good point," Hinjosa said, "So if we take a step back all we really have is Redstone going up on a sand dune, property not his own, and digging a hole. Out of that hole he extracts fifteen sealed boxes. There is nothing in evidence that Redstone's name is on those boxes, and there is only speculation as to what is contained within those boxes. The law cannot presume Redstone even knows what's in those boxes." The judge paused, looked over her notes, then continued. "It's important to note that Redstone does not claim ownership of the contents. Or am I mistaken, Attorney Ayers?"

Ayers was caught in a clever trap set by the judge. If my lawyer claimed I owned the property then when the boxes were opened and money belonging to the bank is found I'd be guilty of possession of stolen property, or worse. On the other hand, if she said I didn't own what was in the boxes then the contents would belong either to the landowner, to the state, or possibly to the bank. But certainly not to me.

"I'm waiting for your answer, Ms. Ayers."

"Your Honor, Defendant is not prepared at this time to declare ownership of the contents, but reserves his right to do so as we move forward."

"Have it your way, Attorney Ayers. Okay, so my finding with respect to the containers found in that sand hole is that we can't know who owns that property until we determine what's contained in those boxes and how they got buried up on that land. At this point there is no presumption that the defendant owns the contents of those boxes. One thing I do know, if I owned a piece of land and someone came and dug a hole on my land and pulled out fifteen containers, I'd have a good argument that those containers are mine. Does anyone disagree so far?"

I was hoping Ayers would pop to her feet. But she sat quietly.

"Moving on then, we will determine ownership at a later date. If we go forward, we will need the landowner of record to weigh in on this matter. Now let me address the question facing this

Court tonight. Should I issue a search warrant for the containers or not? On the one hand, I could postpone such a decision until we hold a hearing on ownership. But if I did that, the Government would be forced to allow Mr. Redstone to go free because they would have no probable cause to charge him with a crime. According to the arguments I heard in chambers, if I did that then any incriminating evidence at his residence would go missing if a warrant were not to issue. This would follow because digging up boxes with nothing more, however bizarre that might be, is not a crime. Disagreement?"

Silence.

"On the question of the warrant. The fact is the cartons in question were dug up in land, actually sand, belonging to someone other than the digger. There is no evidence in the record that the land in question was fenced off. There is no evidence in the record that No Trespassing signs have been posted. From what is in the record, I don't believe anyone has a reasonable expectation of privacy with respect to anything buried in that sand. Furthermore, the true owner of the contents can never be found if we don't know what the contents are. Anyone disagree?"

Hinjosa was on a roll, and it didn't at all sound good for me. My only hope was for my attorney Ayers to say something legally brilliant. Something to stop this runaway train that was coming straight for me.

But Ayers remained silent. A silence that all but sealed my destiny.

"Okay, then," the judge said, "all factors considered, I hereby grant a warrant to open the containers in search for evidence of a crime. If the contents of those containers provide evidence of a crime, or strong suspicion of criminal activity, then the fact that those containers were found in the defendant's possession under strange circumstances supports a conclusion that the criminal activity leads to the defendant. If that proves to be the situation, then the warrant to search the defendant's residence at the Riviera Hotel will be granted." She tapped her gavel for added measure.

My stomach knotted, knowing what was about to follow. I'd be lucky to walk freely for many years to come, if ever. I studied the marshals and the doors, assessing my chances of escaping, knowing they would never be better than they were now. There was only one man who was in a position to stop me. Unfortunately for me he was alert and studying me as hard as I was studying him.

Hinjosa was on a roll and remained on the bench to direct the search—or perhaps just out of curiosity. Highly unusual, but with this judge not totally unexpected. "Bailiff please bring several marshals to this courtroom immediately and alert the supervisor. Wouldn't want to open forty million dollars in cash only to have it...misappropriated."

The marshals must have had their ears pressed to the door. Immediately after Hinjosa requested armed assistance, the courtroom began filling with folks brandishing weapons. Some in uniforms, some in suits and two with large K-9s wearing vests proclaiming them members of the Bomb Sniffing team. This being Texas, one's imagination could easily hear horse hooves clomping in the common alleyway.

"Place the first container on the prosecutor table," the judge ordered.

Two guys, their stomachs long past being confined by their belts, bent to lift the top container and place it where Hinjosa was pointing. When the container was positioned in the center of the table the two men placed their hands on their weapons apparently in anticipation of something bad jumping out.

"Okay, now cut the first seal and let's see what we have."

The two marshals who had walked me into court again gripped my wrists. I value my life too much to have contemplated even for a moment escaping. Even if I had planned to make an escape, now was certainly not the time to try.

On second thought, this actually might be the perfect time. There were so many people packing heat crammed into the small courtroom that a single discharge could have wiped out half of the South Texas federal law enforcement capability.

Talk about the perfect storm. One trigger-happy individual could set off a round-robin massacre.

"Seal's open," Hinjosa announced, excitement in her voice. Perhaps recalling her early days working in the Sheriff's office to pay for law school. "You," she pointed to the closest armed person, "open the top, but do not touch anything on the inside."

The woman, a deputy Sherriff, did as instructed and carefully tried to pry the top upward, her efforts thwarted by sand granules grinding between the container body and its top cover. Watching the Sherriff's efforts, it was immediately clear to me, if not yet to anyone else in the room, that something was amiss. Too much sand was piling up on the table.

"Sand, Your Honor," the woman who slid the top up called. "Looks like this here box is all fulla sand!"

"Bailiff," Hinjosa called, "please examine the container. Everyone else step back."

The money's been stolen. How much was gone, I didn't know. This was now a sensitive topic in my mind. If the money was in the cartons and the serial numbers matched, which I knew they would, I'd be lucky to spend anything short of my eightieth birthday on the outside of prison walls, should I even live so long. But if the money was gone, I'd be free to go. *Except I'd be forty million poorer.*

My father liked to tell the Jack Benny joke about the time a burglar stuck a gun in Benny's ribs and demanded, "Your money or your life?" When silence followed, the burglar demanded, "Didn't you hear me? Your money or your life?"

Benny remained silent a while longer before saying, "I'm thinking. I'm thinking."

I'm thinking.

"It's all sand, Your Honor," the Bailiff called. "What now?"

"Open the next box."

The two burly guys dutifully laid the second box beside the first.

"This here's all sand as well," the Bailiff said a moment later, laughter forming at the corner of his eyes.

"What's so funny over there?" Hinjosa demanded "Share with the rest of us if you will."

"Nothing, Your Honor. Only...only all this legal...legal talk and it's all...all nothing but...but sand. One might be tempted to say...hot sand." He laughed a deep throaty laugh.

THIRTY-EIGHT

W e hadn't yet left the hotel parking lot when Ben-Yuval's cell buzzed. He checked the screen, then turned to me. "Angella, I think you'll be pleased with the judge's holding."

"The judge in Brownsville?" I asked, still trying to get my head around the fact Jimmy had been arrested. "What could be pleasing about Jimmy being arrested?"

"That art back there," Ben-Yuval replied, "was bought and paid for by money my folks just happened to find up island here."

"Define *happened to find* please."

"Full disclosure. Your government located the money a few months back. Electronics these days are better than most people believe—and from a satellite no less. Same technology they use to locate underground launching sites. Tiny tipped us off to your government's operational plans. That tidbit you didn't hear from me. We converted the cash into art."

"Why would you do that? I can't believe to protect Jimmy."

"Not exactly altruistic on our part, I must admit. The operation we were tipped to was the IRS operation I told you about earlier, with your government setting up a sting operation to trap Jimmy. Treasury, namely Carmella Hampton, was concerned about proving Jimmy had possession of stolen money, so their contingency plan was to use the arrest as a pretext to obtain a search warrant for your apartment. Police records in Pittsburgh show the *Bucksbaum* to have been stolen yesterday. As I told you, they planted the *Bucksbaum* in your apartment this morning so that the search would find 'stolen' property. They were taking no chances."

"But you could have simply told Jimmy of the sting operation and saved him being arrested. That's what a real friend would do."

"What's your saying? Don't kill the goose who lays the golden egg?"

Clearly Ben-Yuval wasn't going to debate my *friend* remark. To him, this was all business, and very little, if any, emotion. "I suppose you expect me to say thank you."

"You needn't say anything, Angella. Just make yourself available when I come to collect the debt. And make no mistake, collect I will."

THIRTY-NINE

Judge Hinjosa leaned as far forward as humanly possible, her face radiating anger. "I find nothing humorous about this colossal waste of time! Open them all! And do it now!"

"Third one's sand," one of the marshal's called.

"Fourth's sand as well."

By now they were like kids at a beach. Sand everywhere, as one box after the other was opened to reveal sand in all fifteen. Hinjosa stood to leave.

Ayers called, "Motion to drop all charges against my client, Your Honor. And of course to deny the home search warrant."

Without sitting back down, the judge turned to Federal Attorney Hendrix. "Seeing as though you have no stolen property and a gaggle of inadmissible hearsay evidence that Mr. Redstone even committed a crime, I'd think you would have made that motion yourself."

The prosecutor, his shoulders drooping, slowly turned toward me. "I certainly don't see any evidence of a crime here in this courtroom today, except possibly by the person or persons who stole the money from those containers. If, in fact, money was ever even in those containers in the first place. So I concur with esteemed counsel Ayers; the government moves to drop all charges against Mr. Redstone."

"And to expunge today's arrest record," Ayers injected.

"And to expunge today's arrest record," Attorney Hendrix reluctantly repeated.

Judge Hinjosa, with a twinkle in her eye, said, "I grant defendant's counsel's motion. All charges are dropped and the record is expunged. Mr. Redstone you're free to go. I don't know what you did or didn't do, but if whatever you did was contrary to the law, then after the wonderful public service career you've had, I for one will be greatly saddened." She then spun on her heel and disappeared through the door to her chambers.

No sooner did the door close behind her than several of the lawmen hurriedly pulled boxes toward them and dug frantically through the remaining sand, I suppose in hope of finding a few bills the cash thief had left behind.

I hugged and thanked my lawyer, Merry Ayers, and hurried out of the courtroom, still not knowing if I should laugh or cry.

Jack Benny had it right all along.

Non-Fictional Art Works Investigated by
Jimmy and Angella

Walking Man   *Giacometti*

https://www.artsy.net/artwork/alberto-giacometti-walking-man-i

Portrait of Adele Bloch-Bauer   *Klimt*

https://news.artnet.com/exhibitions/neue-galerie-gustav-klimt-adele-bloch-bauer-paintings-535565

The Painter on His Way to Work   *Van Gogh*

https://www.sartle.com/artwork/the-painter-on-his-way-to-work-vincent-van-gogh

Portrait of an Old Man   *Van Gogh*

https://www.vangoghmuseum.nl/en/collection/s0061V1962

The Pigeon with Green Peas   *Picasso*

http://www.artcrimeresearch.org/pigeon-with-green-peas/

Portrait of A Young Man   *Raphael*

https://www.sartle.com/artwork/portrait-of-a-young-man-raphael

En Canot   *Metzinger*

https://howlingpixel.com/i-en/En_Canot

The Old Man with a Beard   *Rembrandt*

https://www.dailymail.co.uk/sciencetech/article-2069176/Old-man-Beard-WAS-painted-Rembrandt-New-X-ray-technique-solves-art-riddle.html

The Holocaust

The Holocaust was the systematic, bureaucratic, state-sponsored persecution and murder of six million Jews by the Nazi regime and its collaborators. Holocaust is a word of Greek origin meaning "sacrifice by fire." The Nazis, who came to power in Germany in January 1933, believed that Germans were "racially superior" and that the Jews, deemed "inferior," were an alien threat to the so-called German racial community.

During the era of the Holocaust, German authorities also targeted other groups because of their perceived "racial inferiority": Roma (Gypsies), the disabled, and some of the Slavic peoples (Poles, Russians, and others). Other groups were persecuted on political, ideological, and behavioral grounds, among them Communists, Socialists, Jehovah's Witnesses, and homosexuals. (Source: ushmm.org)

Holocaust Center of Pittsburgh

The Holocaust Center of Pittsburgh was created in 1980 as an educational resource provider and a living memorial to honor survivors who came to Pittsburgh to rebuild their lives and to honor local soldiers who helped liberate the camps. (https://hcofpgh.org) There are 80 similar resource centers in the United States and around the world.

Other Books by David Harry

Jimmy Redstone / Angella Martinez Series

The Padre Puzzle

The Padre Predator

The Padre Paranoia

The Padre Pandemic

The Padre Poison

The Padre Phantom

The Padre Phony

General Fiction

(Under the name of David Harry Tannenbaum)

Standard Deviation

Out Of The Depths

General Fun

(Under the name of David Harry Tannenbaum)

Adventures In The Law

Weird And Funny Tales Told By
The Lawyer Who Lived Them

Paragraphs, Mysteries of the Golden Booby

Bob Doerr, David Harry, Pat
McGrath Avery, Joyce Faulkner

Thank You

I want to thank my editor, Meridith Murray, for her outstanding work. My wonderful wife Mary went far beyond the call of duty, when, with pen in hand, she liberally spread green ink across the pages of the manuscript. Thank you wonderful woman for all that you do for me. And most of all, thank you for sharing your life with me.

Special thanks go to Marion Wike for her initial reading and proofing of my many spelling and grammatical errors and to Marnie Monheim, my nonagenarian friend, who served as an early reader, and who called my attention to a major flaw in the story, since repaired.

A big appreciative nod is hereby tossed in the direction of Steve Hathcock, the man who knows everything worth knowing concerning the history of South Padre Island and the environs.

How does one say thank you to a city? Beginning with the terrain, framed as it is by three major rivers and several mountains, and extending to the ethnically diverse people, Pittsburgh is a happy place, not entirely devoid of tragedy, but cohesive despite its over 90 neighborhoods. The chants; Go Steelers, Beat'um Bucs, or Go Pitt are never far from earshot. Pittsburgh, thank you for what you are: A great place to live.

About the Author

David Harry and his wife, Mary, have a home on South Padre Island, Texas. When he isn't writing, David enjoys biking, traveling, and model train building. If David is off the island, he, Mary, and their dog, Franco, can usually be found enjoying their old stomping grounds of Pittsburgh, Pennsylvania, and more recently, Miromar Lakes, Florida.

Communications

David Harry can be reached at authordavidtannenbaum@gmail.com

You can follow David Harry on Facebook: davidharry (or patentguy) and on twitter: david1harry.

Made in the
USA
Middletown, DE